Million Dollar Road

Books by Amy Conner

THE RIGHT THING

MILLION DOLLAR ROAD

Published by Kensington Publishing Corporation

Million Dollar Road

AMY CONNER

KENSINGTON BOOKS
www.kensingtonbooks.com

KENSINGTON BOOKS are published by

Kensington Publishing Corp.
119 West 40th Street
New York, NY 10018

All Kensington titles, imprints, and distributed lines are available at special quantity discounts for bulk purchases for sales promotion, premiums, fundraising, and educational or institutional use.

Special book excerpts or customized printings can also be created to fit specific needs. For details, write or phone the office of the Kensington Sales Manager: Kensington Publishing Corp., 119 West 40th Street, New York, NY 10018. Attn. Sales Department. Phone: 1-800-221-2647.

Kensington and the K logo Reg. U.S. Pat. & TM Off.

eISBN-13: 978-0-7582-9515-6
eISBN-10: 0-7582-9515-4
First Kensington Electronic Edition: June 2015

ISBN-13: 978-0-7582-9514-9
ISBN-10: 0-7582-9514-6
First Kensington Trade Paperback Printing: June 2015

10 9 8 7 6 5 4 3 2 1

Printed in the United States of America

For Zachary:
the best, most astute reader ever.
(And yes. We did.)

Acknowledgments

Once again, I wish to thank the community of souls who helped bring this novel into the world. All of you who were present during the long processes of growth and change, those who held my hand during its birth, are deeply appreciated. I only wish I could thank everybody by name.

To John Scognamiglio, my patient and excellent editor, and to Marian Young, my fearless agent, I owe you both more than thanks. They don't get any better than y'all, and nobody knows that better than I do.

It took a determined gang of fellow writers to help me keep this book on the tracks, and I salute the Nolan Group again for their dedication and professionalism. I especially want to thank the always wise and witty James Nolan, as well as M. A. Sheehan and Grace Frisone—two women with a remarkable ear for what sings and what doesn't. Everybody should have the opportunity to work with people like these.

And to Fionn, for keeping me alive and functioning in that vast, mysterious space known as the Internet, and to Rue, for keeping Baggage and Weasel from starving to death (I know, but that's what they always tell me), I give you my gratitude—and more than gratitude, my love. Being a part of your lives is a privilege, one I honor and treasure more than any other in my life.

Then everything includes itself in power,
Power into will, will into appetite;
And appetite, an universal wolf,
So doubly seconded with will and power,
Must make perforce an universal prey
And last eat up himself.

—William Shakespeare, *Troilus and Cressida*

Late August, 2004

Something within Snowball craved blood and bone.

These were mere abstractions, however, for she had no experience of either. From birth her diet consisted of a milled feed—nutritionally balanced pellets of fish meal, antibiotics, and corn, similar to dog kibble—instead of ligament and sinew, muscle and fascia, rib and vertebrae. Still, within the confines of her walnut-sized brain, Snowball knew as surely as she knew the dimensions of her fifteen-by-twenty, six-foot-deep tank that she had been designed by Nature to smash her mighty hinged jaws around the struggling prey, to dive beneath the surface of her world, and hold the terrified animal underwater until it ceased to breathe. Then she would've been able to feed at her leisure.

A soggy clump of this morning's offering drifted past her massive snout. Snowball snatched at it with indifference, throwing back her huge milk-white head, and the clotted mass of pellets vanished down her pink gullet.

Within the long barn, in all the other tanks, twenty thousand other captives thrashed and smacked the water as they launched upon their feed in explosive hunger, the lesser animals shoved aside in a ritualized choreography of dominance and surly submission. Together they lived fifty-five to a tank in saurian tangles, but Snowball lived alone.

And when the Two-Legs came for the rest of the alligators in the BFG *barn, wound their jaws shut with duct tape, and dragged them out of their tanks onto the cement floor, never to be seen again, Snowball remained after they were long gone.*

The rarest of her kind, a white Alligator mississippiensis, *she would abide.*

CHAPTER 1

Nobody had said a damned thing to Lireinne about any freaking tour.

"Oh, for sure—she's one in a million, Hiro-san." The big plywood doors swung open into the BFG alligator barn, hot yellow sun spilling a wide square onto the cement aisle. Dust motes danced in the light. Tina from the front office ushered a small group of Japanese visitors inside into the steamy air of the long, low structure, while somewhere a peacock called to its mate in an imperial screech. *Ay-yah, ay-yah.* This scorching Thursday morning in August was a headache aborning in Covington, Louisiana.

Lireinne Hooten didn't turn around at the group's entrance. Instead, she kept her high-pressure hose trained on a stubborn crusted pile of gator feed in a far corner of the barn. Spilled pellets attracted swarms of rats, and even the farm's resident cat population, rumored to be somewhere in the neighborhood of fifty or so, couldn't keep up. The cats, all of them orange, feral, and disturbingly inbred, scattered like the rats themselves when Lireinne got to work early in the morning and the hose came out.

Well, every cat had blown the joint this morning and this tour was messing with her routine. She hoped it was going to be shorter than usual. The BFG barn had to get done before she could move on to the other twenty barns.

Tina and the Japanese gathered at the first tank down by the entrance. Tina slid open the plywood access door, showing off the farm's prized white alligator.

"Snowball's not really an albino—she's leucistic. Albinos' skins have no pigment, but Snowball's pigment is white." Four Japanese cameras chittered insect-like whirs. Tina raised her voice in order to be heard over the low roar of Lireinne's hose, relating the short history of Snowball. "The egg collection crew found her eight years ago in '96, part of a clutch of eggs out west, near Morgan City. Out of hundreds of thousands of alligators, she's the only white one we've ever hatched."

The Japanese were bound to have asked the routine questions since Tina spieled on. "These BFG eight-footers will go to a tannery in Paris to make handbags—every purse uses a whole grade-one skin. This barn is part of the 1999-year class, but Snowball's bigger because she's three years older. And no, she's not for sale. She's sort of a farm mascot."

Another low-voiced, polite question. "Oh, right," Tina said. "It's called the BFG barn for Big French Gators."

Bullshit. The crew called it the BFG barn for Big Fucking Gators and everybody knew it. Lireinne stole a glance over her shoulder at the approaching group through the black curtain of her hair. The Japanese, four undersized men in business suits, ties, and mirror-polished shoes, had put down their cameras and were in varying stages of reacting to the intense smell. One of them pinched his nostrils shut against the overpowering reptile reek while the others merely appeared uncomfortable, maybe regretting a big breakfast.

Go on—get *out,* Lireinne thought, lowering her head. Her long hair, glossy as her pink nail polish, swung down to cover the crescent-shaped scar bisecting her right eyebrow.

Get out, go play Pokémon or whatever.

Meanwhile Tina and the Japanese were strolling down the middle of the barn aisle, stopping from time to time to slide open the plywood doors and peer down into the tanks at the alligators. Lireinne didn't turn off the hose, even though if they kept coming her way those tiny, shiny shoes would be ruined. She didn't care. As she saw it, Lireinne was exercising her right to free speech. And besides, instead of her preferred footwear, flip-flops, stupid company policy forced her to wear white rubber shrimp boots she'd had to buy herself. Not even a gator could do damage to those heavy, ugly-ass things.

"Hey." Tina tapped Lireinne on the shoulder of her faded black shirt, a ripped, shapeless New Orleans Saints jersey that had once been her half brother's. "Turn that off. I'm giving a tour." Tina's nasal whine was raised over the powerful *whush-whush* of the hose. She didn't call Lireinne by name, but Lireinne was used to that. For six months, since her first day on the job, the crew and the rest of the farm staff had always looked through her as though she were a ghost with a hose and that was just the way it was. Being a ghost sucked. Lireinne didn't answer Tina and she didn't turn the water off either.

Make me, she thought mutinously. I'm working here and you're not.

"Like, *now,*" Tina snapped.

Okay. Lireinne twisted the hose's galvanized nozzle shut. The barn was suddenly quiet, the silence broken only by the grunts and splashing of the alligators in their tanks and desultory, incomprehensible Japanese murmurs. Tina's narrow-eyed glare promised she wouldn't forget this.

Except Tina would. A hoser was just a part of the landscape, noticed only by her absence if she didn't show up for work.

The tour moved on, the scent of the men's colognes floating like expensive chemical flowers on top of the ripe stench. Well, the stink was a part of the job, and besides, the tour had to be almost over— fourteen minutes, start to finish, the normal time it took to show visitors a couple of the barns and snap some pictures of Snowball—and in Lireinne's opinion these sweating, overdressed Asians looked like they'd seen enough. She could always tell, especially with foreign people: they'd begin glancing at their watches, edging toward the open doors at the other end of the barn and the clean, relatively cooler August air outside. The oh-my-God impact of 250,000 alligators massed in one place always wore off faster than you might think.

The tour group paused near the end of the barn for a shot of the girl with the hose. Irritated, Lireinne turned it on again in a hissing cannon of water, eliciting a glare from Tina and alarm from the Japanese, who scurried out of the doors into the hot sunlight. So what, Lireinne thought. After she finished the BFG barn, there were twenty more to hose; it was payday and Lireinne had plans for her afternoon. It was Thursday. The Dollar General got new shipments in today.

Ten minutes later, the cement aisle was spotless, a film of water slick as mineral oil pooling in the muted sun falling through the skylights overhead. Lireinne coiled the heavy python-like hose neatly around the coupler outside, but before she moved on to the next barn, she opened the door to Snowball's tank, gazing down into the water just below her boots. The eleven-foot white alligator swam up to the edge of the tank, her opaque eyes as blue as twin lapis marbles.

Digging into the pocket of her loose athletic shorts, Lireinne found the dog treat she'd bought at the dollar store.

"Here." She dropped the beige, bone-shaped biscuit onto the surface of the water. Snowball snapped up the floating dog treat with bland ceremony, tribute accepted.

The front office of Sauvage Global Enterprises sat on the hill at the top of the four- hundred-acre farm, next to the gravel road and overlooking the big twenty-acre water retention pond. It was a converted Creole cottage, an old frame house that was much, much nicer than the place Lireinne called home—a green-streaked double-wide on cement blocks. When she went inside the office on paydays, she liked hanging around in there because the air was deliciously cool and smelled like heaven with the aroma of chicken and dumplings, or sometimes spaghetti and meat sauce since part of the regular crew's compensation was a hot lunch. Lireinne, being what the accounting department termed "casual labor," didn't rate even a ham sandwich.

Today the kitchen smelled of fried catfish and collard greens. Big Miz 'Cille, the farm cook, didn't look up from rolling out the biscuit dough when Lireinne clomped through the back door.

"Pay's not ready yet." Perched tremendous on a tall stool to accommodate her swollen feet and ankles, Miz 'Cille ordered, "Get out of my kitchen, you. Go wait in the Big Room and don't touch nothin'." She punched the biscuit cutter through the stiff, floury mass, the pendulous white flesh of her arms wobbling.

So Lireinne sauntered into the adjacent vaulted-ceilinged conference room, the "Big Room," to wait for her money. Bleached alligator skulls, some the size of suitcases, hung in skeletal splendor on the pecky cypress-paneled walls. Above the bar were the antique, sepia-toned photos of immense dead gators suspended from oak tree branches and oil derrick arms. The trappers, posed proudly beside their trophies, looked like small, wrinkled children in beat-up fedoras, dwarfed in the shadows of those record-setting dinosaurs. Like everything else in the room, they were the private property of Mr. Roger Hannigan, the owner and CEO of Sauvage Global Enterprises.

Lireinne knew better than to sit on the long leather sofas or to touch the glittering crystal decanters and highball glasses on the bar. Her place was outside with the gators, the cats, the rats, and the peacocks, but while she waited in here she liked to imagine the family who'd lived in this house before they'd sold their failing dairy farm to Hannigan, seeing them all together in this room watching the Saints on TV. The parents would be sharing a six-pack, the kids eating their dinner on trays, while the Saints, those morons, threw the game away time after time. There hadn't been TV at Lireinne's house for eight months, not since the cable company had discovered the pirated line, and so when she ate her dinner in her bedroom she was limited to the two fuzzy channels she could get on what her stepfather, Bud, called "natural TV." Without cable, the 2004 football season was going to be a total loss. Preseason games started in a couple of days and wasn't *that* going to suck.

Lireinne twisted her hands together behind her slim waist, standing in the center of the Big Room, waiting on the bookkeeper to bring out the payroll. It wasn't like payday was ever going to be worth getting wound up over, though. Seven dollars an hour, minus withholding, came to less than a hundred dollars a week because the job was only part-time. But without a high school diploma that was the best an eighteen-year-old was going to get, especially since she didn't have a car and had to find work where she could walk to it. At least the farm paid her in cash. There was no way in hell she could get to the bank in town without hitching—not such a good idea out here in the sticks.

It was nice, being in the cool Big Room after working outside in the heat since early morning. Her sweat dried now, Lireinne inhaled the mouthwatering smells coming from the kitchen while 'Cille put a plate of biscuits on the table. The back door banged open and the men of the crew began to file inside. Simultaneously, Tina herded the chattering Japanese through the Big Room and out the front door to the farm's black Escalade waiting on the driveway. They wouldn't be having catfish. Lireinne was pretty sure they'd be eating lunch at some ritzy restaurant eighteen miles away down on Highway 190 in Covington, the closest town.

"Hey, 'Cille. Smells good."

That cigarette-ruin of a voice belonged to Harlan Baham, the farm's crew boss. As heavily as a dropped load of lumber, he collapsed his stocky frame into the chair at the head of the wide kitchen table. With a scrape of chair legs on the linoleum, the two Sykes brothers, full-time grass cutters both of them, sat down, too. Mr. Hannigan wanted the four-hundred-acre grounds around the barns and the wastewater retention pond to be manicured as a golf course. In the Louisiana high summer, that was a dawn-to-dusk job for those guys.

"You got some hungry fellers today. Right, boys?"

Lireinne knew the Sykes twins from her years at Covington High—badasses who cut class with the same bored competence with which they cut the thick Bermuda grass—but they'd never acknowledged her with so much as a nod since she'd come to work here.

That, too, was nothing new: in high school, she'd been nobody, just another fat girl with a bad reputation who lived in a trailer. Lireinne had walked the dim, noise-filled halls with her head down, nobody really seeing her unless they wanted to rag on her ass, just like here at the farm except now she had a hose instead of a backpack. In the months since she'd come to work at SGE, between walking to work and the hosing, Lireinne had lost over thirty pounds, and on her fine-boned frame thirty pounds had been a lot. Maybe that was why the Sykes twins didn't recognize her. Sometimes Lireinne looked in the mirror and almost didn't recognize herself.

Her stomach muttered a quiet complaint. It would have been great for Miz 'Cille to hand her a plate of home-cooked food, too. Most of the time nobody cooked at Lireinne's house, not except for Bud, her stepfather. Since he hardly ever got home in time for supper, she and her younger half brother, Wolf, usually got by on frozen Hungry-Man dinners, microwave pizza, and the occasional family-sized box of Popeyes chicken Bud would bring home after work. Bud's meals, when he made them, relied heavily on canned corn and Spam.

Five more minutes passed. At last the bookkeeper came down the hall from Mr. Costello's office. Although she'd seen him around from time to time, Lireinne had never met the CFO. She didn't expect to, though, because he was upper management. Hell, except for being a name on the payroll, she was sure he wouldn't know who she was even if he ran over her with his Lexus. The air was rare up there.

"Here you go," the bookkeeper said, handing Lireinne her pay envelope. "Don't spend it all in one place." Jackie said this same lame-ass thing every payday, her smooth brown face masked by a smile that never quite reached her eyes.

And like every payday, Lireinne took her money without a word. Stuffing the envelope into the pocket of her too-big athletic shorts, she trudged past the table of men to the back door, ready to begin her long, hot walk home.

Her hand was on the doorknob when Harlan jerked his loose-jowled head up from his plate.

"Hey, hoser," he grunted, his mouth spilling crumbs of Miz

'Cille's biscuits. Being the farm's only hoser, Lireinne stopped in the doorway, waiting to see what he wanted now.

"Mr. Costello says we're gonna be killing in Barn Twelve tomorrow." Harlan said this with a loose grin. "You wear good duds like you done today," he said in sly amusement, "and you're gonna be wearing gator blood. It's a *casual* Friday, got it?" Hunkered over their plates as though someone was going to snatch them away before they'd cleaned up their catfish, the Sykes brothers sniggered.

"Hear me? Don't go getting all redded up like you always do, now—purty gal like you wants to keep her clothes nice." Harlan's openmouthed guffaw featured black molars and a missing tooth or two.

By way of a reply, Lireinne twisted the doorknob and stomped out into the heat. Go to hell, she thought.

All of you.

Ancient live oaks stretched fern-covered limbs across Million Dollar Road, so-called because way back during the Depression the WPA had spent a million bucks to get it drained, laid, and paved. The shadowy trees overhead formed a dense, black-green canopy shot through with arrows of afternoon sun.

Lireinne walked on the shoulder and kept her eyes on the gravel under her shrimp boots. At her approach, in the drainage ditch among the blue-starred spiderworts, the peepers ceased their shrill song, resuming as she passed on. Behind a three-board fence, rust-colored cows grazed in boggy fields. It was a long mile from the alligator farm to the trailer, and after six months of walking it twice a day, five days a week, by now Lireinne knew every step of that mile.

Before she'd dropped out of high school in the middle of her junior year, she'd had a car, though. Bud had saved what he could, and bought her a used Buick minivan so she could drive herself and Wolf to Covington High instead of taking the school bus. Now the minivan was up on blocks in the weeds beside the trailer, waiting on Bud Hooten to find the time and money to replace the blown head gasket, but for those three amazing months Lireinne had been free to drive wherever the hell she wanted, whenever she wanted, instead of walking or waiting on her always-working stepfather to give her a ride.

After the van had died in the Walmart parking lot, Bud towed it home behind his truck: it'd been parked in the same place for over a year now. Fifteen-year-old Wolf went back to taking the bus, but Lireinne had had enough of a third-rate education and the endless hassle of high school anyway, thanks for asking. Still, she missed being able to shop at Walmart, the hair-care section especially. Although it was just a forty-minute walk from home, the Dollar General was no substitute.

By the time she turned up the shell road to the double-wide half hidden in the grove of massive live oaks, Lireinne's jersey was once more soaked through with sweat. The yard was empty except for the minivan, and Bud's truck, as usual, was gone. Dripping window air conditioners groaned a bass note to the peepers' song while the crackling drone of the cicadas in the tall pines was like high-pitched radio static. Lireinne wiped her forehead, longing for a shower, but before mounting the cement-block steps up to the double-wide, she headed around back to check on Mose.

The old Thoroughbred was parked under a two-hundred-year-old oak, head down, his knotted tail flicking listlessly at horseflies. "Hey, Mose." Bony and sun-faded, the horse pricked his ears, his liquid brown eyes brightening at her approach. Lireinne's heart lifted as Mose ambled over to the barbed-wire fence dividing Bud's property from what used to be the old Legendre horse farm's hundred acres abutting the back line.

Once Mose had been someone's prizewinning investment, his hooves shod in racing plates and his long black tail tangle-free. Once he'd been bedded down in deep straw and fed oats and alfalfa hay, but now Mose lived in the oak tree–dotted pasture behind the trailer with only the tall scrub grasses to eat. Fifteen years ago the Legendre acreage had been a thriving Thoroughbred breeding operation— until the tax code changed and the great Louisiana racing business hit the dirt like a plane with a dead engine. The Legendres had lost it to the bank and now the breeding farm was a deserted, falling-down ruin with a weathered FOR SALE sign hanging on the gate. Since Mose had lived there for as long as Lireinne could remember, Bud figured he'd somehow been left behind, forgotten when the rest of the stock had gone to the killer sale.

Lireinne scratched Mose along the white blaze of his nasal bone because he liked that. He liked carrots, too, but Bud had forgotten to buy any the last time he went grocery shopping in town. Scratching was going to have to do for today. When the pond in his field had dried up a couple of months ago, she'd bought Mose two mop buckets and tied them to the fence posts with a couple of old extension cords. Lireinne checked them and found they were dry as dust. The hose was too short to reach, so she lugged mosquito-infested water a bucket at a time over from the sagging aboveground pool. Mose drank deeply, his brown muzzle dripping diamonds in the filtered sunlight when he finally lifted his head.

"Payday, Mose," Lireinne murmured. "Maybe I can get to the feed store this weekend, buy you some fly spray, huh, boy?" She scratched the sunken crest of his neck and the horse lowered his head. "Deer flies are freakin' murder this time of year." Her hand came away sticky from the sweat and dirt caked under Mose's thin mane, so she rubbed it on her shorts. Feeling the edges of her pay envelope, Lireinne's leaf-green eyes turned flat and faraway. $147.50 for two weeks' work. Part-time, yeah, right—except she put in over six hard hours a day, five days a week, and only got paid for four hours. Casual freaking labor, my ass, she thought.

Alone except for a now-dozing Mose, Lireinne abruptly yanked the Saints jersey over her head and tossed it onto the fence. Next, her heavy shrimp boots sailed in shallow arcs far into the weeds. The garden hose was full of holes, but the strong pressure from Bud's artesian well turned it into a twisting water serpent when she opened the spigot. Holding the hose above the crown of her head, the cold, clean stream flowed over Lireinne's black hair, over her scarred eyebrow, over white shoulders bare except for her bra straps. For long minutes she stood under the cold water with her eyes closed, her skin gleaming pale as a summer moon in the green light of the oak grove. Gradually, the dirt, the sweat, the stench and ordinary hatefulness of the alligator farm flowed away to pool in the cool gray mud between her toes.

Hoser.

CHAPTER 2

You can't always get what you want.

The Bunsen-blue Lexus circled the parking lot while the savage chords of Bill Wyman's bass thudded guitar gut punches behind its dark, closed windows.

Parking at the Lemon Tree was tight this afternoon, so tight that Con Costello, late again, after one pass gave it up and parked by the front door in the handicapped spot. The instant he turned off the engine, the temperature inside the car felt as though it climbed fifteen degrees. Tall Con climbed out of the front seat, grimacing as he shrugged his wide shoulders into a sport coat. Lunch with the Japanese called for a measure of respectful discomfort, so he'd sweat under a thousand dollars' worth of tropic-weight worsted wool until he could get inside the restaurant and out of the blistering heat.

"Showtime," Con muttered under his breath. He ran his hand over his hair, thick and silky as a setter's coat, flame-red as only an Irishman's ever really is. "Time to Obi-Wan these guys." Con imagined the *Star Wars* Jedi Knight in an Italian sport coat, exerting his powers of mind control over the Empire's Stormtroopers, and grinned wolfishly. *He* was going to cloud the minds of the Japanese. That was what he did best, after all.

Truth be told, nobody did it better.

At the wide front door flanked by blue lilies of the Nile in terra-cotta urns, Con paused, mentally reviewing the files on his desk back at the alligator farm. What was the leader of the team's name again? Tojo? Kirosawa? Was it Hirohito? That was it. Hiro. Hiro-san to you, buddy, he reminded himself.

Today was a big day for Con Costello, the in-house legal counsel and CFO for Sauvage Global Enterprises. After lunch, this deal would be done. Signed, inked, put to bed. Still, after the conclusion of today's business and fulfilling the pending French contract, there would remain over a hundred and fifty thousand alligators back on the farm destined to be belts, wallets, shoes, and handbags, a hundred and fifty thousand alligators eating their heads off and getting their water drained, warmed, and changed out every damned day. The Japanese needed to come to Jesus and pay for their twenty thousand flawless, grade-1 three-footers—a deal worth over four and a half million dollars—just to keep all the plates in the air.

The boss man, Roger Hannigan, wasn't going to be in attendance for today's lunch, or at the contract-signing later on, for that matter. Ol' Rog was in the South of France at the wedding of his youngest daughter to an impoverished *comte,* or some other French guy who was equally titled and broke. Con was somewhat foggy on the details, but as always he was going to carry the big guy's water. It was time to earn his $400,000-a-year salary, so he gave his tie a final tug, swung the door open and strolled into the busy restaurant.

With a connoisseur's eye, Con took note of the girl behind the reservation desk.

"Jennifer, right? I'm with the Japanese gentlemen, honey."

The tall, long-waisted blonde in the black dress beamed as though he'd just handed her an armful of roses, her small, even teeth a testament to scrupulous orthodontia and bleach trays.

"Right this way, Mr. Costello." The Lemon Tree had been open only a month and already all of the hostesses knew him by name.

And that was just as it should be. For all of his forty-three years, Con had possessed the knack of making any woman feel like she was

the only one in the room—the only one who mattered, anyhow—
and over the years this talent had defined him. From his mother and
sisters, to Mrs. Schexnaydre, his kindergarten teacher, to his dental
hygienist, Penny; from his first wife to his second wife to the girls
on the side, Con's talent worked with an impressive reliability on
just about everybody else as well. When what he called the Obi-
Wan Factor came into play, things *happened*. The most moss-backed
old judges fell into line, opposing counsel caved, the farm's clients
couldn't wait to sign on the dotted line, and the girls, well . . . they
melted like cherry Popsicles. To Con that was, hands down, the part
that made everything else worthwhile.

Bottom line, being Obi-Wan was all about paying attention.
People thought they knew what that meant, but Con's formidable
powers of concentration, his ability to draw a laser focus on the un-
suspecting subject of his regard, went far beyond simple attention-
paying.

Take Jennifer, this hostess leading him into the private dining
room, for example. So few women felt like they got the regard they
deserved. Once he turned on the old Jedi charm, women fell into his
Lexus like ripe fruit into a basket, softly, and with a plump sweetness
of dazed gratification. Over the years, Con had come to accept his
ability as a vital, living thing, but he never tried to examine it too
closely. Sometimes it was damned spooky, even to him.

There was this, too: what if his talent quit working? Who would
he be then? Another middle-aged guy with a shit job, yearning for
the pretty girls in their summer dresses, that's who.

Con impatiently dismissed this uncomfortable thought. That was
never going to happen, and in any case, it was time to join the Japanese. The table for six was already well into pre-lunch cocktails. Tina,
drinking iced tea and looking longingly at the bread basket, seemed
glad to see him. She wasn't his type, not with those doughy hips and
acne scars, but Con gave her a flash of the old Obi-Wan treatment
anyway. Why not? Homely women needed attention, too, and since
they usually got so little of it, were always plenty grateful. More often than not, gratitude had a way of coming in mighty handy.

Over his lunch of smoked redfish with a tarragon-butter reduction, haricots verts, and Russian fingerling potatoes, Con went to work and gathered the Japanese around the fire. By the time the crème brûlée arrived, after four cold bottles of excellent Napa chardonnay, they were red-faced and giggling like kindergartners sharing a potty joke. All that intense attention had primed them for the big kill. In fact, Con decided, the clients were on the verge of begging for it.

Pouring the last of the wine into Hiro-san's long-stemmed glass, he said casually, "And of course, we'll want your letter of credit before the close of business on Tuesday. Let's get the paperwork done back at the farm, and then later I'll pick you all up at your hotel. We'll do dinner tonight in New Orleans."

Set the hook, Obi-Wan, you scoundrel, Con thought as he gave the group a broad wink. "You enjoyed Rick's Cabaret on your last visit, right?" Rick's was the ultimate lure, a French Quarter strip club of no small renown where the girls were young, agile, and frisky. "We'll hit Bourbon Street," Con said with an easy smile, "once we've finished our business, Hiro-san."

"Yesh," the older Japanese man slurred. "Very fine, *hai*." He raised his glass in a toast.

Done. All done except for the signatures. Con breathed a little easier, although he hadn't been particularly worried about this deal. The bill for lunch came to $648.09 plus tip, but you had to spend it to make it and Alligators times Demand equals Money. Big Money.

After he paid the check and put the receipt in his wallet, Con waited outside by the Lexus with his jacket over his shoulder, watching while the thoroughly tight Japanese weaved like addled ducklings across the torrid parking lot. Tina's square-jawed face was determined as she herded them toward SGE's gleaming black Escalade, but the Japanese weren't stumbling, not quite, and the farm manager somehow got them all loaded up into the car in creditably short fashion.

Con lit a cigar, tossing the spent match into the Lemon Tree's landscaping, and waved good-bye to Demand as the Escalade pulled out of the lot. Alligators he had. Demand he would satisfy.

Hell, he was beginning to sound like Yoda now. It had been a long, boozy lunch. Con had unlocked the car, letting the pent-up heat escape, when the door to the restaurant swung open. The hostess poked her blond head out, searching for someone. Her professional smile melted into delight as she spotted Con.

"Mr. Costello! I'm so glad I caught you before you left. One of your guests forgot his phone." Jennifer tripped out to the Lexus, her high-heeled sandals exaggerating the length of spray-tanned legs Con had judged to be perhaps a little on the meaty side. She held a tiny, state-of-the-art cell phone in the palm of her hand.

"Thanks, Jenny," Con drawled. He took the phone, his fingers brushing hers. Those hazel eyes were set a blink too close together, but her long, long lashes shaded cheeks the color of sun-kissed apricots. Nice, Con thought. Very nice indeed.

"Say, feel like getting a drink with me sometime?"

Jennifer smiled, looking surprised and happy. "I've got a double shift today, but I get off at eleven tonight." Those shining eyes. "And tomorrow night, if eleven's not too late," she said, her voice shyly hopeful.

Tomorrow? Friday night. Too bad, Con realized. Fridays belonged to his wife, to Liz, but he'd find a way to ditch the Japanese before Jen got off work tonight. Rick's scene was getting a little old anyway. Like a cruise-ship buffet, the club's staggering abundance of girl flesh rendered the spread somewhat less than truly appetizing.

"Maybe I'll see you later tonight." Con's intimate smile was just for her.

"That would be *great*." Jennifer waved on her way back inside the Lemon Tree.

Alone in the parking lot, Con puffed on his cigar for another minute, grinning, and then he climbed in his car. He cranked the engine. The CD player picked up where it left off, Mick Jagger wailing above the Lexus's throaty purr.

But if you try sometimes, you get what you need.

Hey, Mick—Obi-Wan *always* gets what he wants.

★ ★ ★

"Not again!"

A towel knotted around his lean waist, Con surveyed his jaw in the mirror, his red-blond furze of beard shaved close and smooth. He picked up a bottle of Hermès cologne and slapped some on his neck before he answered her.

"Lizzie, baby." Con sighed, marshaling a weary patience. His blue eyes met her angry sherry-brown ones in the mirror. "It's where the money comes from. Strip clubs and drinking are just part of the job." The words echoed slightly in the spacious, travertine-marble bathroom. Con braced his muscular forearms on the edge of the vanity and quirked an eyebrow at her reflection. "You know this, sweetheart."

Liz made a rude noise. She tossed her hair, artfully streaked caramel and gold—the color of the best molasses taffy. "I know you don't have to like it so damned much," she declared. Liz's lips, recently enhanced with some bovine injectable, were turned down in an almost-frown. The Botox wouldn't let her really cut loose and scowl, but Con knew that look. Hell, he didn't have time for an argument. He was running late again.

After eighteen months of marriage, his second wife was proving to be a different animal from the exciting young associate who'd worshipped him as a god. The Mercedes SUV, the new house on the golf course, and her endless trips to the dermatologist's for whatever harebrained procedure was currently rampant among Covington's lunch set ought to have been enough to keep her content, but Elizabeth MacBride-Costello never let a day pass without a new complaint.

Tonight's expedition to Rick's Cabaret was not a new complaint.

"C'mon, Liz," Con coaxed. "Don't be mad, honey."

Lizzie folded her arms, her eyes angry. "It's goddamned sick, those skanky sluts and that disgusting pole. If you think I don't know what goes on there, well, think some more, *honey*."

A couple of months ago Con had taken his wife out to Rick's for an evening so she could see there wasn't much to get worked up about—not within the environs of the strip club, anyway. While at the time she'd seemed to enjoy her lap dance, unfortunately Lizzie's trip to Bourbon Street had only served to provide her fresh ammunition. Now she knew about the pole.

"Why can't that fat son-of-a-bitch Hannigan take them?" she asked angrily. "Why does it have to be you?"

Donning a conciliatory smile, Con turned around to shower his wife with a bigger helping of attention. "Because he's in the South of France, Liz. Because that's why they pay me the big bucks. Besides, Rog never goes on these things anymore." Lizzie's face remained a study in high piss-off. Con, already dragging from the daylong Obi-Wan effort, fought the impulse just to throw on his clothes, pat her briskly on the cheek, and hustle out of the house.

"It's only business, babe."

But as though he hadn't said a word, Liz snapped, "And whatever happened to that bullshit about how you always bring it home to *me,* how I'm the only one who can do it for you? The last time this crap went down I waited up in a *garter belt* and stupid stockings, but you didn't get in until seven the next morning. They don't pay you enough, not if you have to troll the French Quarter whenever these foreigners need a thrill. You should be making at least twice what that jackass pays you, if this is *only business.*" Liz bracketed this last with angry air quotes.

Suppressing his memory of the dancer from that last visit to Rick's, her train wreck of an apartment in dawn's gray light, the messy scene afterward when she'd actually demanded cash, Con crossed the cool marble of the bathroom floor to wrap his arms around his wife. He was a tall man and the top of her head came to just under his jaw, but he noted Liz's mutinous eyes were averted, her arms still folded tight to her chest. He put a fingertip under her chin, lifting it so the oval perfection of her face tilted up to his. Okay, Obi-Wan—once more with feeling, Con thought, hiding a weary grimace.

"Sweetheart, you *know* I love you."

With a deep sigh of defeat, Liz rested her forehead on his broad, sandy-haired chest.

Ah, that was better. "Hey, Mrs. MacBride-Costello," Con murmured, his voice husky and tender. "Guess what? In a couple of months I'm going to take you with me to Paris for the leather show—the Semaine de Cuir. We'll stay at the Plaza Athénée, eat oysters and caviar, drink champagne. We'll go shopping on the Avenue Montaigne. I'll take you to Prada and we'll have a ball." He would. Lizzie's slim-hipped, full-breasted figure was made to wear Prada. And Armani, and Cavalli, and all the other high-end Italian designers. When the French deal was in the pipe he'd be getting a bonus. Hell, they could sure use it. Liz spent money like a Saudi prince and the old bank account would breathe easier for the extra cash.

"So don't worry about Rick's, babe." Con kissed the top of her head absently.

With a sniff of disgust, Liz pulled away from him and stalked out of the bathroom.

Expressionless, Con watched her rigid, retreating back for a second before he went into the walk-in closet to get dressed for the evening.

A ringing clash of metal sounded all the way from the other side of the house—Lizzie, in the kitchen, banging pots and pans with undisguised fury. It sounded like she was unloading the dishwasher, a job he knew she loathed, and she wanted him to hear it. Liz was turning into a real handful lately.

Con shook his head and picked out a tie, debating where he'd take Jennifer, and making a mental note to himself.

Be home before dawn this time.

CHAPTER 3

Arugula. Baby leeks. Cipollini onions.

On Friday afternoon, Lizzie MacBride-Costello dropped a mesh bag of key limes into her shopping cart and wondered what the hell to cook for dinner tonight. Enoki mushrooms, heirloom tomatoes, watercress. She wasn't drawing much inspiration from Maestri's produce department, so she maneuvered the cart around the corner of the narrow aisle to head off into the meat section.

The claustrophobic old grocery store had undergone a recent transformation along with the rest of downtown Covington, a newly fashionable suburban enclave just forty minutes from the outskirts of New Orleans. Before its upgrade, a year ago Maestri's produce had consisted of a few heads of wilted iceberg lettuce, heaps of dusty Idaho potatoes, and bruised apples in plastic bags. In the meat department's cold cases, opaquely frozen foam trays of mysterious animal parts labeled only "service meat" and family-sized packs of turkey necks and hog maws had lurked like suspicious characters. Grimy-linoleumed Maestri's could still use a real face-lift, but in the last month or so the merchandise had certainly stepped up to the plate of the town's upwardly mobile expectations. Liz had only just consented to shop there instead of the Winn-Dixie.

Cornish hen, lamb chops, a beautiful pork crown roast. Lizzie picked up a vac-packed tenderloin selling for $48.98 and studied it without much enthusiasm.

"You'll do," she muttered to the meat and dropped it into the cart. Since giving up her job as a law associate at Milliken-Odom's satellite firm in Covington, she'd come to employ the remarkable, storm-like energy she'd spent drafting litigation into learning to cook for Con, an arrangement growing increasingly onerous. This venture into the culinary arts was an expensive endeavor—scandalous, really—the cost of which was exceeded only by Lizzie's clothing bills.

Well, why not buy the best? To Lizzie, the sight of a refrigerator and pantry stockpiled with exotic foodstuffs (some of which she'd no idea how to prepare and would never get around to cooking) held at bay her memories of the canned soup aisle and all those Lean Cuisines she'd endured before marrying Con. Shopping the sales at the Ann Taylor outlet, T.J.Maxx, and discount shoe stores on her associate's salary had been equally demoralizing. Forty-five thousand a year had sounded like a lot of money—until Liz actually had to live on it. Graduating from law school with a mountain of student debt had guaranteed that she'd be wearing designers' mistakes, clothes other women had passed on the first time, and cheap shoes well into her forties.

When Lizzie was growing up there'd never been enough money for anything, much less clothes. The youngest of four girls whose ages were separated by only six years, she'd even had to wear the same dress her big sisters had already worn to their own proms. As a consequence, it was unfortunately memorable. Lizzie still cringed, remembering the snide comments of the other girls who'd seen that dress making an appearance under the gym's crepe-paper streamers three times before. Even her date had recognized it. No wonder she'd been a depressed kid.

Well, Liz was now a firm believer in money's magical powers to combat depression. And whatever his many faults, at least Con always paid the bills without question.

That tenderloin would be perfect with an asparagus risotto, she decided, forgetting the last attempt that had turned into a pot of burnt-black rice. Back to the produce department. While she was picking up the asparagus, she threw a couple of globe artichokes and a carton of champagne grapes into the cart, too. Risotto was such a pain in the ass—all that stirring—but Con loved it. And to think that once there'd been a time she actually looked forward to cooking for him. Liz's artificially plumped lips thinned at the thought. Last night, even though he *knew* she'd hate it, he hadn't gotten home until four a.m. She'd been huddled under the duvet on her side of their king-sized bed, pretending to be asleep when he came in, listening as Con stripped off his clothes. Then he'd stealthily eased under the covers without touching her, obviously hoping she was so sound asleep she wouldn't wake up. Liz had hated that even more.

It was a little over a year since they'd married and the bloom, as it were, was distinctly off the proverbial rose in the sex department. In the beginning they'd been so hot for each other. Before, Con would have swept Liz into his arms and made incendiary love to her no matter what time he got in, but these days he acted like she was a goddamned IED in their bed. These days, she only changed the sheets once a week.

Maybe some of it was her fault. Lizzie tried the idea on grudgingly. She probably hadn't been as supportive of Con's job as she might have been. Maybe all those evenings out with clients in New Orleans, schmoozing, drinking, and hanging out in strip clubs, was as much of a chore for Con as doing the cooking and cleaning had turned out to be for her.

"Fat chance." Lizzie denied the notion, knowing it simply wasn't possible. She moved on to the dairy section.

Organic milk, heavy cream, a thick slab of French brie. She'd need to hurry home to get the groceries in the Sub-Zero before they spoiled in the heat of the car. Lizzie was debating the merits of sour cream versus crème fraîche when someone tapped her on the back of her white linen sundress.

"Liz!" It was Sally Rayne, one of her erstwhile coworkers at Milliken-Odom. Raw-boned Sally cocked her pinkly blond head, an unmistakable home-cooked dye job gone wrong.

"Haven't seen you since the wedding, girl," Sally said. "What're *you* up to?"

"Just grocery shopping," Liz replied. Hell, that sounded lame— especially since it was true.

Sally nodded though, her no-color eyes blinking behind those narrow half-glasses that, in Lizzie's opinion, had never done anything for her horse-like face.

"Lord, me too," Sally said brightly. "These days, there's never enough time except to pick up a couple of things. Maybe you've heard, but the shop's still a madhouse with the zoning lawsuits— remember those? The world and his brother hell-bent on bulldozing some scrawny pine trees to throw up strip malls, and all the tree huggers wanting them shut down yesterday? Too bad for the tree huggers. No money there, just a few old ladies and hairy granola-freaks. They ain't the Sierra Club, babe." Sally rolled her eyes at the idea of the hapless environmentalists. She shifted the grocery basket on her arm holding only a bag of coffee and a box of Splenda.

"But hey, you know how *that* goes," Sally added.

But the truth was, Lizzie didn't know. Not anymore. She was a housewife now, not a litigator.

When Con had persuaded her to give up her job last year ("Just take care of me, darlin', be my baby. I want you all to myself and I'm making plenty of money at the alligator farm.") she'd never imagined the stay-at-home-wife thing could get so old, so fast. Life might be lush, but this . . . *domesticity* wasn't turning out the way she'd expected it to. Keeping house was a bore, almost an insult, after having been a leading light among the firm's herds of associates. She'd worked hard to become a lawyer, damned hard, and now it was as though she'd been reduced to a glorified maid. Liz had always longed for a maid, but now that she'd married Con and could finally afford one, this arrangement meant she was trapped inside a big house that needed a lot of cleaning.

And even zoning lawsuits would be preferable to grocery shopping.

"Oh, right—can't forget," Liz said, looking down into her full cart and playing with her gold bangles. "One screaming asshole after another." An awkward silence fell as Sally blinked at her. "Those were the days," Lizzie managed with a weak laugh. "Believe it or not, sometimes I wish I was still a part of the ol' Milliken-Odom grind, you know?"

"Well, the shop's not the same since you left." Sally shrugged. "Nobody's out to mop the floor with the other side, not like Lizzie MacBride. Queen of the Carpet-Bomb Discovery Motions, we used to call you. Quite the move, girlfriend, getting out of the rat race, getting married. Tons of green-eyed associates wishing they were you." She glanced at her watch. "Yow, look at the time. Let's get together after this cruel war is over. Have lunch, maybe."

"Yes, let's. That would be *great.*"

But as Sally disappeared with an airy wave into the paper-goods aisle, Lizzie knew that lunch likely wouldn't happen. After she'd resigned, at first she'd had a few get-togethers with her previous coworkers: big salads and too much wine—as well as having to put up with a lot of probing questions about Con and the alligator farm. How was he doing out there in the hinterland since he'd left Milliken-Odom, gone native as in-house counsel? It was a bold, out-of-the-box move—hitching his future to hundreds of thousands of reptiles, much less working for Hannigan, that reclusive, whack-job entrepreneur. When she'd married Con he was solidly on the partner track, a star in the Milliken-Odom firmament of legal talent, and now he was a rocket launched into a blazing, eccentric orbit. Not so her. Those lunches had tapered off when her old colleagues had soaked up all she had to tell them. Since then, nothing had changed.

Lord help me, Liz thought, *who'd have thought I'd ever be envious of Sally Rayne?*

So . . . where did that leave her? Lizzie fingered a wedge of imported Parmesan without really seeing it. She was thirty-one years old, bored, resentful, and restless. Maybe it was time to have that baby

Con mentioned when they'd first married, but lately Con didn't seem to want to discuss that subject anymore. That was fine by her. Lizzie didn't really want a baby—the sickening smells, no sleep, chained like a plantation slave to a howling mess until it finally went away to school. *Be my baby,* he'd said. It definitely seemed like the alligator farm was Con's baby now. One thing was for sure, she wasn't, even though she was faithfully holding up her end of the deal.

The hellish irony of it? Liz had always wished with all her heart to be somebody's baby, somebody's only darling. After a lifetime of hand-me-downs and being last in line for everything, after she'd given Con her life and become the housewife he seemed to want so damned bad, hadn't she more than earned the right to come first with him?

Lizzie tossed the cheese into the cart with a snort. Fine, she thought venomously. *Fine.* Today was Friday, tonight was date night, and Con would just have to take her out. To hell with the risotto and all that stirring, all the tedious prep work, and cleaning up afterward. The tenderloin could keep.

And, Liz thought, planning ahead, she'd make a real effort tonight: she'd surprise him at the door already dressed to go out to that new restaurant, the Lemon Tree. The black Tahari with the low neckline and the big diamond studs he'd given her for her last birthday could work. Liz would put up her hair the way he liked it, too. She'd even flirt with him like a madwoman, just as she'd done back when they were seeing each other on the sly, meeting in New Orleans so his first wife, Emma, wouldn't find out about their affair.

Those had been heady days. Con had moved in on her with such passionate, single-minded intent, and, thrilled at having been chosen by such a powerful player in the firm, Liz soon knew she'd no intention whatsoever of letting their affair end. A part of her had been shocked at how easily she'd dismissed her previous scruples about sleeping with a married man, but nevertheless Lizzie embraced the role she'd always sworn she'd be too smart to play. Mistress to a married man was almost always a losing proposition, but in the end, she won. The fervent, deeply flattering attentions of a powerful man,

Con's money, and what that money would buy—that life was hers now. She'd won and Emma had lost. It was as simple and brutal as that, but Con's mistress, now wife, had known for many years that life was often both simple and brutal.

Okay. So I won the role of the little woman in Con's life, but what the hell happened to my own? Liz wondered.

Picholine olives, cornichons, giant caper berries. Dropping the ridiculously expensive, too-precious jars on top of the heap of the day's shopping, Lizzie headed to the checkout. Little women did the grocery shopping, and everybody knew it. Well, after she'd put everything away, before she embarked on the long processes of showering, shaving her legs, blow-drying and arranging her hair, and putting on her makeup, Liz would change the sheets. She'd put a bottle of Cristal in the fridge and meet him at the door with two glasses; wearing a hey-handsome smile, but no panties.

So these days she might be having some buyer's remorse—maybe more than some—but one thing was sure: there were going to be some changes made. Con would just have to understand, and Lizzie meant to make that happen tonight. If there wasn't going to be a maid, she deserved to be the sole focus of her husband's attention. The strip club action had to stop, at least. She was *over* this stupid housewife routine.

Period.

Where was Con? It was Friday night, *her* night, and he was late again. Lizzie, made up to perfection and wearing her black dress and a killer pair of heels, had finished half the bottle of champagne. The other half was almost flat and no longer as cold as it should have been, in spite of the silver bucket of ice. It was 9:15 and Con was supposed to have been home over two hours ago.

He'd called at 6:30, just as the sun had begun lowering behind the tall pine trees that surrounded their sprawling house on the golf course. "Running a little behind, hon, but I'll be there by seven. Promise."

But seven came and went. At 7:45 Liz popped the cork and

poured herself a glass of champagne. Then another. The champagne went straight to her head, especially since she'd forgotten to eat lunch again. She'd called his cell phone five times already, but it rolled over to his voice mail as soon as it rang. I'm nobody's fool, Lizzie told herself, her irritation turning to something approaching real anger. His damned phone's turned off, she fumed.

And why was that? Liz's stomach fluttered in sudden apprehension so she gulped half her third glass of champagne. What if . . . Con had been in an accident? Maybe he'd crashed in one of those deep drainage ditches out there on Million Dollar Road. Maybe he was in the ER at St. Tammany General in a coma, his handsome face the color of cottage cheese, I.V. tubes sprouting from his arms like sinister plastic vines. If something had happened to Con, Lizzie didn't know what she'd do. I mean, she thought, it's not as if I don't *love* him.

Of course she did.

Okay, the fear slyly suggested, he's probably not dead. What if he's with someone else instead? Some girl? Maybe he's keeping the wife at home on ice—just like he did with Emma? Those questions were unavoidable and somehow more deeply disturbing than the idea of him being dead in a ditch. After all, she knew what Con was capable of better than anyone else.

Liz's mouth turned down, stoutly denying her fears any traction. Unlike her, Con's first wife had been beyond clueless. Two years ago, when Con had asked Emma for a divorce, she'd been so shocked and undone she had to be hospitalized. So what? Lizzie thought. According to Con, Emma was a really good person, but Lizzie knew that sometimes bad things happened to good people. Life was like that; bad things had happened to her all the time. Con had said he felt just terrible about having to divorce Emma, especially after the breakdown, but Lizzie hadn't felt terrible. It wasn't her fault, was it? The Birkenstock-wearing, prematurely gray, all-natural idiot had missed every last one of the signs and that wasn't anybody's fault but her own, right?

But there were times when Liz couldn't help but be uncomfortably aware that despite her one-time rule about married men, she'd been *that* girl. She'd been the ruthless, infatuated twentysomething who'd taken Con away from Emma without a moment's indecision. Still, all that was over now, everything had worked out like it should. Now he belonged to her.

No, there was no way Con would dare run around behind *her* back. Liz was positive about that.

Impossible, she thought. There couldn't be another girl. Unlike clueless Emma, being nobody's fool, Lizzie would *know*.

She'd just polished off the bottle of Cristal when Con finally walked into the living room at 10:15. Slumped on the ivory linen sofa, Liz had taken her shoes off and her hair was starting to fall around her face in loose, taffy tendrils.

"Sorry I'm late, babe," Con began. He sat down beside her with a penitent smile, looking beat on his feet. "I was just getting ready to leave when Roger called from Provence, wanting to know how the Japanese deal went down yesterday. That took an hour, but then we had some kids sneak onto the farm, looking for a place to park and smoke dope. I had to call the sheriff's office so they'd come out and take care of it, and then I couldn't get out of there until the damned deputies showed up and ran 'em off."

It was a smooth stream of reassurance, but Con's face was questioning as with a quick glance he took in the upended bottle in the ice bucket. "And you've been waiting for hours." He kissed her cheek. "Still hungry, babe?"

"Hell, yes. You think I dressed up so I could stay home?" Liz was aware she might sound snotty, but by now she didn't give a damn. "You're gonna take me to the Lemon Tree. *Now*."

"Okay. If you really want to, honey." Not looking as enthusiastic as he should have, Con stood and flipped open his cell phone. "I'll call and see if they can still take us." He dialed. "Hey, Jen, it's Con Costello. Can you handle one last table tonight?"

Con listened for a long moment, his cheeks gradually flushing. "Yeah. Uh, yeah, for sure. Me too." He paused again, looking even more uncomfortable. "Soon, yeah. Well, uh, thanks for taking us. We'll be right there."

From deep in the sofa cushions, Liz glared at him in sullen dishevelment, now wishing she'd given up on Con an hour ago. She wanted to be curled up on the couch in the den watching HBO, but with a labored sigh, she slipped into her heels and let him pull her to her feet.

"You look great, hon," Con said. "Just great."

Oh, right. She'd looked great *three hours ago*.

It was a mostly silent ride to the restaurant and, once inside, the blond hostess at the reception desk seemed overly happy to see Con, in Lizzie's fuzzy estimation. Then, too, she had the impression she was being given a discreet once-over as the girl ushered them to a booth in the bar in a polite hurry.

"They're still serving in here. I hope you don't mind," the blond hostess said with a sideways glance at Liz.

Definitely a once-over, Lizzie thought.

"No, no," Con said a little too heartily. "This'll be fine."

It was most certainly not fine with Liz, but it was clear that the Lemon Tree was in the process of shutting down for the night: all the tables were empty except for a lone party of three paying their check. The bartender came out from behind the wide mahogany bar, wiping his palms on his apron before he reached to shake hands with Con.

"Good to see you again, Mr. Costello," he said. "I'll get you a couple of menus. Would y'all like to order a cocktail to get started? Glenmorangie on the rocks, right?"

Con slid into the booth across from Liz. "No thanks, Chuck," he said. "We're good."

"Oh yes, we would *so* like a cocktail," Liz announced, stifling a belch. "I want champagne." Better not to change horses in midstream, she thought.

Con's face was unreadable. "Bring us a bottle of Cristal, then, please." He shook out his napkin and put it in his lap. After Chuck the bartender had hurried off, Con's tone was dubious when he said, "More to drink, Liz? You sure?"

"Absolutely." Liz tried to sound dignified and almost succeeded. Okay, maybe she'd had a little too much champagne, but Con had been so late that the drinks had sort of gotten away from her. She changed the subject. "Already you're some kind of celebrity in here, aren't you." That sounded like an accusation, not the way she'd intended. A headache was forming inside the clouds in her brain and Liz would have killed for a couple of aspirin. "Everybody knows your name, what you drink even," she said, rubbing her forehead.

"Lunches with clients, hon. It's a nice change of pace from chain restaurants and fried seafood." Con's sea-blue, almost-green eyes studied her. "Not still upset, are you? I know I was late, but that's how it goes out there—especially while Rog is out of town."

He reached across the table to take her hand, but Liz pulled it away. Con might be doing that charm thing he did whenever she was upset with him, but she meant to get down to this evening's real purpose before she was distracted by him.

"Look." Lizzie toyed with the place setting's silver-plated knife. "I thought," she said, choosing her words with tipsy care, "we were going to have more time together when you took this job. That's what you *said,* anyway." Her silverware arranged, Liz looked up to meet Con's grave, attentive gaze. "I mean, I saw more of you when we were working together at the law office, before we got married even. It's just, well, I . . . miss you, okay?"

That last was a painful admission, one she'd only just had to admit to herself. Lizzie despised feeling this way, as though she were somehow diminished by acknowledging a perfectly rightful need.

"For God's sake, Con," she said, determined to have her say anyway, "ever since I quit and turned into Suzy Homemaker, and you took the job with Hannigan, it seems like you're never home." She knew she was whining now, and hearing that in her voice was almost unendurable. Lizzie MacBride-Costello didn't *whine.* She wanted to kick Con's shin under the table for reducing her to this.

Hating her anger, too, she snapped, "You're either at the farm or in some goddamned strip club. You should be making time for *me*. I only agreed to this bullshit arrangement we have because it seemed so damned important to you that I be *home* all the time."

Liz was sure she'd just crossed the line between whiny and bitchy, but in that moment the bartender arrived with their bottle of champagne and a footed silver ice bucket.

"Here we go, folks. Have y'all had a chance to get a look at the menu yet?" Chuck seemed anxious for them to order.

"Not really. Why don't you surprise us?" Con sounded affable, but Lizzie couldn't miss the undertone of exasperation in his voice. The young man in the black shirt and pants looked somewhat confused. Her husband gave him a quick smile then, the same confident smile that had so charmed a twenty-nine-year-old junior associate from Baton Rouge that she'd shrugged off her Methodist upbringing and rule about sleeping with married men along with her second-best dress ($69.99 on sale at Banana Republic), before falling into bed with him at the Ritz-Carlton. On their first date.

"Everything I've had here is excellent," Con said, "so just have the kitchen do what they still can and I know we'll love it."

Her jaw tightening, Lizzie thought of the tenderloin in the fridge, marinating in red wine, crushed pink peppercorns, and garlic. "No, I know exactly what I want," she said with an adamant shake of her head. "A filet, medium rare, with a real béarnaise sauce—not that crap from Sysco—and I want it on the side."

Con closed his eyes for a moment. "I'll have the same, then," he said.

After Chuck the bartender had poured the champagne and hurried off to place their order, Con gave her a long, beginning-to-be-irritated look. Lizzie decided she didn't care. She downed the better part of her glass right away, her head throbbing.

"What the hell's this about, Liz?" Con said in a low voice. "I already apologized. I brought you out. You've got another nice bottle of French booze. You've gotten your way. You always get your way, so can't we just have a quiet meal and go home?"

"*My* way?" Lizzie yanked the bottle out of the ice bucket. "My ass! My way was not on your goddamned agenda tonight. So maybe this marriage isn't turning out how it was supposed to, Con. Maybe we need to get, get . . . *counseled,* or whatever. Maybe I should go back to work and you can keep the house. God knows the firm wouldn't have stuck me in some backwater. I could have been on the partner track, too, if I wasn't being your stupid, unpaid housekeeper."

Recklessly, Liz poured herself another glass of champagne. Foam spilled over the edge of the flute onto the white tablecloth. "Oh, yeah. And maybe instead of carrying on around town, getting cozy with random *hostesses,* you should make it home at a normal hour. Tell the clients to scrounge up pole dancers on their own time instead of using you for a damned pimp!"

She raised her glass to her lips, hot amber eyes glaring at him over the rim. The champagne tasted sour, but she took a gulp anyway. Liz hadn't meant for her evening with Con to turn out like this. Her plans for a civilized discussion had been ruined by too much champagne and her own bitchiness. Con was bound to be fed up with this conversation. She was sickened by it herself, and yet she couldn't seem to stop.

Con didn't look remotely contrite, though, and wasn't that the whole problem? Lizzie suspected meek Emma, that *good person,* had never called him out on his crap. Liz was sure to suffer by the comparison—although she was in the right on this. But the thought of long-suffering Emma tasted as sour to her as the champagne, and even as a part of Liz was frantically telling her to shut up, shut up *now,* she couldn't let it go, not yet.

"And don't you dare tell me I sound like your pathetic ex-wife!" Liz hissed. Being compared to Emma, even in her own head, was beyond galling.

"I wouldn't dream of it," Con said. His voice was contemptuous. "Emma would never have gone off on me like you've done tonight." His mouth was a flat line. "She had too much class."

That old Baton Rouge nerve—being nobody worth noticing, special to no one—had never been successfully buried, and now it flared into life. How *dare* he? She had as much class as anybody, by

God, she most certainly did! Far past being reasonable now, Liz's simmering resentment exploded. Her hand suddenly seeming to move by itself, she snatched her glass and tossed champagne into Con's astonished face.

"Fuck *you!*" she snarled.

The long hours of waiting for her husband to come home to her, his lessening desire for her body, the halfhearted attention, this insulting disrespect. A thunderbolt of devastating certainty split the champagne clouds in Lizzie's brain, bringing months of growing, half-sensed suspicions into a long-denied clarity.

Cheating. Con had to be *cheating* on her.

CHAPTER 4

An empty bushel basket resting in the dirt at her feet, Emma took off her wide-brimmed straw hat and wiped the perspiration from her forehead with a dusty forearm.

Late August in the garden was pretty much a lost cause. There'd been nothing worth taking to town this Saturday morning for the Covington farmers' market. The neat rows of summer vegetables—bell peppers, snap beans, summer squash, tomatoes, sweet corn, and field peas—everything was picked over and almost done.

Except for the okra, of course. In all its hairy, practically carnal exuberance, okra thrived long after everything else gave up in the staggering heat. Emma sighed, resigning herself to bushels of exuberance well on into Christmas.

Born in New Orleans, a child of the Deep South, forty-year-old Emma had always only submitted to the seemingly endless Louisiana summers. Like everyone else, she waited them out, longing for the first days of fall, when being outside felt less like a forced march through the Congo. The flock of gold-brown, fluffy bantams was equally oppressed by the heat. The hens pecked at squash bugs with halfhearted stabs, scratching listlessly in the powdery soil of the garden.

Organic farming, Emma reminded herself, was not for sissies. It was damned labor-intensive and time-consuming, so as an exercise in mindfulness—*be here now*—months ago she'd quit wearing her watch when working in the garden. The sun was her clock now. As the mornings drew on into early afternoon, shadows crept close under the plants' wilted leaves, huddling like refugees from a natural disaster. Then Emma would shoo the chickens into their pen, whistle for Sheba, the mongrel bitch who'd adopted her six months ago, and go home. In for the afternoon, she'd stay out of the garden until well after the sun's burning angle fell oblique to the horizon before venturing out again to do her few evening chores.

The shadows were announcing it was time to quit. Emma put her hat on, picked up the empty basket, and began walking through the garden, back to the house.

The farm was a recent endeavor, one strongly urged by her therapist, Margot.

You need a healthy outlet, dear, one that both fulfills and challenges you.

At first, the challenges were immediately apparent, the fulfillment not nearly so much. The backbreaking days of clearing, tilling, and planting had stretched Emma's fragile equilibrium taut as a thrumming power line, until the jeering voices in her head fell silent from sheer exhaustion. Through the long nights, alone in the too-big bed, she'd slept like a dead woman, and, already more thin than was flattering to her tall, graceful frame, she'd misplaced another seven pounds somewhere along the way. Eighteen months later Emma's high cheekbones now planed sharply, her pale gray eyes grown huge, luminous as moonlit snow under her bangs of shoulder-length silver hair.

In the near-barren garden, an errant breeze lifted the dust in a spiritless spiral. As she took off her gloves, Emma rolled her aching shoulders, brown and smoothly muscled.

"C'mon, guys," she called over her shoulder to the flock of bantams. Like tired commuters, the chickens ambled down the rows, heading for the coop's fenced yard under the live oak's deep blue shade. Emma whistled for Sheba and the rangy black-and-tan dog came trotting from the woods that bordered the field, panting, her tongue lolling.

"Catch anything?"

The dog seemed to shrug at her question, as if saying, "What's to catch in this heat?" Sheba, some mixed breed of hound, often brought home big dead field rats, a wide variety of snakes, and the occasional fat raccoon, apparently sharing the carcasses with Emma. Hunting was sure to be a survival skill learned from living off the land, but when Sheba had wandered up to the porch one frigid evening last February, Emma had felt as though she'd discovered a kindred soul—lost or abandoned, hoping for one last chance before she wound up as roadkill. It never occurred to her to turn Sheba away, and so digging holes to bury the dog's victims seemed a small price to pay for her loyal company.

Sheba at her heels, Emma trudged up the steps of her front porch. The rambling old farmhouse promised the cool relief of central air-conditioning, a guilty pleasure, one she'd found she couldn't bring herself to sacrifice on the altar of sustainable farming. The low, wide eaves and long windows, her flower garden's morning glories, shrub roses, and sunflowers, the crows perched on the gabled roof— all of it was as it always was: a place she'd had to teach herself to call home.

Once inside the blue-painted front door, Emma was greeted by the ethereal echo of Mozart's *Requiem* playing on the radio's NPR station. Music made the house seem less empty, and she'd conceived a deep and abiding fear of silence. Emma raised the volume, and after making sure Sheba's water bowl was filled, she went down the long center hall to her spare, cream-painted bedroom, as neat, simple, and solitary as a nun's cell.

Gathering fresh clothes from her closet, Emma tossed her sweaty shirt and shorts into the hamper in the old-fashioned bathroom while she ran a bath. With a groan of pleasure she slid under the lukewarm water in the claw-footed tub. Emma scrubbed her knees and under her fingernails with a brush, lathered her hair with organic, cucumber-scented shampoo, and soaked for long minutes. Her thoughts drifted in a rare peace as the soprano's pure, soaring voice sang of loss from another century, until, after half an hour, when her hands and feet began to wrinkle, Emma got out of the tub. She dressed in what had become her summer habit of khaki shorts and a plain white T-shirt, running a comb through her wet hair before she twisted it up in a clip.

And now it was time for the exercise in hard discipline that followed the afternoon's ritual bath.

Taking a deep breath, Emma forced herself to look at her reflection in the medicine cabinet's wavy mirror, at the long straight nose, the dark eyebrows feathered like moth wings. Startlingly pale in her tanned face, her gold-flecked gray eyes looked back, grave and wary.

Emma summoned an unconvincing smile for the woman in the mirror. Her reflection was still there. For today at least, she was seeing what was real.

"You cooled off yet?" she said, turning to the dog.

Sheba, stretched out on the planks of the bathroom floor beside the tub, thumped her tail in response. With a grimace, Emma dry-swallowed her Prozac tablet and two fish-oil capsules before she slipped on her watch. She glanced at it. Only 12:45.

She'd hoped it was later than that.

This was the treacherous part of the day, the long hours between morning's end and evening's chores. Reading left Emma's mind untethered, the intrusive thoughts and unsought memories slyly inserting themselves into what had once been safe, measured passages of Austen and Proust. They popped up around corners in the histories she'd once loved. The old house was isolated at the end of a gravel road, and all its rooms were so fearfully quiet. Emma feared hearing the low voices, insidious whispering voices, both familiar by now and yet still dread-invoking. There weren't *really* any voices, she knew that, but Emma heard them all the same. Over the past year she'd come to leave the NPR station on all day, whether she was in the house or not, hoping the constant classical music and the calm, competent voices of the news cycle would make the whispers leave her alone.

But even Nina Totenberg was no defense against memory. Emma lived side by side with stubborn memory reminding her of the way life had once been. Memory led to melancholy, futile dreams of the paths her life might have taken if only things had turned out differently. Perhaps if the baby had lived, instead of being alone in this house Emma and her daughter could have passed the summer afternoons making gingerbread, going shopping, or just, just . . . being together. Her child would have been eighteen years old this summer, and if she'd been born there might have been three of them here, a family. Three instead of only her, alone.

Cultivate gratitude. It was another of her therapist's affirmations.

Catching hold of the thought, with a flash of her formerly characteristic, philosophical good humor, Emma reminded herself that, yes, she could choose to be grateful. She'd come a long way in the two years since her breakdown. For one thing, she could look in the mirror now, even though it was still difficult to work up the nerve to do it.

"There's this, too—I've got you, old girl, for company," Emma said, looking fondly at the dozing dog beside the bathtub. Sheba lifted her head for a second and went back to sleep.

Padding barefoot into the big, sunny kitchen, Emma poured a tall glass of lemonade from the frosted pitcher in the fridge. She sipped at it while looking out the window at her twenty-acre farm, paid for with the divorce settlement. The herb parterre bounded by flower beds, the grassy alleys stretching under the sun-spotted shade of the pecan tree grove, the iris-ringed pond where a great blue heron waded—it was an ordered, beautiful place, but at moments like these, Emma felt the emptiness of every solitary acre. Beauty could be lonely, too. She sighed.

So what to do now with the rest of her afternoon? Emma wondered. She'd cleaned the house yesterday, her laundry was done, and she wasn't hungry. Emma glanced hopefully at the cell phone charging on the kitchen counter beside her hand, although hardly anyone called her anymore except for Sarah Fortune.

When the old woman had come by over a year ago to welcome

Emma to the neighborhood, Sarah arrived with housewarming gifts: a loaf of homemade bread and a bottle of discount vodka. Oblivious to Emma's nearly mute shyness, she'd made herself at home in the kitchen and stayed for two hours. Now possessed of an unlooked-for friend, over the months Emma had come to appreciate Sarah's blunt company. The acquaintances she'd made in Covington before the divorce had done a slow fade since she'd been single, as though divorce were catching and she, having contracted the disease, was a carrier. Consequently, more often than not, checking the phone was a waste of time.

But then time was something Emma had more than enough of, miles of it.

Still, she picked up the phone anyway and for once this Saturday morning there'd been an unusual two missed calls and a voice mail, besides. Emma noted Sarah's regular morning call, reminding herself to ring her neighbor back, but then she recognized the rare second number and it set her heart to banging like an unlatched screen door in a high wind.

Con.

Her knees going abruptly slack, Emma had to sit at the scrubbed cypress table. She was breathless at the approach of her old enemy— a panic attack. Instinctively, she began Margot's breathing exercise, frantic to head off the sudden, unreasoning terror stalking her before panic brought her down once again and tore her to pieces.

But Con had called. God help her, *Con* had called and panic was winning.

"Breathe!" Emma grabbed at the air in gasps, struggling to find a rhythm. Gradually, her racing heart slowed. After long minutes, her breaths deepened. As if sensing something amiss, Sheba trotted down the hall into the kitchen, toenails clicking on the pine floor, and heaped herself like a load of laundry at Emma's feet under the table.

"I can . . . do this." Although calmer, Emma still panted. Her hand went down to Sheba's dark head and found the long, silky ears. She stroked them. "I'm okay . . . I'll be okay, Sheba. It's just . . . a voice mail."

A voice mail from *Con.*

Still, Emma knew she'd retrieve it. She always did. She was going to listen to his voice again. She had to, it was a compulsion, as inexplicable as phantom pain from a lost limb, but now Emma was fighting to turn back the unbidden memory of her ex-husband's once-beloved face, his mouth, so dear to her, saying those terrible, terrible words.

I want a divorce.

They'd been together since the start of her sophomore year at Tulane, meeting outside the library when Emma had discovered a flat tire on her bicycle and Con had stopped to help.

He'd fixed the leak, asked her out for a coffee, and from that afternoon they were inseparable. A handsome, popular twenty-one years old to her solemn, quiet nineteen, he'd pursued her with a bewildering ardor and she was helpless to resist him, even if she'd wanted to. When Emma contracted mono that fall, Con came to her dorm room every day with newspapers, magazines he knew she'd enjoy, class assignments, and silly haikus he'd written for her. Until she recovered, he weekly brought her fragrant armfuls of lilies he'd picked up at a discount market down in the Warehouse District. Both on impossibly tight budgets compared to the majority of the other, more privileged students, most nights they studied together in Emma's dorm room before falling asleep in each other's arms, twined together in her narrow bed.

Sometimes Emma wondered why Con had chosen her, an agonizingly shy, orphaned girl raised by an elderly aunt and uncle in their decaying Garden District mansion. They'd died during her freshman year. Utterly alone then, she'd had no one—until Con found her. And so the weeks turned into months before Emma could at last believe it: she had fallen in love, she began to trust that she was loved in return, and over the course of that year she began secretly framing what had been a solitary life in unfamiliar, exciting terms of *we, us,* and *ours.*

One cold December night washed with a gentle rain, Con asked her to marry him. They'd been walking in the French Quarter, and he'd just given his last five dollars, unasked, to an almost invisible woman who'd been huddled in a doorway.

"Marry me, Em?" His face was grave, but his tone was light.

Oh, how Emma had loved him then for his generous heart, how she had loved him ever after. They were married a year later, and as the years passed, except for the shattering grief of the miscarriage and Emma's subsequent inability to have another child, theirs became a happy life, gilt-framed by marriage. Without the possibility of the large family she'd longed for, it was always going to be just the two of them, but Emma Costello had felt safe in that frame. She grew lilies in her garden, looked after her husband, and their life together was so very, very good.

Emma had believed with all her heart that it was forever, that life.

Forever lasted until the afternoon when Con told her their marriage was over. At first she couldn't believe what he was saying to her. Like firebombs, his words hung in the air of their old, painstakingly renovated house in Covington, falling like a rain of napalm in her kitchen.

"What?" Emma faltered.

"I said . . . I . . . want a divorce."

Emma's head was slammed with a vast ripping sound, as though a world-sized sheet of canvas had been torn in two. She couldn't hear Con's halting explanations, his reasons for what he was going to do to them, going to do to *her*, because that monstrous rupture brought Emma to her knees. Her hands covered her ears as she gasped for breath, lost in the throes of her first full-blown panic attack.

Con went to his knees on the floor beside her. Gently, he pulled her hands away, his tear-filled blue eyes searching her face.

"Please listen to me, Em. Don't blame Lizzie. She's not the first. I-I've never been faithful to you and I can't lie about it anymore. I know I'm a bastard. You deserve better." A tear ran down Con's cheek. "Please try to see that this is for the best, honey."

"Is this because of the . . . baby?" Speaking was almost impossible. "If somehow she'd . . . lived?"

"God, no. A baby wouldn't have made any difference. It's not about that." Con knuckled his streaming eyes, moaning, "Oh, Em—I *hate* this."

And on her knees, Emma comforted him. God help her, she'd comforted him then even as she'd labored to breathe. But when he was done crying, Con rose to his feet and left, driving away to his girlfriend's apartment to begin his new life. His bag had already been packed.

Now Emma's golden frame was broken, the picture she'd so loved wadded up in a discarded ball. In the days after Con left, she'd known herself only as a wavering outline floating in a solid world, vanishing like a gray fog in the bright light of day.

And soon came the morning when, following another long sleepless night, she'd wandered into the bathroom to wash her tear-swollen face, looked in the mirror, and seen nothing—nothing—no reflection whatsoever. Too breathless even to scream, Emma had hit the limits of what she could take: she checked herself into the hospital that morning. Thus began the nine months of Emma's pregnancy of loss, a term of heavy therapy, the search for the right pills, and the fight for her tenuous sanity. Nine months, and at the end of it, she'd given birth to solitude.

You'll have to reinvent yourself. It was more of Margot's advice.

So although she was crippled inside, in dogged determination Emma took back her maiden name—Favreaux—and got her own bank account. She changed her address at the post office, signed reams of legal papers, and did all the usual divorce things her lawyer told her to do.

The house went on the market.

She began looking for country property.

It was a halting start to a journey she'd have given the earth not to take, but later Emma learned Con would be working for Hannigan at the alligator farm, only a few miles away from her new property. So close she could feel him, could almost hear his ringing laugh.

But with no other choice, not if she wanted to go on living life as a semi-sane woman, Emma doubled down on the therapy and began the work of renovating the old farmhouse. With a heroic, blind effort, somehow she learned to forget for hours at a time how near he was.

And yet, Emma never forgot for long that she only had to walk out her door, go across the countryside through the fields, and she would see him again.

Just . . . see him. Sometimes it was the only thing on earth she wanted.

Other times, it was the last.

And today, as he occasionally did, Con had called, burning through Emma's carefully constructed and vigilantly maintained defenses like a prairie grassfire. As always, there'd been an episode at the mere sight of his number on her cell phone. This panic attack was no worse than the others, but even after all this time, it wasn't getting any easier either.

Ah *God,* this had to stop, Emma thought in despair. It had been years of days since that day.

But she'd listen to his message; she was going to do that now. It was just a voice mail, just a collection of words, and panic attack or not, she wasn't really going to die if she heard it, would she? Her forehead in her hand, her shoulders tensed, Emma pushed the voice mail button and held the phone to her ear.

"Hey, it's me," Con's voice said. "Call when you get a minute, will you, honey?"

Emma gripped the phone in her hand, staring at its blank screen for minutes. Relieved to discover that her heart remained more or less steady and her breath stayed even, she wondered if she dared return the call. Talking to Con didn't seem to be getting any less painful, but . . . he might need to tell her something important, right? Then, too, her alimony check had been due days ago. So . . . she shouldn't put it off, should she?

It would be pointless to try. With a sense of helplessness, Emma knew from experience she was going to do it because she wasn't going to be able to stop herself.

Be here now.

Yes. Okay. Her finger trembling, Emma dialed her ex-husband's number from memory.

Con answered on the second ring, his familiar voice warm. "Emma!" He seemed delighted it was her.

Oh, she'd done this to herself *again.* Immediately, Emma imagined her emotional walls, high stone walls keeping her safe.

"Hello, Con." The walls were up. "What can I do for you?"

Con chuckled. "Nice to talk to you, too, honey. What, I don't even rate small talk with one of my favorite people?" he said.

Against her will, Emma's generous, full-lipped mouth turned up in a half-smile. He was doing that Obi-Wan thing of his. Since seeing *Star Wars* together back in college, Obi-Wan's famous line—*these are not the droids you're looking for*—had been something she'd laughingly repeat when, once again, he'd won someone over, a difficult professor, a cautious client. But *she* was the one being Obi-Wanned now; he was doing it to her instead of some stranger.

Walls. Emma began to pace the wooden floor of the kitchen, the phone cradled to her ear. Remember the walls.

"Sorry." She traced an aimless design in the lemonade glass's ring of condensed moisture on the table. "What do you want? I'm . . . sort of in the middle of something." Sure I am, she thought, sneering at her lie. Except I have nothing to do until it's time to feed the damned chickens.

"I was wondering if I could borrow your truck," Con said, his tone breezy. "Just for a couple of hours this afternoon."

"My truck?" Emma was startled by this unexpected request. "Um, doesn't the alligator farm have a bunch of trucks you could use instead of mine?"

"Well . . ." Con hesitated.

She could almost see him, his hand at the back of his neck, his long, big-knuckled fingers buried in his red hair. Emma bit her lip, struggling to unsee that image, imagining the walls instead.

"So?" she asked hastily. "Why *my* truck?"

Con sighed. "This is kind of personal. Lizzie wants a damned trampoline, of all things, and there's a sale on at Western Auto. Cash and carry. If I can borrow your truck, I could get it home and set it up in the backyard this afternoon." At least he had the grace to sound a little embarrassed. "It'd be a big help, Em. What do you say?"

A *trampoline*? For his new *wife*? Brilliant, white-hot pain almost slipped past the walls. Emma drew a shaky breath before she could answer.

"Sorry, I don't think my insurance will cover it if you have an accident," she said quickly, crossing her fingers against another lie. She couldn't bear to see Con if he came out to get the truck. It had been bad that last time at the attorney's office: she'd had a breakdown in the parking lot and hadn't been able to pull herself together sufficiently to drive home for an hour. Since then she hadn't been near Con in a year. Talking on the phone today had proved to be perilous enough.

High, rough stone walls covered with hanging trumpet vines, the scarlet blooms nodding in the breeze. "Wish I could help," Emma managed. The stone was cool as she pressed her ear to the wall to hear Con on the other side. "Sorry," she said again, her voice quiet.

It was Con's turn to be quiet. After a pause, he said, "No, I'm sorry to have bothered you."

"It's okay. Um, is there a problem with my check this month?" She had a right to ask, of course she did, Emma thought. And talking about money felt safer, as though it was a neutral territory in a country hollowed out with land mines.

"You haven't gotten your check yet? Sorry, I'll get to it on Monday." Con lowered his voice. "Hey, Em? You doing all right?" He really seemed to want to know. "I missed you at the farmers' market this morning. I was looking for you."

Emma's already rapid heartbeat shot skyward in an explosion of wild wings. Con and his wife at the market, buying free-range eggs and lingering over organic blueberries, holding hands, laughing. Except for Margot's office and the farm, the market had been the one

48

AMY CONNER

place where she'd imagined herself safe from running into him. Her throat threatened to slam shut. Emma swallowed with difficulty, her breath running fast to keep up with her heart.

"There wasn't much to bring to town, that's all," she croaked. "Just okra."

"Oh, right," Con said. "Okra. Well, don't work too hard, honey. I bet it's hotter than hell's doorknob out there. You know how I worry about you."

The concern in his voice sounded so genuine, so intimate, Emma's stone walls were swaying as though they were made of cardboard.

"I'm fine. Sorry . . . I couldn't help." Her *breath,* scraping in her throat.

"It's okay, Em. Hey, maybe we could get together soon, have lunch? It's been a long time. We could catch up. I'd love to see you."

"No." Emma choked. "'Bye."

She stabbed the "end" button and placed her phone on the table like it was a stick of dynamite, feeling almost as if she should throw it outside in the yard before it blew up her kitchen.

Oh God, no—what was that? Somewhere in the house, just under the last haunting notes of the *Requiem,* Emma was suddenly sure she heard a murmur, a voice just out of earshot, a low laugh. With a shiver, she turned and hurried out of the kitchen, down the hall, and into the bathroom.

Thighs braced on the edge of the sink, her hand shaking, Emma spilled a handful of Xanax into her palm and swallowed two tablets in a gulp, begging the tranquilizer to hurry, to please, *please* quiet the steel hammer of her heart.

And Emma didn't look in the mirror because she was heavy-limbed with a deadly certainty that if she dared a glance, she'd see nothing.

Nothing at all.

CHAPTER 5

Con, sartorial as ever in a polo shirt that almost matched his eyes, a pair of pressed jeans, and gleaming alligator loafers, fired up his cigar before he rolled down the window of the Lexus. As always, he was driving too fast on his way down the highway, heading out to the alligator farm to collect one of the pickups from the SGE fleet this Saturday afternoon.

Son-of-a-bitch, he thought irritably. What's *her* problem?

Con hadn't wanted to remind Emma that her precious truck was bought and paid for with the money he'd given her in what anyone would have called a rather generous settlement. That was sure to create conflict and Con hated conflict. He hated conflict so much he was going to take said SGE truck back into town to buy a goddamned trampoline for Lizzie. Then, with any luck, she'd bounce her ass into a better mood. After the scene in the restaurant last night, Con had wanted nothing more than to walk out and let his drunk wife find her own way home, but instead he'd wiped the champagne off his face and eaten his subsequently tasteless dinner in silence.

And yet . . .

This morning they'd woken up, rolled toward each other in the bed, and made love as though the whole embarrassing incident had never happened—a confusing but all-too-frequent pattern these days, especially following an alcohol-fueled disagreement.

Something, Con thought, was going to have to be done about Liz and her drinking. She'd never had a head for it, but lately that fact didn't seem to matter to her worth a damn. It had once been hot, the way a glass of wine or two made her giggle and flirt, but there wasn't any of that happening *now*. Instead of a sweet, sexy giddiness, Liz's recent boozing was turning into a real problem to deal with; hell, it was becoming damned unpleasant. Con wanted Lizzie back, the fun, adoring girl he'd fallen for, not this new, narrow-eyed, fault-finding version.

Where had that girl gone?

And what in the hell was going on with Em? Con's thoughts circled back to that phone conversation with his ex-wife. It had been disturbingly distant in its tone, Emma's noncommittal responses sounding as disengaged as if she were talking to some Republican Party phone banker seeking money for Bush's re-election. So her check was late, okay—he was having a temporary cash-flow issue—but she'd been barely polite. Up until that last call she'd been still, well . . . Emma. Still reachable, still in love with him even though they weren't married anymore.

What, Con mused as he made the turn onto Million Dollar Road, was up with Emma?

He hated to lose more than he hated conflict, and after that phone call he sensed the ground might have shifted. Con didn't like to admit to it, but two years after the divorce he continued to miss Emma's keen, coolly worded observations, her graceful acceptance of him in all his complicated energies. He missed the easy conversation, the intimate understanding—comforting as balm blended with single-malt scotch—waiting for him when he came home. She'd welcomed him like he was a buccaneer, returning ragged and triumphant from the high seas of the courtroom. Sometimes her habitual gravity, her terminal shyness, had been stifling and something of a bore, but certainly life with Emma had been more restful than it was of late with Lizzie.

After two damned years, couldn't he and Emma at least be friends? Of all the women before, during, and after Emma, there'd never been another one like her, Con thought with nostalgia. He took a deep puff of his cigar. Sometimes he wondered if leaving her had been one of his better ideas, but then he remembered how so often he'd felt, well . . . *constrained,* tired of laboring under the weight of Emma's unrealistically high expectations of him. To keep her good opinion he'd had to pretend to a monogamy he'd never once practiced, a subterfuge that had grown to become a pain in the ass. The fifth boy in a family of eleven children, Con had always needed the comfort of a woman waiting for him at home, someone who'd belong to him and only him. He needed a constant moon, a green and fertile planet to his wandering comet-self.

After his affair with Lizzie began, though, Con had found he wanted all that and more. More sex, more fun, more of this superb girl who seemed to get him, all of him, all the way down to the ground. He'd wanted less seriousness, less introspection, and less of the work involved in taking care of Emma's tender—sometimes too tender—feelings. To be sure, when he really thought about it Con always calculated that he'd made the right move, even though he missed his first wife more often than he'd ever imagined he might.

But his new wife wasn't under any illusions about him. Con puffed his cigar in renewed complacence, smoke billowing out the open window. Liz had known exactly who he was when she'd boarded ship—known about his affairs, his excesses, his pirate nature. She just didn't want to have her nose rubbed in it, that was all.

And even if she suspected that he continued to wander afield (which she almost certainly didn't), Lizzie was sure to get it: his other women didn't threaten her position as his wife in any material way. Hey, she was Mrs. Con Costello now. That champagne-in-the-face business last night was bound to be just a glitch in the system, only one of those rough spots in the road. He'd indulge her like he always did, she'd come around, and life would return to its usual satisfying rhythms once more.

Liz just needed to ease off the sauce. Ease off the sauce and quit bitching.

So preoccupied with his thoughts of his wives, past and present, Con didn't see the girl on the side of the road before he nearly ran over her.

Slewing around the blind curve, he was throwing the soggy butt end of his cigar out of the window into the drainage ditch and then, unexpected as a heart attack, there she was—a half-seen, open-mouthed figure scant inches from his front bumper.

"Shit!"

Con's excellent reflexes swerved the Lexus in a screeching *S* across the road. Two wheels went into the ditch before he got the car under control and back onto the asphalt. He slammed it to a stop, leaving twenty feet of burned rubber in his wake.

Shaken, Con looked in the rearview mirror.

She hadn't budged from the spot where he'd almost hit her, a young, dark-haired girl clutching an armload of yellow, plastic Dollar General bags to her chest. Cursing under his breath, Con unsnapped his shoulder belt and got out to see if she was all right.

"You okay?" he called to her as he approached.

When she didn't answer, he commanded his legs, still trembling with the aftershock of his near miss, to walk back down Million Dollar Road toward her. The girl remained motionless, rooted to the spot as though she were planted in the gravel beneath the underwater gloom of the live oak trees.

"Hey, are you okay?" Con asked again, drawing closer.

Her pretty rose-leaf lips parted; her green eyes were huge in her white face . . . her extraordinary, heart-shaped . . . *face.*

Con's eyes raked the perfection of it, noting that her pale, poreless skin was marred only by a small crescent-shaped scar through her right eyebrow.

And Jesus, her *body.* Slim-waisted, slender, lithe as a mermaid clothed in a white tank top and short, frayed cutoffs, Con's breath caught at the wonder of her thighs, the sweet curve of her calf, the remarkable architecture of her ankles, the high-arched feet in red rubber flip-flops.

The girl shifted her stuffed Dollar General bags to one hand, pushing a cascade of blue-black hair behind a seashell ear.

"I'm okay." Those green eyes narrowed, those lips turned down in a lovely frown. Light and rippling as cool water, her voice trembled ever so slightly as she said, "Like you coulda killed me, you know, driving like your ass was on fire."

At that, Con's lawyerly instincts woke up at last. "Well, now . . . I think you had a duty to walk farther off the road—legally speaking, of course. And," he added quickly, "I *was* doing the speed limit."

The girl shrugged one white shoulder. "Sure you were," she said. The tremble was absent from her voice now.

Con found himself almost tongue-tied in the face of this girl's self-possession, those amazing eyes appearing to see only a middle-aged guy in a fancy car trying to talk his way out of a potential lawsuit. If she weren't so arrestingly lovely, that self-possession would be a challenge. Most men would pass on a challenge like this one, but not Con.

In self-defense he offered, "Well, I wasn't speeding. Really."

The girl shrugged again, re-grouping her plastic bags with a sharp rustle in the country quiet. "Whatever, okay? You didn't hit me. I get it." She turned away from him, ready to resume her walk down Million Dollar Road. "Just slow down, okay?"

It seemed as though the afternoon's sunlight faded. Quick, Con thought. Do something, you idiot. Don't let her go!

"Hey. Uh, listen," he said loudly.

She paused, that gorgeous, disinterested face turning to look back at him over one shoulder.

"Can I give you a ride at least?" The corners of Con's mouth lifted in his trademark smile. "It's a miserable afternoon for walking, anyway. I could give you a lift, get you out of the sun." He paused. "And those bags look heavy," he added. "C'mon. I'm safe."

The girl seemed to think it over for a moment, as if weighing his offer of a ride against resuming her walk in the stifling heat.

"You sure?" she said cautiously. "Like, I don't know. Maybe."

Now that's better, Con thought. The girl didn't seem overly anxious at the notion of accepting a ride from a stranger who, five minutes before, had nearly killed her with a Lexus.

She said, "I've got another mile to go from here, just up the road from the alligator farm. I guess . . . I *maybe* could."

Upon hearing the words *alligator farm,* Con seized the opening. "SGE? Great! I'm headed there anyway. I'm Con Costello."

They were walking toward the Lexus now and the girl hadn't said anything more. Con opened the passenger door with a courtly suggestion of a bow and she arched a scarred, disbelieving eyebrow, as though he'd summarily dropped his pants and was hanging around in the middle of the road wearing only his boxers.

"I mean, you can trust me. I'm no ax murderer," Con volunteered, belatedly regretting the bow.

Saying this only seemed to make matters worse, though: gauging from the look on her face, he was positive she found him even more ridiculous now. "I work in the front office at the farm," he added.

The girl dropped her Dollar General bags on the floor of the front seat in a yellow heap. "I know who you are," she said shortly. "No offense—you might still be an ax murderer, but you said it. It's hot." And she got in, drawing her long, long legs into the car.

At once Con found himself undone by lust, imagining those legs wrapped around him. This wasn't going by the rules. For God's sake, he was teetering on the brink of an embarrassing tumescence, beginning to be hard as a zit-ridden kid holed up in the bathroom with a Victoria's Secret catalog.

Goddammit, Con thought. He shut the passenger door in a hurry. "Get a grip, guy," Con muttered under his breath as he hurried to the other side of the Lexus. She's just a pretty girl, not some, some *goddess.*

But easing himself into the driver's seat, Con discovered he couldn't take his eyes off the vision sitting next to him, so close he breathed in the sweet mingled scents of girl-sweat and some subtle perfume, fresh as the memory of long-ago rain. He tightened his hands on the wheel, shocked by the overpowering urge to press his lips to the tender skin behind her exquisite knee.

The girl shifted the plastic bags under her flip-flops as the car slowly accelerated in a smooth meshing of gears.

"So, what's *your* name, and uh, how do you know who I am?" Con asked, trying to make conversation.

"Lireinne Hooten." She adjusted the air-conditioner vent, her profile pure as a marble water nymph's in a Roman fountain. "I work at the alligator farm, too."

She lifted her long, silky hair off the back of her neck, un-self-consciously fanning the chilled air toward her chest. Con wrenched his gaze away from those beautifully proportioned breasts, a pair of ripe peaches hammocked in the tight-fitting tank top. Trying to feign a coolness he didn't feel for an instant, he forced his eyes to stay on the road.

"Really! You work at SGE?" Con cursed himself for sounding so fatuous, so ham-handed. Where was his goddamned charm when he needed it most? And if she was a farm employee, why hadn't he noticed her before now?

"That's quite a coincidence," he said. He was struggling to think of where she could be hidden on a four-hundred-acre alligator farm with fewer than twenty employees and coming up with nothing. "Let me guess, you're a . . ."

"Hoser."

A hoser. Con quit wondering because that explained everything. He had no idea who hosed. He didn't even sign hosers' checks— Jackie handled the casual labor out of petty cash. And of course their paths had never crossed. He rarely went down to the barns. The smell in there was so awful that one minute spent in the stench insured you would reek until you could shower it off. Liz even had to wash the clothes he wore in there by themselves, separated from the rest of the laundry.

"So you're the hoser?" Con said. "Wow."

Wow? Oh, that's good, jerk. She might think I'm making fun of her, he thought. Being a hoser was such a crappy gig that the farm gobbled them up like hot wings. He'd been given to understand that nobody lasted in that job for long, especially since the pay was so lousy.

So turn up the Obi-Wan Factor, Con thought with renewed determination.

"Summer job, huh? Home from college?"

"I'm not in college," Lireinne Hooten said, her voice flat and bordering on antagonistic. "I've been working at the farm, like, six months. You just never saw me 'cause you're front office, but I'm there most of the freaking day, five days a week."

"Well, I sure wouldn't have forgotten if I *had* seen you." Heavy as a chunk of firewood, Con's attempt at flattery fell into the conversation with a dead thud. And did he sound creepy? He must have, because now she looked uncomfortable. One long-fingered hand tightened on the door handle.

"There! It's just up ahead, there on the right," she said suddenly, pointing. Reluctant to let the girl out of his sight, Con nonetheless pulled the Lexus onto a potholed, weedy shell drive.

"Thanks for the ride." The hoser—Lireinne, her name was Lireinne, it could almost be "Lorraine," but wasn't—opened the door and collected her plastic bags. She swung those incredible legs out of the car, her red flip-flops coming to rest on the white shells as she glanced back at him. "And thanks for, like, not killing me back there, I guess."

"You're welcome, Lireinne." She seemed awfully young to Con, now that he thought about it. "Say, uh . . . how old are you, anyway?"

There was an unfamiliar, previously unimaginable note in his voice that sounded an awful lot like pleading for crumbs, but Con was on fire. He had to know more about her; he couldn't wait until he got to the office today to pull up her employment forms.

"Eighteen." She got out of the car.

Only eighteen.

Jesus.

"See you around the alligator farm, then," Con said, feeling in-effectual, and worse, *old*.

With a toss of her hair over her shoulder, Lireinne looked him straight in the eye with a wry-mouthed assurance.

"No, you won't. Nobody does." She shut the car door in a *thunk* of finality.

And then she was swaying up the shell road with her Dollar General bags and Con still had to go buy a damned trampoline for his wife. He'd gotten nowhere with this girl, worse than nowhere, and that was more humiliating than a glass of champagne in the kisser. He hadn't struck out so thoroughly in a very, very long time. Obi-Wan sure needed to put more effort into this girl.

But he'd see her again. By God, he would. She worked at the farm, didn't she? Hell, a girl like this one must hate being a hoser.

Maybe . . . Con mused as the car idled. Maybe if he brought Lireinne out of the barns and into the office? He could give her a promotion. What position he could promote her to was a good ques-tion, but that way he'd see her every day. That might work.

It was definitely worth a shot, Con decided, watching Lireinne's graceful back receding into the trees. In fact, it might be the only shot he was going to get: he couldn't very well try to make time with this girl while she was hosing the barns.

Lireinne disappeared, hidden by the dense brush and live oaks around the bend in the road. Help me, Obi-Wan Kenobe, Con thought.

You're my only hope.

CHAPTER 6

G*reat.* After Mr. Costello had dropped her off, Lireinne opened the door to the trailer, stopped dead in the entrance, and was instantly aggravated by the scene inside the front room.

How freaking great.

Her younger brother, Wolf, was hanging out with his lame-ass friend Bolt. Both of them were camped in front of the TV, wired like idiots into that lame-ass EverQuest video game they were always playing on Wolf's lame-ass Xbox.

Disgusted, Lireinne dropped the Dollar General bags of toilet tissue, laundry detergent, and paper towels on the worn sectional sofa and planted her hands on her hips. When Wolf and Bolt were hooked into that stupid sword-and-sorcery crap, it was like they were buried alive, deep underground in a plywood box with only an air hose connecting them to the world above. With an aggrieved sigh, Lireinne crossed into the kitchen area, heading to the refrigerator to look for something cold to drink.

And could this crap get any greater? The fridge was empty except for a lone bottle of Pabst Blue Ribbon and a half-empty jug containing orange juice of a dubious age. Wolf and Bolt had drunk up all the Coke. The empty liter bottle was on the floor next to them, as well as a crumpled bag formerly containing chili-flavored Fritos.

The rest of the results of their foraging expedition lay on the sticky countertop in a debris-field of dirty Tupperware, lunch-meat packages, an empty bag of bread, and an open jar of mayonnaise with a fly in it.

"You're a freaking *slob*, Larry."

Lireinne's half brother's given name was Larry Duane Hooten, but he wouldn't answer to anything but "Wolf" anymore, not since he'd been a freshman. That was when he'd started hanging with the Goth kids at Covington High and had gone all black clothes, Doc Martens, and death-obsessed. Lireinne called him Larry whenever she was pissed off at him and wanted to get his attention.

Well, she was getting pissed now. With rising indignation, Lireinne began to clean up the mess. Looks like somebody's gotta be the girl in the house, she thought. That's me.

"Did you remember to check on Mose?" she snapped, gathering up the trash and stuffing it in the garbage can.

The Xbox thundered in response. On a mountaintop somewhere in the land of Norrath, an army of orcs fell upon Wolf's sword-waving avatar and arms and legs flew. Wolf grunted. Whether that was a reply to her question or a reaction to being vastly outnumbered, Lireinne couldn't tell.

"So be that way, *Larry*. Hey, Bolt," she said, feeling snide. "I can see your ass-crack."

Without looking away from the TV, greasy-haired Bolt yanked his black T-shirt down to cover his Crisco-white buttocks.

"Bite me, Scar-face," Bolt sniggered, his hands busy on the control pad. "I can see your tits."

What a loser. At least he couldn't call her fat anymore. Whenever he wanted to mess with his big sister, Wolf swore Bolt had a huge crush on Lireinne. Some freaking crush.

"Leave her alone," Wolf muttered, fingers flying on his own control pad. Orc body-parts scattered across the TV screen like wood chips from a giant buzz saw.

Lireinne shrugged. She'd risk a glass of OJ since the Coke was finished, but when she looked in the cupboard she discovered all the glasses were used and dirty. "You two make me sick." Piling everything into the sink, she squirted dish detergent on the mess and ran the faucet to cover it.

"Hey, Wolf?" Without much expectation, Lireinne tried again. "Hey—like, Mose's *water*? Hello?"

Purple lightning erupted in answer. Lireinne gave up. Be fair, she thought. It's not like it's Wolf's job anyway. She stomped back outside into the heat and humidity to go check on Mose. Sure enough, the old horse's buckets were dry and dusty. She filled them from the swimming pool, wishing for the thousandth time she had a hose long enough to reach.

"Still haven't gotten your fly spray yet. Sorry, boy."

By the time Bud got home this afternoon from work, the feed store would be closed, probably. Poor Mose. The flies were like a disease this time of year, a buzzing summer head cold. Lireinne slapped at a big horsefly biting the old Thoroughbred's shoulder while Mose sucked the water down in big gulps. The bug was reduced to a smear, her palm coming away bloody. Hah! she thought. Take *that*.

"One down, a zillion to go. See you later, Mose."

Back inside the trailer, Lireinne gathered her own bag of shopping—some more dog biscuits for Snowball, cotton balls, and nail polish. She stalked past the two boys without speaking and headed to her room to put a door between her and all that monster slaying and treasure collecting.

Getting to shut the door was the only advantage to being the girl in the house: her stepfather got the other bedroom while Wolf slept on the sofa, something he'd done once Lireinne and her brother had gotten too big to share a room. This summer, that had seemed to suit Wolf just fine. He'd stayed up practically all night, every night, playing EverQuest like a skinny, black-clad bat with an Xbox.

Lireinne worried about Wolf's being alone so much, except for that creep Bolt. Why couldn't her brother have some normal friends? It would be September soon. When was he going back to school?

Lireinne hoped he'd meet a nice girl this year, maybe one who was into band, played the clarinet or whatever. Someone who didn't have multiple piercings or a shaved head. Like, did Goth girls *try* to be ugly?

On her single bed beneath the faded travel posters of Paris and Oslo Scotch-taped to the wall, Lireinne settled herself to paint her toenails. She'd rescued the posters from the Dumpster behind the school a couple of years ago when the World History teacher had thrown them out.

For years, Lireinne's big, secret dream had been to go to Paris. The posters were supposed to be a reminder that sometimes people were so freaking lucky—or rich—that they got to get on a plane and go wherever they wanted. The taped-up pages from *Vogue,* the ones of cool, superthin models hanging out on the Champs-Élysées and at the Eiffel Tower, were like an invitation to a party she knew she'd probably never get to attend, but Lireinne harbored a secret hope that someday, somehow, she'd find herself there. It was a stupid hope, though: unlike her, those hyper-elegant, racehorse girls were, like, so totally in charge of their own lives. They'd never find themselves hosing at an alligator farm, not them. They wouldn't be caught dead in shrimp boots instead of Jimmy Choos.

"*Bien sûr, chérie.*" Lireinne had taken French her sophomore year and still tried to remember the little she'd learned, just in case she made it to Paris before she died.

She'd just finished painting her toenails with a new neon-pink polish when through her closed and locked door she heard her stepfather come home. The walls in the trailer were so thin that even over the racket of the Xbox, Bud might as well be talking in her room.

"Hey, Wolf. Yo, Bolt. What y'all up to?" Bud sounded worn-out.

His Saturday job with the well-diggers over at the Pentecostal church was a bitch and a half. Poor Bud never got a day off. He worked all week for the Walmart distribution center in Hammond unloading freight on the dock, and then he'd spend his nights and weekends doing part-time work with the well-drilling outfit. Oh, once in a while he'd get a Sunday free, but then he went all comatose in his room like he was a freaking turnip.

Bud had always said that if you worked hard you got ahead. Lireinne had her doubts about the truth of that. Bud Hooten worked harder than anyone Lireinne had known in her whole life and he was always, always behind.

Outside in the hall, his heavy footsteps set the trailer floor to shivering on its cement blocks. The footsteps stopped outside her door when Bud knocked gently. "Lireinne? You in there, honey?" Bud had always been really great about her locked-door policy.

Lireinne screwed the top back on the bottle of pink lacquer. "Coming." Careful not to smear the wet polish, she walked on her heels across the matted shag carpet over to the door and opened it to her stepfather. "Hey, Bud. How's it going?"

"It's going." A heavily muscled, bald-headed man, his hairy arms covered in faded merchant marine tattoos, Bud Hooten leaned against the door frame and smiled. "I got off early, for once. You need to run into town today?"

"Hell, yes!" Elated, Lireinne threw her arms around her stepfather, breathing in the not-unpleasant, familiar smells of clean sweat, Red Man chewing tobacco, and motor oil. "I really, really need to get to the feed store before it closes, but can we go to Walmart, too? I'm out of my shampoo, conditioner—like, girl stuff, you know? My hair always gets frizzy if I don't have the right conditioner for it, and I want to buy this month's *Vogue,* too."

Rubbing his stubbled jaw with a grease-stained hand, Bud said, "Hold up there, sugar. I got to get clean first. Can't take my little girl to town smelling like a goat." He opened the door to the cramped, shared bathroom off the hall. "Just give me a minute and we'll go. Swear."

"Whatever. Get clean," Lireinne said with a wave. "My polish needs to dry anyway."

Twenty minutes later, after Bud had reamed Wolf a new one for leaving the kitchen a wreck, giving him strict orders to wash up the dishes in the sink and put away the paper goods Lireinne had bought, they walked out to the truck in the hot, oblique sunlight of the late August afternoon.

"Don't you be worrying 'bout the feed store. We got plenty of time," Bud said, throwing up the truck's rusted tailgate. "Ol' Ricky never closes much before six on Saturdays, waiting on all the farmers to drag their asses into town, and Walmart never closes anymore."

He opened the passenger door for Lireinne the way he'd done since she was a little girl, just as though she were someone special, a lady or something. She climbed inside the truck, shifting a pipe wrench and a jumbo roll of duct tape from the bench seat onto the floor with the other crap, taking care to avoid the plastic spit cup riding on the hump of the gearshift.

"Weird," Lireinne mused out loud as Bud got in behind the steering wheel.

She was remembering Mr. Costello. He'd opened the door for her, too. He'd even done that out-there, embarrassing bowing thing. She tried to imagine Bud with a Lexus and just couldn't see it, but his opening the door for her was always nice. Bud did stuff like that without making a big deal out of it, but Mr. Costello had been just sort of, well, *weird*. Maybe not weird in a scary way, but weird all the same.

"What's weird?" Bud asked, backing down the drive.

"Nothing."

Lireinne didn't want to talk about her near-death experience. Bud wasn't all that cool with her walking to the Dollar General as it was: the last thing he needed to hear was how she'd almost wound up smushed like an armadillo and gotten a ride with the weirdo who'd almost hit her, a weirdo who was her boss. She probably should've been nicer to Mr. Costello, but she'd never even met the guy before. It had been taking a chance she only rarely risked, catching a ride with a man, but Lireinne had already walked three miles to the Dollar General and two more on the way home. The bags had been so heavy that she'd decided that taking the chance was worth it. Besides, it wasn't like she'd been *rude* to him.

There hadn't been any trouble, not really. Everything had turned out okay, Lireinne decided.

"How's the well going?" She rolled down her window. The truck's air-conditioning had quit earlier that summer and chances were it wouldn't be coming back. The air tangled her long black hair around her face, the warm rush of wind making it hard to be heard in the cab.

"That job's a cluster-fuck, pardon my French," Bud shouted. "We got down another thousand feet, the drill shaft sheared off, and then that dumb-ass Ottis tried to back it out but . . ."

Bud's update on the ill-starred Pentecostal well went on for nearly the whole ride into Covington. Lireinne tried to act as though she was really listening while she ran down her Walmart list in her head. A copy of *Vogue,* shampoo, conditioner, razor blades, a box of Tampax.

Don't forget deodorant, she reminded herself. At least the old guy this afternoon had smelled good—hell, Mr. Costello had smelled *rich,* him and his Lexus both. And for sure he'd barely been able to keep his eyes on the road, she thought, uncomfortable at the memory of his sidelong, hungry glances. Maybe accepting a ride from him hadn't been such a hot idea after all, now that she thought about it.

Once, Lireinne had sort of dated a guy who'd looked at her just like that. Lanky, chinless Brett Schenker had eyed her that same way the afternoon he'd asked her to go with him to the basketball game.

Like she was a piece of meat, and he was a starving dog.

In high school Lireinne had been a shy, plump bird on the outermost edge of the vast flock of other students, never called on in class and wanting it that way, sitting by herself at lunch while everyone else seemed to have a crowd.

Maybe it was because she'd grown up so far from town that making friends seemed impossible, perhaps it was because she had no mother at home to teach her the ways of making friends. But whatever the reason, by the time Lireinne was in high school by herself was just the way it was going to be. By herself and practically invisible.

When the older boy had asked her out, though, Lireinne couldn't believe her luck. She hadn't understood that all Brett had wanted from her was one thing. Television sitcoms and chick-flick videos hadn't prepared her for that particular trap. She'd been stupidly thrilled, assuming this date might be the beginning of something special. Again, if she'd had a mother, an older woman in her life, maybe someone would have warned her how single-minded, how determined some boys could be when in pursuit of that one thing.

But nobody had warned her and Brett had gotten the one thing he wanted on the dark edge of the parking lot, in the cab of his truck after the game ended. In the most matter-of-fact way possible, he locked the doors. Then . . . he was all over her. Frightened and confused at first, Lireinne tried to fight him off, but he'd been too strong. In the end, she just gave up, quit struggling, and let Brett do it to her. She could only sob through her terror, her humiliation, and her pain. Outside the fogged windows of the truck in the cold January night, the other kids were getting in their cars, laughing, and shouting directions to one another to the postgame bonfire. Brett had casually put his big-knuckled hand over her mouth when she'd tried to scream out loud, calling to somebody, anybody, to help her.

Nobody would have cared anyway, not even if they'd heard that one cry. Who the hell was Lireinne Hooten? Brett hadn't even bothered to take off his LSU cap when he raped her, just ripped off her panties and held her down. Then, when he was done he'd driven back to the trailer without a word, as though Lireinne were something he'd picked up on the way, a blubbering bag of groceries slumped beside him on the front seat of his truck. He didn't even say good night.

And then the next day at school Brett had looked right through her like she was invisible again. That had been only what she expected, but she soon discovered that the word had rapidly gotten around that she was easy—whispers and mocking remarks, catcalls and the occasional shove into the lockers. Lireinne thought that her morning couldn't be any more of a nightmare, until she screwed up her courage and went to the school guidance office.

"You say Brett *Schenker* assaulted you?"

The counselor, wide-hipped Mrs. Cooper, had peered at Lireinne over the tops of her rimless glasses. The Schenkers, a huge clan entrenched in local politics, was an important Covington High booster family, always showing up with trays of cupcakes for bake sales and running the concession stands at the games. Nobody at school had ever known Lireinne Hooten from Adam's freaking housecat. This was her first trip to the guidance office in the two years she'd been at Covington High.

"Why didn't you call the police?"

Mrs. Cooper got up, turning her back to Lireinne to pick dead leaves off the discouraged philodendron on the sill behind her desk. "It seems . . . *odd* to me that you didn't."

How was Lireinne to explain that she'd been terrified, nearly out of her mind with the paralyzing knowledge that if she called the cops, Bud would have to be told?

Talking about it to Mrs. Cooper had been bad enough, and nothing came out of *that* but a piece of paper with the date-rape crisis-counseling hotline number on it—oh, and a Kleenex to wipe her eyes. No, if he found out what Brett had done to her, Bud would've killed Brett for sure, and when he did, Lireinne had no doubt that he'd have ended up in jail for the rest of his life. Her stepfather hadn't even known she'd gone out with a boy. He'd been working late again, so she'd had to leave before she could tell him about her date.

Besides, whatever evidence to the rape there might have been was washed away. Trembling, white-faced, and tearstained, that night Lireinne had disappeared into the bathroom as soon as she stumbled in the trailer's door. Wolf was so deep into his Xbox he barely looked up, but she'd been glad for that. She wasn't going to talk about what had happened to anybody, not if she could help it.

Under the rain of the shower, Lireinne sobbed her disbelief and shame into her hands until long after the hot water had run out. The tears hadn't run out. Tears fell silently throughout the night until just before dawn, when her stepfather had headed off to work. As soon as the sound of his truck on the shell road faded, Lireinne ran outside and threw what she'd worn—her underwear, her nicest sweater, and a practically new pair of jeans—onto the burn pile, doused everything with diesel, and tossed a match on her clothes. Stony-eyed,

Lireinne had decided that was the only way to begin to put Brett's assault behind her.

So, no evidence, not that it would've done any good anyhow. Nobody was going to believe her, now that everyone was calling her a whore.

And after a couple of hopeless anger-and-shame-filled months, the talk did die down some. But having to see Brett in the halls, strutting his newfound reputation as a ladies' man like a rooster, his life untouched while hers had been ruined, was one of the reasons—the main reason, really—dropping out of Covington High became a no-brainer for Lireinne. It wasn't any part of the reasons she'd shared with Bud. God, no. By then she only wanted to forget that night had ever happened. Lireinne had learned it wasn't that great, being noticed.

Already more than a few pounds overweight, those hateful months had been the start of the binge-eating, too. Food was a poor comfort, but it was better than none at all. She gained another fifteen pounds before she left school, as though she was hiding behind the layers of fat from the knowing, giggling whispers and dirty sniggers that had followed her in the halls. A reputation for being easy was bad. Fat and easy was worse. No, Lireinne had fled Covington High. That was the truth.

It was one thing working at the alligator farm had done for her: she'd lost the shame-weight and then some, and finding her body again after having lost it for a year had been . . . liberating.

Not as good as that night having never happened, but it was better than nothing.

Today her boss had freaked Lireinne out some, but at the same time the experience had been, well, kind of heady—as though she could have snapped her fingers and he'd have sat up like a dog. It was an unaccustomed feeling, one she'd never felt before in her life, but it probably didn't mean much. She was just a hoser. Would Mr. Costello look at her like that again if they ran into each other at the alligator farm? Lireinne wondered how she'd feel about it if he did.

"Hey, Bud." They were in town at last. The old truck's tires crunched across the gravel as they turned into the lot at Ricky Montz's feed store. "Do you think I'm pretty?" Lireinne asked, trying to sound as though his answer wouldn't be important to her.

Bud didn't hesitate. "Sure are, honey. Pretty as a picture." He shut off the loud roar of the diesel engine. In the sudden quiet he looked out the bug-streaked windshield, his eyes fixed on nothing, his face still.

"Just like your mother," he said after a long moment.

That was way unusual, Bud bringing up the subject of her mother. Normally, he didn't volunteer much about his ex-wife and Lireinne was more than good with that. She knew all she needed to know about that bitch already.

Her mouth twisted. "Like, not exactly what I wanted to hear, but thanks anyhow."

Lireinne's no-good mother had left Bud eleven years ago, left him for another man and a job as a blackjack dealer down in Biloxi when the big casinos had opened. She'd walked out on her kids, too, and never called, never even sent them so much as a Christmas card. Her daughter from an anonymous, previous liaison and her son by Bud were left behind like a litter of kittens that nobody wanted. Lireinne had no idea who her real dad had been and neither did anyone else. From the little she knew, she'd surmised that there had been too many men to count before Bud had stepped up and married her mother.

Lireinne herself had only a few memories of the woman who'd given birth to her. She remembered her mother had smoked, that she spent a lot of time on the phone, and she knew how to make fudge. That was about it, if you didn't count the fact that she'd been beautiful. According to the reluctant, spotty information Bud had let drop, though, before he'd been in the picture, ever since she was born, Lireinne had been passed around from relative to relative up in Tylertown, Mississippi while her mother, still a teenager, had run wild across three counties.

Apparently, she'd blown through those family relationships like a twister before Lireinne was three and her mother turned twenty. This was why none of Lireinne's Mississippi relatives wanted anything more to do with the irresponsible, unwed mother, nor with the solemn, quiet toddler who was dropped off for months at a time without even any money for her care. Lireinne only had a few memories of those years: the cramped trailers and small houses with too many kids in them, being hungry a lot, how nobody ever came to see what was wrong when she cried. Only her grandmother had been kind to her, giving Lireinne hugs, pieces of candy, and once, a pink stuffed bear. The bear was long gone, and her grandmother was dead now.

No, after they were shut of her, nobody else from Tylertown had wanted to know Lireinne, and now Lireinne didn't want to know anything about them or her mother either. Every bridge had been thoroughly burned, which was likely the only reason that bitch had bothered to marry Bud at all. She'd needed him to support her, and then when she found a new sucker, she just took off without a backward glance.

Except for Wolf, Bud was the only one who'd given a damn about Lireinne since she was three. If it hadn't been for Bud, the two of them would have been raised in foster homes, probably never seeing each other again. The double-wide wasn't much, but Bud made sure they were never hungry, and when he had money to spare—which wasn't often—he spent it on them, never on himself. The dead minivan, Wolf's Xbox, the aboveground pool nobody used anymore. Bud had done his best.

Lireinne unexpectedly knew an intense wave of affection for this man, this plodding, responsible man who'd always stood by her and her half brother, no matter what.

"Well, a course you're pretty," Bud said now, turning to look at her with a smile. "Always have been to me, anyway. *Real* pretty since you slimmed down so much." His honest face turned quizzical, horizontal lines creasing his sunburned forehead. He dug his bag of chewing tobacco out of his hip pocket. "Why you askin'?"

Lireinne shrugged, feeling embarrassed. "No reason. You coming in?" Shouldering her purse, she opened the truck's door and climbed down onto the gravel lot.

"I'll wait. You need money, baby girl?" Bud stuck a pinch of Red Man under his lip and reached for his spit cup.

"No, I got the rest of my pay. I won't be long." In the scorching sunlight, she paused by the truck's open door.

"Love you." Even as the words left her mouth, Lireinne was surprised at herself for saying them.

"Huh?" Bud said absently. "What'd you say?"

"Nothing." She shut the truck's door and turned away. Lireinne didn't know why she'd said that in the first place.

Love was a rare word in the Hooten household. Bud and Wolf became almost visibly uncomfortable whenever it came up. To Lireinne, saying *I love you* felt like one of those half-remembered French phrases—*la plume de ma tante est sur la table dans le jardin*—unfamiliar, wondering if she'd gotten it right. It seemed almost stupid to say it, as though she could have just ordered a well-done tractor or something equally ignorant from a snooty waiter.

Like she'd ever been to that kind of restaurant anyway, or ever would.

No, love must be what you *did,* like the kind of good stuff Bud was always doing, not something you said. Anybody could say, "I love you," Lireinne reflected as she walked up the wooden steps of Montz's Feed Store. For all she knew, even her loser mother might have said it to Bud once upon a time.

And yet, having uttered the word *love,* Lireinne found herself wanting to say it again, wanting to feel the taste of it on her tongue once more. It was a painful, sweet wanting that was all the more compelling for that word, *love,* being a relative stranger to her.

Before she pulled the screened door open to go inside the store, Lireinne shaded her eyes, looking down at Bud, patiently waiting for her in the stifling truck.

She waved to him. Bud waved back.

Je t'aime.

CHAPTER 7

It was late in the day. When Emma's truck had pulled up to the feed store, the only other vehicle parked in the lot was a rusted red pickup. A big man was slumped on its front seat, dozing in the heat.

"Hell of a scorcher, Emma." Sarah Fortune and Emma had gone inside and were waiting at the counter made of rough planks while Ricky Montz, the owner, was busy with another customer.

"Thanks for the ride into town," Sarah added.

"No problem at all. You're on my way. What's the story with your car?" Emma asked.

"It's a piece-of-shit Mercedes, that's the story." As always, Sarah's conversation was larded with profanity. "Goddamned parts take years to come in, even when it's a *new* car. My piece of shit's an antique."

At first, eighty-year-old Sarah's casual, salty language had shocked Emma when the epithets dropped from those wrinkled old-lady lips in a shower of flaming horse-apples. Over the past year, though, she'd become accustomed to it and now this eccentricity barely registered.

"Damnation, isn't it ever going to rain?" Sarah complained. She took off her green John Deere cap and fanned her face, setting her wiry gray hair to wafting like Spanish moss in the warm air of the store. "My goddamned pond's drying up. I'm gonna have to haul water out to the damned horses. Always gets me down in my back." She rubbed her bowed shoulder with a resigned smile. "Getting old, Em."

"Ouch." Emma smiled in sympathy. "My pond's not looking so good either, but it's got to rain soon."

Cultivate gratitude.

Gratitude.

Well, Emma was grateful summer would soon be winding down. She was grateful for Sarah's company. She was grateful for Xanax, too, even though the two tablets hadn't seemed to help very much. For several hours after talking to Con, she'd been too shaky to do anything more than pace and randomly pick up books and magazines, straightening an already obsessively clean house while praying, without much hope, the voices would be silent. Sheba had followed her from room to room, seemingly uneasy about this turn of events. Emma hadn't had a panic attack as bad as that one in over a month, not since the last time she'd talked to Con.

But thanks to the Xanax and time's passing, she'd eventually found a measure of calm once again. Feeling more herself, she got around to returning Sarah Fortune's call, and after hesitating for a long moment, Emma had agreed to take the old lady into Covington that Saturday afternoon. Sarah needed to buy oats for her horses, and Emma remembered she needed to go to Ricky Montz's store for chicken feed anyway, so this neighborly duty wasn't really a burden.

Then, too, driving Sarah into town should act as a remedy for her usual low spirits attendant upon a panic attack. The old woman had become surprisingly good—if sometimes abrasive—company, and Emma had learned from bitter experience it wouldn't be wise to be alone with her memories in the empty house, especially following this afternoon's harrowing conversation with Con.

"Thank God for air-conditioning," Emma said. "But it's August. Fall will be here before we know it."

"Can't come soon enough for me." Sarah sniffed. "I'm turning into a goddamned raisin."

Ricky Montz's feed store was housed in an old converted barn near the middle of downtown Covington. It was a dimly lit, confusing place with no apparent order to its fifty-pound bags of dog and cat food, plastic owl scarecrows, chainsaw parts, grass seed, sacks of oats and bales of hay, insecticides and fertilizers, garden tools and hoses, terra-cotta pots and watering troughs, tomato cages and stakes. All of this merchandise and more ranged haphazardly along the knot-holed plank walls and was piled in casual heaps on the dusty floor, as though it had been dropped there and forgotten as soon as it arrived. Trying to compete with the big-box "companion animal" emporiums, Ricky carried a fair assortment of pet products as well: leashes, collars, doghouses, and food bowls, plus a small selection of basic horse equipment like halters and lead ropes. At the moment, he was busy in the horse section helping a customer—a striking young girl, a heart-shape-faced beauty with long black hair. She was examining a bottle of fly spray with a dubious eye.

"I want some stuff that'll, like, kill the disgusting things *dead*," the girl was saying with some vehemence. "Keeping flies off him's just a start, you know?"

Ricky shook his head. "Don't know of any spray what kills 'em outright, not what's safe for horses, nohow."

Emma never really knew which eye she should focus on when she talked to Ricky, a big, gray-bearded man in bib overalls. One brown eye seemed to head east while the other wandered west. She hoped she didn't make him feel self-conscious about his walleye, but patient Ricky never seemed to notice. Generous with his time to a fault, he could be counted on to steer Emma through the bewildering array of farm products, always providing what answers he could to her usual laundry list of questions.

Ricky reached to get another spray bottle off the shelf. "Now this here stuff's the top of the line, claims to work longer."

"What you *need* is some goddamned LarvaStop." Sarah advanced on Ricky and the girl in wizened determination, her dentures clacking with enthusiasm. Bossy by nature, the old woman positively lived for the opportunity to give unsolicited advice to anyone who'd listen to it, and even those who wouldn't.

"Gotta kill the little bastards before they hatch out in the shit," Sarah announced. She folded her arms across the sunken bosom of her faded print housedress. "Me, I use it all the time out at my place. Expensive as hell, but it's worth every damned dime if you hate flies—and who the hell doesn't?"

Emma covered her mouth to keep from laughing out loud at the girl's wide-eyed reaction. Meet my friend, the incomparable Sarah, she thought. She never met a cuss word she didn't like.

Ricky looked pained. "Okay, Miz Fortune," he said. "Thanks for your usual ladylike input." He turned to the girl. "She's right, though. I got some LarvaStop right here." He handed a bright yellow plastic container down to her from the overhead shelf.

"How much is it?" The girl's scarred eyebrow lifted as she looked at the box. She handed it back.

Ricky studied the label. "Forty-four ninety-nine. Like Sarah said, LarvaStop ain't cheap, but it sure works good. Put a scoop of this in your horse's feed and the flies'll die before they can hatch out in the manure. You really ought to get the fly spray, too, if you want to do it right. That should fix you up fine."

The girl compressed her lips, frowning as though she faced a tough decision.

"Feed? I don't know about *feed*," she said uncertainly. She was quiet a moment. "It's just . . . he's so miserable, you know?" She paused, then the words tumbled out of her mouth in a rush. "Like, it sucks for him. Every summer, it's the same. I *hate* seeing him get all bit up."

"Who's this 'he,' young lady?" Sarah demanded.

"Mose." With a shake of her head, the girl took only the bottle of fly spray from Ricky. "He's not really mine, though. Mose's just an old horse, but nobody looks after him but me. He's a good person— never tries to bite or kick."

Sarah nodded in sage agreement. "Most of them won't, not if you're easy with 'em. Where's Mose stabled, anyhow?"

The girl hesitated again, seeming to weigh her words. "You're not going to call the Parish on me, are you? I'm doing my best, okay?"

"No ma'am," Sarah said emphatically. "If you're looking after him, there's no need."

The girl looked relieved. "Okay. Mose doesn't have a stable. He's behind our place, out off of Million Dollar Road, on back of the old Legendre property. I think they forgot about Mose when all the other horses went to the sale. He's been, like, all by himself in the field ever since I can remember."

Sarah's sharp little eyes lit up like road flares. Emma knew Sarah's real passion was the low-key rescue operation she ran out of her farm, taking in abandoned and abused horses and finding them homes, one horse at a time. "Grew up with 'em," she'd always said. "Isn't right, letting these old horses die of goddamned starvation when their idiot owners don't want to look after them anymore." There were plenty of hard-luck cases in the Parish and so Sarah's pasture always had at least a couple of rescues grazing the lush grasses while they waited for what she called their "forever homes."

"Holy shit!" Sarah crowed. "I *knew* there had to be another horse out there after Sammy Legendre quit the business. His old place is just down the road from Emma here and me. You're Bud Hooten's girl, Lireinne, aren't you? Well, you're doing the right thing, you know, by feeding him. That shit-for-brains Legendre up and went to stay with his son way the hell over to Bunkie after the bank took the farm. Sent all his stock to the killers himself, so you know *he* doesn't give a good goddamn anymore."

"The pond in the field's gone dry, so I've been watering him every day," Lireinne said. "But . . . he's *really* skinny." She lowered her eyes—extraordinary, clear green eyes fringed with long, sooty lashes—and shrugged, her expression shamed. "Didn't know Mose needed *feed,*" she muttered. "There's a lot of grass, tons of it, and he eats it all the time."

"Oh, that'll keep him alive, but that horse needs more than damned grass if he's pulled-down some. Look, take this." Sarah dug into her ancient, cracked-leather pocketbook, strewing crumpled Kleenex, stub-ends of pencils, odd pieces of paper, assorted change, and half-used rolls of antacids by the wadded handful across Ricky's countertop. With an air of triumph, she located the wallet buried somewhere in the chaos of her purse.

"Here." Sarah offered Lireinne a crumpled hundred-dollar bill. When the girl only stared at the money, the old woman flapped the note at her impatiently. "Go on, take it. Get rid of the goddamned flies and buy him some feed, too. He needs to *eat,* girl."

Lireinne licked her full lips and furrowed her brow, obviously deciding if she should take Sarah's hundred dollars. Slowly, seeming distrustful as a kicked cat, she reached and took the bill, smoothing it between her fingers. She looked up from the money, her face luminous with a huge smile. Those amazing green eyes were shining, and in that instant Emma was startled anew by the girl's extraordinary looks.

"What kind of feed should I get?" Lireinne asked. "What do horses eat, anyhow?"

That was all Sarah needed to hear.

Emma exchanged a rueful glance with Ricky Montz. It would be a solid half hour before her neighbor was done managing the Hooten girl's business because, aside from rescuing horses, there was nothing in the world Sarah Fortune liked more than telling people what to do.

Later, after they'd gotten the bags of chicken and horse feed loaded up and were in her truck on the way home, Emma was still turning the encounter at Montz's over in her head.

The low, lush strings of a Dvořák symphony filled the cool, spacious cab of the big Ford, a counterpart to the hushed whisper of the air-conditioning vents. Wanting to talk, Emma turned down the volume and turned to her friend.

"I've been thinking about that girl," Emma said. "It was so generous, what you did this afternoon. I feel like I ought to have done something, too, like . . . oh, I don't know. I never know, but *something,* at least. She seemed like she wanted to take good care of her horse, but she didn't really have any idea, did she? Or money to spare. You were kind to help her out. I wish I could have thought of a way to help, too."

Sarah leaned forward in the deep leather passenger seat and switched the radio to the country music station she preferred. She also raised the volume: a pair of twanging guitars and nasal, syrupy lyrics replaced the Dvořák. Somebody was having a very bad time getting over somebody named Retta, communicating a nasal feedlot misery. The singer sounded as though he was ready to hurl himself, wailing, under an eighteen-wheeler to put an end to it.

"Shoot, honey," Sarah said loudly over the redneck dirge. "That hundred dollars wasn't much at all, not to me. My dear, old, departed daddy owned most of the frontage out there on Highway 190. That was way before the shit-stupid New Orleans invasion rolled in over here and bought it all up. Hell, I've got *plenty* of money." Sarah cackled, probably not regretting in the least the lost pastures, marshes, oak, and pine trees that were now chain restaurants, auto dealerships, and strip malls.

"Besides, I believe that child's doing the best she can," Sarah went on. "Know her father, too—stepfather, that is. Bud Hooten's a hell of a good man who's been dealt a shitty goddamned hand." Sarah's feet, shod in a pair of child-sized cowboy boots and dangling inches above the truck's carpeting, swung in apparent indignation at the thought of Bud Hooten's luckless state.

"How so?" Emma asked, curious.

The old woman snorted. "Known Bud since he played halfback for Covington High, purt near twenty-two years ago. Poor bonehead bastard got himself hooked up with a trashy piece from Tylertown when he was working for the Parish. No-count bitch took off like they always do and left him with two little kids to raise all on his own. Now that gal would be the oldest, Lireinne. She'd be about eighteen by now. Real looker, isn't she?"

Emma kept her eyes on the road and nodded. "She's . . . *beauti-ful*. Unusually so. Even with that scar, she's just plain gorgeous. Beauty like that must come with its own set of problems, I'd think."

"No doubt." Thankfully, Sarah turned the radio down. "Sure has lost a pile of weight, that one. You should have seen her before. I seem to recall she'd always been a kid with a little more meat on her bones than was good for her, but for a while there she ballooned up like a goddamned life raft. Don't know why. Lord knows her asshole mother was never fat. Nowadays I'd almost say Lireinne's the image of her mom, only better lookin'. Classy, somehow, where her mother was always got up like a whore, no better than trash with a coat of paint slapped on it. No, that Lireinne could be a gal in one of those old-fashioned pictures, like the kind they got over in Europe. Good-looking as hell, except you can't miss but that she'd have a story to tell, too."

Emma said thoughtfully, "And only eighteen. No matter how pretty she is, though, it can't have been easy for her, having no mother when she was growing up. I admire that—her wanting to take care of an abandoned horse, especially when you can tell money's a real problem for her."

"Ain't *that* the goddamned truth."

Emma thought some more as the truck barreled down the highway past the turnoff to Million Dollar Road, a mile or so from Sarah's farm. She knew about being eighteen years old with no mother. And, she remembered once more with a pang, her daughter would've been eighteen this year, too. Emma had always been sure that her child would have been a girl, even though she'd lost the baby before the ultrasound could positively confirm it. What hope she'd had when she learned she was pregnant, what elation. Coming so soon after Con's graduation from law school, the pregnancy had been un-looked for but full of joy nonetheless. An only child, Emma had al-ways wanted lots of children, and this baby was the beginning of her big family.

But one overcast day in her second month, Emma had been planting snapdragons and pansies in the yard and felt a sudden cramp in the small of her back, a bad one that grew rapidly worse. Somehow making it to the house, she'd called Con and they'd rushed to the obstetrician's office as the pain threatened to become unbearable. The tests at the hospital soon destroyed all her hope: it was an ectopic pregnancy, one that would never have come to term without killing Emma and her baby. Now the tiny life inside her was dying. The fetal monitor's faint *whush, whush, whush* stuttered, stalled, and then it was gone.

It was the last time she would hear the music of her daughter's beating heart.

"There'll be other babies," Con had said. He was crying, holding her hand as the hospital staff prepped her for surgery. Emma had been numb, facing the procedure that would separate her from her daughter, but she squeezed his hand. Trying to be strong for his sake, all she wanted was to turn her face to the wall and wish for death to take her, too.

"Lots of babies," she said faintly.

But there hadn't been any more babies. After years of trying, that chance of a child had been Emma's one and only chance. Perhaps—no matter that he'd said it wasn't the reason—perhaps that was the reason he'd left her. Con had found someone else because she hadn't been enough for him by herself.

But still . . . Eighteen years ago, Emma had had a child of her own, however briefly.

Motherless Lireinne Hooten was eighteen.

"Do you think she'd be offended if I . . . offered to do something for her?" Emma wondered out loud. Not wanting to be misunderstood, though, she added quickly, "With some more money for the cause, I mean. I could do that. I never spend all of my alimony check, and the farm's almost pulling its own weight these days." Emma's natural reticence prevented a more personal involvement, but if money would make a difference, she was certain she should do it.

Sarah's wrinkled, age-spotted face turned reflective.

"Don't know 'bout that. Those country folks can be prideful. Lireinne only took that money from me because she wanted it for

Mose. Damned horses are expensive to keep. She'll blow through that hundred dollars in a hurry, although I'm sure it seemed like a shitload of cash to her. It'd be best to get that old horse moved off the Legendre place before too much longer, find him a real home before winter comes. Didn't sound like he was doing so goddamned hot."

Emma slowed the truck, making the turn off the highway and onto the gravel road leading to Sarah's forty-acre farm. "Well, you could arrange a rescue for him. Then he'll be fine, right?" Hearing Sarah's proposed plan, however, she felt a sudden, obscure disappointment.

"I could do that, surely," Sarah agreed. "And I likely will, sooner or later, but that's a ways off yet. I've seen this kind of situation before. Right now that child feels responsible for him, she loves him. You heard her—he's been a big part of who she is, ever since she was a little thing. Lireinne won't want that horse to go, even though she can't afford him. Shit, if you really want to help out, go over there, get to know her. Haul feed to Bud's place while we wait on her to come around. Besides, I'm mortally certain money's not the only problem there. Transportation's got to be a real bitch for those folks, and I'd bet my damned pacemaker Lireinne needs somebody besides an old horse in her life, too. Someone of the female persuasion."

The big silver truck rolled to a stop in front of Sarah's neat farmhouse, the dust a gritty cloud hanging over the gravel road. Seven cats leapt off their perches on the porch railings and came trotting across the yard to meet them, their tails erect as furry flagpoles.

"Back the truck up to the shed, why don't you," Sarah said, sounding tired. "These days, a hundred goddamn pounds of feed weighs more than it used to. I'm turning eighty-one next month."

"Happy birthday," Emma said absently. She was still thinking. "About the girl, Lireinne—I'm sure she won't want someone butting in." Actually, her strong, fierce beauty had been fascinating, but a little intimidating as well. Emma hadn't been able to bring herself to offer more than a shy nod to the girl during the whole feed-store encounter.

The two women got out and walked around to the back of the truck.

"Besides," Emma said with a dismissive shake of her head, "I know next to nothing about horses, and you know me, I'm so stupidly shy, it's embarrassing. Can't I just give you some money for her?" The cats twining around her ankles, Emma dropped the tailgate and swung the first bag of feed over her shoulder. "Where do you want this?"

Opening the door, Sarah pointed to a wooden pallet in the corner of her relentlessly organized shed. "Over there," she said. "Look, Emma, I already told you money's not Lireinne's only problem. Shit, if that was all that's wanted here, I'd do it myself. Now *you*—you've got nothing at all going on until it's time to put in your fall garden. It's too damned hot to do that yet, so get off your ass and drive out to Bud's place. It's just over there on Million Dollar Road. There's a damned mailbox on the road, says 'Hooten,' so you can't miss it. You've got a truck, Lireinne needs help keeping that old horse fed, and I know Bud's hardly ever home before dark—if he gets home at all, which seems unlikely. Man's a goddamned fool for work."

"But I'd need . . ." Emma was appalled at the idea of calling on people she didn't even know. She dropped the heavy bag on the pallet, turning to face her friend.

Sarah said, "What you *need* is to get out more. You're too damned young to spend the rest of your life cooned up on your farm like you do. For crap's sake, it's not natural."

Emma's reluctance was wavering—until she remembered Con. He was working at the alligator farm on Million Dollar Road, and it sounded likely the Hootens' place was close. Seeing him, even in passing, wasn't something she could withstand. Emma was sure of *that*. Look what had happened after only a phone call. Her fragile equilibrium had been reduced to ash, months of hard-won coping scattered far and wide.

"I don't know, Sarah. Con works out there on Million Dollar Road, you know. What if, what if I ran into him?" It was another reason, Emma thought, to avoid venturing into the Hooten girl's backyard. "I don't think I can afford . . . seeing him, not without a lot of medication." She laughed, but there was no humor in it.

Sarah made a rude noise. "What you can't afford is *lonely*. Get over it, Emma. It's been two years, hasn't it? Quit hiding out from your ex, quit burying yourself in that damned little organic hole. Make an effort to know your neighbors at least, since it looks like you're never going to try to get to know a *man*."

This was a warning shot, a promise of more advice to come. Getting out more and meeting men was one of the old woman's constant harangues, one that always left Emma feeling frustratingly tongue-tied. Any further resistance would soon collapse in the face of Sarah's bullying anyway: besides, Emma knew her friend was only pressing her to do what *somebody* needed to do—no matter that Sarah's somebody did it under friendly duress—and so she capitulated at last.

"Okay, okay! Since you're so godawful pushy, I'll try to go out there."

"When?" Sarah demanded.

When indeed, Emma was thinking as she heaved the second bag of horse feed over her shoulder. Look at it this way, she told herself. Wouldn't you have wanted someone to help your own daughter if she needed it? Of course you would.

True, too, it had been a long time since she'd reached out to anyone, Emma realized, even in simple kindness. Much too long a time. That, she knew with a new beam of understanding, wasn't a part of herself she should be willing to give up at any price. Helping Lireinne Hooten could be good for her as well. Doing a small favor, costing her little or nothing, would be scary, yes, but it would be . . . *new*. Hadn't she already decided that her life needed to change?

You'll have to reinvent yourself, Emma.

And surely there'd be little chance of running into Con if she made the trip out to Million Dollar Road when he wasn't likely to be there. He'd never worked Saturdays, right?

"Maybe Saturday?" Emma murmured, thinking out loud. She

dropped the bag of feed on the pallet and rejoined Sarah outside. A black-and-white-spotted cat lay flat on the warm metal truck bed, stretching its sinuous length beside Emma's bag of chicken feed. She picked up the cat, stroking a fingertip under its silky chin. The cat purred, its eyes half closed in pleasure.

"Maybe on Saturday," Emma said. "I'll think about it."

"Hmmph." Sarah slammed shut the door to the shed. "Don't think too long. She'll be out of feed by next Saturday. Take a damned bag of oats out there. The piece-of-shit Mercedes won't be fixed by then so I flat can't do it. Somebody needs to help Lireinne out, and that person ought to be *you*, Emma. Be good for you both."

The warm, pink summer evening was flaming into a cyclamen dusk. Emma's chickens and Sheba would be waiting back at the farm, as hungry for their dinner as though they'd not been fed for a week. With a tired nod, she put the cat on the ground and gave Sarah a quick hug.

Before climbing into her truck, Emma wondered what she was getting herself into, but deep inside she knew Sarah was right. She could do this small thing for someone else. Childless, alone except for a stray dog and a bunch of chickens, wandering around her house terrified of voices that weren't there—something needed to change, and soon.

Emma rolled down the power window. "Next Saturday for sure," she said. Sarah's stubborn, lined face relaxed into a gratified smile.

"Good," she said shortly.

"But just the one time," Emma warned. Just this once, she'd make herself do it. "After that, your car will be fixed and you can take over."

"Bullshit," said Sarah Fortune.

CHAPTER 8

The alarm clock had gone off an extra thirty minutes earlier this past week, but to Lireinne that lost half hour of sleep was well worth getting up with the sun.

She'd learned to love this new part of her routine, hanging out with Mose while he scarfed his breakfast. Sharing that time with him made her long day at the alligator farm seem a little shorter, too, knowing that she was going to get to feed him again after work. Like, that horse *loved* to eat. He'd hoovered up almost the whole sack of oats already.

This Friday morning in the kitchen, she scooped Mose's feed with a big plastic measuring cup from the scant layer of oats on the bottom of the bag. Lireinne worried that Bud wouldn't be able to take her to Montz's tomorrow. He'd said he'd try, but still: while Lireinne knew he'd do his best, some things just couldn't be helped. Bud's freaking work schedule was one of those things.

It was 6:30 in the morning, the early light a pearled, luminescent gray. Her half brother was still asleep on the sectional and Bud was long gone for the Walmart distribution center when Lireinne walked out back with Mose's breakfast. The old horse eagerly buried his nose in the golden oats, snuffling and chewing in deep contentment until the last kernel was gone. Lireinne waited until he was finished, then dragged the Dollar General dishpan back under the fence.

She climbed carefully through the barbed wire to the other side where Mose waited for her. "Hold still, boy." Lireinne covered his body with the fly spray, the horse's skin twitching under the mist of fine droplets. Sarah Fortune had said it might be a week or so before the LarvaStop began to work, but already the repellent was helping. A big black horsefly buzzed around Mose's ears but didn't settle on them. Muttering angrily it flew off in search of something more hospitable to chew on.

"Showed you!" Lireinne jeered. "Got to get to work, Mose. See you later."

When she brought the dishpan back inside the trailer Wolf was still sprawled under the blankets on the couch, snoring. Good for him, Lireinne thought as she pulled on her shrimp boots, trying to be as quiet as possible. School was bound to be starting any day now, and he should get all the rest he could while he was still on summer vacation. Let him sleep, she thought with a fond smile.

Lireinne was at the door and ready to start walking to the alligator farm when Wolf rolled over and rose on one elbow. He blinked sleepily, his head backlit by the pale morning sunlight just beginning to filter through the dusty window.

"Hey, sis," he said with a yawn.

"Hey," she replied softly. "I was trying not to make too much noise. I figured you'd want to sleep in. What're you doing up so early?"

"I dunno." Rubbing his eyes, bare-chested Wolf sat up on the sofa and gathered the blanket around his waist. Sometimes, especially before he put on his black Goth getup and Doc Martens, Lireinne could see the little boy he used to be—a skinny kid, too lonely, anxious around people he didn't know well—and that made her heart ache. Except for the acne, the peach fuzz on his cheeks, and the prominent Adam's apple, he hadn't changed so very much from the shy younger brother she'd helped raise. Lireinne totally understood that shyness: her mother's leaving them hadn't been easy for him either, even though he'd been only four when she'd walked out. It was like there'd always been a woman-shaped hole in both their lives.

But unlike her, now Wolf had *some* friends at least. Before he fell in with the Goth crowd, he'd been as alone as Lireinne and that had been hard for her to take, harder than her own isolation. Pain in the ass or not, he was her little brother, the only blood relative she had who gave a damn about her. She might not say it often, but she loved him and Wolf loved her, too, even though she couldn't remember the last time they'd said it to each other.

When she'd been going through her bad time last year, Wolf had been good to Lireinne, even in the midst of his own self-absorbed sojourn through high school. She'd never talked to him about what Brett had done, but he was bound to have heard the rumors. He never mentioned it to her, but months later, Lireinne learned through the school's grapevine that he'd gotten into it in gym class with some kid who'd shot his mouth off, calling his sister a whore.

Wolf had gotten the worst of that fight. Black-eyed, split-lipped, and sullen, he'd refused to tell Bud the real reason he was suspended, stoutly maintaining it was over bullshit. He wouldn't say another word about it, and Lireinne had been beyond grateful for Wolf's closed mouth. She hadn't felt quite so alone then, knowing that her brother had stuck up for her. Further, without her having to tell him, like her, he knew better than to let Bud find out the truth. No, she and Wolf had never talked about the whispers around school, but that was better than okay with her. Sometimes Lireinne looked after Wolf, and sometimes he looked after her.

But it was past seven and time to get walking to work. Lireinne had opened the door to the damp morning air when it occurred to her that there was something she'd been meaning to ask her brother. "So, when's school starting up?" she said.

"Started three days ago," Wolf said with another big yawn.

"What?" Lireinne stopped dead in the doorway. Had the summer really gone by that fast? "So why the hell aren't you there, then?" she demanded.

"Not going." Wolf shrugged, his eyes narrowed in defensiveness.

"What's that?" Lireinne couldn't take this in. Surely she'd misunderstood.

"I'm not going back, okay?" He fell back on his elbows, shaking his head. "Finished tenth grade, but so what? It's not like I'm going to learn anything, nothing that's going to get me anywhere, I mean. We all know I'm not gonna go to college. This way, I can get a job like you. I can help out and bring in some more money around here."

But Wolf *couldn't* drop out. Lireinne was aghast. Not *Wolf*.

"You can't!" She shut the door, leaning against it for support. "Don't quit," Lireinne pleaded. "You've only got a couple more years of high school. Maybe you can get a scholarship or, or . . . a grant when you graduate."

Wolf lowered his head despondently, his longish black hair tumbling around his acne-pitted face. "C'mon, Lireinne—get real, okay? They don't give scholarships away to guys like me. Gonna end up just like Bud. That's a fact no matter how you want to look at it. Two more years of high school won't change a damned thing for me."

Shaken by his fatalism, Lireinne sat down on the sectional beside him and slipped her arm around his thin shoulders.

"Don't do it!" she said, giving Wolf a rough hug. "Don't be stupid. Dropping out is dumb as hell. You're good at math, and science, and, and other stuff—not like *me*. You could maybe be an engineer someday. You'd make a ton of money then." Lireinne warmed to her subject, thinking of all the ways Wolf's life would be different from her own if he went to college.

"You can get TOPS, go to LSU in Baton Rouge," she added. TOPS was a state government scholarship program for Louisiana high school kids who held at least a 3.0 grade average and scored above a 27 on the ACT. Wolf would easily qualify for having his tuition paid, at least. He was so smart, unlike her. Even before the rape, Lireinne had come to dislike school so much that the only A she'd ever made was in French.

"Yeah?" Wolf countered. "Even if I did, how the hell would I pay for books, and . . . a, a room in the dorm, and all the other shit you gotta have? Like Bud's ever going to have that kind of money.

Not." Her brother pulled away from her, his mouth mutinous. "And I'm not taking out any student loans either. Not gonna go into debt just so I can say I went to college. Fuck no, I'm done with school."

Wolf gave her a sullen glance. "Leave it alone, okay?"

Lireinne was exhausted even before she set out on her mile-long walk to work.

Already running behind, she'd argued with her brother until she couldn't wait any longer, but Wolf was adamant, refusing to consider returning to Covington High no matter what she said. Lireinne had been forced to give up because she couldn't afford to be late again. Harlan Baham, the crew boss, would make her morning even more miserable if she came in after eight. Sick with frustration, she slammed the door on her way out. Lireinne knew her kid brother was making the same argument she'd made to Bud when she'd quit school. He'd tried to talk her out of it, too, just like she'd just done with Wolf. Now she knew how Bud must have felt—sick with frustration and worry.

But her situation had been totally different, Lireinne tried to tell herself as she hurried down Million Dollar Road under a rapidly clouding sky. Wolf didn't understand that there weren't any real jobs for people with no education, none that paid worth a damn. He made mostly A's and B's in school; sometimes he even made the Honor Roll. He could *do* something with his life—if only he didn't give up before his life even began. That couldn't happen. One of them had to get out of here. Anybody with half a brain could see it wasn't going to be *her*.

She'd be hosing for the rest of her freaking life.

It was nearly eight o'clock. Lireinne was already worn out from the confrontation, but somehow she made it to work on time and the omnipresent reek in the barns greeted her. At least it's Friday, she thought, in a weary attempt to find a bright side to this already terrible morning.

Better get on it, Lireinne told herself, and so with a grim industry she got busy hosing, taking it out on the cement floors all through the long morning and the early afternoon, barn by barn. Soon the men left for lunch up at the house and she was alone with the BFG gators, making sure she left the floor spotless before she moved on to the last five filthy floors waiting for her.

No matter how many times Lireinne tried to puzzle out what she could do about this latest trouble, she was left with the same miserable sense of failure, sure that she was letting Wolf make the mistake of a lifetime. She was the only big sister he had, and if she only knew how to explain this to him, he'd *have* to see she was right.

But if there was a gap in Wolf's faulty logic, today Lireinne couldn't freaking see it. Kids dropped out all the time for the same reasons, and it wasn't like she could do anything to help with the money anyway. She only made enough to pay for crap like paper towels, toilet paper, and the occasional bag of dog treats.

A long twenty minutes later, the BFG barn was finished. At the far end down by the entrance, Lireinne slid open the plywood access door to Snowball's tank. The massive gator drifted in ivory somnolence, only the tip of her snout and bony eye ridges visible in the dark water. Lireinne gazed down at Snowball, moodily wondering what, if anything, went on in that big white head day after day. In a long-ago biology class, she remembered the teacher describing reptilian brains as being similar to oversized computer chips, registering only an "on/off" switch.

"A gator is 'on' when it's hungry, or for only a week or so during breeding season," the teacher had said. "Any other time, they're essentially turned off. That's it. Hungry—on. Not hungry—off. Sex, on. No sex, off. There's no higher brain function in those animals. They're big, scaly appetites. Period."

Lireinne didn't know why she'd always been so fascinated with Snowball. Perhaps it was because she was special. The only white gator, at eleven feet she was the largest animal on the farm. Lireinne had always wanted to be special. But maybe it was because the big lizard was all alone, trapped, and seemed pissed off about it, too—qualities Lireinne could identify with, especially today. So . . . what if she and Snowball were both free to do whatever they wanted?

Lireinne considered that for a moment. Snowball released into the wild would have a big old time for a little while, at least until some trapper discovered her during the gator-hunting season and killed her for the money her hide would bring him.

But Lireinne couldn't run away to Paris even if through some miracle she got the opportunity because she couldn't leave Wolf, not since he seemed hell-bent on destroying his future. Like she'd do him any favors by staying anyway. She was no role model. She was such a loser, she hadn't even realized it was September, that school had already started.

I mean, look at me, Lireinne thought. Eighteen years old and the only job I can get is hosing crap. Oh, and don't forget that my best friends are an eleven-foot gator and a beat-up old horse.

Mired in these depressing reflections, an inescapable gloom fell upon Lireinne, mirrored in the clouds lowering in the sky outside. They were metallic gray and dense, like a layer of lead painted on the sky, and threatened rain, the rain everyone Parish wide had despaired of seeing ever again after the long, dry summer. She wished it would cut loose and freaking pour. The humid air was like breathing a thick soup of dust.

Below Lireinne's feet, Snowball's length slowly undulated to the edge of the tank. The big gator floated, motionless, until she dropped the ritual dog biscuit into the water. "Here." Lireinne didn't stay to watch Snowball snap it up, but slid the access door shut and locked it. What was the point? Five more barns; another hour and a half. Not looking forward to going home, not even to feeding Mose his dinner, she lugged the hose outside the entrance and began coiling its heavy length around the iron coupler before she moved on.

Lireinne was almost done, just another ten feet left to wind, when without warning, from behind her someone approached. She turned around, holding the hose's nozzle at her hip.

"Hey, girl."

It was Harlan Baham, the crew boss. She'd been so preoccupied she hadn't heard him coming, and now he was so close he was practically on the toes of her shrimp boots.

"You done in there?" Harlan's big, work-scarred hand descended on her shoulder. Lireinne couldn't hide her involuntary flinch, but she nodded in wary agreement.

"Yeah," she said. She wanted him to take his hand away, but knew she couldn't tell him to knock it off. Harlan was her boss. She couldn't risk making him mad at her for any reason, not if she wanted to keep this hateful, desperately necessary job. Harlan seemed to be enjoying her discomfort, too, and that was somehow worse than his touching her.

"What's up?" Lireinne asked cautiously.

"Been thinkin 'bout you," Harlan said with a greasy smile. "Thinkin 'bout how you're bound to be feeling the pinch, hosers getting paid shit, and don't I know it." His hand moved lower and closed around her upper arm, squeezing in a mindless rhythm. Squeezing, squeezing. He licked his thick lips.

Lireinne froze, her heart suddenly thundering. Harlan was reminding her of Brett in the truck, right before he'd locked the doors and grabbed her. All that was missing was the LSU cap.

"I could help you out some," Harlan whispered, a world of intent in his throaty rasp, "if you want to play nice."

They were alone in the doorway of the BFG barn, alone at the back of the property: the rest of the crew was up in the house eating lunch. Lireinne's mouth went dry. Her hands clutched the hose's nozzle in an unthinking death grip. Harlan was too *close;* he had her by the arm. His nauseating smell—cigarette smoke, days-old sweat, and rancid hair oil—was like a poison gas, worse than the barn reek. She was totally *freaking* stupid. She should have seen this coming. She should *never* have let herself get trapped like this.

Lireinne looked wildly over Harlan's shoulder, but there was no one in sight. She was on her own this time, too, she realized with a sinking heart, just like before with Brett.

His mean little eyes dancing, Harlan's low, hoarse voice thickened with insinuation. "What you say? Want to come over to my place later on?" He slid his hand down to her waist, pulling her toward him.

Lireinne's paralysis broke. She jabbed her elbow in Harlan's side, as revolted as though his hand were a cottonmouth moccasin. "You jackass," she snarled in desperation. "Don't you *dare* grab me, or, or . . ."

"Or what? Look who thinks she's a big ol' gal." Harlan leered as he let his hand fall. He wiped his dirt-grimed, perspiring neck and raised an eyebrow in speculation.

"We ain't gonna be friendly, huh," he said. He turned his head and spat. "Well, I just might let ol' Mr. Costello up to the house hear 'bout you getting sloppy, messing shit up in the barns with that there hose you got. Believe you me, your ass'll be outta here in no time. I even got somebody in mind for the job, you don't give me a piece of what you're keepin' so close. My sister's gal, Chimene, got laid off at the gas station just last week. Come here, you."

Harlan hitched up his work pants before he lunged. He was quick for a big man, but Lireinne leapt like a startled doe and he grabbed nothing but air. Thick lips split in a confident grin, Harlan reached for her again as she backed away, still clutching the hose.

"Hold still," he said with a laugh. "You little whore, I got you now."

The hose! Lireinne's mind screamed. With a twist the nozzle opened full bore. Water exploded, the hose a live thing in her hand. "Get back—I *mean* it." The pressurized flood tore the ground at Harlan's white rubber boots. Fat brown chunks of mud shot upward, clotting his stained pant legs.

"Get the fuck back, I'm telling you!" Lireinne shouted.

"Shee-it," Harlan laughed. "Ain't afraid of a little water. C'mon, honey—give ol' Harlan some sugar." Lunging again, he had her shirt. "Let's see what you got under this here."

With a wordless shriek, Lireinne raised the cannon of water to Harlan's gray-stubbled face. The powerful stream clobbered him solidly on the nose, flooding his astonished pig eyes. Harlan's head shot backward over his shoulders like he'd been sucker-punched. Arms flailing, Harlan slipped on the slick ground, and toppled flat on his ass with a splat. At the same moment the sky overhead shattered in a great crack of thunder. Covering his face with his hands, Lireinne's would-be rapist was pinned under the water hammer pummeling his chest and shoulders.

"*Bitch!*" Harlan's howl was muffled, but there was no mistaking his rage.

Lireinne didn't stop to watch. She wasn't waiting to get grabbed again. She flung the hose away from her, and freed, the long rubber cylinder was a twisting anaconda hurling angry spirals of water. With a single white-faced glance over her shoulder at her attacker, Lireinne almost slipped in the mud herself, but she was running now, running for home as fast as her shrimp boots would let her.

She was leaving five barns unhosed, there was work remaining for her on this terrible Friday, but she ran.

Nobody was home when Lireinne fell inside the trailer door, sobbing for breath from her headlong flight down Million Dollar Road.

"Wolf?"

But her brother was gone, embarked on being a dropout. He was probably riding around with Bolt or some other loser from Covington High—someone with a car and a fake doctor's excuse to get out of class. She was alone in the trailer. Lireinne threw the dead bolt, knowing that it would be of little use if Harlan went crazy with rage and came after her. The trailer would be easy to break into. Should she call the distribution center and get them to send Bud home? Should she call the police?

Thoughts of Bud and the cops sobered Lireinne. Her breath slowed, her racing heart pounded down. Lireinne collapsed in a boneless heap on the sectional, holding her bowed head in her hands, her fingers buried in her long black hair. She couldn't call Bud at work. He'd go postal and beat the hell out of Harlan, for sure. After Brett's assault, hadn't she endured Bud's questioning glances, his unspoken worry for just that reason—keeping her step-father out of the Parish lockup? Besides, Bud had enough to worry about already. He needed the hours on the loading dock: the last thing she wanted to do was screw that up, too. There'd be September's bills to pay soon.

And forget the police. Her mouth trembling, Lireinne almost sobbed with the frustration of knowing what would happen if she called them. The police wouldn't believe her, not if it was her word against Harlan's. She'd figured that out the hard way when she'd tried to get the school counselor to at least *listen* to her. No, nobody ever believed the girl, especially if the girl was just some hoser who lived in a broken-down trailer. Lireinne had no doubt Harlan would have a good story ready should the cops even bother to come out to investigate her allegations. It had been a near thing, but he hadn't actually raped her. Oh, he'd talked rough and grabbed her shirt, but Lireinne wondered if that was enough to get Harlan into real trouble. Calling the police would probably stir shit up worse, with no good to come of it.

Her job was bound to be shot after this, Lireinne realized, twisting her hands uselessly. After getting hosed, Harlan was sure to follow through on his threat. Remembering the look of soaked astonishment on his brutal face, though, her mouth involuntarily turned up in a halfhearted grin. He'd looked so freaking *lame,* rolling around on the ground in the mud. If Lireinne didn't need the job so bad, that would have been worth laughing at now. She had to admit it felt good, having defended herself for once, having taken care of a would-be rapist.

But . . . her *job.*

Outside, after nearly ninety days of drought, the rain began falling with a slow tack-hammer beat on the trailer's fiberglass roof. Lireinne hugged herself as she got up and peered out of the window. The first drops were streaking the dusty windshield of the minivan in the weeds. It was really raining at last.

It was raining and there was Mose to feed before these first drops turned into a downpour. Lireinne didn't know if wet feed would hurt him, but she couldn't take the chance.

Hurrying, she found an umbrella behind the door, three of its ribs broken and dangling, but it would do to keep the oats dry while the old horse ate his dinner. With still-shaking hands, she poured a measure from the last of the feed into the plastic dishpan, added the LarvaStop, and dashed out back where Mose was waiting for her by the fence.

Eyeing the umbrella with wary suspicion, but drawn by the scent of grain, he sidled closer, snorted, and then got to work on his dinner. The rain was falling in heavy, slow drops. Lireinne held the umbrella over the dishpan as the dust of the parched ground popped in dry explosions, and the steady fall swiftly intensified until it turned to streams of water, to a river, and then the rain was a cataract, cold and clean and life-giving as oxygen.

Her long hair dripping into her eyes, Lireinne shivered in her wet T-shirt and shorts. While Mose was busy eating, she confided in him about Wolf's dropping out, the hosing of Harlan, and at last she broke her long silence about Brett. Mose was only the second person she'd ever told, the first being useless Mrs. Cooper, who hadn't believed her.

"What the hell am I gonna do now?"

Lireinne knew Mose didn't have any answers, but he was the only person she could trust with any of her troubles. She didn't dare share a thing with Wolf because he might not keep his mouth shut this time. He might tell *Bud*. Where would they all be then?

Bud would be in jail, that's where, and then they'd be out on their asses, Lireinne thought grimly. She swiped her soaked hair out of her eyes. Without Bud's income, she and Wolf would be *fucked*. No, there was no one but her old horse to tell about Harlan, but thank God he'd waited until Friday before trying to jump her behind the barns. She'd gotten a full two-weeks' pay yesterday, but the specter of Monday loomed. Monday was going to come around like it always did. Come Monday, she'd almost certainly be out of the only shitty job she could get. She'd be an unemployed hoser and Wolf would still be a dropout.

"Sorry you're getting wet, Mose." Lireinne stroked the horse's rain-soaked neck, wishing he had a warm, dry place where he could wait out the downpour. Was she imagining his liquid brown eyes returning her defeated gaze with sympathy? Probably so, but right now, she'd take it where she could get it.

Lireinne hurried back inside the trailer, out of the rain.

In spite of her wretched day, after a frozen dinner and a hot shower Lireinne fell fast asleep that night to the sound of the steady drizzle pattering on the roof and the faint thunder of Wolf's Xbox in the front room.

She slept without dreaming, awaking the next morning to washy, pale sunshine and a chill in her room: the rain had stopped during the night and a cool front had moved through. Lireinne sat up in bed and stretched, yawning. Her clock said it was after nine. Somehow she'd slept through her alarm. Lireinne frowned, feeling as though she'd forgotten something important, until she remembered what had happened yesterday afternoon.

Harlan. Her job. Wolf's dropping out.

And as those appalling recollections sank in, Mose whinnied out back and Lireinne remembered that the bag of oats was almost finished. There was barely enough feed left to give the horse his breakfast this morning, but then it would be done.

Before Lireinne knew she ought to be feeding him, she'd never had to worry about how she'd pay for it, and now that she was doing right by Mose, she was going to be broke. There was a word for this feeling, if only she could figure out what it was. It was on the tip of her tongue, a word from her last English class. *Ironic,* Lireinne thought. That's it. I'm ironic now.

Overwhelmed by the notion of her life being ironic before she could even have a legal *drink,* Lireinne threw the covers over her head, wishing she were seven years old again, having no cares beyond how to spend her Saturday. Like, would she take her Barbie down to Tiger Branch and play *Gilligan's Island* on the rain-swollen creek bank? Would she climb the live oak by the fence to see if the crows' nestlings were still there? As a child, Lireinne had been used to these solitary pursuits. Isolated in the country, with other kids few and far between, it was a very rare day when someone was around to share the life of her imagination with her.

When Lireinne was three, she and her mother had moved into the trailer with Bud. She remembered her mother had occasionally spent time with her—for a little while. Her mother would drink Diet Coke and smoke cigarettes while Lireinne carefully poured out tiny cups of make-believe tea for her and the pink bear, but those tea parties never seemed to last for more than a few minutes. Soon her mother would be on the phone again, pacing, smoking, and talking to someone named Duane. The tea party was always over after that.

"Hush up, Lireinne, go away. I'm not gonna play with you now. Mommy's *busy*, okay?"

Often Lireinne's mother left the little girl behind, by herself in the trailer, when she caught rides into town with a man in a white truck. Being alone was frightening, but then her mother grew big with the new baby. She'd stayed home then, complaining bitterly about her lost figure, and making fudge—that is, when she wasn't taking long naps. Her mother had left for good, though, a little over three years after Wolf, known then as Larry, was born. Then Bud had to pay the neighbor woman, Miss Penny, to look after Lireinne and her little brother while he was working.

Lireinne remembered that arrangement had been okay. She'd liked Miss Penny because the old woman pretended to drink the make-believe tea. She also drank out of a brown bottle she kept in her purse. While the stuff in the bottle would put her to sleep on the sofa, Miss Penny had been fun when she was awake. She used to make Lireinne sugar-and-butter sandwiches, too. There'd been plenty of salty potato chips and discount-brand soda, lunches of canned pineapple rings dotted with maraschino cherries and mayonnaise. Those calorie-dense, nutrition-poor meals and snacks had tasted better than good to Lireinne. They tasted of safety, of caring. She ate and ate and ate, remembering the sweets her grandmother in Mississippi had sometimes given her, and her mother's warm fudge.

And living so far out in the country as Bud did, until Lireinne grew older there'd been only a couple of other children to play with, like Miss Penny's niece Shayla who'd come to visit her aunt sometimes. Then, too, for a few months there'd been another little girl who lived down on Million Dollar Road in a trailer, one lacking indoor plumbing, but with a pack of cur-dogs in the yard. The little girl had given Lireinne a case of head lice before one of the mean dogs had bitten her and consequently Bud put an end to Lireinne's visits to the other trailer. Anyhow, soon the little girl moved away.

So, for the most part, Lireinne had grown up with companions who lived in her toy box—the pink bear, the Barbie Bud had bought her—and her friends who lived in the trees and fields, like Mose and the crows. After he got to be old enough, sometimes Wolf had joined her. Those times had been the best, climbing and exploring, and making up compelling, dramatic adventures. Her brother had been a prince, she'd been a princess, and Mose had been a noble steed. Wolf outgrew those games before Lireinne did, although he'd loved it when she read him the gorier stories from the old, dog-eared book of fairy tales Miss Penny had left behind when she went to live with her sister in town. Lireinne's favorite story had been the one about Cinderella, but now she knew better than to hope for a fairy godmother. Now, she knew *more* than enough to believe Prince Charming was a nice guy. There were no real princes in the world.

Only Bretts.

Mose nickered again outside her bedroom window. Lireinne groaned, wanting to put her pillow over her ears. Under the covers the bed was warm, smelling of laundry detergent and the scent of her own body. Unwilling to rise and face the day, she'd have loved to escape into sleep again, but there was Mose to feed. Only a scant pan of oats left in the bag, Lireinne thought again. How was she going to get to town to buy more? That worry and the sound of hooves splashing in the mud along the fence line finally drove Lireinne out of bed. She couldn't escape her ironic life forever.

Lireinne had just pulled a sweatshirt on over her nightgown, figuring that Mose wouldn't care what she was wearing, when Wolf knocked on her door.

"Yo—sis, somebody here to see you." His muffled, sleepy voice on the other side of the door sounded deeply aggrieved at the early-morning visitor who'd disturbed his rest.

"Oh, yeah?" Who in the hell would have come out to the trailer this early on a Saturday morning? Lireinne wondered. Nobody ever came here, nobody who wanted to see *her,* anyway. It couldn't be somebody from the alligator farm, could it? No, she decided, they wouldn't bother to come to her house to fire her: there'd be plenty of time for that on Monday, after all.

"Who is it?" Lireinne called through the door.

"I dunno—some lady in a truck. She's waiting outside, so, like, hurry up. I was trying to *sleep.*"

"Okay, okay. I'm coming."

Lireinne threw a pair of jeans on underneath her sweatshirt and nightgown and combed her tangled hair with her fingers. Wolf was a grumbling heap underneath the blankets when she hurried past the sectional. "Sorry," she said, opening the door to the cool, fresh-smelling morning. Once outside, she blinked in the bright sunlight at the rare visitor.

Wolf had it right. There was a woman in the yard, waiting be-side a big, shiny truck, looking like she was freaked out some and maybe a little bit lost. She seemed familiar, and after a confused second or two, Lireinne recognized her as the quiet lady from the feed store last Saturday—the gray-haired one who'd been there with the old woman, Sarah Fortune.

Hanging out in the yard next to the burn pile and all of Bud's other junk, the gray-haired lady was ridiculously overdressed: her soft cotton sweater, khaki shorts, and brand-new-looking Top-Siders screamed of the casual luxury women like her always seemed to take for granted. What was *she* doing here? Lireinne shut the door and paused at the top of the cement stairs. She folded her arms over her sweatshirt, wishing she'd taken the time to put on real clothes. She was still wearing her nightgown, and was sure she looked like a lazy slob.

"Yeah?" Lireinne said to the woman, feeling resentful. "What do you want?"

"Hello." The woman from the feed store smiled an anxious, wavering smile. "Um," she said, swallowing. "We, uh, haven't actually been introduced, have we? I mean, Sarah told me how to find your place, but I was afraid I might be at the wrong, uh . . . house."

With a quick, barely disguised glance of apprehension at the old green-streaked trailer, at the minivan on blocks in the weeds, and all the other crap Bud hadn't gotten around to hauling to the dump yet, the lady said, "I'm, uh, um, Emma Favreaux." She sounded unsure, like she didn't really believe that was her own name.

"Okay," Lireinne said. "I'm Lireinne. What do you want?" she asked bluntly. Emma-whoever widened her pale gray eyes, her fingertips going to her mouth.

"I'm so sorry—am I here at a bad time?" She sounded more nervous than ever. "I mean, I could come back later if that's more convenient for you. I didn't realize it was that early. When I went to the feed store first thing this morning, I had no idea so many people would be there. It seemed to take such a long time to get the, uh, oats, that I guess that's why I thought it was later than it is. Ricky helped me get the right kind of feed, but I had to wait for him to finish with a big line of customers who were there before me, and so I'm sorry if . . ."

Oats? Lireinne thought. The feed-store lady, Emma-whoever, hurried on in a breathless babble while obviously trying not to stare at the chain saw stuck in the oak tree stump, or at the random collection of engine parts and bald tires scattered around the clearing like a sale day at the salvage store. Lireinne hadn't ever really given much thought to how bad the yard might look to strangers, not until this woman had showed up this morning. Well, who the hell did this Emma think she was, anyway—the freaking feed fairy come to visit the poor?

Still, Lireinne's practical side reminded her, the woman *said* she brought oats.

Ignoring Emma's endlessly repeating how *sorry* she was, Lireinne marched down the cement steps to the truck, skirting the big puddle in the middle of the yard, the rain-soaked dirt cold and wet under her bare feet. Sure enough, there in the truck bed was a fifty-pound bag of oats. Maybe this lady really *was* the feed fairy, Lireinne thought, marveling at her luck. Now she could be sure Mose got fed this week. As if he'd heard her thoughts, the old horse whinnied behind the trailer. Lireinne noticed there was a big brown paper sack in the back of the truck, too.

"That's for you, too," Emma-whoever said. "Sarah told me you needed basic grooming equipment and something called a hoof pick. It's all in the bag. Sarah told me . . ."

She was off again, yapping, but now Lireinne didn't care because inside the sack she found some brand-new brushes and a small, sickle-shaped, metal tool that had to be the hoof pick. *Awesome,* she thought. Perpetually itchy Mose was sure to love this stuff, although it might take a little while to get the hang of using most of it. Lireinne ran her fingertips over the soft plastic bristles of a brush, imagining how good it would feel on the old horse's face.

"I could bring the oats inside for you," this Emma person offered. "Since you don't have a barn. I always carry Sarah's feed for her because she's getting on—eighty-one this month. It'd be no trouble to take it in your, um, house, no trouble at all."

Before she could say another word about getting inside the trailer, Lireinne cut her off. "No!—I mean, that's okay. I got it." She wasn't about to ask the woman inside the double-wide, even though Bud would've wanted her to be polite to a visitor. It was a total mess. She'd been too worn out last night to pick up after her brother, and anyway, this woman looked like she'd pass out from suburban trailer-horror if she set foot in the double-wide, even if it was hospital-clean in there.

Lireinne dropped the tailgate and grabbed the fifty-pound bag, slinging it over her shoulder with a grunt as it heavily settled. Emma hovered beside her truck, twisting her hands. It was like she was at a party where she didn't know anyone, like she wanted to leave, but couldn't get away yet without being impolite. People like her were always big on acting polite when they didn't know what else to do.

"Hold on, I'll be back to get the brushes and stuff." Lireinne headed for the steps. Still glancing around the yard as though there were something dangerous lurking there, the woman nodded in distracted agreement.

Inside the trailer, Wolf groused from under the blankets. "Aw, c'mon! What's that all the hell about?" he said, his voice muffled. "Is it the septic tank again? She from the Parish or something?"

"Nope. Just a feed delivery." Hurrying, Lireinne dropped the new bag of oats in the corner of the kitchen with a rustling thud. She poured what was left of the old bag into the dishpan. "Don't come out, okay? Go back to sleep." She slid her feet into her red flip-flops and stepped outside again, shutting the door behind her firmly. On top of the steps, she balanced the dishpan on her hip and surveyed Emma with a skeptical eye.

"So, like, why'd you do all this?" Lireinne knew she probably sounded ungrateful, but she didn't much care. "I can't pay for it."

In her experience, the world was full of people who wanted to get their noses into your business if for no other reason than to find out if something smelled bad. Her grammar school teachers had always been asking nosy questions about Lireinne's family, wondering why her stepfather never made it to back-to-school night and couldn't attend conferences. It didn't do any good to explain that Bud was *working*, that he couldn't get time off. One of the teachers had called the Child Protective Services people, sending them out to the trailer a couple of times to investigate. Bud had been forced to take an expensive day off to meet with them. Even as a little girl Lireinne had known that these visits could be dangerous for her family, that she and Wolf could get taken away. People like her old teacher were so smug, so positive they had a right to poke around in your life— no matter how much trouble they caused. Worse, they expected you to be *grateful* for it.

Emma hadn't answered, so Lireinne asked again. "Why'd you do this, huh?"

Looking as though she wanted to jump in her truck and drive back to suburbia, nonetheless Emma swallowed hard and, after a long beat, she said, "Because . . . I like horses?"

"Right. I bet you go around delivering feed all over St. Tammany Parish, just 'cause you get a bang out of it. Merry freakin' Christmas—only it's not Christmas, huh."

Emma seemed crestfallen. Dropping her eyes, she shrugged and wrapped her arms around her waist, looking so defeated and miserable that Lireinne couldn't help but pity the woman. She did seem kind of nice, if only she wasn't so damned nervous all the time. Maybe this Emma was really okay, like Sarah Fortune. Lireinne liked Sarah. Even though she was full of advice, it was different: that kind of nosy person was useful, they actually *helped*.

Shoulders drooping, Emma opened the door to her truck. "I'll go now," she said, her voice dispirited. "Sorry to have woken you up. It won't happen again."

"It's all right." Lireinne suddenly decided it was, in fact, all right. "You're not too early, not really." She was feeling generous now. "You want to meet Mose?" she offered. "I'm going around back to feed him. Bring the grooming stuff, will you?"

Emma-whoever prudently stayed outside the barbed wire while Lireinne fed her horse and knocked the caked mud off his legs and back with the stiff-bristled brushes. She used the soft one on his face, and Mose lowered his head with obvious pleasure.

The woman didn't seem as nervous anymore, Lireinne reflected as she carefully brushed Mose's dusty ears. Maybe she'd finally gotten used to the trailer and all the crap in the yard, or maybe she felt more at ease, now that she was a little less clean.

"You seem to have a way with horses," Emma said, her tone respectful. Her smooth brown legs were splashed with mud and her cotton sweater had a dirty smudge on it from hungry Mose's curious nose. As soon as Lireinne had put the feed on the ground, he'd buried his face in the dishpan, so ready for breakfast he ignored her as she ran the new brushes over his body. Emma said, "I confess I'm completely ignorant. Horses are so big, they scare me."

"I don't know a whole bunch about them, not like Sarah does," Lireinne confessed. "Mose is kind of like, well, *family,* but until the other day I didn't even know he needed feed. Did Sarah say what I'm supposed to do with this hoof pick? I've never seen one before."

"Me either." Emma's tanned face was almost comically perplexed, but then it brightened. "Maybe you're supposed to use it to clean the bottom of his feet somehow."

"How am I supposed to do that?" Lireinne looked at the horse's hooves, unsure. "Do I just tell him to pick 'em up? Like, 'Stand on three legs, boy—it's good for you'?"

"You've got to know more than I do," Emma said, her mouth wry. "Why don't you try touching one and see if he knows the rest? He used to be a racehorse, didn't he?"

And sure enough, as soon as Lireinne ran her hand down the back of Mose's front leg and touched his heel, the old horse lifted his hoof off the ground as though he'd been doing it every day. "I guess I better hold on to it so he won't put it back down." The packed mud came out in a big chunk, and when she let go, Mose rested his foot again, looking over his shoulder at Lireinne as if asking her to get on with it. His hind feet were a little trickier, but in no time she got them picked out, too.

"He seems like an old pro at this," Emma observed with a short laugh. The morning had quickly warmed up and she'd taken off her cream-colored sweater, tying it around her waist over her white T-shirt. She ran her fingers through her shoulder-length silver hair and stretched her arms upward in the brilliant sunlight filtering through the live oak leaves. "What a lovely day. I'm so glad it finally rained. Aren't you?"

Ignoring the question, Lireinne straightened and shot Emma a direct glance. "Why'd you do this? I mean . . . okay, it's cool, but you didn't have to."

Emma blushed under her tan, lowering her shy gray eyes to the mud on her Top-Siders. "I thought . . . I'd like to get to know you and Mose, that's all," she said, a hint of the old nervousness returning. She paused. "We're neighbors, you know, since I live just a few miles from here. But that's only if you don't mind—me getting to know y'all, I mean." Emma raised her gaze then, her expression uncertain and earnest, as though she was afraid Lireinne would say that she did indeed mind—minded a lot, in fact.

But as she crawled back through the barbed wire, Lireinne said, "Sure. It's okay, I guess. I can't pay you for the feed and all this stuff, though, not right away. I think I'm gonna lose my job." She stood and stuffed the brushes in the paper bag. "I could sign a paper or something, promising to pay you back," Lireinne said, wanting to make sure she went about this in the right way. Lireinne was adamantly opposed to owing anybody anything, ever. Life was hard enough, Bud always said, and debt was the worst way to make a hard life even harder.

Emma's gold-flecked eyes were wide with sympathy. "I'm sorry to hear that—you losing your job, I mean. Please don't worry about paying me. I'm happy to help," she said softly. "Really. And I can bring Mose's oats out here next week, too. You're sort of on my way home from the feed store. I've got, um . . . plenty of time."

Lireinne bit her lip, thinking this offer over. She hated counting on anybody but herself and Bud because, sooner or later, people always let you down. She was remembering the teachers and their intrusive questions, of how before she'd wised up, they'd called the Parish on Bud when she'd answered their questions like the trusting little dumb-ass she'd been back in grammar school. Then there was Miss Cooper, who was supposed to be on her side, only to have turned out to be no help at all. Her mother's family, turning their backs on their own kin, was no better. Except for Bud and maybe Miss Penny, nobody had ever wanted to give her a hand when she needed it. Even Miss Penny had never come by to see her again, not after she'd moved back to town.

But Emma had *said* she wanted to help with hauling feed. Lireinne looked at Mose. Fed and groomed, he was parked under his tree, resting a hind leg in contentment. Already the prominences of his hip bones had become less like stark, rocky outcrops under his faded brown coat, and his long neck seemed less sunken and thin. His eyes were bright, his ears pricked at the sound of their voices. He even smelled healthier after his grooming.

Yes, Lireinne thought, Mose was worth taking the chance. For sure.

"Just the same, I'll pay you back one day," she said briefly. "Thanks."

"You're very welcome," Emma said, sounding as though she meant it. "I'm happy to help with Mose." A brief silence fell between them, broken only by the muttering calls of the crows high in the top of the live oak tree, and the rumble of tires as a car sped past on the road at the front of the property.

Emma sighed, but it didn't sound like a sad one, not like before. It sounded almost happy—satisfied, even. "I should get on home," she said. "It was great meeting you and Mose. I'll be sure to come back next week, but if anything comes up before then, just let me know. I'll give you my number."

They were walking around the trailer, back to Emma's shiny truck. As soon as they reached it, she grabbed her fancy leather purse off the passenger seat, found a pen, and wrote her name and phone number on a piece of paper, just like she'd said she would.

"Here," Emma said. "Please call if you need me, for any reason. I'm just down the road."

In spite of the disaster Lireinne was sure she'd be facing on Monday morning, in spite of Wolf's lame dropping-out idea, the day now seemed bright and fine. Emma-whoever didn't act like some nosy bitch, not really. You couldn't ever be sure, but she was probably a nice person, maybe even a good one—like Sarah.

After what seemed like a lifetime of disappointments, maybe, *maybe* this Emma might be for real. As random and as out-of-the-blue as her promise might appear, she'd sounded like she was really planning to help. These were thoughts that triggered Lireinne's usual suspicions about the untrustworthiness of do-gooders, but at the same time they offered something else, something that felt like . . . well, hope.

What if?

"Hey—you ever go to Walmart?" Lireinne asked.

CHAPTER 9

"Mr. Costello?"

In the logy aftermath of the farm's usual Monday calorie-bomb of a lunch—'Cille's fried ham steaks, hot sausage, and white beans—Con was alone in his office this afternoon. Back from France at last, the boss, Roger Hannigan, was currently away from the farm and meeting with his personal CPA in town. Con was standing at the window with his hands shoved in his pockets, deep in thought.

He was staring out at the expanse of the wastewater retention pond, a great tear-shaped body of aggravation sited down the hill from the house. Discharging was a never-ending problem for the farm. The barns consumed tens of thousands of gallons a day emptying and filling the deep-water tanks. Whenever the twenty-acre pond was full and threatened to climb over its banks—which it was now doing after Friday night's big rain—there was no option: they'd have to discharge into the branch on the edge of the property, one ultimately emptying into the Bogue Falaya River. Con was waiting on a call from the farm's D.C. lobbyist for an update on the looming EPA litigation, but as he gazed at the deceptively innocent water's brown surface, his thoughts were elsewhere.

Lireinne.

In spite of the headache of discharge issues and a desk piled high with other pressing business, just as he had been for the past nine days, Con was thinking about Lireinne, daydreams of the extraordinary girl that were as seductive as the remembered fragrance of her scent.

"Excuse me, Mr. Costello?"

"Yes?" Con answered, returning to the here and now with a jolt. He rubbed his head in an effort to clear it. Lireinne considerately retreated to the background with a "Later, baby" flash of her green eyes, a toss of her hair, and a private smile.

"Harlan Baham's in the kitchen, asking for a word with you." Jackie, the farm's bookkeeper, waited in the doorway of Con's office. Her brown, pleasant face was expectant.

"What's he want?" Con said. He turned away from the window, his tone short at the mention of Baham, that goldbricking bastard. Although he was a fair hand at bossing the crew, in every other way that mattered, the man was an unmitigated, lazy waste of a human being. Con was still disgusted with himself for having made Harlan a five-hundred-dollar loan last year to help him buy a used truck. The loan had yet to be repaid.

Jackie lifted her shoulders under her neat blue blazer, letting them fall with a noncommittal expression. "It's something about the hoser. Harlan says she's being careless, doing structural damage to some of the barns. Apparently, he tried to talk to her about it last Friday, but he says she cussed him out, turned the hose on him, and somehow he ended up falling down. He says his back hasn't been right since and he wants her fired. I can handle it, if you want."

The scumbag probably got himself hosed for hitting on her, Con thought in disdain.

"No, I'll look into this," he said, stifling a grimace at the thought of the man anywhere near Lireinne. Poor kid.

But wait—hold on a minute, Con thought, struck by a happy realization. Here was the answer to the question he'd been pondering for better than a week, the way to create an opportunity to get closer to Lireinne. "In fact," he said quickly, "tell him to send her up to the house so I can talk to her."

Jackie turned to go. "Sure thing, Mr. Costello."

"Oh, and Jackie? Bring me Lireinne's employment file and pay records, will you?"

As soon as she'd shut the door, Con hustled into the attached bathroom to check out his reflection in the mirror. Unzipping his khakis, he straightened his polo shirt, tucked it in again, and buckled his alligator belt. He ran a comb through his red hair, drew his lips back from his teeth to make sure he wasn't wearing an errant speck of lunch on an incisor, and examined his nails. Then he began to pace the office, anticipation sparking like a lit bottle rocket inside his chest.

Distracted with his evolving plan, Con couldn't pretend to work, not even when Jackie brought the files he'd asked her to get for him. He roamed restlessly around his office instead, straightening the Audubon prints on the cypress-paneled walls, shuffling papers, moving his chair from behind his desk around to the front, putting it back again. Normally, he'd have been relaxed and at ease as he waited to do what he did best. Con was almost amused at his excitement, wondering if even Lireinne was worth all this attention to detail.

She was. A long twenty minutes later Lireinne had answered his summons and was standing in front of Con's big antique partners' desk, her shrimp boots shedding mud on the Oriental carpet. She glared at him in sullen defiance.

"Hell yes, I hosed him." Lireinne spit the words from her lovely mouth. "Harlan's a pervy creep who doesn't freaking get it—like he never heard that *no means no*?" She tossed her black hair over the shoulder of her faded Saints jersey. "Bet he left out the part where he grabbed me, how he told me that if I didn't 'give ol' Harlan some sugar,' he'd see me fired. Isn't that the way this bullshit is gonna go down?"

Her low voice was rough with hostility, but her eyes gleamed with unshed tears.

Con came out from behind his desk smiling his very best smile, the one that radiated good will and good feeling. If you're gonna take a swing at this, Obi-Wan, don't miss, he reminded himself. His own motives were one thing, but if Lireinne filed a sexual harassment suit against the farm because of Harlan Baham, Hannigan wouldn't be pleased. Not at all.

"I'm sure we can work this out, Lireinne." Con gestured at one of the leather club chairs arranged around the conference table. "Please, sit down. How've you been lately?"

"How've *I* been?" Lireinne raised a wary eyebrow, but after a moment's hesitation, she clomped over to the chair and perched on the edge of it like an elegant waterbird in shrimp boots, poised to take flight.

"I've been okay, I guess," she muttered. "Except for Harlan." Lireinne crossed her amazing legs, one white-rubber-covered foot swinging in nervous arcs. Con pulled up another conference chair and sat down across from her, smiling still.

"I'm sure that . . . incident gave you a bad turn, but ever since we met the other day I've been thinking that a bright girl like you is wasted as a hoser here at SGE." Con looked deep into her guarded, still-water eyes, his voice reassuring and confident as he said, "You could be so much more useful to the company in another position. What do you think about becoming my personal assistant?"

Lireinne frowned, her brow knit in confusion. "Your personal assistant?"

"I'm offering you a promotion," Con said, bright and warm as a host of candle flames. "A girl like you—so smart, so . . . attractive—would be a big help in the front office."

"Me?" Her expression disbelieving, Lireinne folded her arms and collapsed against the back of the chair in a graceful slouch. "I mean, why me? I'm, like, a *hoser*."

With a deliberate calculation, Con angled his broad shoulders toward her in a subtle invasion of her space. He rested his elbows on his knees and, wearing a thoughtful frown, nodded as though she'd said something rather more intelligent.

"I think you could be more than that, obviously. It would mean additional responsibility, of course, but there'd be a commensurate raise in pay."

At the mention of a raise, Lireinne's exquisite face was immediately alight with interest. "A raise? I'd get a raise?" She uncrossed her legs, her hands clenched the arms of the chair. Lireinne sat up, straightening her back, and her breasts lifted under the shapeless Saints jersey.

Con's breath caught, his pulse racing. Holy shit, Obi-Wan, he thought. He reached to the desk behind him, picking up a manila folder to cover his reaction.

"I see you've been netting . . . what?" Con opened the file and pretended to scan the time sheets, as though he hadn't known for the past nine days exactly what the farm was paying her.

"Less than four hundred dollars a month," Lireinne stated, her face discouraged now. "That's it. I tried to get on full-time, but Tina said y'all didn't need me for more than four hours a day. Like, that's just not *right*. I always have to put in at least six hours to get it all done, but I don't get paid except for four. That sucks, *big time*," she said with hot vehemence.

Con nodded, emanating sympathy. "Boy, I understand—do I ever. Unfortunately, Tina's right. That's farm policy regarding casual labor. Usually a hoser's just not worth that kind of outlay, so we call the job part-time even though it's basically full-time work—when someone's doing the good job you've been doing, that is. I agree. That does suck."

Lireinne looked away. Her voice was small and bitter as she said, "Nobody can live on that."

Taking a calculated risk, Con placed two light fingers on her knee. She gave him a startled glance, a question in her doubting eyes.

"But if you take this promotion, Lireinne," Con said, "instead of an hourly wage, you'll be getting a salary—say, two thousand a month? You'll net about sixteen hundred, after taxes. That's a big jump up." Con removed his fingers and leaned back in his chair, watching as the girl absorbed this offer. Now, it was only two thousand dollars, a sum closing in on the bottom line of Lizzie's monthly grocery allowance (not counting wine, a separate budget), but even that modest amount was bound to seem a fortune to a girl like Lireinne.

"Really?" Her eyes were wide. "Two thousand dollars a month? But, like, what's a personal assistant do, anyway?" Lireinne asked cautiously. She shifted in her chair, those new-leaf eyes doubtful again.

It was a question Con had contemplated ever since he'd hatched the idea of how to bring Lireinne into his orbit, especially since he didn't actually need an assistant.

"Good question," he said, nodding in affirmation. "I'm a busy man, ridiculously busy. I spend hours on the phone, selling skins all over the world, handling the farm's legal issues. You could be a big help to me, Lireinne. Keeping up with my correspondence, screening my calls, updating my calendar. You're comfortable with computers, aren't you? There'll be some data entry, too."

Absently rubbing her crescent-scarred eyebrow, Lireinne didn't answer for a minute. "I had a class in school, before I quit. We don't have a computer at home, though. I might need a couple of days to get my head back into it, if that's okay."

This was hardly a deal-breaker. Con had known it was unlikely she'd be worth a damn right away, but keeping his calendar wasn't why he'd offered her the job in the first place. Just sitting across from her now was a promise of almost unimaginable pleasure—if only he could be patient. He'd known instinctively that propositioning her wasn't a successful ploy. Not with this girl. After nine days of deliberation and daydreaming, Con had become certain that when it came to Lireinne, the long game would be the only game.

Meanwhile, her uncertain expression had grown thoughtful. "I can't come to work up here in the house dressed like this." She gestured at her faded jersey and shorts. "I'll have to buy some new clothes, won't I."

It wasn't a question, but Con was prepared for this as well.

"Yes, of course. I'm okaying an advance on your new salary for more, uh, professional clothing."

Actually, he'd give a hell of a lot to go shopping with her, to oversee the Cinderella-transformation from Lireinne the hoser to the glorious girl of his daydreams, but for now he was going to have to wait to indulge that deeply enjoyable notion. Later on, after he was sure of her, he'd take Lireinne to Saks and do it right.

Con was sure now that he'd pursue this seduction without haste because this girl was the real deal. During this meeting, Con had realized she wasn't like his other girls, an ordinary conquest. Some casual . . . *thing* with this girl held no appeal to him; the thought was almost distasteful, to tell the truth. He sensed there were depths to Lireinne he couldn't have imagined before and that made her even more wildly desirable. Con surreptitiously rubbed his damp palms on his pants legs with a quickening of hungry anticipation.

"But I'm probably going to have to get a car, too." Lireinne's cool voice broke into his thoughts. She was biting her full lower lip speculatively, her slim hand playing with her long black hair. "If I'm all dressed up," she said, "I can't *walk* here from the house, not in real shoes with heels. I mean, y'all don't want me showing up for work in flip-flops." It was a self-possessed suggestion.

Clever girl, Con thought with an inward smile. Of course she'd need a car.

"There's a farm vehicle, one of the older Explorers you can use for now," he said smoothly, as if he'd already thought of a car—which he hadn't. "We'll call it a loan, but once you're on the company's insurance, you can drive it until you can afford one of your own."

Con didn't dare sweeten the offer any more without asking for trouble with Hannigan: already he could imagine the raised eyebrows in the office when the hoser showed up tomorrow morning as his new personal assistant. It was a piece of luck that Roger and his wife were coming to his house for something like a working dinner tonight: there was a lot Roger had missed while he was away and he needed to be brought up to speed on the waste-water issue before Tuesday's staff meeting. Con could casually drop the news of Lireinne's promotion into the conversation instead of springing it on

Roger in front of Tina and Jackie. A couple of months from now, after he'd won her, Lireinne could have a little SUV. Nothing too
flashy, but she'd probably fall in love with anything with a CD player
and that new-car smell.

"What do you say?" Con relaxed in his chair, confidently await-
ing her answer with the satisfaction of knowing that he'd played this
hand to perfection—as well as a new admiration for Lireinne's unexpectedly having driven a better bargain than he'd meant to offer her.

The girl met his eyes, and Con was gratified at the way hers
were shining. "We can use the extra money, for sure," she said. Her
smile slowly dawned. "Swear to God—I won't let you down, Mr.
Costello."

"Please." Con laughed in pure delight. In that instant he couldn't
help imagining her in his arms, how delicious she was going to feel,
how happy he was going to make her. "Call me Con. 'Mr. Costello'
was my dad."

Lireinne, not smiling now, nodded. "Um, okay. Thanks, Mr.
Con."

Mr. Con. Well, that was going to have to be enough for now, he
thought. The time wasn't right to push anymore on that front. He
could wait.

"Take the rest of the day off, why don't you?" Con said. "Pick
up that check from Jackie and go shopping."

"Yes *sir*," Lireinne said. She gracefully rose to her feet. "Thanks
again. I really appreciate the chance."

Con watched her leave, experiencing an intense appreciation for
her slender, retreating back that was mixed with a fine impatience.
Sighing as she shut the door, he picked up the phone and dialed
Jackie's extension.

"I need you to cut a check, made out to Lireinne for six hundred. It looks like we're going to be needing another hoser," Con said
affably, lighting a cigar. "Harlan can take over Lireinne's job until we
get someone new. Give Manpower a call, why don't you. This time
around, let's have a guy for the job if we can get one."

Done. Satisfied and keenly looking forward to tomorrow, Con

hung up the phone and leaned back in his chair. He had this, he thought. His plan was well-begun.

In his hand, the cigar's ember glowed like a banked fire.

The September afternoon was mild and dry; the rich, dusty scent of oak mast, wild asters, and goldenrod an aromatic promise that fall would be coming soon.

Unaware of her surroundings, Lireinne walked home with the carefully folded check for six hundred dollars in her hand, glancing at it in dazed elation from time to time. She couldn't seem to feel certain yet it was real.

How freaking amazing, the way life could turn on a dime!

When Lireinne had left the trailer this morning, her jaw had been clenched with the surety that today was the day she was going to be fired. All morning she'd hosed the bad Monday barns, bad because no one ever cleaned them over the weekend, and the five she'd had to leave undone on Friday were enough to have made her gag. Sick with apprehension, Lireinne struggled to ignore Harlan's sniggering comments, his talk about how she was going to be out on her ass by the end of the day.

But against all her dire expectations, this afternoon she'd been promoted instead!

Even the squirmy memory of Mr. Con's fingers on her knee couldn't mar this oceanic relief, this feeling of *freedom*. Her new boss might be a toucher, but he probably didn't mean anything by it, she thought. In Lireinne's book of all-time-worst experiences—Brett and Harlan—the bad guys didn't mess around. They grabbed you, and then they took what they wanted. No, Mr. Con was just a little pervy that way, and hadn't she taken care of herself with one creep already? So what if her boss tried anything more? She'd find a way to handle that, too, because she had something real going for her now. Lireinne had a real *job*.

"Two thousand dollars a month!" Even said aloud, the words couldn't seem to make the outrageous amount of money any less impossible-sounding. Two thousand dollars a month was like winning

the Powerball, or digging up a trunk full of gold in Mose's field behind the trailer. *And* she was going to get a car. Suddenly, the world's
front doors were opened wide to her, a limitless horizon stretching
as far as she could see. A *car.*

Lireinne stopped in the middle of the road, her arms outstretched, her face tilted up at the cloudless sky of deepest blue.

"Two thousand dollars a month!" she sang to the astonished
cows in the field beside her.

"A car!" Lireinne called in triumph to the startled crow perched
on the power pole overhead. "And *two thousand dollars a month.*" With
money like that, she could save for Wolf to go to college. He couldn't
drop out now, not when she'd have an honest-to-God salary coming
in just like somebody with an education. Lireinne's heart beat a strong,
happy rhythm as she resumed her walk home, imagining the flabber-
gasted looks Wolf's and Bud's faces would wear when she told them
her news.

And as if her day wasn't already great enough, she had a check to
buy new clothes, right here in her hand.

Lireinne sobered at that thought, remembering that the bank
closed at five—it must be nearly three o'clock—and after she cashed
the check she'd still need to go shopping. She was going to need special clothes now, clothes unlike any she'd had before. Jackie at the office and Tina the farm manager dressed in skirts and tailored pants;
they wore nice shoes. She bet they had purses that cost a lot, too. No
way she could find real clothes like that at the Dollar General, probably not even at Walmart. In fact, she didn't even have the first clue
as to where to *begin* to get that kind of stuff.

And more importantly, without a car, how the hell was she going to get everything done before tomorrow morning? She owned
nothing that might work for her first day at her new job.

Bud was going to be late getting home; he'd told her so yesterday. "Going to be a long one on Monday, honey. That well over to
the Pentecostals' has got to get done and over with before they run
out of money to pay us." So, getting a ride from Bud was out, she
realized in discouragement.

Lireinne hadn't thought to ask to take the promised Explorer home, and anyway, hadn't Mr. Con said she'd have to be on the insurance first? She couldn't bring herself to call him now. What if he told her the promotion was a mistake, that he'd thought it over and she wasn't right for the job after all? No, Lireinne decided. That was out, too. She'd have to find another way.

Then she remembered that lady, Emma Favreaux. She could ask *her* for a ride, couldn't she? Emma had *said* she could call if she needed anything. Lireinne had kept the slip of paper, the name and number printed on it in an elegant hand, in her wallet.

Well, why the hell not? She had nothing to lose by asking.

Lireinne struck out walking faster than before, hurrying toward home to find out if Emma had been telling the truth.

She *did* say she wanted to help.

"Oh, yes!"

After listening to Lireinne's excited news, Emma seemed completely down with the trip to town. "A *promotion*?" she exclaimed. "How wonderful for you, how happy you must be! I'll be there in thirty minutes, okay? We'll have to get to the bank before they close, but then we'll head to New Orleans, to the mall at Lakeside. They're open until nine so we can take our time."

Lireinne hugged herself in giddy relief, cradling the phone between her shoulder and her ear. "Oh, wow, *thanks*. I've never been to Lakeside, like ever. Sometimes I used to hear the girls at school talking about shopping there. Holy cow, now *I* get to go."

Emma chuckled. "I'm looking forward to it, too. See you in thirty minutes, then."

After she hung up the phone, Lireinne dashed outside and fed Mose without taking the time to hang out with him while he ate. Instead, she ran back inside to the trailer's cramped bathroom for a quick shower to lose the stink of the barns, afterward blow-drying her long hair at the speed of sound.

Lireinne looked at her reflection in the foggy mirror, debating whether she should put on some makeup. No, there wasn't time, and besides, she almost never bothered with it. Makeup did nothing to cover her scar, never had. So, dressed in her best pair of jeans and a fresh white tank top, she was just sliding her feet into the red flip-flops when there was a light rap at the door.

"Coming!" Grabbing her old purse, Lireinne ran to the front of the trailer and slipped quickly through the door, hoping to keep Emma from seeing inside. The sectional was covered in rumpled blankets and she hadn't had a chance to pick up after Wolf, who was MIA again this afternoon. She hadn't needed to worry, though. Emma, wearing a shapeless gray linen dress and clunky sandals that made her look kind of dumpy, in Lireinne's opinion, was waiting for her down in the yard and was nowhere near the door, thank God.

"Hey, let's go!" Lireinne said happily. She rushed down the cement steps and climbed up in the front seat of the shiny silver truck, the interior rich with the smell of new leather. She was already buckling her seat belt before Emma had even gotten in on the driver's side.

"Take a deep breath." Emma smiled reassurance at Lireinne. "We're going to have enough time." She slid the key into the ignition and the truck's diesel engine turned over with a well-tuned rumble. Classical music filled the cab, an atonal cascade of complicated notes that Lireinne found bewildering. Who listened to this stuff?

"Change the station if you want," Emma said as she backed the truck down the drive. "Oh, and by the way—congratulations on your promotion. You know, I'm embarrassed to realize that I forgot to ask where you work."

Lireinne was looking for another radio station. "I didn't tell you? At Sauvage Global Enterprises, down at the alligator farm." Her usual music station acquired, she was applying lip gloss in the truck's vanity mirror and didn't notice Emma's interested face turning stony.

She was going on a shopping trip with six hundred dollars to spend!

But after a flying trip to the bank, during the trip across the Causeway to New Orleans, Emma was almost wordless. Lireinne didn't think much of it. She was too busy telling Emma all about how freaking awesome it was, getting that humongous raise, how the money was going to change *everything* for the Hooten family, so those murmured, single-worded responses didn't really register.

And once they were at the mall, Lireinne couldn't wait to begin shopping. In Dillard's, after avoiding a trio of scarily made-up women shoehorned into black dresses who threatened them with atomizers of perfume, Emma and Lireinne took the escalator—another new experience—upstairs to a section called "Career Separates." Lireinne was surprised by how much everything cost there, even something as simple as a skirt. She'd thought six hundred dollars was a lot of money until she looked at the price tags. At this rate, she wouldn't be able to buy more than a couple of things, she thought in discouragement, much less a whole new wardrobe for work.

Now that she was no longer looking, Emma's preoccupation was impossible to miss. Emma didn't seem to see that Lireinne had stopped shopping for what she couldn't afford, that she was reduced to hanging around, feeling depressed. Instead, Emma flipped through the racks of clothes without saying anything to Lireinne at all.

Finally, Emma glanced at Lireinne. She cleared her throat. "I think you're going to get more for your money if we go out into the mall," she said. "And all this is too old for you, too severe." She looked away, frowning at a pair of black slacks. "Let's go try Banana Republic. There's always a sale there, and for the money, the quality is fairly good. Clothes matter, you know. People treat you differently when you're well dressed." She seemed to say this with an effort, as though she'd rather not be talking at all.

Emma's clothes came off as pretty dumpy to Lireinne. Still, Emma must have better taste than she'd originally thought: she'd seen the automatic respect the salesladies had given her, but Lireinne had assumed it was because she was older. Maybe that dress of hers was as expensive as the rest of the merchandise and Lireinne just didn't get it. She nodded, relieved that Emma must really know what she was doing when it came to clothes.

"I don't know what to buy anyhow," Lireinne said. "Not really."

"Let's go," Emma said quietly.

She didn't say anything more after that, but in mutual agreement they walked out of Career Separates and went downstairs out into the mall. It was an enormous, dazzling corridor of stores, shops, kiosks, and crowds.

Trying to stroll nonchalantly through Lakeside's wide marble aisles among the throngs of other shoppers, Lireinne was rendered almost speechless at the choices before her, the cool places she'd only seen advertised in the pages of *Vogue* and *Cosmo*. There was an Abercrombie & Fitch ("too casual and way too expensive," Emma said), a Gap ("mostly cheap jeans"), and a Talbots ("not really your style, I don't think").

They passed at least fifteen shoe stores, a candle shop expelling a thick, almost visible fog-bank of competing smells through its open doors, glitzy boutiques selling evening gowns, swimsuits, and ski clothes, an Apple Store with what seemed like a million people in it, a Build-A-Bear store with nobody in it, an opulent jewelry gallery where the windows were draped with ropes of pearls, chalcedony, and gold, a Victoria's Secret, and a JCPenney. She could have window-shopped for weeks at Lakeside and never have gotten tired of it, no *way*, Lireinne thought in mounting excitement as they walked through the aisles of the enormous mall.

At the Godiva chocolate shop, though, she tugged at Emma's sleeve. The older woman had been striding along in her thick-soled sandals through the crowds, showing no interest whatsoever in the wonderfulness surrounding them. It was like she was on some kind of superimportant, special-ops mission with no time to spare for plain old window-shopping.

"Hey—I'm going in there," Lireinne said firmly. The Godiva window display was piled high with tantalizing golden boxes, promising rare delights. She was dying to have one chocolate, just one. It had been a long time since she'd eaten chocolate, and never anything from *this* fabled store.

"Come with me?" If the salespeople were snotty, Lireinne didn't want to go in there without backup.

With a shrug, Emma said, "If you want."

She didn't sound like it was a big deal to her, but there were so many delicious-sounding choices in the Godiva store that after five minutes of agonized indecision, Lireinne let Emma choose for her— a champagne truffle that tasted like what she imagined rich angels could afford to eat in heaven.

Outside in the mall Emma finished her own chocolate quickly. She hadn't seemed to enjoy it much. Lireinne tried to make hers last, taking mouse bites until the truffle was gone.

"Oh my God, that was, like, so freaking yummy! How was yours?"

"Fine," Emma said. In passing the food court she went to throw the Godiva store's little glossy bag in a nearby wastebasket, but Lireinne held out her hand.

"Can I have that? It's so pretty, I hate to just throw it away." She could use the black-and-gold bag to hold her cotton balls. Besides, black and gold were Saints colors.

"I'm sorry." Emma's closed expression changed, softening as she said, "Of course you can." Lireinne carefully folded the Godiva bag and put it in her purse.

Emma watched her intently, as if she had something on her mind, then looked away. People streamed past them into the food court like a human river. Finally, Emma turned to Lireinne with a forced-looking smile.

She said, "When we get done at Banana Republic, before we head home we could have dinner afterward, if you want. That would be a nice way to wind up our trip, and we could . . . get to know each other better."

"Here?" Lireinne was a little intimidated by the loud, busy crowds of diners laden with trays, the raucous gangs of teenagers camped at the tables, by all the fast-food choices of the food court. A yeasty, mouth-watering aroma of pizza floated out into the mall. That would be *awesome*, Lireinne thought. She couldn't remember the last time she'd had pizza that wasn't frozen: this smelled like it would be a huge improvement over a pepperoni-studded floor tile from Wal-mart.

"I could go for some pizza."

"If you want," Emma said diffidently, "but I was thinking we'd go all out and have dinner at P.F. Chang's. It's a pretty good Chinese restaurant on the other side of the mall. My treat."

They walked on, but Emma's silence didn't feel so strange anymore, and, approaching the Banana Republic store, Lireinne's spirits rose once again. The wide windows displayed groups of headless mannequins, all of them draped in the kinds of clothes Lireinne had hoped she'd find for her new work wardrobe, only much, much cooler. *This,* she decided as they walked in the doors, was the place!

And, as promised, there was a sale on.

An hour and a half later, a hostess led Emma and Lireinne past P.F. Chang's long bar, packed three-deep with chattering, well-dressed people sipping cocktails. They sat down in a booth, piling Lireinne's white paper bags on the seat beside her. The shopping at Banana Republic had been resoundingly successful. One bag held a very special purchase: a sleeveless sheath in a green silk, a perfect dress the color and texture of sea foam.

"Can I wear this to work?" Lireinne had asked Emma doubtfully in the changing room.

"No—it's just for fun," Emma replied. "I'll buy it for you."

Lireinne demurred, but Emma insisted, and now the beautiful dress was hers, all hers.

P.F. Chang's smelled like there was something wonderful going on in the kitchen. Except for the few times Bud had taken her and Wolf to the Pakistani seafood place up by the gas station in Folsom, Lireinne had never been in a real restaurant before. McDonald's didn't count. She watched Emma carefully, wondering how to act. She didn't want to look like country-fried trailer trash out on the town, not in here.

Emma unfolded her napkin, a heavy black linen square, and put it in her lap. Lireinne did the same. Emma took a sip of water. Lireinne did, too. They both studied the menu and Lireinne realized she'd never heard of anything on it: the descriptions seemed strange, like the food might taste weird. Like, who ate cashews and broccoli together? And what the hell was oyster sauce? Nothing sounded good. She put the menu down and took another nervous sip of water. Emma hadn't offered anything in the way of conversation, and after a few minutes of increasingly awkward silence, to Lireinne's relief the waiter in his black pants and white shirt came to the table. He asked for their drink order. Emma said she wanted hot green tea.

"Can I have a Coke?" Lireinne asked, wondering if green tea would taste like soap. Some of the shampoos at Walmart were made with green tea. They smelled nice, but nothing like regular tea.

"Sure thing." The waiter winked at her. "Be right back." With a flattering smile, he hurried through the maze of tables to get their drinks.

After that, Lireinne found herself beginning to relax. That guy had been supernice to her, even if Emma had decided not to talk again. Soon their drinks arrived and they got their dinner order placed with the now openly flirting waiter—something called Vegetarian Mu Shu for Emma and some mysterious chicken-and-rice-noodle dish she recommended for Lireinne to try.

Lireinne sipped her Coke and tried to act as though she ate in nice places like P.F. Chang's all the time. Even if Emma didn't seem to be enjoying herself, this, she decided, was turning into *fun*. That table of guys over there was definitely checking her out with sidelong, appreciative glances and she wasn't even wearing her new clothes yet.

"So you're working at the alligator farm." Emma took a sip of her green tea. She looked into the cup, not meeting Lireinne's eyes. "I wonder if you know . . . Mr. Costello?" She put her cup down and some tea slopped over the rim onto the table. Her hand was shaking.

Lireinne was surprised at her question. A lady like Emma, knowing Mr. Con? she thought in some confusion. The alligator farm was one dirty, messed-up place, the opposite of what she imagined being Emma was all about. People like her had the kind of life where everything worked out just fine all the time and nothing ever, ever went wrong. A creep like Harlan wouldn't even dare to *speak* to someone like Emma.

"You mean Mr. Con? Yeah, he's my new boss," Lireinne said, cautious now. Why would Emma care who she worked for? "You know him?"

"Yes. It's a small world, isn't it." Not looking at Lireinne, Emma arranged her chopsticks neatly in front of her on the shining teak tabletop. "He's my . . . he's my ex-husband," she said, her voice low. Emma clasped her hands tight together, gazing across the crowded restaurant, her face tense and troubled.

Lireinne, however, felt much more at ease. So that's it, she thought. Everybody has an ex-husband these days—even Bud's an ex-husband—and most people aren't on the best of terms with their exes anyway, right?

"Wow," Lireinne said. "Who knew? Small freaking world, for sure."

"Who knew," Emma agreed, and her voice was grim. She met Lireinne's eyes at last and it seemed as though she was ready to say more, but at that moment the waiter showed up with their food.

"Here you go, ladies." He began mixing three different kinds of sauces, adding vinegars and chili oil, explaining what each one was like. It was a complicated process and a lengthy one.

No big deal, Lireinne reflected, picking up her fork. Too bad about Emma and Mr. Con, though.

Her dinner, as it turned out, was delicious.

CHAPTER 10

"So then that frog bastard had the brass-balled nerve to ask me to put my money in his vineyard! Now what in the hail am I going to do with a got-damn vineyard?"

Fat Roger Hannigan threw back his head with a self-satisfied roar of amusement at his new French son-in-law's expense. Sitting next to Lizzie on the recently acquired living room sofa, his wife, CoCo, lean as an Italian greyhound in a pair of skintight black pants and a hand-painted silk tunic, added her own two cents.

"I was plain knocked for a *loop*," CoCo said. She placed her icy pre-dinner tumbler of vodka and very little tonic on Lizzie's prized antique end table. It was sure to leave a ring, but Liz didn't dare hand her a coaster. Dinner with Con's boss was an Occasion, so tonight CoCo Hannigan could put her glass down wherever the hell she wanted.

"I mean, there he was," the boss's wife said, "looking just like a little bug in those funny glasses they all wear over there—kind of like that Buddy Holly, you know?—and don't you know Henri got right up in Roger's face, wanting a loan!"

CoCo's practically pupil-less hazel irises glittered in her taut face, her jawline as sharp as the Chinese cleaver in the kitchen knife block.

She appeared to be trying to raise her eyebrows while her disdainful glance implied Liz was bound to know all about the travails of being so wealthy that everyone of your acquaintance wanted a handout, *tout suite.*

"Um." Lizzie wanted to be agreeable. In her newly gained experience, however, the seriously rich were so close with their money that, like squirrels, they might as well keep it hidden in the walls. Despite their miserliness, they still wanted to act as though they never gave all that money a thought and neither should anybody else. Liz knew she'd never have *that* much money, not enough to forget about it. She'd never be able to forget all those degrading moments before marrying Con when her credit card had been turned down. She'd had to watch her own mother suffer that same ordeal on more than one occasion. Raising four girls on her husband's schoolteacher salary had been hard—especially when that schoolteacher had a little gambling problem. Mrs. MacBride often had to return half a basket's worth of groceries to the shelves and get back in line, humiliated. Little Lizzie had been even more embarrassed than her mother, learning to dread having to go with her to the supermarket. She'd been determined that miserable experience wouldn't happen to her, ever, not once she was a lawyer and making a salary that had, at the time, seemed more than adequate. But after the first excruciating moment when the saleslady had run Liz's Visa three times with no success and handed her back her card, she'd been forced to relive her mother's humiliation more times than she wanted to recall.

"I can't imagine how you must've felt," she said to CoCo. "What nerve, asking y'all for money!"

From where he was lounging in the armchair in front of the marble fireplace, her husband crossed his sockless ankle over his knee and chuckled.

"Damn, Rog," Con said easily. "You're plenty liquid. Buying into something like a vineyard wouldn't hurt your bottom line at all. Besides, you knew your son-in-law was a deadbeat when you met him. This could be a win-win situation, you know. If he's busy making wine, he won't have time to get himself into trouble with your little girl."

At that, Hannigan howled with laughter, *har har har*. CoCo's face stretched horizontally into a different kind of grimace.

Con exchanged a glance with Lizzie from across the living room, recently redecorated out of the Restoration Hardware catalog. It was a crowded upscale photo shoot of white linen slipcovers, vintage-inspired lamps, and oversized, distressed pine furniture. Liz had been thrilled, seeing the glossy pages re-created in her own living room—down to the silk orchids in pots, domed bell jars, and coordinated architectural drawings in ebony frames. The space was *perfect* now, except for these Hannigans in the middle of it. Liz peeked at her watch. It was only seven fifteen. This evening was never going to end.

"Don't you need to check on dinner, honey?"

Lizzie looked up with a start to meet Con's questioning gaze.

"I think our guests would like a refill," he said. "I'll join you in the kitchen."

Damn. There'd be no quick, surreptitious drink for her now. "Dinner's only about ten minutes away, y'all," Liz said, a resigned smile on her numb-feeling lips.

Three glasses of white wine on an empty stomach were probably two too many, but she'd needed the clandestine, golden calm to settle her nerves before the Hannigans had showed up at the front door and Con went into that overdrive thing he always did. Nothing in Lizzie's previous life had prepared her with the skills necessary for these dinners, where all the details were in her unequipped hands. Supper at her parents' house had always been a grab-and-go kind of meal: you had to snatch it while you could before someone else got there first and there was nothing left for you except scraps, crumbs, and burned pieces.

CoCo held out her glass as Con rose from his chair. "Remember—just a splash of tonic, sugar," she simpered.

"Coming, Liz?" Con asked, picking up Roger's empty beer bottle.

Lizzie didn't answer, focused on trying to rappel her way up out of the deep, upholstered sofa. Halfway to her feet, she almost toppled like a downed tree onto the Berber carpet because her long, voluminous hostess pants were trapped under the cork soles of her high-heeled sandals. Liz tugged the hems free, only to find herself swaying alarmingly. With an effort she recovered her shaky balance, hoping no one saw the slip.

Con followed her into the butler's pantry on the way to the kitchen, much to Liz's aggravation. So far he hadn't seemed to notice she was a little tight. After that memorable night at the Lemon Tree, he'd been a real ass about her drinking.

"Look, Liz—don't screw up *this* dinner," he'd said. "Roger's hinting he might retire to Provence in a year or two. It'll mean a promotion for me, so keep your goddamned drinking under control for a change. The last thing I need is him thinking my wife's a lush. The way you spend money, we need every damned dime I make."

Positive that drinking—copious drinking—was going to be the only way to get through this dinner, still Liz had to ignore Con's unfairness if she didn't want a repeat of several recent arguments. So, even though she was still more than halfway convinced Con was running around on her, Lizzie had backed her suspicions into a corner with a whip and a chair, swearing piously there'd be a fabulous meal and a tranquil atmosphere for this all-important dinner party. Since it wasn't as if she had a choice anyway, she'd thrown herself into the preparations, hoping for the best.

Once in the kitchen, though, hoping for the best proved pointless when Lizzie discovered Con wasn't fooled at all. "What's your problem?" he demanded in a low voice. "You're sitting there like a damned stuffed animal. Didn't you hear CoCo asking you to be on that Downtown Arts committee of hers? Really big deal, Liz, she was serious about it. What, are you drunk?"

"I most certainly am not." Somehow Lizzie managed to keep her voice even. "I can't help it if I'm not thrilled about CoCo's stupid committee. Covington's art scene is bush-league anyway. I swear, if I get dragged to another opening and have to *ooh* and *ah* at one more bad watercolor show, I'll . . . I'll do a performance art piece of my own. I'll rip off my clothes and run naked down Boston Street, screaming. Even the wine is awful at those things. And for your information, I'm not *drunk*."

"Good. Be sure to accept, tell her thank you, and act happy about it. How's dinner going?" Con was busy getting ice for CoCo's vodka.

Lizzie peeked in the oven. The quail were browning faster than they should—they were practically burned. She'd have to take them out right away or they'd be reduced to charcoal. The Marchand de Vin sauce had separated in its copper saucier while waiting on a dinner that had been too slow to cook and now was black on the outside and probably raw on the inside. The potato gratin was soggy, the salad wilted. It had turned out to be a very bad idea, cooking something she'd never attempted before on this night of all nights. What had she been thinking? Liz thought, filled with a wobbly panic.

Her only hope lay in the fact that CoCo was a perpetual dieter, rumored to live solely on vitamins, weight-loss drugs, and vodka, and Roger's palate was pure country. Con said he loved lunches of fried bologna sandwiches made with Miracle Whip and pickles, that Hannigan had Miz 'Cille out at the farm prepare him three of those revolting sandwiches every day without variation. It was an appetite left over from the old days of his one-man operation, Con told her, back when Wife Number One had packed his lunch.

It was too goddamned bad, Liz thought with a mounting sense of her own doom, there wasn't a flap of bologna in the house to feed him if the quail proved inedible.

Unaware of the culinary disaster on the horizon, though, Con raised an eyebrow. "We ready?"

"Go on—bring them another drink," Lizzie hissed. She gave him a shove. "Would you *go*? Don't leave them in there by themselves!"

With a shake of his head, Con took the fresh drinks out to the Hannigans. Alone in the kitchen, Liz made a frantic attempt to resurrect the Marchand de Vin sauce and ran the potatoes under the broiler, vainly hoping to re-crisp the gratin's Gruyère topping. She could do nothing about the salad.

"Soup's on!" Lizzie called to the living room with forced gaiety. "Y'all come and eat."

Dinner was a lugubrious affair. Roger talked business nonstop to Con at one end of the table, leaving Lizzie to make desultory conversation with CoCo. The other woman was rearranging the food on her plate in obvious distaste, having discovered the underdone quail as soon as she'd sliced into one burned breast. CoCo didn't even pretend to eat anything else, although she'd worked her way through better than half the luscious bottle of cabernet Con had decanted.

Now CoCo leaned in Liz's direction, her gravel-road contralto lowered in tipsy confidentiality.

"It's not easy, being a second wife." CoCo was Roger's third wife, actually, but that didn't stop her from dispensing advice on being a second one.

CoCo said, "You two are *such* an attractive couple, but you should never agree to let him take business trips without you, darling." She swigged the last of the wine in her glass. "And if he's coming home later than he should, well . . . I wouldn't tolerate it, not if you know what's best. Even though you two are practically newlyweds, you've got to keep an eye out for all the little whores in this world. Those gold-digging bitches—they'll try to steal what belongs to *you*."

CoCo looked meaningfully down at the other end of the table where Con and Roger were absorbed in talk of kill-schedules, alligator parasites, and someone called Lireinne who'd just gotten a promotion.

"It's sad but true—all men cheat. They're such dogs, always sniffing around." CoCo lowered her voice further. Liz had to strain to hear her. "I hate to say it, sugar, but I've heard some . . . well, *things*. Now that's probably just the usual nasty old gossip from the usual nasty old people, but even though I'm sure Con is madly in love with you, Lizzie dear, it's better to be safe than sorry. Believe me, I know."

Things? Con's second wife had twisted the linen napkin in her lap until it was a damp, shapeless rag.

"More wine?" Liz asked, changing the subject in a flustered hurry. *Things?* Appearing unconcerned about this revelation took enormous self-control. Lizzie blinked, forcing herself to concentrate on getting through this interminable dinner. *Things* were going to have to wait until after these Hannigans finally left. She'd have to swallow her outrage over this disturbing gossip of CoCo's now.

Oh, but there definitely needed to be more wine to chase that outrage, Lizzie thought, her eyes narrowing. Like right this minute.

"Con, honey, can you open another bottle of wine, please?" she said, her tone syrupy. "CoCo could use a refill." Her own glass was empty, too: her mouth was as parched as dryer lint.

"What's that?" Con looked up from across the dining table's crystal wine goblets and silver candelabra, the Limoges plates full of mostly uneaten food. He looked especially handsome tonight in the white-on-white patterned dress shirt Liz had bought for him on her latest shopping trip in New Orleans—the collar open at the throat, the cuffs folded back above his elegant wrists. "Did you say something?"

"Another bottle of wine, dearest?" Liz said sweetly. CoCo's empty glass was a godsend. Now she could have more wine and Con couldn't blame her, that bastard. She was being *such* a good hostess, she thought, suppressing a fresh wave of fury. *Things?* Damn him, what was *that* all about?

"Sure, honey." Con got up to go to the wine rack in the kitchen for another bottle of Chateau Montelena.

As soon as he left the dining room, Roger fielded a very small forkful of quail.

"Mighty fine dinner, Miss Lizzie." Hannigan took a gulp from his glass. "Never had these here lil thangs done quite like this before." He looked down at his quail dubiously, as though they were some alien species come to a bad end on his plate, far from their home planet.

"I'm so glad," Liz murmured. She tried not to look at the remains of her own dinner, a heap of sad little bones and too-pink, watery flesh. "It's a new recipe." Never again, she decided. Quail were on her list of Big Mistakes now, like a great many other things.

Things.

Roger wiped his mouth, putting his fork down with an air of finality. "Yes, ma'am, ol' Con says you're learning to be a gourmet cook. Now, I admire that in a woman. Too many of these gals today gotta have housekeepers, or, or . . . what d'you call 'em? Nannies, that's it. Way back when, we called those 'nannies' babysitters. No ma'am, nowadays young ladies don't want to run a house or look after their man. They just want to go out to lunch and spend money all day, shopping. I told my Lacey that if she wants to keep that French husband of hers happy, she'd better learn to cook her some of that *cuisine*. Like my old mother used to say—"

"—Kissin' don't last but cookin' do," CoCo finished for him, sounding bored. "There's nothing wrong with having help, Roger. Don't you have a maid, Lizzie? I'm sure I don't know how I'd get along without our Consuelo."

Con walked back in the dining room with the wine in time to answer her question.

"But you're so busy, CoCo," he said good-naturedly. "You really *need* a housekeeper. It's different for Liz and me. Back when we got married, we decided that since she's taking time off from work anyway, she could keep the house better than some Mexican could. It's a regular old, traditional marriage that way. I bring home the bacon, my wife's got my back, and we're both happier for it. Right, Liz?" Con picked up the corkscrew and stripped off the bottle's deep maroon foil.

Liz eyed the cabernet with longing. Would he please hurry the hell up? "Right," she murmured. But that *wasn't* right. Ever since she'd left that cramped, disorganized house in Baton Rouge, where everybody sacrificed constantly to keep it from falling down around their ears, she'd promised herself that one day she'd have a nice house and a maid to take care of it for her. But in the heady days of Con's courtship she'd agreed to everything to close the deal, including laundry. At least none of her three older sisters had ever been well off enough to have a maid, but this fact afforded Liz little satisfaction. No maid, and now there were *things*.

"Aw," Roger Hannigan sighed. "Ain't that the best thang ever? A hardworking man needs a smooth-runnin' home and a little woman in it, looking after him. It was just the same with me and my Aggie."

Roger's first wife, Agnes, had died years ago after giving Hannigan five daughters, but before the farm had taken off like a cruise missile. Lizzie was certain long-suffering Aggie would have wanted a maid. Wife Number Two, Roger's blond trophy wife, had done a bunk with her Pilates instructor after only nine months of marriage: Roger was still paying ruinous alimony for that one. Burned once, he'd waited a few years to marry again and had settled on CoCo, an older, socially connected widow with her own money. Lizzie wondered if CoCo had had to sign a prenup, but at least she had gotten help around the house.

"Yep, those sure were the days," Hannigan reminisced, leaning back in his chair, his wineglass almost disappearing in his wide paw. "I worked my behonkus off like a big ol' mule, so tired I couldn't even get to sleep some nights. Hail, I could go days at a time without talking to nobody but the gators. And do you know, ain't a soul ever give me a break I didn't make for myself. Did it all without those high-hat investors or the banks—sum-bitch banks wouldn't give me the time of day back when I was getting off the ground."

He took another gulp of wine. "Well, no regular banks, that is. There was the ol' Ex-Im Bank and the SBA, a course. They might of put me on the map, but those guvment agencies didn't raise the gators, did they? No sir, just me and my Aggie, all on our own, and look at me now. I'm a got-damn millionaire, twenty times over! People today want everthang handed to 'em, don't know what hard work is anymore. Got so's a workingman can't hardly breathe with all the regulations and damned taxes y'gotta pay to keep these lazy welfare queens in cigarettes and beer. Now, those Bush tax cuts was a fine beginning, but there's gotta be a whole lot more, a whole lot. Bunch of folks who keep this country great are gonna make it happen, you just wait and see, ol' son. I'm hearing good news 'bout the election, good news. Now where we at on that wastewater thang?"

Con had finally gotten around the table after filling the Hannigans' glasses. He'd poured Liz's only half full.

Half a damned glass.

"We're working on it." Con clapped Roger on a ham-like shoulder before he sat down again. "A couple of significant donations to the senator's re-election PAC and he tells me the whole problem's going to be buried in paper at the EPA. And I hear you talking, Rog, about how only some of us actually *work*."

With that smooth segue, Con remarked, "You know, I was the seventh kid of eleven children, part of a big New Orleans Irish-Catholic family. My mother always used to say to me, 'Work hard, Con, and grow up to be somebody.' Well, I took her words to heart. I figured I wasn't ever going to be lucky, since if it weren't for bad luck, we'd have had no luck at all."

"I've always wondered, Con," CoCo drawled, openly drunk now. Those glittering hazel eyes were having trouble focusing. "Your name's so unusual. Is it a family name?"

Con laughed. "Hardly. By the time my mom had me, the fifth boy, she'd run out of family names so she named me for her gynecologist at Charity Hospital—Greek guy, Dr. Hercules Constantine. Took a lot of flak for that when I was a kid, so when I got out of the neighborhood and went to Tulane, I decided to call myself Con instead of Hercules."

Hannigan guffawed. "*Hercules*. Charity Hospital! I had no idear. Here I was, thinking you was some kind of Garden District, white-columns boy—you with your fancy law degree. I mean, look at what you got here."

He waved his hand in a wide, encompassing gesture at the lavish dinner service, the spacious, high-ceilinged dining room dominated by Lizzie's full-length portrait over the gleaming walnut buffet. "I was just a-seeing you growing up on St. Charles Avenue with all the other New Orleans' society muckety-mucks."

Taking a sip of wine, Con smiled. "St. Charles? Hell, no. Think the corner of Constance and St. Mary Street in the Irish Channel. We were so poor, Rog, sometimes all we had for dinner was day-old bread soaked in hot milk—powdered milk, at that. Dad died the day I turned ten and by then my older brothers were already offshore, tool-pushing out on the rigs to help the family get by. They never made it to college. I had their Holy Cross hand-me-downs to wear to school, but my feet were bigger than theirs and so I never had a pair of shoes that really fit, not until I went to college on Pop's Social Security. Money was tight, but I graduated top of my class at Tulane Law and it wasn't easy, making that happen. I treated school like a job, worked my ass off, and didn't owe anybody anything when I was done either."

He sounded so irritatingly self-satisfied. Remembering her own student loans that had forced her to skimp and economize until Con had paid them off, Lizzie swigged her half-glass of cabernet. No Social Security survivor benefits had paid *her* way, she thought hotly.

"You're leaving out the part where Emma put you through law school," she said with a tight smile, "working in the kitchen at Brennan's. You never had to borrow money, thanks to her and those thousands of Eggs Benedicts."

CoCo leapt upon the remark, those glittering eyes focused now in avid curiosity. "And just who," she drawled, "is Emma?"

"His first wife." With a boardinghouse reach, Liz captured the bottle of cabernet and refilled her glass. "She's the reason we're all here tonight. Isn't that so, Con? I mean, she held down a job working the breakfast shift for four years while you were in law school and studying for the Bar."

Con's face was immobile. Roger frowned. CoCo, however, looked intrigued for the first time all evening.

"Why, I never met her, did I? I'm sure I would have remembered if I did."

Con shifted in his chair. "Oh," he said casually, "we were divorced before I came to work for SGE, that's all."

"And where is she now?" CoCo pressed.

"Running some kind of organic vegetable operation out in the country—not far from the alligator farm, in fact." Con waved a hand in dismissal. "Emma's much happier."

It was midnight and the Hannigans had finally gone home. Settled deep in a lawn chair, Con was outside on the brick patio smoking a cigar, a crystal glass of single-malt scotch held loosely in his hand. Lizzie was in the kitchen, washing up after dinner with what seemed like a lot of unnecessary banging and clanging of restaurant-grade copper cookware.

Con hadn't turned the floodlights on, wanting the night and the solitude unbroken. Hell—the food tonight had been well nigh inedible. Emma, Con reminisced, had been an excellent cook, due to her tenure at Brennan's. But the bad meal aside, what had gotten up Lizzie's ass, talking about his first wife at dinner? For a man who was on his third go-round, Roger was as uncompromising as the Pope about the sanctity of marriage. At least Con could write the whole evening off as business entertainment: these days, with all the new expenses and Emma's alimony, every little bit helped.

A soft breeze was blowing out of the west, fresh with the clean resin smell of the surrounding pines. The low landscape lighting illuminated the lush plantings of camellias, azaleas, and sweet olive, the banked beds of liriope and white impatiens stirring in the gentle wind. Its underwater spots glowing, beyond the lap-pool's slender aquamarine oblong Lizzie's new trampoline hulked like a moon lander.

Con stretched in his chair, turning his gaze upward. Tonight the sky was a mix of high clouds and stars, diamonds and translucent gauze stitched on a black velvet shawl. He yawned, settled deeper into the lawn chair, and took another long pull on his scotch.

Con was deep in thought. Yeah, it was nice and peaceful out here, but he honestly couldn't fathom Liz's damage. Except for the maid, he gave her every damned thing she wanted. Why had she turned into such a bitch? For the first two years they were together she'd been an ideal partner—hungry as he for all of life that she could grab, sexually adventurous, worldly far beyond her twenty-nine years.

They'd had such fun, Con thought with nostalgia. He remembered staying up till dawn playing poker—a game Liz was surprisingly good at—hitting the New Orleans bar scene until the wee hours, eating caviar on crackers and drinking champagne in bed. Bed. Con had enjoyed plenty of women in his life, but nothing had prepared him for Liz's inventiveness. Christ, she'd kept him wound so tight that even his own unparalleled libido had to sprint to keep up with her. He hadn't wanted another woman for the first six months of their relationship, and for him that was some kind of record.

But Lizzie's real attraction, Con saw now in hindsight, had been the *fun*. Life with Emma had never been about fun, and as he'd turned forty, Con found he needed fun, needed it badly enough to begin to think about making some changes. The daily grind of his law practice had become an ox yoke around his neck, his otherwise solid marriage unremarkable and stale. Even before he'd met Liz, Con had known he wasn't ready to surrender his youth to middle age. The deep, uncompromising bell toll of his fortieth birthday had rung, announcing that almost half his life had passed.

And Liz was a hell of a lot of woman, built like a Swiss bank, a damned good-looking armful, and he was the guy who'd landed her. It was a real triumph, being seen around town with Lizzie on his arm. But now, although she was as magnificent as ever, it was as though marriage with Liz had become a five-course meal from an overly ambitious kitchen—too much on the plate, too much to digest, just . . . too much of an unhappy muchness. He was damned tired of it all.

But he could never tire of Lireinne. Con's thoughts turned happily to his new personal assistant.

Lireinne. Wearing that enigmatic expression (and, truth be told, rarely anything else) once again she was waiting for him inside his head. No matter how many times he told himself it would only be sensible to forget her, a girl so far out-of-bounds as to be laughable, she was always there.

She was much too young for him, of course. Con knew that. He was no cradle-robber, for God's sake. Con took a sip of his scotch and grimaced, reminding himself that his girls had always been at least old enough to have a legal drink. Then there was the difference in their circumstances: before he'd managed to promote her, Lireinne had been the farm's *hoser*. She lived in a trailer, was a high-school drop-out, was maybe on drugs—all circumstances that ought to have made this infatuation of his a no-brainer. Con really ought to forget about Lireinne before this got out of hand. He really should.

Except he couldn't. Oh, hell, tell it like it is: he wasn't even re-motely going to forget about her. He would get to see her again to-morrow, and he could hardly contain his impatience.

With a faraway smile, now Con imagined Lireinne here in the backyard, swimming nude while he watched, slowly climbing up the steps out of the glowing lap pool, water streaming down her beauti-ful body, coming to sit on his lap in the lawn chair. He shook his head, already half aroused. Down, boy, he thought with an inward laugh. At dinner, only a concerted Obi-Wan offensive had saved the dinner party from becoming a total disaster because he couldn't seem to quit thinking about Lireinne. During that delicate, all-important conversation with Roger about the EPA and the bribable senator, Con had almost forgotten how much money that matter was going to require—a substantial amount. While Roger droned on about wastewater, he'd been daydreaming like a moony teenager. Con grinned. This thing with Lireinne really was like being a kid again.

But after the Hannigans finally left, Liz had hit him with some shit CoCo had said to her, some stupid gossip. *That* had required some major Obi-Wan action, too, but in the end a conflict with his wife had been averted. It hadn't been easy, dismissing what people were saying around town. People were always going to talk, he'd told her, especially about a couple as attractive and interesting as they were.

People misconstrued so much, they had dirty minds, they wanted to believe the worst.

Et cetera, et cetera.

In the end, at last he'd managed to convince Lizzie there was nothing to worry about. Con had no intention of ever divorcing again, not even for Lireinne. She was staggeringly lovely, yes, but he already had a wife, however rocky things were at present, and alimony was a bitch. Liz's damage was that like all women, she needed reassurance and attention. Well, he'd given her all she wanted, all right. That part was easy—he really did love her. Con lifted his glass to Obi-Wan, toasting Jedi victory all around today.

No, he never intended to go through a divorce again, but this crazy, unreasonable attraction was something new and that was a fine thing all on its own. Lireinne made all of his previous conquests seem too easy now: the same breasts and thighs, the same sighs of completion and release, the same girls again and again. All of them— overripe as dropped fruit. When he thought of his latest girlfriend, Jennifer from the Lemon Tree, with a hint of distaste Con admitted he was bored with the affair after fewer than a couple of weeks. He'd get around to ending it soon, because he was prepared to wait for Lireinne. After all, when they'd worked together for a few weeks she was bound to come around. They always did.

The back door swung open onto the patio, the stark yellow light from inside the kitchen falling over his right shoulder.

"Whatchu doin' out here in the dark, huh?" Above him on the brick steps, Liz stood backlit in the doorway. Taking a swallow from the glass of wine in her hand, she sounded impatient. And drunk. So much for the healing properties of reassurance and attention, Con thought, resigned to this long evening's predictable denouement. Back in the saddle, Obi-Wan. Before he answered her, he finished the last of his scotch, melting ice cubes sounding a muted clink in his glass.

"I was looking for a little peace and quiet," Con said shortly. He wasn't going to get into it with Liz again, not if he could avoid it. She'd had better than a bottle of wine this evening—and that was only the wine he knew about because he'd poured it for her. A drunk Lizzie was an oftentimes argumentative Lizzie.

His wife stumbled down the steps and dragged another lawn chair across the patio to sit beside him. The screech of metal on the bricks was shrill and piercing, like the scream of the brakes that Saturday, the day when he'd almost hit Lireinne with . . .

"Con? Hello-o?" Lizzie poked him in the ribs. "Earth t'Con!"

"What?"

"Hey, I'm trying t'tell you I want a *puppy*. Hell, it's like you're in 'nother world. For crap's sake, d'you ever lissen t'me?"

A puppy? Was that it now? Liz had proved to have not a nurturing bone in her body, but if a dog would help keep the peace, Con would gladly sacrifice it before the gods of domestic tranquility in a heartbeat. Good thing he'd decided against having children with her. Once, years ago, he'd been an expectant father for about six weeks, hardly enough time to get used to the idea. And, truth to tell, he'd been ambivalent then about becoming a parent—another thing he couldn't share with Emma. She was so blissfully happy, so radiant with joy, he flat didn't have the heart.

But Emma had miscarried and could never get pregnant again. That had been a strange time for Con, finding that he could feel such pain at the death of a child he'd never even held, but now, years later, he was satisfied with the way things were. All the signs pointed to Lizzie's disinclination to being a mother, in any case. No, kids were definitely out, so a dog was inevitable, he supposed.

"Sure." Con took a deep puff on his cigar, expelling the stream in a plume of acrid smoke. The end of a cigar was never the best part. "So just head down to Mr. Fish and get whatever mutt you want, honey."

He tossed the butt over the pool, its ember arcing into the flower bed, a meteoric shower of orange sparks.

"Ooh, *really*?" Liz squealed. Leaping out of her chair, she threw herself into his lap. Her wine sloshed the rim of her glass but, with that particular drunken deftness of hers, somehow his wife flung her arms around his neck without spilling a drop.

"Oh, Con Costello—I jus' *love* you!"

Burying her face in the side of his neck, Lizzie commenced nuzzling in a gale of enthusiastic, loose-lipped kisses. "Thankyouthankyouthankyou. To hell with ol' CoCo and the shit she says, you know? That bitch. I'm getting a puppy!"

She was heavy as a mound of sandbags across his lap, too warm in the balmy night, too insistent with her kisses. Con shifted uncomfortably in the lawn chair, buried under a soft avalanche of attention-demanding woman.

"I'm gonna call th' breeder in the morning," Liz announced. "I want a Beesh, a *Bichon* Frise. Gonna call him Lima Bean. Don't y'think thass cute?" Mercifully, she struggled up out of his lap, commencing a gleeful, teetering dance around the flagstones bordering the pool. "I'm gettin' a puppy," she sang.

"Lima Bean. Adorable," Con said, sourly wondering if she was going to stumble and fall into the water. He'd probably have to jump in and save her from drowning, she was so hammered, but at least she was over being difficult for now.

"I'm gettin' a puppy, I'm gettin' a puppy." It was an off-key, little girl song that was irritating to Con, but somehow, a little . . . well, sad.

Disconcerted by that realization, Con debated having another drink and decided it was a good idea: he might as well get sufficient scotch on board to get to the place where he didn't care anymore. He wanted to tell Liz to please shut the hell up and go to bed, but *that* would create a conflict for sure and he'd already had enough of being Obi-Wan for one night.

Tired and a little drunk himself, Con got up from his lawn chair and was in the brightly lit kitchen, pouring himself a Glenmorangie, when outside Lizzie was suddenly screaming as though she were being hacked to pieces with a garden shovel.

His drunk vanished. With a crash of splintered Irish crystal, Con dropped his glass in the sink and ran to the back door. He bounded down the steps onto the patio. Next to the trampoline, Liz lay in a hysterical heap, pitifully moaning in a mass of crushed impatiens and liriope. Con knelt beside her in the flower bed. He lifted her shoulders and Lizzie flung her arms around his neck in a panicked, suffocating grip. She screamed in his ear.

"Con!"

"Calm down, babe. *Please,*" Con said with difficulty. "Come on, tell me what happened, sweetheart."

She couldn't answer him. Her inarticulate, breathless shrieks were shrill as a steam engine on a steep grade: the neighbors would be calling the police if she didn't stop soon. Shaking his head in disbelief, Con scooped his wife up and carried her back inside the house where slowly, through a storm of tears, the story emerged. Even though she was so drunk she could barely see, Lizzie had nevertheless somehow climbed onto the trampoline, wanting to express her delight at the prospect of her new puppy. Bounding with elation, she'd somehow bounced right off the damned thing over the azalea bushes into the impatiens, landing on her ankle. Swollen alarmingly, it was twice its normal size.

Liz swore it was broken.

"It's probably just sprained," Con said, feeling thoroughly helpless.

"Fuck *that*—it hurts, it hurts, oh, Con, it hurts so bad, it's *got* to be broken." Lizzie was weeping and adamant. "Take me to the hospital!"

There was nothing to do at that point but to load her up in the Lexus amid her sobbing and swearing at him for jostling her ankle ("Careful, Con! M'God, you trying to make things *worse*?"), and hurry to the St. Tammany General Hospital's emergency room for an X-ray, an evaluation, and then, finally, a cast.

"Tole you it was broken!"

In the ER, her doctor wouldn't give Liz a shot of Demerol for the pain—two hours later, she was still obviously shit-faced—and then there was the matter of the HMO's requiring a blood test before he could administer the local anesthetic prior to setting her ankle.

Lizzie, as it happened, was pregnant.

"*What?*" the proud parents-to-be screamed in unison.

CHAPTER 11

"I only *said* I'd do it the one time, Sarah." Emma lifted her arm and wiped a fine film of sweat from her forehead. "Don't tell me you don't remember."

The blistering, oven-like days of summer had passed and this Saturday was a bright, mild mid-September morning, ideal for working outside in the garden. Emma sifted the loose dirt over the seeds lying in the row of mounded earth, taking care not to cover them too deeply. She deliberately didn't look up to meet her neighbor's accusing gaze. Across the row, Sarah's shadow obscured the future kales and collard greens, as dire as a bowed-shouldered hanging judge. When Sarah didn't reply, Emma glanced up at her friend.

Sarah's return glare was stony.

Oh, come on, Emma thought with some impatience. Just let it go, why don't you?

The row finished, she picked up her trowel, hoe, and seed basket, stood, and moved on to the next. Sarah could disapprove all she liked, but the garden wasn't going to plant itself this morning. Emma had work to do. She chopped at the ground with her hoe, breaking the dirt into dusty clods, all the while wishing the old woman would talk to her instead of just . . . *glaring*.

But Sarah remained stubbornly silent. The woman's sharp eyes on Emma's profile felt like being poked in the head with a stick, and much to her irritation, Emma found herself somehow compelled to defend her decision again.

"Look, your car's fixed, and in any case she told me she's going to get the use of one of the alligator farm's vehicles. Lireinne doesn't need *me* to haul feed out to the trailer. She can get it herself."

Clods dispatched, Emma began to loosen the soil, preparing it for the leeks and artichokes she'd planned for her fall garden. Damn Sarah, Emma thought. When it came to Lireinne, she offered Emma all the understanding of a glowering garden gnome in a John Deere cap.

With a stifled sigh, she put the hoe aside and knelt again in the dirt, working the soil with her gloved hands. "I'm busy putting these seeds in today," Emma pointed out, as though Sarah couldn't see that for herself. "And besides, in a couple of weeks I'll be back at the farmers' market every Saturday. I won't have time for toting feed all the way out to Million Dollar Road, even if Lireinne still needed me to."

The still of the morning answered her, quiet except for a mock-ingbird calling high overhead, its piercing lilt the only sound besides the scrape of her trowel. After a few minutes more of the silent treat-ment, Emma conceded defeat. She sat back on her heels and looked up at her friend, shading her eyes against the hazy sunlight with her gloved hand.

"Come on, Sarah. You hear what I'm saying, don't you?"

Her arms folded, Sarah Fortune nodded curtly, her wrinkled mouth pinched.

"Oh, I hear just fine. You're cutting out on Lireinne," she said. "You're going to wrap yourself up in this goddamned twenty-acre womb again." She kicked an errant hunk of dirt with the toe of her diminutive cowboy boot. "What I don't understand, though, is why the hell you keep saying Lireinne doesn't need you anymore." Sarah eyed Emma contemptuously from under the worn green visor of her cap. "If I'd thought you were going to act like a damned baby about this, I'd never have put you two together in the first place."

"I'm not acting like a baby! And why do you care, anyway?"

Sarah snorted. "Because you're a lonely goddamned mess and she's a good girl who needs a woman in her life. When I was a kid, my own mother raised me like a yard dog, but even that was better than what Lireinne's mother did to her. These excuses of yours are bullshit. You know better, even though you're acting like a cold bitch."

Stung, Emma threw down the trowel.

"Oh, all right, then!" she cried. "Here's what I know. Lireinne's working directly for my ex-husband. She's his *personal assistant*. That's just too close to home, Sarah. That's more than I ought to have to take, okay? I've done the best I can up till now, but this is too much." Emma bit her lip, wishing Sarah would give her a break.

"Do you know how hard it is for me, just hearing his name?" she went on, trying to explain. "God, the other night she couldn't stop talking about him—Mr. Con this and Mr. Con that. It was like she'd been enchanted by him or something. You couldn't possibly understand since you've never met him, but Con has this huge . . . *effect* on people." Emma looked away, muttering under her breath, "Especially pretty young girls."

"Huh." The old woman sniffed, unimpressed. "Sure seems to have one hell of an effect on *you*. Poor kid doesn't know why you won't talk to her anymore. She called me, you know, wanting to find out if you were mad at her or some stupid shit like that. You've got no damned call acting that way. Lireinne thought you two were friends and then you go and cut her off just because she got a promotion? Big deal, she's working for your ex-husband. You know that's not goddamned right, no matter what you say."

Hearing that, Emma's heart swelled in not-unwilling sympathy. Poor Lireinne. Of course she wouldn't understand. Of course she'd think she'd done something to have offended her new friend. Sarah wasn't wrong about that—this really wasn't kind at all. In a way, it was almost . . . cruel, and she didn't want to be cruel to anyone, not ever.

But Emma hadn't been able to bring herself to talk to Lireinne since she'd let the girl off at the trailer that Monday night, nearly two weeks ago. The girl's happy chatter on the long drive home about her new job and her new boss had been well-nigh unendurable, and while Emma hadn't had a panic attack in the truck, it had been a constant, silent struggle.

And later, when she'd come home to her darkened house, there'd been only Sheba, an unusually large dose of Xanax, and the radio standing between her and the voices whispering that it was only a matter of time before Con focused his attentions on Lireinne—if he hadn't already. She was terribly sure he had: Con wouldn't see any reason not to. For days afterward Emma couldn't bring herself to listen to Lireinne's many voice mails, erasing them unheard even as she knew she was being both childish and cowardly. She'd hated having to do that, but Emma had already fought too hard for her precious equilibrium to put herself voluntarily in the way of more pain.

No, she'd been right to cut off this entanglement before things got any worse.

With an uncomfortable shrug, Emma went back to work with her trowel. "I'm sorry, Sarah, I know you don't believe me, but it's better this way. In the long run. Really."

Sarah grunted in response. She took a giant step over the row between them, sitting down in the dirt beside Emma without ceremony. The folds of her housedress billowed around her skinny shanks as she settled on the dusty ground like one of the broody hens.

"No, it's not 'better this way,'" Sarah said, blunt as a mattock. "You're still letting that asshole ex-husband of yours mess around in your life, even though he doesn't seem to give a good goddamn about *you*. Think he goes around giving a shit about what you're up to? I doubt it, Emma, I sincerely doubt it. Running away from your damned divorce—'cause that's what this is, running away—isn't helping you worth a rat's ass. Listen to me."

Sarah drew a deep breath, apparently preparing for some serious ordering-around. "Woman, you need to do something different 'cause this crap of yours isn't working."

Emma crumbled the rich soil in her hands to avoid saying what she really wanted to say, that Sarah had no idea, no idea at all. She had no right to judge her.

"So what would you suggest?" Emma answered instead, gritting her teeth in what was turning into real anger. "Shall I call Con up? Do *lunch?* Invite him and his new wife over for dinner? I don't think so. Shall we all become great friends, do a little barbecuing, share a bottle of wine on the patio? Wait—I don't have a goddamned patio. So that's out, too."

Her breath was running rough and fast, hot in her chest. She didn't have to defend her decision, not to anyone. No matter how Sarah tried to bully her this time, Emma had no intention of confiding the truth about the death of her marriage, the tearing, constant agony and humiliation of it, but if Sarah didn't shut up soon Emma was going to need a Xanax just so she could finish planting her damned garden.

"So back off," Emma muttered with a vicious stab of her trowel. *"Now."*

"Ooh, you're getting mad, aren't you? Good! It's high time you let yourself in on a little secret," Sarah said, nodding self-righteously. "You're so pissed off with your ex that it's making you crazy as a betsy-bug, but instead of letting him have it, you're holed up out here, hoping you won't ever goddamn hear his name, even. *He's* the one you should be giving the business to, not some motherless girl who needs a friend! You don't know a damned thing about what might be going on between Lireinne and him. And even if there is something to that, you can't do shit about it anyhow."

"I can't . . ." Emma began anew, determined to make Sarah understand.

"Oh, grow the fuck up."

Motionless, Emma stared down at her gloved hands, stricken mute with this injustice.

Meanwhile, Sarah Fortune had managed to struggle to her feet.

She shook out her skirt, briskly dusted her hands, and adjusted her John Deere cap.

"I'll be going now," she said. "I'm headed out to Bud's place to see if I can't convince Lireinne that it's high time Mose gets his ass out of that piss-poor pasture. If he's as quiet and easy as she says he is, those handicapped riding folks up to Folsom say they can take him. It's a good place for an old horse. I think she's ready to see that now, 'specially since she's got a new job. That's a real opportunity for a girl like that, and you should be damned glad for her, you hear me?"

Emma didn't raise her eyes from her work, although she was keenly aware of the scuffed toes of Sarah's cowboy boots planted beside her in the dirt. She was afraid that if she looked up at the old woman she'd burst into tears. Instead, Emma reached into the basket beside her, squinting at one of the feed store's small brown paper bags of seeds because her eyes were too wet to make out Ricky Montz's careful grammar-school printing. If she wasn't going to try to understand, then *why* wouldn't Sarah let this alone?

A slow minute passed.

Finally, Sarah exhaled a disappointed-sounding sigh. "Guess I'll see you around the feed store, then." She reached down and put a gentle age-spotted hand on Emma's shoulder, rested it there for a moment, and then she was hobbling back through the garden, where her old Mercedes was parked under the shade of the live oak.

"Get the hell out of the way before I run you over, you idiot birds," she scolded the meandering chickens. "Think about it," she called to Emma as she climbed into the front seat of the car. "You sure need to."

Emma didn't answer.

The old diesel coughed to life, and then Sarah was gone in white plumes of gravel dust and oily gray exhaust.

Indeed, Emma thought about it. Try as she might, she couldn't stop thinking about it. The rest of the morning drew on while she doggedly prepared the ground, planting her seeds, her unhappy thoughts skipping from Lireinne's glowing face in the Banana Republic store to the searing echoes of Con's devastating confession, from her therapist Margot's advice to Sarah's shrewd—and intrusive—observations.

When she'd finished the last rows of fennel and arugula, Emma rose to her feet with a groan, her hand pressed to the small of her back, feeling as though she were a woman standing on the edge of the earth, tired and alone with no road ahead of her.

Come on, none of this matters very much, Emma chided herself, seeking the elusive peace of dispassion. Sarah will get over it eventually, and Lireinne's bound to be so happy with her new job and . . . whatever else, that she'll forget all about you. Call the dog, put up the chickens, take a bath, clean the house. There's still the rest of a long day to get through, so be here now, why don't you?

But *here* was a lonely place, and *now* felt guilty, somehow emptier than ever.

"Sheba! Come, girl." When the hound didn't come trotting across the pasture, Emma whistled for her, waiting in the newly planted garden. The bantams were still having a high old time, pecking at the bugs and worms turned out from their life underground: the busy flock was reluctant to leave the rows when she herded it back to the pen. To Emma, their clucks sounded almost as disapproving as Sarah had.

"Shoo. Hurry up—go home."

After the squawking brood was cooped safely under the live oak, though, Sheba still hadn't returned. Emma shrugged and headed to the house, a little disquieted. The dog almost always came within a few minutes of Emma's call. Where could she be?

The afternoon passed as slowly as it ever did, and still Sheba didn't come home.

Even though Emma tried to tell herself that the dog was probably out on an extended hunt, nonetheless she was becoming uneasy about her absence. The farm was far enough off the highway that she'd never been much concerned about Sheba getting hit by a car, but what if her ranging had taken her too close to that well-traveled road? She'd been spayed, so it wouldn't be likely that she'd taken up with a roaming male, even less likely that she'd gotten lost.

Emma tried to think that there wasn't any reason to be worried. Sheba would be back for supper.

But as the day drew to a close, Emma's worry was growing, and when the sun dropped behind the tops of the tall pines bordering her farm and Sheba hadn't turned up yet, she knew with a sinking heart that something had to have gone wrong. Maybe very wrong.

"*Sheba*—come, girl!"

Emma was out on the front porch, calling into the gathering dusk. The air was turning cooler as the sun westered in banked clouds of orange, scarlet, and violet-rose. She wrapped her arms tightly around herself, shivering, but stayed out on the porch until well after dark. Sheba didn't return and after a tasteless meal that Emma forced herself to prepare and eat, after one last solitary wait outside on the porch under the cold stars, she finally went to bed. She didn't rest well, though, for her dreams were full of a terrifying confusion, of Con and Sheba walking away from her down the gravel road while she called after them.

Come back, come back.

And contrary to her usual habit, Sarah didn't call the next day, not even once.

Now Emma regretted having quarreled with her friend—but refused to admit that Sarah might have had a point. Lireinne was well on her way, she insisted, unwillingly reliving her argument with the old woman. Sarah would just have to make her peace with that. Instead of driving out to Million Dollar Road where a panic attack was sure to be waiting for her, Emma had a missing dog to find. She needed to get in the truck and go look for her, call the SPCA and the Parish animal shelter. Sheba had to be somewhere.

But after five days of searching, on Thursday, Emma had to face the terrible truth: Sheba was almost certainly lost for good—or dead.

Without the dog, the house had never seemed more threateningly still to her. Now even her garden, a place of hard-won peace, seemed like a shoe-box diorama of a farm complete with cardboard cutouts of trees and papier-mâché chickens. Sheba, Emma's sole companion, was gone and she was truly alone.

Emma gave in to grief then, grieving for the friend who'd never offered her anything but love and a steadfast loyalty, who'd kept her company when she needed it most and then, like everyone else, abandoned her. Unable to look at the reminders, Emma put Sheba's bowls away and threw out the last of the dog food while she sobbed helplessly, blindsided by her unrelenting, profound sorrow. When Emma forced herself to think about it rationally, she knew this tearing pain was out of all proportion to her loss. Sheba was only a stray dog, for God's sake.

But in the house it was just her own echoing footfalls now, the constant stream of classical music—and the emboldened voices. Emma couldn't seem to stop crying, no matter how she tried, until her tears gave way to a numbness almost more frightening than the constant tears had been.

So it was that when Con's car pulled up in front of the house late that Thursday afternoon, Emma found herself letting him in. He came carrying an armful of lilies and a bottle of her favorite wine, a fine old Bordeaux that she remembered tasting of cherries and still, dark earth; of honey, amber, and sunshine.

In the way Con had always possessed, he seemed to know something was wrong right away. Without their having to say very much to each other, Con sat in the kitchen with her while she trimmed the stems of the flowers and arranged them in a cut-crystal vase that had once belonged to her mother, and then he opened the wine. Carrying their glasses, they moved to the front porch and sat in the rocking chairs, looking out across the farm where a light rain had begun to fall. Even in the depths of her sorrow, Emma took the comfort of his understanding gratefully. How right it seemed, Con being there with her now. The quiet between them seemed necessary. It was a gift to her sorrow, a sharing without words.

The bottle was nearly done before Emma could tell Con about losing Sheba. She was weeping again, and so dazed from the unaccustomed alcohol that she poured out much more than she meant to say. He listened to it all, though, really listened in the way that only Con could. Oh, his listening was another loss, one that had haunted her for two years, but wrapped in that perfect attention Emma felt herself finally accepting that Sheba, whom she'd also loved, was never coming back. As Con gave her this safe, quiet space for full acceptance, she abandoned herself to him, dismissing whatever other reason it had been that had brought him to her farm that day. It didn't matter.

And so when Con got out of his chair, crossed the porch, and knelt beside her to take her into his arms, Emma gladly surrendered her mouth to his, drinking him in, as hungry for him as the dry ground hungered for the steady-falling rain.

She knew better, God knew she did, but it was Con at last, it was her husband and she didn't care anymore about the past. After all the years of solitude, for this one moment Emma wasn't alone.

Later, much later, as they lay in Emma's bed, Con held her close while the rain pattered overhead on the tin roof. The radio was playing Verdi's *Aida* in the other room: it was opera night at the NPR station.

Con pressed his lips to her forehead, stroking her silver hair in the lamplight. In this so-familiar aftermath, Emma threw a long leg over his and propped herself on one elbow, looking down into Con's beloved face. Her fingertip traced the line of his jaw. He smelled of his Hermès cologne, the smoky incense of his cigars, and their lovemaking.

"I didn't expect this," Emma murmured with a tremulous half-smile.

"Didn't you?" Con looked up at her, his eyes warm and fond. "Oh, we're forever lovers, Em. You know that."

Ah, yes. She had known that. Always.

"I guess so . . . yes." Running her fingers through her hair, Emma sat up in the bed, drawing the sheets to her to cover her breasts. "Yes," she said again, willing a firmness to her voice. But with Con here now, here again in her bed, she was filled with a thousand sudden questions she couldn't bring herself to ask, not right away. Not just yet. Things were so new between them. Emma pondered, biting her lower lip, until she thought of a question so obvious that it had to be safe.

"By the way," she said lightly, "I didn't ask before. What brought you out here today, anyway?"

Con frowned, lacing his fingers behind his head on the pillow. He sighed, his expression rueful.

"Oh, Em." Con turned his eyes away from hers. "God, how can I say it? I came out to see you because I knew that if I called, you'd just blow me off like always. I, uh, wanted you to hear this from me and not from someone else, but then you were so broken up about Sheba, I . . . I forgot everything but you." He felt for her hand and Emma clutched his, feeling the long bones, his warm, broad palm. She pressed his hand to her lips.

"You know I hate it when you're unhappy, sweetheart. I can't stand it," Con said. "When you're sad it makes me feel like hell, especially when it's something I can't fix." His sea-blue eyes were sparkling with unshed tears in the lamplight.

As Con spoke, Emma's breath caught as though her throat had been crushed. She let go of his hand, raising her own to her mouth. It was an echo of a long-dreaded memory, the resonance of annihilation, of betrayal. From a long way away, from the border of Breakdown Country, Emma heard her own voice ask, "What is it, Con?"

He hesitated, his beloved face pleading and almost shamed.

"Lizzie's pregnant."

Outside the rain continued to fall, but inside her bedroom the voices shrieked all around her, the voices were a monstrous flock of birds, and from the whirling center of that vast, twittering chorus of jeers and blame, Emma could only repeat it, the thing Con had just said.

"Lizzie's . . . pregnant."

Con reached to stroke her cheek. "Yes." He sat up next to her in the bed and put his strong arms, his smooth, well-muscled arms that had always made her feel safe—so safe—around her trembling shoulders.

"I know it's a shock," he said soothingly. "I couldn't think of a better way to say it. God knows I didn't want to hurt you, but this is . . . what it is. You needed to know, sweetheart."

You're so pissed off with your ex that it's making you crazy.

It was Emma's last, fully realized thought before she slapped him.

And then she couldn't breathe, the light fled the room, and a storm fell like a rain of rocks around her.

There wasn't enough Xanax in the medicine cabinet to do the job right, and Emma had a horror of killing herself merely sufficient to render herself brain-damaged instead of genuinely dead. Using the truck's tailpipe was out—she didn't have a garage—and the oven was electric. She'd been meaning to buy a gas range for a while because she preferred to cook with gas, but it was too late for that now. Emma knew she'd never screw up the courage to step off a kitchen chair, her bathrobe belt tied around her neck, and hang herself from the light fixture. It probably wasn't strong enough to support her weight anyway. Thanks to Sheba's hunting, she'd never bothered to keep rat poison on the farm either.

In the end, then, Emma found herself in a warm bath armed with the sharpest knife she could find.

Con, of course, had left long before.

But then the voices inside the house were gone, too. She was really by herself now, totally alone. Soon to be alone forever.

And in a gift of exquisite, midnight irony, *Madame Butterfly* had followed the Verdi opera on the radio. The soaring notes of Cio-Cio San's final aria seemed far away, floating down the hall in a music that was as liquid and pure as the water lapping Emma's knees, promising an end to pain.

It was time. Probably past time.

Setting her jaw, Emma dug the tip of the knife into her wrist. She dragged the edge upward, but while the blade was keen enough to slice a thin red line up the inside of her arm, when she pressed harder the scratch grew ragged. It hurt. It hurt a *lot.*

For God's sake, Emma thought in weary disgust. She used to be a chef. How could she have let her knives get this dull? But now she was reduced to sawing at her sturdy, traitorous skin, and the pain grew so fierce, so hot, that Emma hissed, reflexively flinging the knife away from her as though it were a snapping rat. The blood-smeared blade fell outside the tub with a clatter on the bathroom floor.

A narrow trail of crimson ran down her arm and swirled in the warm bath like wine mixed with water in a chalice. Emma stared at the red, drifting ribbon.

Who would it be? she wondered dully. Who would discover her after she was dead? Who would have the awful responsibility of calling the police? Would they wait here with her body until the cops and the ambulance arrived? It was hard to muster the energy to care about the answer, but she ran down the short list of who might be the lucky one anyway. It could only be Con or Sarah. There was no one else. Her aunt and uncle had died years ago and she hadn't any other family.

Con would cope—he'd cry, but he'd cope—but the thought of Sarah finding her was a bad one. Emma didn't want her friend to have to deal with this mess, even though Sarah was a self-acknowledged tough old bird. No, this should be Con's job because he'd been the one who drove her to this. She ought to call his cell phone right now before she finished killing herself, leave him a little voice mail of her own. Like, "Hey—I'll be dead when you get this. Thanks for keeping me in the loop, by the way."

You're so pissed off with your ex it's making you crazy.

"Right as usual, my friend," Emma murmured to the memory of Sarah in the garden.

The water was pink-tinged and beginning to cool. Her left arm burned, throbbing in time with her heartbeat. No, Emma knew she wasn't going to call Con. The thought of him standing over her naked body . . . *crying,* was too much for her to bear thinking about. It might even be her last thought. Oh, damn him and his easy tears. It would have to be Sarah, who would be bound to come by any day now. Poor Sarah. Still, it couldn't be helped.

Better get on with it now, this last part.

"Here goes." With a tired groan, Emma reached out of the tub to find the knife, to pick it up and finish the job, but the knife wasn't under her wet fingers. She peered over the side of the deep bath and didn't see it anywhere.

The knife must have bounced and skidded underneath the old claw-footed tub. Emma was going to have to get out and hunt for it. The unbidden image of herself, bent on suicide and naked on her hands and knees fishing around under the tub for a knife, was so ludicrous that when poor, tragic *Madame Butterfly* ended and the muscular, mountaintop sopranos of Wagner's Valkyries commenced their skirling chorus, she almost laughed at the absurdity of it all. Almost.

"Hell." Emma collapsed against the cool porcelain back of the tub, exhausted. This killing yourself is harder than it looks in the movies, she thought bitterly. So . . . go on. Get your ass out of the bath and look for the knife. Better yet, just go in the kitchen, find the steel, and put a decent edge on another one if you're really hell-bent on this. Make it easy; make it fast.

With an effort, Emma hauled her now-shivering body out of the water and grabbed a towel. The long, ragged scratch on her forearm bled sluggishly, leaving a bright red smear on the white cotton.

She caught her reflection in the bathroom mirror and stopped, surveying it with a numb indifference, not giving a damn anymore whether she saw herself or not. Look: there she was, like a ghost. The face looking back at her was ashen, her full-lipped mouth slack with the emptiness of this, her last gesture to the world. Emma noted without much interest the deep hollows above her collarbones, the long thin column of her neck. She should try to eat more, except, except . . . she was killing herself tonight instead.

You're so pissed off with your ex it's making you crazy.

"No."

Full-throated with sudden, unthinking fury, Emma slammed her fist into the mirrored cabinet. A frieze of cracks exploded her reflection into a hundred pieces.

"*Hell,* no!" Her fist hit the mirror again, harder this time. The cabinet door flew open and the bottle of Xanax tumbled out into the sink.

"What did you think was going to happen?" Emma demanded of her splintered face in what was left of the mirror. "Did you really think he'd come to tell you this has been a . . . a bad dream? That he'd changed, that he was leaving her and coming back to you? You *idiot.*"

Emma grabbed the plastic pill bottle in the sink, hurling it violently away. The vial shattered against the wall. Xanax hit the floor in a narcotic rain of peach-colored sleet.

In addition to her arm, now her hand was bleeding steadily from the broken glass—blood in the sink, blood on the floor, a splatter of blood on the wall. In rage-filled impatience Emma ransacked the contents of her medicine cabinet until she found the box of Band-Aids. She tore it open, spilling little bandages everywhere, and with shaking fingers patched up the heel of her hand.

"That son-of-a-bitch!" Naked and not caring in the least, Emma stomped down the hall to her bedroom, leaving a line of wet footprints on the pine floor behind her.

"Damn him, damn him, damn him," she muttered under her breath as she threw on her soft cotton robe. "That *shithead.*" The sleeve bloomed a pinkish stain from the deep scratch on her arm, but she didn't notice. Clutching her fingers in her hair, closing her eyes, Emma vowed to strip her bed and throw those rumpled sheets, still smelling of him, into the garbage.

"How could I have let Con do this to me again? How? I *hate* him!"

Saying that, suddenly Emma went still, openmouthed. That felt good, she realized in surprise. It felt . . . really *good* to be furious at Con, to hate him for all he'd done to her.

The Valkyries had reached the windswept climax of the mountain and were screeching their way across an ancient German sky in a thunder of spears and flying blond braids. "And I hate stupid Wagner!" Emma ran out of her room and down the hall to the front of the house. She stabbed the radio's power button. The room's silence was complete and utter, except for the steady fall of rain on the roof.

"*There*," she said defiantly. "I'm not afraid of you anymore!" She was talking to the voices. In the answering quiet, Emma cocked her head, narrow-eyed and listening. There were no voices, not even a whisper. "Cowards," she sneered to their absent echoes. "Don't ever come back. Ever."

Filled with a restless energy now—she was going to see to those goddamned *sheets*—in that blessed hush, Emma heard it. Emma heard what she'd been unable to hear over the water running in the tub, over the radio, the rain, and her unlooked-for, surprising rage.

The soft, insistent scratch of a patient paw at the front door.

"Sheba!" Her heart leaping, Emma threw open the door and her dog, thin, wet and dirty, limped into the house, her tail wagging hesitantly. "Oh, my girl—you came *back*." She fell to her knees, throwing her arms around the hound and burying her face in the warm neck. Sheba licked Emma's jaw and whined in contentment. She was home.

After she'd rubbed the dirt off with a towel and examined Sheba to see if she'd been injured, Emma and her dog went into the bright, warm kitchen together. "Oh, honey—I threw out your food. Whatever am I going to feed you?"

It was late, past one o'clock in the morning, but Emma didn't feel tired at all. She searched the refrigerator, hurrying to find something to throw on the stove for the two of them. Sheba was so thin she had to be starving, and to her astonishment, for the first time in what seemed like decades, Emma was ravenous. While she cooked a huge meal of sautéed chicken and rice, from time to time she'd stop, bend down, and hug the dog at her feet. She was cultivating gratitude while the chicken browned and filled the kitchen with the scents of sharing, of friendship, of a real peace.

Tomorrow she'd call Sarah. And soon, Emma sternly declared to her fears, she'd go out to Million Dollar Road to see Lireinne again. She'd known for weeks that the girl had needed her. By denying Lireinne, she knew now she was denying herself. Too, it was long past time to face up to answers instead of running from them.

Contentedly watching Sheba bolt her food in wolf-like gulps, in quiet amazement Emma found one answer.

This, she realized, was what it meant to be here now.

CHAPTER 12

The swamp maples were vermillion-and-gold fires in the cool morning sky, and the wild asters burned a blue haze in the fields. When she got in the car, Lireinne turned the radio to her favorite station for the short drive to the alligator farm. Looking in the rearview mirror, she put on her lip gloss, making a sultry pout since she was alone, and then laughed at her reflection. Lireinne wondered if maybe this was what a million other career women did every day: striking poses when no one could see before they had to be responsible and went to their jobs. The thought made her feel . . . solid, somehow, almost like a grown-up.

Bud and Wolf had left already—Bud to the Walmart loading dock and Wolf to Covington High. That had been a righteous battle, but in the end she and Bud had pounded some sense into her little brother's head. Lireinne had explained it over and over: with her new job, she could save enough to help out with college expenses. All Wolf had to do now was keep his grades up. Bud insisted he could cover the rest, so now her little brother could go to LSU.

That was *sweet*.

Lireinne was wearing her new sweater this Friday because the weather had turned chilly overnight, and that was sweet, too. She loved cool weather. When she'd fed Mose earlier, the old horse's summer coat had been as puffy as a fake fur against the damp early-morning air. She really ought to hang out with Mose while she still could. Sarah Fortune had found him a new home up at the therapeutic riding center in Folsom and he'd be going soon. Saying good-bye to Mose wasn't going to be easy: the old Thoroughbred had been a part of her life for almost as long as she could remember. He'd been the friend of her childhood and soon he wouldn't be waiting for her behind the barbed-wire fence when she came home anymore.

But Mose was going to have plenty to eat and a warm barn to live in for the coming winter. Sarah said that at his age, that kind of care would keep him alive and healthy for a long time. Probably Mose was going to like being ridden by the handicapped kids. She'd send his brushes with him so they could keep up with his grooming, and Sarah had said she could visit him whenever she wanted. Much as she'd miss Mose, it was the right thing to do by him and she could use the money she was spending on feed to add to what she was saving for Wolf, too.

In any case, Lireinne couldn't take the time to hang out with Mose while he ate his breakfast anyway. Getting ready for work took a lot more time when you were getting dressed up every day, Lireinne reminded herself, as she backed the Explorer down the driveway. She'd need to hurry: she'd wasted enough time, mooning over her reflection and woolgathering.

When Lireinne pulled up to the alligator farm at eight and parked beneath the big live oaks, Mr. Con's Lexus wasn't there yet. He must be running late again. Since she'd started working up in the house, she hadn't seen nearly as much of her boss as she assumed she would. The day she got her promotion, that same night Mrs. Costello had broken her ankle in some weird trampoline accident. Mr. Con was often away from the farm taking care of his wife, but when he was there he was nice enough. Hardly handsy at all.

Besides, Lireinne didn't mind having the big office to herself when he was gone, and she got along fine with Mr. Hannigan— although the same couldn't be said for the women in the house. She'd caught Tina, Jackie, and Miz 'Cille giving her the stink-eye when they thought she wasn't looking. Oh, well. Lireinne shrugged carelessly and grabbed her purse off the front seat. They'd come around or they wouldn't. For sure, none of them was lining up to be her best friend, but that was so not her problem. After her years at Covington High, she was used to unfriendly females.

Lireinne got out of the Explorer, tugged at her trim gray skirt and navy merino sweater, and smoothed her hair before heading up the sidewalk to the front door. This was the first time she'd worn this outfit and she knew she looked good in it. Emma had told her that blue suited her, she remembered, saying that it brought out the green in her eyes.

So . . . like, why hadn't she heard from Emma since that totally fun shopping trip?

That had been weeks ago. Lireinne paused on the cement path. She gazed across the parking area, staring at the peacock roosting in the oak tree without really seeing it and thinking about the visit to the mall. After that night, Lireinne had called nearly every day for a while, then given up when the older woman neither answered nor returned her calls.

Okay, so Lireinne had been totally taken in by Emma, how she'd acted like she wanted to be friends. So she'd been stupidly happy and flattered to be noticed by such a classy lady, but Emma had turned out to be just another one of those obnoxious do-gooders, getting her kicks out of messing around in people's lives and then dropping them like a hot rock when she got tired of them.

Lireinne already knew from do-gooders: in the first grade there'd been the lady in the school's office who'd signed her up for the free lunch program. That hadn't seemed like a bad thing, not until that same lady had given her a hard time in front of the other kids for eating not only her own lunch but also the leftovers on nearby plates. She'd only done that because she'd been so damned hungry, Lireinne thought resentfully. Those other kids had been wasting their food and wasn't that supposed to be wrong? Then there had been the teacher's aide who'd called the Parish on Bud after Lireinne had told her about

Miss Penny and her brown bottle, as well as the social worker who came out to inspect the trailer when seven-year-old Wolf had explained to some other kid's parents that he slept on a sofa: they'd notified Child Protective Services. It wasn't like any of those hateful people had ever done anything real for her or Wolf, nothing that made a difference anyway.

No, Lireinne should have known better than to trust someone like Emma. She'd been so dumb, on the way home that night she'd even told her about Paris. Emma must have laughed herself sick later at the thought of trailer trash going to France. Well, Her Royal Highness, Queen Emma of St. Tammany Parish, could go to hell. She didn't need her for anything. She had a *real job* now, with a salary and a car. Everything was going to be just great for her from now on. After three frustrating weeks Lireinne was finally comfortable, working at her new position as Mr. Con's assistant.

For sure, the first few days had been what Mr. Con called a "transition." Some transition. Initially, the computer programs had been a real bitch. Flustered, Lireinne had lost files, found them again, re-lost them, and re-found them until she got the hang of it. She'd dropped a couple of important calls and forgotten to update Mr. Con's calendar, but those days were behind her, Lireinne thought with a sense of accomplishment. She hadn't needed some freaking busybody do-gooder to get her this job, had she? No, Lireinne had gotten here all on her own, and besides, she was good at what she did. Mr. Con told her so all the time.

The peacock launched off the oak limb, flopping to the ground in an ungainly heap and breaking her reverie. She wasn't a hoser anymore, she was a personal assistant, Lireinne reminded herself, banishing the angry, depressing thoughts of Emma. Besides, what was this? Woolgathering Day?

She turned and hurried up the walk to the office. *Bien sûr, chérie!* Lireinne was looking forward to a big cup of coffee with plenty of milk and sugar, planning to sip at it while she filed the week's expense reports this morning. She'd never liked coffee much before coming to work in the front office, but now she thought it was sort of cool.

People working in real offices always drank lots of it, she'd learned. Then, too, it helped to pass the time because, to tell the truth, most of what she did was pretty boring—although it beat the snot out of hosing.

Lireinne opened the front door and stepped inside to the warm aromas of coffee and baking biscuits.

"Hey, Miz 'Cille," she chirped as she walked into the kitchen.

The older woman was busy cutting up chickens for Friday's lunch. 'Cille, wearing a fall-weather getup of plus-size maroon sweats and fuzzy pink house slippers, didn't turn around and she didn't return Lireinne's greeting either. With a crack of bones, she smacked the cleaver into a plump chicken breast.

Okay. Be that way, Lireinne thought with a raised eyebrow. Whatever. A hot, fragrant mug of coffee in hand, cream and sugar added, she was ready to leave the kitchen and get on the morning's filing when 'Cille finally spoke.

"Hope you're proud of yourself, you little mink!" she muttered.

Lireinne almost dropped her mug on the floor. "What'd you say?" she asked, incredulous, sure she'd heard the other woman wrong. "Mink" meant a female who indiscriminately slept around with any-body, a girl with no sexual scruples whatsoever. Of all the names that Lireinne had been called in the past, no one had ever accused her of being a mink. It was that bad.

Miz 'Cille didn't look away from the chicken carcasses spread out on the cutting board, but laid into a thigh joint with her cleaver. "You heard me," she said loudly, her broad back to Lireinne. *Whack.* "Making a hardworkin' man lose his job so's you can cut loose with the boss, and him married, too! I just hope you're proud of yourself."

"Hold on one minute," Lireinne said, confused and suspicious. "What do you mean, 'cutting loose with the boss'? And what the hell is this, 'making a man lose his job'?"

"What I mean, you slut, is you made it sound like Harlan done something bad—which he didn't do and you know it—so he had to quit when they made him go hose. His bad back flat couldn't take it. Now he's out of work and it's all your doing."

Like an ocean liner correcting its course, 'Cille turned her enormous bulk to face Lireinne. She wiped her hands on the bloodstained apron stretched across the expanse of her hips before she announced, "I'm a God-fearing, churchgoing Christian woman. I don't hold with what's going on at this place since you come in here, not at all. Wearing those tight skirts, making up to Mr. Costello like you do. I know *all* about your kind, missy." Miz 'Cille's fat lips were a self-righteous, fleshy bud of contempt. "Hoors of Babel-land."

Stricken voiceless by 'Cille's accusations, Lireinne was struggling to find the words to tell the cook that this wasn't the way things had gone down, that it hadn't been that way *at all,* when Tina walked into the kitchen.

"Whore is right." The office manager shoved past Lireinne to join Miz 'Cille. She folded her arms across her sagging bosom and sneered, "Yeah, I bet you put out like a broke Coke machine. It's the only way a hoser like you could end up being some . . . *personal assistant.*" Tina's eyes turned ugly in her acne-scarred face. "Now I bet you think you're going to run to Mr. Costello, tell him lies about me, too. Don't even dream on it, you slut. Roger Hannigan gave me this job his own self and only he can fire me."

Deep in rolls of fat, 'Cille's gaze was likewise flat with naked hostility. "Yeah, me neither. The big boss tells me every day I'm the best cook in St. Tammany Parish. Tell all the lies you want, but Mr. Roger won't believe word-one 'bout me, not from somebody like you."

Not *this* again, Lireinne thought, her heart thudding in her ears. They couldn't call her a whore for something she hadn't done. This was just, just . . . *wrong.*

"You're wrong!" Lireinne cried. Her throat was thick, she was almost choking. "Harlan, he, he . . ." Once more she was without words, so upset that she couldn't begin to tell them the truth about Harlan's assault. This was what they thought about her? That she'd lied to get him fired and worse, that she'd gotten her job because she was sleeping with *Mr. Con*?

Meanwhile Tina and Miz 'Cille sneered, clearly satisfied at having made her feel so bad. Their hate was as plain as if they'd slapped her. Lireinne abruptly slung her coffee mug in the sink and stalked out of the kitchen. Shaking, she stormed down the hall into Mr. Con's big office, slamming the door behind her before she burst into furious tears.

She'd just been called a whore. *Again.*

Somehow this was so much worse than when everybody at Covington High had called her names. This was happening at her *job.* Lireinne had figured that Tina and the other women in the office wouldn't take to her right away, but she hadn't known they hated her.

Her back pressed against the door, she sank her teeth into her knuckle until it hurt. Slowly, the tears stopped and Lireinne took a deep breath, trying to get a grip because she'd be damned if those dirty-minded bitches would make her cry. Lireinne never cried. She didn't deserve that kind of shit from anyone, much less those two ugly-ass old women. For God's sake, except for that one time with Brett, she was practically a virgin. That shouldn't count, right? Besides, she didn't want to have sex with anyone, *nobody,* least of all her boss.

Lireinne collapsed into one of the conference chairs, staring out the big window at the retention pond while the women's sickening words shrilled a taunting chorus in her head.

Mink. Slut. Whore.

Lireinne sat for another ten minutes, fighting the stubborn tears that wouldn't leave her alone. She was remembering those names, the way they seemed to follow her wherever she went. Why were people so . . . *mean* to her?

Lireinne was forced to admit she didn't know why. She never had, and probably never would. With a slow, unhappy shake of her head, she made herself get out of the chair to commence filing the expense reports: they were waiting and she needed to get to them before Mr. Con showed up at the office. If she didn't want to give up and go home like a loser, she had work to do.

Lireinne wasn't going home.

★   ★   ★

Mr. Con got in twenty minutes later that morning, but Lireinne didn't say a word about the confrontation in the kitchen. Instead, an impotent anger and a kind of sick acceptance warred inside her while she filed and typed on the computer and he talked on the phone at length with somebody way up in Washington, D.C., about the waste-water situation. Although she couldn't stop thinking about her own trouble, it didn't sound like things were going so well for Mr. Con this morning either.

"What the *hell*?" Mr. Con growled. "What do you mean, we're going to court?" He pounded his fist on the desk and shouted at the person on the other end of the phone. "What about the senator? I thought we had this shit wrapped up. You gave me your word, you lying son-of-a-bitch—worse than that, you took the money!"

Ultimately, Mr. Con hung up on the guy, but Lireinne couldn't hang up on the scenes replaying in her head. She could only give half her attention to the flow data from the wells until lunchtime finally rolled around at 1:30. Today lunch was out of the question. Lireinne had made up her mind to keep to the office instead of going out to the kitchen to eat with the rest of the staff. Why sit down with Tina, Jackie, and 'Cille when everybody hated her?

"Ready for lunch?" Mr. Con asked, getting up from his desk.

"No thanks," Lireinne said, trying to find a smile. "I'm not hungry."

"Sure?" He raised a questioning eyebrow. "It's 'Cille's famous chicken and dumplings today. C'mon, Lireinne—you don't want to get too skinny."

Mr. Con was standing behind her chair. He touched her lightly on the shoulder. "You're much too pretty for that." Almost before she realized what he was doing, he casually brushed her hair away from her face before returning his hand to her shoulder. That felt . . . wrong, his touch felt really wrong, especially today.

Lireinne suppressed the strong, sudden impulse to push him away. "No, really. I'm good." She sat in her chair, frozen, until Mr. Con removed his hand. With a perplexed shake of his head, he left the room.

What if Tina had walked in and seen Mr. Con acting like that? Lireinne could bring her own freaking lunch from now on and eat in the office instead of at the table with everyone else, but she couldn't avoid Tina forever. That bitch came in and out of the office whenever she felt like it and Lireinne knew she'd take Mr. Con's handsiness as proof there was substance to her accusations. No wonder he and Emma were divorced, Lireinne thought with a tight, humorless smile. She's a freaking fake, and he must have run around on her something chronic.

She'd never say a bad word about Mr. Con to anyone, though. He'd given her a chance when nobody else ever had. That made him a good person in Lireinne's book, even if he was a toucher. She just wished he'd stop it because it felt creepy. It looked bad, too.

No, she'd find a way to handle up on this mess somehow. There was too much riding on this job not to.

After lunch, Mr. Con had to leave the office to go home and check on his wife.

"We've got a new puppy, too. Have to let the little guy out of his crate sometime. Why don't you take the rest of the afternoon off?" he said, shrugging into his light, buff-colored suede blazer. "You've been hard at it all day. It's Friday. Go on, get started on your weekend."

Even though leaving early was sure to cause more talk, Lireinne couldn't wait to take him up on his suggestion. She'd go home and spend some time with Mose for a change, and then when Wolf got back from school maybe they could go into town and hit the Walmart. The thought cheered her, so much so that when she walked past Tina in the hall on her way to her car and the farm manager hissed *slut* under her breath, Lireinne could pretend she hadn't heard it, although her hand itched to backhand the other woman. She, at least, knew how to behave like a professional, even if Tina didn't.

When Lireinne got in the car, though, her hands clenched the steering wheel till they ached. She was still seething when she got home and changed into a pair of jeans and a T-shirt. Feeding and grooming Mose didn't take the edge off her mood either: in fact, the more Lireinne thought about it, the madder she got. This persecution was high school all over again, and once more there was nothing she could do about it. Nothing. It didn't matter a damn that she wasn't a hoser anymore, because just like always, she was powerless to do a damned thing to defend herself.

Those career women Lireinne had been thinking of earlier this morning, the legions of them getting in their cars, putting on their lipstick, driving to work: had they ever had to face being called whores, simply for doing their jobs? Lireinne didn't think so.

The rest of the afternoon passed with glue on the soles of its shoes. Night had fallen by the time Wolf came home and knocked on her door. Lireinne was lying on her bed, not really watching the fuzzy movie on the TV, but was staring moodily at the ceiling instead and imagining ways for 'Cille and Tina to die—slowly, painfully, with a lot of pleading for their lives. At Wolf's knock, expelling an aggrieved sigh she got up to crack open her door.

"Where've *you* been?" Lireinne asked, feeling peevish. "I was thinking maybe we could check out Walmart, but I don't want to anymore."

"Chemistry project," Wolf explained briefly. "I missed the bus but I got a ride home." Wearing his favorite Goth gear laden with tons of zippers and chains, faded from black to almost gray from too many washings, he leaned inside the door. His normally taciturn expression seemed more animated than usual.

"Hey, sis, can you drive me to Bolt's house? His folks are gonna be gone till tomorrow so we got the whole place to ourselves," Wolf said with a grin. "Party in the Parish, you know? It's already going on, got started about an hour ago."

"Fine," Lireinne said. She shrugged a listless acquiescence. Okay, so giving Wolf a ride into town beat lying around on the bed with all that bad stuff echoing in her head like a stuck CD. At least she wouldn't be by herself for a while. "When do you want to go?"

Wolf's grin widened. "Whenever *you* do. I'm ready whenever," he said, turning to leave. He paused in the doorway as if struck by a thought. "Hey, why don't you come party with us?"

A party? Lireinne hadn't been to a party in years, and this was the first time Wolf had asked her to go to one with him. A teenage party might be an improvement over hanging out in the trailer by herself—not much of an improvement, but still better than being alone. If anyone called her the old names, she could just leave, right? It would be something to do, even if it meant trying to hang with Wolf's lame-ass Goth friends.

Lireinne shrugged. "Whatever. I guess I could stay out for a little while."

"Cool," Wolf said, nodding approval. "You're working too hard anyhow."

Lireinne almost confided in her little brother then about what the women had said to her, but decided she wouldn't. Wolf could probably get how bad that bullshit had made her feel, but she didn't feel like explaining the troubling problem Mr. Con's handsy-ness was for her, not to her little brother. He didn't need to be worrying about her anyway. She would take care of herself like she always did.

"Just don't let that creep Bolt get any big ideas," Lireinne warned. "One drink, then I'm outta there, okay?"

It was late, surely after midnight, and the cool air had turned warmer. Lireinne hadn't meant to stay out this long, but she'd run into a girl she half remembered from French class at school, she'd had a couple of drinks, and now she was on her way to being shit-faced.

Bolt's house was in a run-down section of Covington, not far from the feed store, and the party had outgrown its cluttered, low-ceilinged rooms that smelled of microwaved nacho cheese dip, boiled hot dogs, and Bolt's pet ferret, Black Death. Inside the house five diehard EverQuest gamers were camped out in front of the big-screen TV while another factionalized bunch of kids was arguing loudly about whether they were going to play Dungeons & Dragons, or Magic, the new card game. Everyone else, a fluid mix of some fifty teenagers, was hanging out on the front steps or standing in groups in the road under the streetlight, drinking from plastic cups and smoking weed.

Far from the small party she'd imagined, it was as though half the high school had turned out for this gathering, and to Lireinne's surprise it felt kind of, well, *okay,* being here tonight. The kids all seemed so young, so harmless now. Hardly anybody seemed to remember that she'd once been the fat chick Brett Schenker had nailed in his truck. Several of her nodding acquaintances told her she looked incredible, saying they almost didn't recognize her since she'd lost the thirty pounds, and that felt pretty great. Too, in another boost to her cautious self-confidence, most of Lireinne's former tormentors had gained a lot of weight in the last year. Like string-tied pork roasts, now the hot girls who'd giggled over her undeserved reputation bulged with rolls of arm fat, back fat, and muffin tops spilling out of their tight, abbreviated shirts and low-slung jeans. In the yellow pools of streetlight, their makeup was so heavy, so thick, they seemed to have aged ten years. Like, they could be their own mothers.

What goes around comes around, Lireinne thought with some satisfaction. Her old enemies were staying out of her way tonight, probably knowing they'd only look worse if they stood next to her. Too, she'd learned her nemesis, Brett Schenker, had dropped out himself and gone to Hammond to work for the International House of Pancakes there. He was a freaking *busboy.*

What goes around comes around, for sure.

Carefully, Lireinne set her cup down on the hood of her car. The party's refreshments had boiled down to a couple of cases of warm, cheap beer somebody's big brother had bought, or the alternative: a plastic garbage can full of punch made from the tail ends of various bottles kids had hooked from their parents' liquor cabinets. This alcohol-riot was mixed with the new Mountain Dew product, Live Wire, a high-octane, fluorescent orange soda that, like a toxic river, looked as though it could burst into flame at any minute. The taste of the punch was constantly shifting as people arrived with bottles of amaretto and peach schnapps, bourbon and rye, blackberry brandy and last year's muscadine wine, but the spooky orange glow stayed the same no matter what else got poured into the garbage can.

Lireinne wasn't sure how much she'd had to drink, but her previous low, angry mood had been replaced with a fine hilarity. The punch—"vat," the kids called it—fizzed through her veins like savage butterflies, making her fuzzy head feel as though it was filled with solid plans for revenge.

Like, what about pretending she'd gotten food poisoning from 'Cille's cooking? No, Lireinne decided, that wouldn't be near good enough. Wait, she could take a bag of Mose's newly fly-free manure to work and hide it under the front seat of Tina's car. It might be days before that bitch figured out where the stink was coming from. Now *that* would be cool.

Lireinne threw back a big gulp of orange inspiration. Too bad she couldn't get any kind of payback with Emma Favreaux. *Call me anytime.* Yeah, I call bullshit, you fake.

"Hah!" Lireinne snorted.

"Hah what, sweet thang?" It was Bolt. He was stumbling over to the car, Black Death the ferret clinging to his shoulder. With a belch, Bolt propped himself up against the Explorer's front end. He was looking about as stable as a truck perched on a cheap jack, as though being vertical wasn't going to be an option for long.

"Nothing," Lireinne muttered, finishing her drink. "Beat it, Keanu." Bolt was got up tonight like Neo, Keanu Reeves's character from *The Matrix*. Wearing a long fake-leather overcoat and sunglasses, he was totally lame-ass like always because Neo was majorly hot and Bolt was about as sexy as a burping recliner, draped in black Visqueen.

"Go pass out someplace else," Lireinne ordered. "And get off my freaking car before you puke on it, you loser."

"Aww." Bolt belched again. He stroked Black Death's fuzzy tail. Back arched, the ferret chittered anxiously. "Don't be that way, L'reinne." Bolt took off his sunglasses, his vague little eyes blinking in the dim streetlight. "I ain't gonna bite, am I, Deathy? Y'know, babe, you're looking *fine,* now that you're not fat anymore. Hey—you wan' a hit?" He fumbled in his overcoat's big pocket. "Yeah, here we go." Bolt flourished a homemade pipe made from a half-crushed Live Wire can, a ring of ice-pick holes starring the hollowed, middle part of it. "Got some killer weed, good-lookin'." After a few fumbling passes with a lighter, Bolt got the dope lit and took a deep drag from the can's slot.

"Here." He offered her the makeshift pipe.

Already feeling more than a little trashed, Lireinne regarded the smoldering can for a moment, nonplussed. It had been forever since she'd been stoned—not since that couple of times behind the school, when she and that weird girl from French class had cut fourth period and gotten high. It hadn't been that big a deal.

Oh, why the hell not? Lireinne took the pipe, held it to her lips, and inhaled the herby-tasting smoke. Bolt was right: it seemed strong, burning when she held the hit for a few seconds in her lungs.

"Whoa, I'm feelin' it now." Bolt happily fell backward across the Explorer's hood, his weighty collapse propelling the squealing ferret from his shoulder. Black Death landed on the roof, slipped, and slid down the windshield. "Man, that's some good shit," Bolt commented.

Black Death untangled himself from the windshield wipers and scrabbled down the Explorer's fender, springing onto Lireinne's shoulder in a practically visible cloud of greasy shed fur and pheromones only another ferret could love.

"*God*—like now what?" Lireinne exclaimed in disgust. "Hold on there, you little whacko." She was *so* not going to wear a ferret. "C'mon. Let's get you back in your cage."

Weaving through a crowd of stoned kids in full Goth regalia, Lireinne climbed the front steps into the house. Almost hidden in her long hair, the ferret's claws stuck to her shoulder like Velcro as she picked her way through the groups on the floor. The dark, narrow hall was full of oblivious couples groping each other and making out, but once in Bolt's totally gross room Lireinne managed to peel the frantic ferret from her shoulder and returned him safely to his cage. The rancid reek of dirty socks and Black Death's home was so intense

in there it was like being gassed, so with an ick-grimace, Lireinne
shut the door on Bolt's chaotic mess and found her unsteady way
back outside to her car. Under the streetlight the air was fragrant with
the smell of marijuana, the faint scent of patchouli oil, and the damp
September night.

"Want 'nother hit?" Miraculously upright again, Bolt held out
the smoking Live Wire can.

Why not? Lireinne thought again. It had been a shitty day, but
the punch and the pot made everything seem outrageously funny.
Ridiculous, even. Her, with Mr. Con, of all people. Sometimes he
was a little pervy, and even if he wasn't, he was *old*. So not going to
happen! She couldn't think of him that way without giggling. The
full silver moon riding in the sky overhead seemed to laugh along
with her. Like, those bitches were *crazy,* Lireinne thought. She could
almost feel sorry for them—now that she was stoned. Tina and 'Cille
were ancient; freaking ugly, too: no wonder they had to make stuff
up. Dirty thoughts and mean mouths. That was pretty sad.

Bolt was okay, though. He wasn't such a bad guy, not for a lame-
ass freak who didn't have any real friends—not except for Wolf. She
could almost feel sorry for him, too. Lireinne thought for a moment.
Was she leaving anyone out? Oh, yeah, Emma. She didn't feel sorry
for Emma. Not one bit. Lireinne shook her head in contempt. At
least Tina and 'Cille were upfront with the hate thing; she knew
where she stood with *them.*

"Fuck you, Emma Favreaux," Lireinne muttered. The next time
you play your "I-want-to-be-your-friend" game, go find someone
else to lie to. This last came to her with a sense of finality, as though
she'd put paid to her hurt feelings. Her deeply felt resentment faded
and Lireinne decided she didn't need to think about Emma anymore.
Her cup was empty and she needed a refill.

And so went the night, until the party began to wind down, the
kids piled in their cars, and drove off to find their way home through
the dark streets.

Lireinne stayed till the end.

★   ★   ★

In the way of so many disasters, it seemed like a good idea at the time. Around four in the morning, somehow Lireinne had found herself driving Wolf and Bolt out to the alligator farm.

After stopping at an all-night convenience store for microwave burritos and snacks, once at the farm the giggling trio tumbled out of the Explorer and sneaked onto the property in the country night, as black as the spaces between the stars. Thank you God for the moonlight, Lireinne thought in a brief, cold moment of real clarity. There was a good chance they might wander into the retention pond, it was so dark out here. She ripped open the bag of cheap cookies she'd picked up at the gas station: no dog biscuits for Snow-ball tonight.

"White gator," Bolt was saying. "Thought they were just some bayou cowboy bullshit." He'd left his long vinyl coat in the car, the night having turned balmy and humid. A warm front was moving in and fog was rising off the water, its pale fingers of mist groping toward the dam. Like always, Bolt's T-shirt wasn't long enough to cover his huge stomach. In the darkness his revealed gut was a big white slice of honeydew melon, jiggling above the waistband of his baggy jeans as he struggled to keep up.

"Y'gotta get some longer shirts, Bolt," Lireinne said, drunkenly disapproving. "You're almost as big as freakin' Snowball."

Behind her in the dark, Wolf giggled. "*Snowball.* Helluva name for a gator." He stumbled in his Doc Martens, lurched alarmingly, and recovered at the last moment. The three were crossing the foggy dam of the pond in a ragged line and the ground here was uneven, the grass slippery with dew.

"She like some kind of freakin' pet?" Wolf's voice was loud in the mist.

"Shhh!" Starting to sober somewhat and wondering if this was such a great idea after all, Lireinne led the boys beyond the dam.

"Not so *loud,* Wolf. She's no pet—she's not even scared of peo-ple like regular gators are. C'mon. We gotta get to the BFG barn."

Bolt was lagging behind, having stopped to take a piss in the re-tention pond. "Hey, wait up, y'all," he said. "What's . . . the story on this . . . BFG barn?" Puffing as he zipped his jeans, he was trotting to catch up with Lireinne and Wolf on the other side of the dam.

"Like, for Big Fucking Gators, okay?" Lireinne snapped.

"No . . . shit." Bolt's breath rasped, labored as an exhausted dog's. "We ever . . . gonna get there? We been . . . walking like a . . . *mile*."

"I said, keep it down." They were finally at the doors to the BFG barn. "Listen up, y'all," Lireinne said in a low voice. "Quiet, 'member? Don't want the whole damn barn to go bat-shit. Nobody comes out here at night so I can't turn the lights on." She eased open the doors and slipped inside.

"This way," she whispered. Through the open doors a wavering silver puddle of moonlight spread across the cement floor. A couple of rats scurried out of sight into the blackness. Lireinne, Wolf, and Bolt tiptoed into the barn, blinking and wide-eyed in the dark relieved only by the faint glow from the skylights overhead.

"Can't see," Wolf said, his voice hushed.

"Give it a minute. Your eyes'll work soon." Lireinne fumbled at the barrel latch on the access door to Snowball's tank.

"God*damn,* it stinks in here," Bolt said, holding his nose.

"Like you'd notice." Lireinne sneered softly. "Your freaking room is like a thousand times worse, you slob." To tell the truth, after weeks in the office she thought it smelled rank in here, too. The reptilian reek was as thick as 'Cille's gumbo. The other nineteen thousand nine-hundred and ninety-nine gators began to stir in their tanks, alarmed at this interruption in their normal, changeless routine of feeding, water-changing, hosing, and silence. It was weird, almost horror-movie scary in the unrelieved dark of the barn, filled with all that invisible splashing and grunting, thinking about the hundreds of unseen rats, the crushing jaws lined with savage teeth.

With a shiver, Lireinne slid open the door to Snowball's tank. "She's in here. Y'all hurry, 'kay?"

The water below them was a light-swallowing hole in space, until a huge white head rose out of the black. Snowball swam toward the front of her tank, floating like a horn-backed surfboard until she paused below Lireinne's flip-flops and the boys' Doc Martens on the cement ledge, only inches above the dead, empty holes of her eyes.

"Here," Lireinne said in a low voice, doling out the cookies. "She's gonna love these." One by one, the three trespassers dropped their offerings onto the tarry surface. Snowball snatched the soggy sandwich crèmes up while they watched in wordless fascination.

"Man, this is, like, *ill,* it's so cool. Hey—you think she'd get loose if you left the door-thing open?" Bolt's voice seemed too loud in the quiet. "Whoa, like that shit would be like fucking . . . *doom* or something."

"Maybe," Lireinne said shortly. She dropped another cookie. Before it hit the water, Snowball's maw snapped it out of the air, like an immense mousetrap slamming closed. "The tank's pretty deep, but she's strong as hell. The crew always used to say the gators sometimes climbed into the aisle if they forgot and left the doors open." She handed the boys another cookie apiece.

Giggling, Bolt dropped his cookie on top of Snowball's monstrous head and Wolf guffawed.

"Here, gator, gator, gator." The boys were goofing around like they were at a freaking petting zoo.

Lireinne wished Bolt and Wolf would hurry the hell up, wondering what she'd been thinking, agreeing to bring her brother and his lame-ass friend out here in the middle of the night. Snowball had never come this close to her before. Damn, she could step on that big white snout and stand on it if she wanted to. Snowball might even let her—before she bit her leg off and ate it.

Lireinne shuddered, suddenly chilled.

"Let's go." She was ready to get out of there, like *now.* She was getting a really bad feeling about this.

The boys grumbled, but agreed. With a sense of relief, as though she'd reached the other side of four lanes of speeding cars, Lireinne tried to slide the access door shut. It was stickier than usual in the humid night air, and she struggled with the moisture-warped plywood, panting with a sudden, imperative need to *hurry.*

Just as the door creaked and splintered in its track, Snowball's head and shoulders shot out of the water. She stretched a clawed, webbed foot upward, pawing at the lip of the tank. Before Lireinne could react, those claws had dug into the cement next to her flip-flop.

"Hey!" she shrieked. The boys jumped, nearly falling to the cement floor. They scrambled away, their astonished faces white ovals in the dark. Frantically, Lireinne shoved at the door. It was broken; it wouldn't move. "Help me," Lireinne cried.

Then she froze, her jaw dropping.

Both the alligator's front legs were out of the tank. Opening her pink jaws wide as the door to a stretch limousine, her ivory teeth like rows and rows of twelve-gauge slugs, Snowball *hissed*. Her head swung into the aisle; her scaled shoulders followed.

It all happened so fast!

Now halfway to freedom, Snowball raised her massive tail, smacking the water with a great splash and a hollow *boom*. She grunted, straining to leverage her huge white body out of the tank, over the concrete lip, and into the barn.

Boom. A hind leg was seeking purchase. It was in the aisle. *Boom.*

"Jesus!" Wolf's voice was a breathless scream. "Bitch's coming for us!"

Her paralysis broken, Lireinne grabbed her brother's arm and dragged him toward the door of the BFG barn. "Quick, you assholes—*run*," she cried. So desperate to get the boys away from Snowball's sure pursuit, she didn't notice the torn mouth of the plastic cookie bag because Lireinne was shoving Bolt and Wolf out of the door. The bag still clutched in her nerveless fingers, she didn't notice the cookies that had fallen on the floor behind her, like a scattered, vanilla-sandwich-crème trail.

But when Snowball slammed the mighty length of her tail on the water's surface a final time and launched into the aisle, *she* noticed.

Indeed, she did.

In her slow high-walk, her tail lifted and swinging, eleven terrible feet and twelve hundred pounds of dripping white-scaled alligator followed the cookies to the open doors, consuming every one with a swipe of her insulation-pink tongue.

In the doorway, Snowball paused in the hazed moonlight for the space of a breath, and then she was loose in the night, leaving the barn where she'd been imprisoned for more than a decade. The thousands of other gators roiled the water in their tanks, snapping and bellowing in frenzied confusion.

And while Lireinne, Bolt, and Wolf, stupid with smoke, vat, and terror, raced through the fog across the dam of the retention pond, Snowball followed the moonlit trail of cookies like a saurian Gretel, finding her way home through the woods.

Dawn was a ruby glow in the east. Across the farm, the doors to the Explorer slammed. The engine cranked, sputtered, then roared as the car peeled out of the driveway. Rocks flew when the back end fishtailed in the gravel, but now the Explorer was racing down Million Dollar Road, flying away from the farm.

Away, away, away.

Snowball slid down the sloping dam into the retention pond and the viscid, wet dark received her white girth with barely a ripple. The water was a near-perfect temperature for this time of year, just above 87 degrees. Sensing the almost imperceptible slowing of her metabolism, Snowball swam across the pond, making for the thick stand of willow trees at the far end. The deep mud there was still warm from the sun, and Snowball found that good, too. So, half submerged, she settled herself to wait for the animals that were sure to come down to the edge of the water at dawn.

Every atom of her senses informed her that she would find plenty of prey in this most satisfactory place. The scent of rat was strong, almost as strong as it had been back in her tank, but not nearly as vivid as the smells of cat, peacock, rabbit, nutria, deer, and all the other creatures that came to drink at the retention pond. Snowball would feed well here until the days shortened and turned cold. Then, she would claw out a burrow in the dam, sleeping there undisturbed until the heat returned once more and it was time to breed.

Hatched into climate-controlled captivity, fed on an unvarying schedule, and never having had to hunt a day in her life, all this and more was revealed to Snowball within seconds of her escape. The eons had done their job well. The season, her immediate environment, and her own nature was a knowledge as perfect and complete as her ancestors' had been. Millions of years ago, back at the dawn of time as men reckon it, alligators were simple monsters, models of uncomplicated, unparalleled efficiency.

Yes, this was a good range, unclaimed by others. If more dared come she would drive them off, for this was her territory now and she would defend it.

Snowball planned to stay.

CHAPTER 13

Just as she had been for the past two weeks since she broke her ankle, this Monday afternoon found Lizzie MacBride-Costello ensconced on the leather Chesterfield sofa in the den, her bulky plaster cast propped on the ottoman. She was idly switching channels on the big-screen TV and wishing she could have just one glass of pinot grigio.

Over the course of her confinement, Liz had become bored witless with daytime television, but her cast was such a pain in the ass that even *Oprah* was better than hopping around the house like a three-legged dog. She hated her crutches more than her cast: the crosspieces dug into her armpits and the rubber tips had a tendency to catch on the rugs and edges of the furniture in hair-raising challenges to her precarious balance.

No, the crutches were bad enough, but then there was the wretched morning sickness and all those trips to the bathroom to throw up. Showering was an ordeal, and she couldn't have even a single glass of wine to help her relax. Why, oh why did she have to be pregnant, especially now? Handicapped and pregnant was a miserable combination. Thank goodness Lima Bean was quiet in his crate beside her on the floor, probably worn out from his constant whining and crying.

It was yet another piece of bad timing. Con had brought the puppy home a week ago, "so you'll have some company." This was the first time Lizzie had owned a dog, although she'd always thought she'd love having one. At home in Baton Rouge there'd never been enough room, much less money, to spare for a dog, and later she couldn't afford her car payments, let alone a pet. So, the evening Con had brought the puppy home, she'd been prepared to be enchanted by the little Bichon Frise, adorable as a sugar-white, furry windup toy—until it was time to put him in his crate. Caged Lima Bean had commenced a miseried, ear-piercing complaint that lasted for hours. Her new puppy, Liz declared, hated his crate. How was she to get any rest with this hideous racket?

Con had said reasonably, "But, hon, we're not going to let him wander all over the house to pee on the rugs. Hell, they're not even paid for yet. It's just until he's housebroken. He'll have to get used to it."

But Lima Bean wasn't getting used to it. Neither was Lizzie.

Well, he was asleep now, so for once she could have a nap—if she didn't have to hobble to the bathroom again. Liz settled deeper into the down-filled pillows Con had arranged for her on the sofa, but couldn't seem to get comfortable. Damn this cast, damn this pregnancy, and damn Consuelo, too. Where was she when Lizzie needed her?

CoCo Hannigan had lent the Costellos her maid, Consuelo, for a few weeks while Liz was going to be on crutches, but the maid only came in for the mornings, leaving before noon. If Consuelo hadn't already left today, Liz could have told her to fetch a glass of ginger ale ("cracked ice, not cubes") and some saltines, the only food she could keep down these days.

What was the fun in finally having a maid if she couldn't go out to lunch with friends and leave the housework for the domestic? With just a few more hours at her disposal, she could have made Consuelo drive her somewhere, Liz supposed, but the maid spent every minute she was there on housework. Lizzie sighed in aggravation and tried again to find a better position. A glass of wine or two would have been just the ticket, but that was going to be a thing of the past until after this pregnancy was over, eight long months from now.

Lizzie refused to think about that eventuality today. She'd just begun to doze off when Lima Bean began whining and pawing at his crate again.

"Oh, *hell*." Lizzie fumbled for the remote and turned up the volume on *The Jerry Springer Show,* where four obese transvestites were slapping one another's faces, each jowled face spackled with Kabuki-style makeup. They screamed in strings of hoarse, bleep-ridden vitriol, demanding to know who was the biggest slut, anyway? The audience erupted in uproarious bloodlust.

"Go back to sleep, you stupid dog," Liz muttered. Lima Bean whimpered mournfully instead. Lizzie pulled a pillow over her head, covering her ears. It didn't help. Finally, irritated beyond endurance, she sat up on the sofa, her taffy hair wildly disordered, her expression murderous.

"All right!" With a groan, she heaved her cast off the ottoman. "If you want out so bad, here you go, you pain in the ass. You're out of there!" Stretching over the edge of the sofa, she lifted the latch. Lima Bean tumbled out of his plastic cage, his entire tiny body wriggling in ecstasy at being freed. Liz dragged her cast back onto the ottoman and threw herself into the pillows with another groan.

"Now beat it. Pee wherever the hell you want," she declared. On the television the slap-fest had turned into a group hug: somehow the queens had resolved their differences. In the last thirty seconds, all was forgiven and she'd missed it. With a darling shake of his white fluffiness and a curled-tongued yawn, Lima Bean trotted purposefully down the hallway and disappeared into the living room.

"There goes the goddamned Berber," Liz announced, not caring in the least.

She was just beginning to drift downward into sleep when she felt the soft, wet tickle of the puppy's cold nose on her cheek.

"What now?" Liz exclaimed. Stretching on his hind legs, Lima Bean whimpered, pawing at the leather sofa with his itty front feet. "You want to be on the sofa? Will that shut your ass up?"

She reached down and lifted the dog by the scruff of his neck, dropping him without ceremony at the end of the Chesterfield by her right foot. Lima Bean sniffed around for a moment before he wriggled his way along the cushions, and then climbed on top of her. He circled a few times, sighed, and curled up in adorable contentment just below her chest.

Bemused, Lizzie stroked the puppy's head—only slightly larger than a Ping-Pong ball—with a gentle fingertip. Really, she thought, he was *such* a cute little thing. To hell with the rugs. No more crate for Lima Bean, Liz thought as she finally eased into sleep. Her nausea had vanished and her digestion wasn't at war with itself for the first time in two weeks: apparently, the cure for morning sickness was a warm puppy, sound asleep on her stomach.

But Lizzie soon learned that Con wasn't pleased with this development when he came home that evening, nor was he in a mood to listen to the reasons for Lima Bean's release. It had been a bad day at the alligator farm. The wastewater problem with the EPA was escalating, Hannigan was asking pointed questions about the campaign donations' usefulness—or the lack thereof—and the French deal for the BFG skins was stalled. The crown of Con's frustrating day? Over the weekend the farm's giant white alligator, Snowball, had somehow escaped her tank and taken up residence in the retention pond. The crew had discovered her there, the first thing that morning when they'd turned up for work.

"I'm going to have to hire a security guard after this," Con griped, fixing himself a large scotch at the wet bar in the den. "Somebody had to have let her out, probably some goddamned kids. The guys were at it all day with ropes, duct tape, and dead chickens for bait, but it's like that bitch knows better than to let them get close enough to lasso her ass."

Con sat down beside Liz in the big leather wingback chair, looking exhausted, his glass already half empty. "It was a complete waste of time." He took a long pull on his drink. "I must have reached out to the nuisance hunter twenty times today, but the son-of-a-bitch isn't returning my calls. I just hope he can catch her. *We* sure as hell aren't having any luck."

Prone on the Chesterfield, Lizzie cuddled a dozing Lima Bean in her arms. Ever since she'd given in and let him out of his crate, he'd been so sweet that she couldn't bring herself to put him down unless he acted as though he needed to pee.

"Well," she said carelessly, "why don't you just shoot her and get the whole mess over with?"

Frowning, Con shook his head at her suggestion. "God, Liz— no. In the whole world, there're only maybe another seven like Snowball because wild leucistics die almost as soon as they hatch. When she can't get out of the sun, she'll be dead. With no pigment, she'll overheat and her organs will burn up from the inside out. We got lucky over the weekend. It was overcast and maybe tomorrow will be, too, but Roger's going to blow like a cheap tire if we lose her. She's like some . . . goddamned *totem* to him. I know it sounds absurd, but she's been on the farm almost as long as he has."

Con finished his scotch, rose to his feet, and stretched with a yawn. "I'm going to go see what Consuelo's cooked for dinner. You want me to bring you a plate?"

"No," Liz said. "I never know when I'm going to feel like throwing up."

"Still," Con said. "You need to try to eat. What about a glass of ginger ale? Some crackers?"

Even though her nausea appeared to have taken the day off, Lizzie couldn't think of a single thing she wanted to eat.

"No, you go ahead and have dinner. Lima Bean and I'll be just fine, won't we, sweetie?" She pressed her lips to the top of the puppy's head, and when Con started yelling about the ruined Berber rug in the living room, she couldn't help but smile. The weight of the sleeping puppy filled her with something very like real contentment. What was a stupid rug compared to that? In fact, for the first time in days she didn't even want a glass of wine.

And that night, over Con's protestations, Lima Bean slept next to her in the big bed, his wee belly full of canned dog food that cost almost as much as escargot, his precious puppy breath purring in precious puppy snores. Liz sighed, stroking the warm white ball of fluff snuggled into her armpit.

Why on earth hadn't she done this before?

Lizzie rested better that night than she had in days and woke late Tuesday morning. Con had considerately made no noise at all leaving for work, although he'd managed to remove Lima Bean from the bed without waking her.

He put the puppy back in his crate, Liz thought in muzzy recognition, her tousled head emerging from under the duvet. Well, *that* rule was at an end. Once she got up, she'd let Lima Bean out. A glance at the clock told her it was well after nine and Consuelo would already be in the kitchen, washing up Con's dinner dishes.

Better you than me, Liz thought with a luxurious stretch. The first whiff of morning sickness announcing itself, she grabbed her robe draped over the foot of the bed, slipped it on, and swung her cast onto the floor. After last night, she'd slept so well that even her crutches didn't seem so onerous as she hobbled into the bathroom to throw up.

Half an hour later, laboriously bathed (she had to wrap her plaster cast in a garbage bag and keep it outside the shower stall) and dressed in a light cashmere sweater the topaz color of her eyes, gold bangles, wide-legged slacks, and one silk slipper, Lizzie came back into the bedroom where the maid was arranging the pillows on the just-made bed.

"Oh, don't do that," Liz ordered. "Change the sheets instead. Use the linen ones from Ireland."

Consuelo's brown face was carefully blank. "*Sí,* Miz Costello. I change." Without hesitation she began stripping the bed she'd just finished making.

It was about time for changing the sheets. Lizzie hadn't wanted Con at all that way, not since that awful night in the emergency room at St. Tammany General two weeks ago, but after her delicious night's sleep she might be in the mood again. Her cast was certainly less than seductive, but she had no doubt that Con wouldn't notice it enough to matter, not if she put her mind to distracting him. Liz smiled privately at the thought, and then realized that she was hungry. In fact, she was starving. That, too, was a welcome change.

"Oh, and before you get started on the sheets, go make me some decaf." Lizzie thought for a moment. "And I want scrambled eggs and bacon, too." This morning she wanted real food, not saltines and ginger ale.

Yes, this was shaping up to be a *great* day. Lizzie hopped into the den to free Lima Bean.

Wriggling with joy to be out of his crate, the puppy immediately tinkled on the antique Sarouk rug.

"Want some of Mommy's yummy breakfast, sweetie?" Liz said lovingly. "Consuelo!" she called over her shoulder toward the kitchen. "Lima Bean's had an accident. Grab the paper towels when you bring my breakfast in here." She gingerly lowered herself onto the Chesterfield, arranged her cast on the ottoman, and then scooped up the dog to sit on the cushions beside her.

"What a good puppy you are. Mommy's darling little baby, aren't you? Now, where's that stupid remote?"

The television remote wasn't to be found on the sofa, nor on the big teak coffee table in front of her. Liz called to the maid again in frustration.

"Consuelo, come in here right this minute and find the remote." It was almost time for the morning's Classic Movie on TCM to start— *A Letter to Three Wives*—and she was looking forward to watching it while she ate breakfast. Beginning to be irritated at the delay, Liz spied the slender plastic wand of the remote, wedged in the cushion of the wing chair where Con had been sitting last night. Consuelo hurried into the den, carrying the decaf and a plate of bacon and eggs on a tray. A roll of paper towels wedged under her arm, she set the tray down on the coffee table.

Honestly, Liz thought, how can she be so *slow*?

"The remote's over there in that chair," she said, pointing. "Give it to me before you clean up after the puppy." Lizzie broke off a piece of crisp bacon. "Here you go, honey-bunch." After an intrigued sniff or two, Lima Bean took it from her fingers, his shoe-button eyes avid when he gobbled up the bacon. He licked his lips, begging for more.

Consuelo handed Liz the remote. "Miz Costello?" she said. "I a-finding this, too." The maid was holding Con's cell phone, of all things.

It must have fallen out of his pocket and gotten stuck down between the chair and the cushion, Lizzie realized as she took the cell phone. Won't he be pissed off when he can't find it? With an amused shrug, she was ready to put the phone on the coffee table and tuck into her breakfast, until she noticed the red message light blinking its slow rhythm.

Con had voice mail.

Meanwhile, moving slowly as though her knees hurt, Consuelo scrubbed at the wet spot on the Sarouk with the paper towels. Finished, she struggled back to her feet.

"Is okay, Miz Costello? You need more es-something?"

"What? No," Liz replied, barely hearing the maid's question. She was still looking at the pulsing message light, wondering about that voice mail. Consuelo, appearing relieved, bustled out of the den with the damp paper towels clutched in her hand, hurrying back to the kitchen as though the border patrol was after her.

Who had called Con in the middle of the night? Lizzie wondered. The phone had been in the chair cushion until three minutes ago and would've been so muffled that Con couldn't have heard it ring. Liz held the phone in her palm, watching its slow red blink, the thunderhead of her suspicions growing higher and darker the longer she looked at it. Unnoticed, Lima Bean jumped from the sofa to the ottoman onto the coffee table. He began eating the neglected eggs and bacon off her plate with great enthusiasm.

Golden-brown eyes narrow, full lips compressed in a hard line, Liz pressed the voice mail button and held the phone to her ear.

★ ★ ★

"She's over there!" Con shouted.

The day was overcast again, layered with high, scudding gray clouds. The steady breeze blowing out of the east would carry the ripe smell of the barns for miles. When the wind gusted, the two men rowing the flat-bottomed skiff struggled to oar it across the width of the retention pond where, in the middle of the brown, rippling water, Snowball's white length was just visible beneath the surface, a specter of an alligator.

Con stood on the dam with his hands on his hips, watching in frustration as Snowball once again dived deeper and vanished from view.

"Son-of-a-*bitch,*" he muttered under his breath. Below his feet at the water's edge, two dead chickens floated next to a piece of trash—a plastic bag that had once held cookies. Con nudged it with the toe of his alligator loafer. Roger was adamant about keeping the farm free from any kind of litter. Once they finally caught Snowball, he'd have to speak with the grounds-maintenance guys, the Sykes twins, about this sloppiness.

The waterlogged, feathered corpses were today's bait, but the truant gator had ignored the chickens with an almost eerie canniness, just as she had yesterday's chickens. The Sykes brothers had had no luck this morning either. When Snowball came up for air, she'd hang motionless in the water while they strenuously rowed in her direction, only to sink out of sight and resurface on the other side of the pond.

It was as though the gator was *taunting* him, Con thought, but that was ridiculous, wasn't it? She was just a big-ass lizard, for God's sake.

"A hundred bucks to you guys if you catch her!" He was reduced to offering a reward for Snowball's capture. The nuisance hunter had finally returned Con's calls, but wasn't going to come out since he was laid up with a bad case of gout and wasn't going anywhere soon.

What awaited Con back in his office was no better—a recent stop order from the EPA that was disturbingly confrontational in its tone, a new lawsuit from yet another environmental defense organization, and a long list of phone calls, none of them boding well. There were his bills to pay, too, Emma's alimony chief among them.

With a stab to his conscience, Con's thoughts turned to Emma and that Thursday night last week when he'd gone out there to break the news that Liz was pregnant. He ought to try to call Emma soon, but was pretty sure she wouldn't be ready to hear from him yet. Con winced, remembering the solid slap she'd laid on his face. Okay, so Emma was upset, so maybe they shouldn't have slept together, but it wasn't as though they didn't still *love* each other. It had been a mistake in judgment, but that was a horse that, like Snowball, had bolted from the barn and was long gone.

And to add to his aggravation, Con had managed to forget his cell phone today, too. In his hurry to get to work to get the Snowball mess under control before Roger showed up for lunch, he'd uncharacteristically walked out of the house without it this morning and would have to retrieve his phone when he went back home this afternoon to check on Lizzie. Now there was a chore he was coming to dread, for Liz was demanding and difficult with her lack of mobility and the pregnancy. Con hoped her ill temper wasn't a harbinger of the next eight months because if this was how she dealt with being pregnant, how bad would life be when the baby came? Life, he felt certain, was going to change and probably not for the better. At forty-three, he was going to be a dad whether he wanted to or not. Con had done the math: he'd be all of sixty-five when the kid graduated from college.

It was a not-so-great thought, being the old man at the T-ball games, back-to-school nights, and sleepovers. In years past, he'd assumed he was going to get around to wanting children someday— not more than one or two, though. Being one of eleven kids had shaped Con in more ways than he wanted to think about: the constant poverty, his parents' exhausted distraction making it impossible for him to stand out anywhere except at school, never having anything he could really call his own. He'd even shared a bed with his brother until he was thirteen and Bobby went offshore to work on the rigs.

One kid would have been plenty, but after Emma had lost the baby Con had begun to secretly wonder if the years of caring for a child were worth it. He asked himself if there'd still be enough attention left over for *him* if she'd carried her baby to term. At that time in Con's life, he'd thought becoming a father meant turning into a dour, silent man like his overworked and distant dad, a city worker who filled potholes all day and drank Irish whiskey all night. With a role model like that, how would *he* handle being a parent? Could he? Did he even want to?

As things turned out, Emma's barrenness rendered these questions moot, but now here they were again, only with Lizzie this time. Con had needed the kind of devotion Emma had brought to their marriage. He'd had no doubt she'd have been equally devoted to their child (if not more so; that had been a worrisome notion), but he had a hard time seeing Liz in the role of madonna. Hell, babies needed a lot of attention and Con was suffering from a lack of the attention he craved *now*. What if his child likewise languished, getting only the professional ministrations of a series of babysitters and nannies?

Con didn't know what to think anymore, although it appeared he was going to have eight months to figure it out. Then, ready or not, there was going to be a baby.

But despite this heavy weather, there was the increasing pleasure of seeing Lireinne every day. She'd fast become the sole grace note in the midst of his recent troubles. Brightly efficient and organized, she was lovely, lovely, lovely. To Con's delight, this morning she'd turned up for work in a pair of pants that hugged her slim hips as though they'd been tailored for her, wearing that great V-neck sweater, the one that showed just a tantalizing hint of her perfect breasts. Lireinne even smelled fragrant as rain-washed lilies: a faint, subtle perfume that soothed the tense air back in the office where all the hell waited for him.

Little by little, with infinite patience, Con had initiated a slow dance of intimacy with his assistant—the seemingly casual touches, the lingering eye contact, the careful questions that showed he was interested in her personal life. He was virtually certain that all this Obi-Wan effort was paying off, although she was more difficult to read than he'd thought at first. Perhaps it was because she was so young, Con mused. Well, he'd prepared himself to be more patient than usual with this one. Lireinne was going to be more than worth it.

The wind picked up. "Hey, you guys," Con shouted to the men in the skiff, disgusted at this fruitless expense of time and manpower. "Let it go. Bring the boat in and get back to work."

He was turning away to head up to the office when he saw Lireinne coming down the hill from the house. Skirting the group of three male peacocks that had gathered to watch the alligator-round-up activity, she walked to the pond. Con waited for her on the dam, unwilling to go back to his office now that she was out here with him. His discouraged, darkly questioning mood lifted at the sight of that graceful swaying walk, the long, glossy black hair blowing in the wind, even as he realized she wouldn't have come out here unless there was some piece of new and doubtless problematic business.

"Mr. Con?" Lireinne raised her voice as she approached. "Mr. Hannigan just called. He said he needed to talk with you as soon as possible." She was frowning when she joined him on the dam. "I told him you were trying to catch Snowball, but he said . . ." Her voice trailed away as she gazed across the surface of the pond, her green eyes searching.

Con could only imagine what Roger had said. In addition to his agitation over his pet Snowball's escape, the hefty campaign donations were proving to have no discernible effect on the EPA matter. Hannigan was as outraged as any man who had thought he'd bought a whore only to discover that in reality she was a Presbyterian soccer mom. It wasn't a conversation he was looking forward to having with ol' Rog, especially since Con had promised that the sizable baksheesh was going to turn the tide of their discharge issues once and for all—and that Snowball would be returned to her tank by day's end.

Nonetheless, Con smiled at Lireinne, focusing all the flatteringly seductive power of his attention upon her. "Thanks, I'll call as soon as we get back to the house." He wrapped his fingers around her fine-boned wrist and squeezed it lightly, letting go with reluctance. "I appreciate you coming out here to tell me." Lireinne smiled a nervous, tight smile. Con wondered if she was afraid of the loose gator.

"It's my job, Mr. Con." Her gaze swept the brown, wind-ruffled expanse again, but then she dropped her eyes and quickly bent to pick up the plastic cookie bag in the mud. Crumpling it into a tight, crackling ball, she said, "No luck, huh?" Since yesterday morning when she'd learned of the white alligator's escape, Lireinne had been unusually anxious about the progress toward her capture. In the office she'd turned to the window often, watching the men on the pond, her slender back rigid, her arms folded close to her chest.

"I hope they catch her soon. This is *awful,*" Lireinne said. She paused. "Especially now, when there's so much else going on, I mean."

Ah, that's got to be it, Con thought with satisfaction. She knows I've got a ton of crap on my plate already and wants this to get resolved as soon as possible. Lireinne's really coming around. That's my girl. "We'll get her," he said. "Don't worry."

Cheered, he was beginning to fill Lireinne in on the morning's gator-hunting expedition, intending to frame the whole infuriating exercise as merely an amusing adventure, when the back door to the office flew open. It slammed the side of the house with an explosive bang that carried all the way down the hill. The three peacocks scattered across the grass crying jungle screeches of alarm, dragging their brilliant, impossible tails behind them in eyed bundles of shimmering greens and blues.

Now two women hurried down the hill to the pond. The one in the lead was Lizzie, Con realized in surprise. Her crutches stabbing the soft ground in wild swings, she was followed at a distance by a

heavy-set, brown-skinned woman in a black maid's uniform—
Consuelo—who was holding what looked like Liz's new puppy under her arm. The maid was scrambling to keep up with his wife's
relentless march.

Lireinne forgotten, Con called to his wife. "Liz! What are you doing here? This is no place for you, not in your condition!" Struck with
a sense of uneasy foreboding at his wife's unusual visit, Con wasn't
anxious to meet her, but that didn't matter because Lizzie wasn't stopping. Somehow she'd made it down the uneven slope in no time and
was hustling across the dam. Consuelo stopped some fifteen yards
back, prudently remaining at the edge of the pond with the dog
while her mistress barreled onward.

The closer Lizzie got, the madder she looked.

"What is it, babe?" Con asked, his apprehension sharp. "And
why'd you bring the dog?"

"At least he loves me, you shithead!" Liz shrieked. The wind
gusted. Her hair blowing in molasses-taffy-colored snakes, she leaned
on one crutch and hunted for something deep in the pocket of her
slacks.

"Now hold on a minute, Liz—what's this about?"

"*This,* asshole!"

His missing cell phone was in her fist. Without an instant's hesitation, Lizzie heaved the phone at Con's head like a drunken pitcher
from the mound. Unbalanced by the effort, she dropped a crutch and
almost fell off the other one as the cell phone hurtled past Con's head
and sailed into the pond with a splash.

"Who in the hell is *Jennifer?*" Liz's face was rigid with fury. She
had reclaimed her crutch and pointed it at him with what felt like real
menace.

Jennifer? Oh, fuck me, Agnes.

Con had been meaning to break things off with the hostess from
the Lemon Tree, but had completely forgotten she even existed
because he'd been so wrapped up in Lireinne, Lizzie's condition,
Lireinne, Emma, Lireinne, farm business, and Lireinne. The last time
he'd seen Jennifer—ten days ago?—she'd been a little clingy, but why

had she called his cell phone? What had possessed her? What had she said?

Meanwhile, Liz had regrouped and closed what little distance remained between them. Behind her on the edge of the pond the hysterical dog struggled in the maid's arms, yapping its little jaws off at the screeching peacocks.

"Es-stop it!" Consuelo clutched the wriggling puppy tighter, her round brown face annoyed.

"Answer me, you bastard." Toe to toe with Con, Lizzie's eyes were dangerous sherry-gold slits, her knuckles white on the crosspieces of her crutches. "For the last time, who's this *Jennifer*?"

What could he say to her that wouldn't make this worse, especially since he had no idea what Jennifer had said in her voice mail? Buy time, Con ordered himself even as the dog's shrill barking and the peacocks' alarmed cries threatened to drive all thought from his brain.

"What do you mean, 'Who's Jennifer?' " he asked loudly.

"Don't you dare try to lie your way out of this." Liz's rage-filled contralto turned high and poisonously sweet in an imitation of Lemon-Tree-Jennifer. " *'I miss you, Con darling. Why haven't you called me? I bought us some naughty underwear from Victoria's Secret.'* That Jennifer!" Lizzie swung at him with her crutch, cracking him across the shin. Con nearly fell to his knees at the shock of it, stunned by the sudden, vicious pain.

"You cheating son-of-a-bitch—I hate you!"

This was worse than he could've imagined. The situation was moving too fast to control. His shin throbbing, Conn felt his mouth fall open uselessly, all his talent, all that miraculous Obi-Wan-Kenobe-mind-control action failing him in that singular, critical moment.

"And who's *this*?" Lizzie sneered. She pointed her crutch at Lireinne, forgotten but likewise agape and frozen in place.

But before Con could answer—and how could he answer his wife, how could he explain the gorgeousness that was Lireinne without laying it all out there? *She's the girl I left Jennifer for, darling, I gave her a job*—the maid cut the humid air with a fire-alarm scream.

"*Madre de Dios! El perrito,* he es a-loose!"

And sure enough, Lima Bean was pelting away from Consuelo lickety-split, flying as though the gusting wind had lent him fluffy white wings to sail free above the mud at the pond's edge.

"*No,*" Lizzie wailed. "Lima Bean, come back. You'll get dirty!"

"I'll get him!" Desperately grateful for the distraction, Con seized his chance and took off after the dog.

But he was hampered by his throbbing shin—Christ, it felt like Liz had fractured it—and Con had only gotten off the dam when Lima Bean had run almost halfway around the pond. Before Con was even close, panting and swearing breathlessly, Lima Bean had come to a stop at the far end down by the willow trees. His tiny legs braced, the puppy was barking shrilly at a huge presence, the white, knobbled head the size of a floating Kenmore dishwasher that was parting the water and swimming straight for him.

Snowball.

Praying he could reach the puppy in time, Con put on an extra, limping burst of speed. Behind him on the dam the women were shrieking for him to hurry, hurry! Fifteen yards ahead of him Lima Bean was standing his ground and yapping at the gator. Con's labored breath sang in his ears.

Almost there, he thought with a frantic determination. Still running, he reached for the puppy to snatch him to safety.

But then his alligator loafer got stuck in the muck at the water's edge. Arms wind-milling to recapture his balance, Con just missed catching Lima Bean, went to one knee in the mud, and sprawled, falling fully prone with a dirty splash in the shallows of the pond.

Just as he raised his head and wiped his eyes, Snowball crawled out of the water not two feet away from him. The milk-white leviathan's massive pink jaws opened wide as the doors to hell itself, her breath a rank, miasmic cloud.

Con, mud-caked from his eyebrows to the tip of his remaining shoe, looked directly into the deadly blue-lapis gaze of the gator.

Strangely not feeling anything other than a hair-raised awe at this primordial threat, still Con raised his left fist in futile protest at the grotesque irony of it. He was going to die here, die now, mangled to death by the one alligator he could never doom to slaughter.

"Wait!" Con screamed.

She lunged.

Snowball's jaws slammed shut and Con felt an enormous, excruciating *pressure* across the edge of his left hand. Bright blood exploded in a plume of gore. He rolled away through the mud in a horrified, gagging reflex, clutching his bleeding hand to his chest. Snowball lumbered out of the water. Throwing back her head, she gulped her mouthful of his flesh.

Con knew then this was the end of him. He was a dead man.

But there was a God. Con would never know why, but unaccountably Snowball changed her awful course. She waddled away from him, pursuing the still-yapping puppy instead. Soaked in blood and mud, grasping what was left of his spurting hand as he tried to struggle to his knees, Con turned his face away with a sick horror because he couldn't bear to watch.

"Boss!"

Out of nowhere, strong hands grabbed his shoulders, dragging him to his feet and up the slope, away from the eleven-foot alligator. Churning mud-curds, foul-smelling fume, and sheets of brown water into the air, Snowball thrashed through the shallows after Lima Bean.

"Hold on—I got you!" The hands on Con's shoulders belonged to a Sykes twin, one of the grass cutters. Heedless of his boss and his brother, the other Sykes twin ran down the hill waving a coil of rope and a roll of silver duct tape, his normally bored face wild-eyed with excitement.

"Holy shit, Ricky—help me get a handle on her," he shouted. "That's a hundred bucks! *Goddamn!*"

In the ensuing epic struggle to wrestle Snowball into submission, to wind her jaws shut with the tape and hog-tie her, no one had any attention to spare for the wailing pair of women on the dam down at the other end of the pond. Lireinne had somehow vanished. Then, sobbing as unrestrainedly as though it had been her own hand in the gator's teeth, Tina loaded Con up in the Escalade and drove him to the emergency room while Lizzie and Consuelo followed. The Sykes twins dragged Snowball back to her tank.

None of them ever saw Lima Bean again after that eventful Tuesday.

Snagged in the corner of Snowball's terrible jaw, a white gossamer strand of fur was all that remained of the most adorable puppy in the whole wide world.

Chapter 14

"Well, hell! Come on in. I just this minute took a loaf of bread out of the oven."

Sarah Fortune, wearing a flour-smudged, rickrack-trimmed apron over her faded blue housedress, held the kitchen door open for Emma on this Thursday afternoon.

"I was wondering when I'd see you again," Sarah said, sounding satisfied that, just as it always must, her will had triumphed again. "You took your time. Now, what's all this?"

Standing on the back steps, four of Sarah's seven cats winding around her ankles, Emma smiled with an embarrassed lift of her shoulder. "Kind of a peace offering, I guess." She held out the bouquet of late zinnias—deep magenta-pink, golden-orange, and yellow—and the small tin pail of brown free-range eggs. "I, well . . . I missed you."

Her old eyes sharp in her lined face, Sarah squeezed Emma's arm briefly. "Shit, you're a stubborn woman, Emma, but then, so am I. I missed you, too. Here, let me put those in some water." She took the flowers over to the sink, gesturing at Emma to come inside.

"Well, don't just stand there on the doorstep like one of them tract-waving Jehovah's Witnesses. Get in here and sit. I've got a jar around here somewhere."

The cats came inside, too. Putting the pail of eggs on the counter, Emma drew a caned chair up to the white-painted table. The kitchen smelled of fresh-baked bread. Taking a deep breath of the fragrant air, Emma smiled, remembering Sarah's housewarming gift of a home-made loaf and the bottle of cheap vodka. Sarah was right: it had been too long.

"I'm sorry," Emma began, but her friend interrupted her.

"You haven't talked to Lireinne yet, have you."

Sarah squashed the zinnias into an old Mason jar and added water from the tap. Turning to look at Emma, she planted her hands on her hips and cocked her head like a wizened mockingbird. "I was out there yesterday afternoon with those crazy damned therapeutic riding folks, picking up Mose. You'd have thought it was some kind of come-to-Jesus, tent revival meeting, the way those people carry on around horses. Shit, it's a wonder Mose got on the trailer at all with the amount of fuss they made, but he was the only one of 'em with any sense. Like I said, he's a good old creature. But I noticed Lireinne didn't mention hearing from you."

Sarah sat down across from Emma and put her elbows on the table. Her eyebrows were raised, waiting for an explanation.

Emma shifted uncomfortably in her chair. A gray tabby jumped into her lap and she stroked it before she answered.

"I know. That's because I haven't talked to her yet," she muttered. In the intervening days, resolving to see Lireinne had turned out to be simpler than actually doing it.

"I'm going to go see her," Emma said more loudly, abashed. "I guess I wanted to start with something a little easier, such as coming to visit you to apologize. You were right, Sarah. Cutting Lireinne off the way I did was a wretched thing to do. I, I mean to head out there the day after tomorrow, on Saturday, to catch her when I know she'll be home."

And on Saturday Con wouldn't be out at the alligator farm, just a mile down Million Dollar Road from the Hootens' place, but Emma didn't mention that. While she'd finally learned to deal with the hard truth of how deeply angry she was with her ex-husband, she was still leery of seeing Con face-to-face. Remembering that last night and what had happened between them, Emma knew she didn't want to be near him again until she felt she was strong and composed enough to look him in the eye without slapping him a second time. Finding such a balance would require a measure of forgiveness, Emma knew.

And that might take a while.

Too, as far as her other question was concerned, Emma wanted to believe that perhaps her suspicions about him and Lireinne were only that—suspicions. It was still possible that she was wrong. Even if she wasn't, though, wouldn't the girl need a friend now more than ever if she'd become one of Con's many conquests? The real question, one Emma wasn't quite ready to answer, was whether she could get past that possibility and survive. Her memory of how close she had come to killing herself over him was still raw enough to make her flinch.

"That's my plan, anyway," Emma said with a self-deprecating tilt of her head.

Sarah Fortune nodded slowly, her expression considering.

"Good," she said at last. "Goddamned good for you, and good for Lireinne, too. It's going to be hard for you, but you can do it, Emma—I know you can." Sarah patted Emma's hand and nodded in approval. "That's a nasty scratch you've got there," she remarked. "And an ugly cut on your palm, too."

Involuntarily, Emma's hand moved to the self-inflicted wound on her arm.

"Oh, I did that to myself by accident . . . gardening," she lied. "I wasn't paying attention." That, at least, was true—in a way.

"Well, just don't let that shit get infected. You want some coffee?" Sarah got up and put the kettle on to boil without waiting for a reply. "I'll cut you a hunk of new bread."

The two friends sat in the kitchen together for another hour, sipping coffee, eating warm bread with honey, and gradually mending the rift, until Emma glanced at the clock on the wall.

"I need to go," she said. "But this has been . . . so great. Thank you for being patient with me." Emma pushed the purring cat off her lap, got up, and gathered her keys.

With a muted pop of eighty-one-year-old knees, Sarah stood, too.

"I'm damned proud of you, Em. That girl was mighty sad when they loaded Mose up, you know. I think she's going to be needing a friend while she gets used to him being gone. Told me he'd been back there in the field behind their piece-of-shit trailer for as long as she could recall—the only friend she really had when she was grow- ing up. Hell, that'd make Mose at least twenty, twenty-five, and that's getting on for a horse. Lireinne did right, seeing him off to a new home, even though it was hard for her to do. Now you go on and do the right damned thing, too. Let me know how it goes."

The zinnias were bright as a sunrise on the kitchen counter as Emma hugged her friend, bright as her renewed resolve to do what she could to repair her fledgling friendship with Lireinne. Her fear- ful questions wouldn't stop her this time.

But as Emma drove home, she couldn't help turning it over endlessly in her head—the possibly unfair but nonetheless threaten- ing suspicion that had reared its head the instant she'd learned of Lireinne's elevation from lowly hoser to Con's personal assistant.

Lireinne.

Con.

How long before the inevitable came to pass? Despite her resolve, Emma was sure in her bones that Con's appetite was at the bottom of the girl's promotion. True to his nature, her ex-husband wouldn't be able to resist the temptation.

Would Lireinne?

CHAPTER 15

*C*rippled.

It had been five days since the horror on the pond's edge. In room 447 at St. Tammany General, the flower arrangements, balloons, and cards all served as hollow reminders to ensure that Con awoke to his new reality. Now that the hospital staff was stepping down the Demerol, every time he opened his eyes, reality, that beast, inexorably buried its sharp teeth in his consciousness and shook it like a rat. This Saturday morning as he drifted upward through the fog of his narcotic doze, Con sensed the snarling beast was ready to pounce.

Crippled.

But still, everybody kept saying, it could have been so much *worse.* Refusing even a glance at the white gauze-swathed lump that was once his left hand, Con set his jaw and stared out the window at the hospital parking lot.

So much worse? Easy for the un-crippled to say. They were complete while he was going to have to manage without his little finger, his ring finger and nearly half of his palm. For the rest of his life, Con would have to endure the averted glances, the pity, the inevitable questions, as well as this uncompromising fact: he wasn't himself anymore. He never would be again.

Con had lost a lot of blood, undergone two surgeries, and so was still weak as Arkansas coffee. But oh, don't forget—it could have been so much worse, right? Everyone cheerfully reminded him how lucky he was that Snowball had eaten his left hand, so lucky that he was right-handed. As though he wasn't going to have to re-learn how to feed himself, to button a shirt, to do even something so simple as unlock and open his own front door. To drive his car. To open a bottle of wine.

To make love.

With a violent shudder, Con shoved that last thought into the back room of his mind, slammed the door, and locked it. Don't think about that, he thought, fighting the panic. Don't let yourself wonder if it might be impossible that a cripple with a deformed hand could attract *anyone,* even Thanksgiving turkey–thighed fat chicks with unibrows.

And whatever he did, he couldn't let himself think about Lireinne. Don't, Con begged his stubborn, heedless desire. Think of . . . nothing. It's safer.

Daring a glance at the lump on the end of his arm, he wondered wearily if having a mangled hand wasn't somehow worse than having no hand at all. At least there wouldn't be as much to stare at, Con thought in sour humor. Then, too, maybe if he had only a stump he could've been outfitted with a steel claw, like that immortal pirate, Captain Hook himself. Hell, he'd always thought of himself as a pirate, but now he was a . . . cripple.

A grotesque.

In the hospital since that fateful Tuesday afternoon, Con's risk of infection was such a threat his surgeon didn't want to remove him from the super-high-power antibiotic, dripping one stratospherically expensive drop at a time into his saline IV.

"Wouldn't want you to lose the whole limb to gangrene, or a staph infection," Dr. Binnings, the plastic surgeon, had said.

For a small mercy, at least Binnings had agreed that he didn't have to wear the catheter anymore: Con and his bladder were on their own now. He groaned, realizing he needed to crawl out of his hospital bed, drag his IV pole into the adjacent bathroom, and take a piss. This simple act was fraught with clumsiness and pain, but being catheterized had been a constant irritation—and humiliating, too. Con writhed, remembering the disgust on Lizzie's face when she'd come by for one of her obligatory visits, when her eyes had gone to the bag of urine hanging from the bed frame.

So far, though, Liz hadn't broached the subject of Jennifer. Con had avoided it as well. It seemed there was some kind of uneasy truce between them for the time being, an unspoken pact not to open that nuclear can of worms until he was back on his feet again. He was grateful for the reprieve, whatever the circumstances. Con was certain there'd be some bad weather ahead, but for now dealing with his injury was eating up all of the small energy he could muster.

Like now: simply getting to his feet was a major effort. Using his right hand, Con drew back the cotton blanket and swung his bare legs over the edge of the bed. His vision grew gray and spotty, and for a long moment the room slid disconcertingly sideways. Demerol could suspend the normal laws of physics, he'd learned, and so Con waited for the corners and the ceiling to stop switching places before he tried to stand.

Okay, he could get up now—if he didn't mind the gaping hospital gown, exposing his backside to anyone who might be looking in his window from the parking lot. Women had always admired his ass, Con thought with a wince, but in this case revealing it wasn't a choice. Being one-handed had narrowed his options down to the critical: that is, to hanging on to his IV pole with his right hand, the useless left one held protectively to his chest.

Con's bladder sent him an urgent message. With a low moan, he stood. The room revolved again.

"Damn it to hell," he muttered, swaying.

His right hand clutching the cold steel IV pole, like an old man Con shuffled barefooted across the linoleum to the adjacent bathroom. Under the yellow overhead light, in the mirror his unshaven face revealed new lines of pain and fatigue. It was the face of his dad before he had died at sixty, as ravaged as an underpass bum's. Con could swear that the few silver threads at his temples had crept upward into his red-gold hair overnight. He was distinctly grayer, and his beard was coming in gray, too. Crippled and old to boot, he shuddered as he turned away from his reflection.

Con emptied his bladder with a groan of relief, and had just laid the fingers of his right hand on the toilet's handle when, outside the door to his room, in the hospital hallway, he heard them talking.

"But how are *you* doing?" His plastic surgeon, Binnings.

"It's been . . ." There was a catch in Liz's voice. "It's been . . . very hard."

In the bathroom, Con froze, holding his breath.

Binnings was an irritatingly self-possessed young man in his early thirties with the misfortune of being short, a full head shorter than Con's wife, but he also bore a striking resemblance to a young, baby-faced Tom Cruise. Even under the influence of five hazy days of heavy narcotics, Con had picked up on the fact that Binnings thought Lizzie was hot. Here was another undeniable fact: although she was handicapped by her crutches and cast, Lizzie was doing her damnedest to encourage the doctor in that opinion.

Outside in the hall, Liz sniffled. "I don't know what else to do. I guess I shouldn't feel like this, not when he's hurt, not even after he, he . . . *cheated* on me, but half the time he doesn't seem to know I'm here at all."

So Liz had shared that, had she? Con flushed, wondering why. And that business about him not knowing she was there? Bullshit. She'd followed the usual good-wife guidelines and come to the hospital all right, but they'd been acutely aware of the other's presence, uncomfortably aware, no matter how doped up he'd been. Lizzie had never stayed more than five minutes—unless the surgeon was there, too, checking on his patient.

"Look, Liz," Binnings said. He lowered his voice and Con's ears strained. "Please don't cry. You've got to do . . . what you've got to do. No one could blame you for that."

"Oh, Skip."

This was something new to Con as well. Until now his wife and the plastic surgeon had been scrupulous to call each other "Doctor" and "Mrs. Costello"—in front of the patient, that is. Con's lips drew back from his teeth in a humorless grin. She wasn't letting any grass grow under her feet, not at all. That's the Lizzie I know and love, he thought with a grim twist of his mouth. Con wondered if she'd told Binnings she was pregnant yet.

"Fuck it," Con said under his breath. With a savage yank of the handle, the toilet erupted a loud cataract of water. Let 'em know I'm in here and listening to every goddamned, backstabbing word, he thought, anger flaring.

Grasping his IV pole, his support and anchor, Con gave up on retaining any particle of dignity and emerged from the bathroom. Liz and Binnings were just outside the doorway of his room. Binnings, red-faced, was pretending to study a chart.

But Lizzie lifted her chin and met Con's eyes in defiance. She raised her hand to tuck a stray strand of caramel-streaked hair behind her ear, and with a jolt, Con realized she wasn't wearing her wedding band. Her three-carat diamond engagement ring sparkled on her finger, but now it was on her right hand. When had she done that? And, he wondered uneasily, *why?*

"Y'all will have to excuse me," Con said, recovering and raising one sardonic eyebrow. "Can't hold this damned gown closed and drag my pole at the same time. Avert your eyes, darling."

Liz's face was as cold as a blast of winter spiraling from the frozen plains of Canada. "By all means, Con. We wouldn't dream of looking. Would we, Dr. Binnings?"

The little doctor cleared his throat, his tone now professional as he said, "Glad to see you up and around, Mr. Costello. I was just telling your wife that we're going to release you tomorrow morning."

The hell you say, you suck-up weasel in green scrubs.

But his anger deserted him as the linoleum heaved under Con's feet. Struck with the unalterable certainty that he needed to get back into bed as soon as possible, he had to turn away from them, keenly aware that his backside was hanging out of the hospital johnny with every halting step.

The bed looked like a bear had been wallowing in it. The blanket was twisted and hanging halfway to the floor, but when Con sank into the rumpled sheets he felt as emptied of fight as a wounded soldier coming home. The ruined hand had begun to throb again, but Con would be damned if he whined in front of these two.

Well, well, Con observed wearily. During the last five days Liz had become significantly more accomplished with her crutches, winging across the hospital room with confidence. She must have had plenty of practice since he'd been laid up in the hospital and hadn't been around to fetch and carry for her. With something almost like grace, Lizzie propped her crutches on the end of his bed and settled her shapely ass in the room's sole chair.

Taking his place beside her, Binnings almost laid his hand on her shoulder, but hesitated and shoved it in the pocket of his scrubs instead. His baby face revealed a fleeting guilt, just like a thief who'd spotted a cop the instant before he lifted a wallet from a clueless mark.

Things were moving fast now, Con suspected. "When do I get out of here?" he asked.

"Soon, but there's going to be a day or two more of adjustment, Mr. Costello." Binnings recovered his surgeon's smile. "I've made an appointment for you with the hospital's physical therapist later on today. She'll acquaint you with the protocol for your sutures. You'll need to return to my office on a regular basis, too, so I can check your drains."

"The hand still hurts like hell," Con griped, hearing the petulant tone in his voice and hating it.

"It's going to for some time, I'm afraid," Binnings replied. "Lots of nerves in hands. They tend to be painful when they're damaged. You're looking at several weeks of recovery."

The doctor turned to gaze down at Lizzie's upturned, rapt face. "And you, Mrs. Costello—with those crutches you're hardly in a position to help your husband, so I recommend hiring a home nurse for the next few days."

At the mention of the words *home nurse,* Liz's eyes turned hard as brandy-colored agates. With the demeanor of a woman facing an un-pleasant but necessary task, she got right to it.

"We need to talk," Lizzie announced to Con without preamble. Her expression probably would've been unreadable to anyone else, but he knew the set of her mouth very well: his wife was going to have her way in this, whatever this was. There was going to be no opting out of this conflict, no Obi-Wanning her even if he'd felt up to the challenge. It seemed the Jennifer discussion was now on the table.

Binnings, looking less self-assured now, glanced at the pager clipped to the waist of his green scrubs. "I've got another couple of patients to see," he said quickly. "That'll give y'all some privacy. I'll be back later on today for a wound check before we get cranking on the discharge process, so rest up, hear?" The smarmy dwarf exchanged a complicit glance with Lizzie, one loaded with an unspoken, mutual admiration. "Try to have a nice day . . . Mrs. Costello." With a sug-gestion of a swagger, Binnings left the room.

After the doctor was gone, the gloves came off.

"So, you want to tell me what *that's* about?" Con asked, his voice carefully neutral.

Liz didn't bother answering his question. "You won't be coming home, Con." She ran a hand—a perfectly good hand, the one with the diamond—through her chestnut-gold hair and stared at him without a shred of feeling. "I've arranged one of those residential suites for you, down at the Marriott on 190, until you can find a new place to live."

Surprised that he wasn't more shocked by how fast her plans had advanced, still Con was walloped with an emotion strikingly similar to the one he'd known in the instant before Snowball's deadly strike. *Wait.*

He was too damned ennervated to attempt the tremendous ef-fort required to change Liz's mind, though. After absorbing this lat-est turn of events in what had been a long week of unexpected and unwelcome events, he was exhausted with life and its insults. Living at the Marriott hadn't been the way he'd envisioned his recuperation.

"I see you're not wearing your wedding ring," Con said, his mouth wry. His own ring would likely remain in Snowball's stomach for years. Alligators' digestive tracts rarely processed metal objects like license plates, Coke cans, or boat propeller parts without a decades-long struggle.

"No, I took it off yesterday," Liz said. "And I'm going to have this one made into a necklace." She regarded the diamond on her finger, her mouth pensive.

There was a long pause while Con took this in, what it implied for him. Being thrown out of the house was just the lead-up to something more . . . final.

"I take it you've already talked to a lawyer," he said eventually. "Who're you using?"

Lizzie's quick, hostile glance was a stiletto between his ribs. With a brittle smile, she said, "Jerry Soames."

Letting his head fall back against the pillows, Con closed his eyes and nodded. "Good choice."

It was. Soames was an old *compadre* at Milliken-Odom, one of the most affably savage legal sharks swimming the bloodied waters of divorce court. Emma had resisted getting a lawyer, Con remembered. She'd trusted him to do the right thing by her and he had—but then, as he'd known for some time, Lizzie was a different animal from his first wife. Liz would be out for his balls, and Soames, a guy with a genuine enjoyment for his work, was the ideal man for the job. Con couldn't help being bitterly impressed at how quickly she'd moved, especially for a woman on crutches.

"Can't we try to work this out? You've mentioned counseling before."

Liz shook her head in emphatic denial. "Absolutely not. I'm not going to spend hours in some therapist's office rehashing the disgusting details. You fucked somebody named Jennifer. I'll never forgive you for it. Period. End of story."

"I never meant for you to know, but Liz . . . I honestly didn't think you'd be so upset as to divorce me over something so, so . . . trivial."

"Trivial?" Liz raised a disbelieving eyebrow. She shook her head again in disgust. "There's a lot you didn't think about. It's too late to start thinking now," she said drily.

"What about the baby?" Even though Con wasn't sure how he would feel about her answer, he had to ask. "Won't he be needing a father?"

For the first time, Lizzie's cool confidence seemed to slip a notch. She turned away and stared at the sumptuous arrangement—hothouse lilies, red spray roses from Chile, lipstick-pink Shasta daisies, and white tulips—on the windowsill beside her. It was the alligator farm's gesture of support, one of half a dozen other, lesser bouquets. A shiny Mylar balloon hovered above the flowers like a miniature purple blimp, the directive "Get Well Soon!" emblazoned on its slick surface in aggressive cheer.

Her lips compressed, Liz took a deep breath, releasing it in a sigh. "I don't know yet, Con. If I decided to go through with having it, that would mean you being around for the rest of its life, you know? Neither one of us was exactly thrilled when we found out I was pregnant." She reached over to the bouquet and fingered the fragile ivory petals of a tulip. "But right now, one thing *is* sure. I don't want to see you anymore, not after we're done today. I'll make up my mind about . . . this other problem . . . later, when I've had time to think."

Con had been halfway expecting something like this, and Liz was right: he was ambivalent about becoming a parent to a child that was, as yet, only an idea to him. Still, with no warning, Con felt a bitter stab, a deep, disquieting sense of poignant loss.

Wait.

"So it's all your decision. This means I don't have a say at all," he said, his voice heavy.

Liz shook her head, plucking the tulip's petal and crushing it in her fingers. "No, you don't. It's not your choice anymore. Don't try to fight me," she warned. "You'll lose."

She was right; he almost certainly would, even if he decided to try. Con lay in the bed, stricken silent with the weight of his powerlessness, leaden with a kind of confused despair. He didn't know how to feel about any of this. Ever since the accident, his life had seemed to have slipped away from him. Lizzie regarded him impassively as the minutes passed.

"So that's it, then?" Con said at last. "We're done?"

"All but the paperwork. I'm going to get the house and the Mercedes, Jerry says, and fifty percent of everything else. That'll have to be enough." Liz folded her manicured hands in her lap. Somehow, she'd managed to craft her flat gaze into a convincing expression of deeply wronged dignity. "I filed two days ago. You'll be served tomorrow and then six months from now, we'll be over for good." There was a sheen of moisture in those familiar eyes, but no tears glistened amid her thick, dark lashes.

Underneath Liz's stellar acting job, though, Con thought he could read a malignant satisfaction. Louisiana, a community property state, was perfectly clear on the law: without a prenup (something it genuinely hadn't occurred to Con to ask for in the crazy-about-each-other, not-yet-married part of their relationship) Lizzie would be entitled to half of everything he owned, half of what was left over after paying Emma's alimony. Jennifer from the Lemon Tree had proved to be a very expensive lay indeed.

"I wasn't trying to hurt you, Liz." It seemed like something he needed to say to her. Con didn't have the words for a better apology, although he wished he did. Still, he was going to make the gesture. "I'm sorry," he said simply.

Liz smiled, all her sadness replaced with sudden, blithe good humor.

"Don't be," she said, her tone airy. "I'm not." With a glance at her Rolex, Liz gathered her crutches and rose to her feet. "And now I've got to go. Consuelo's waiting downstairs to drive me home. When I get back to the house, I'll arrange a nurse for the next week or two. She'll see to . . . whatever you need at the Marriott."

She glanced at his bandage with barely disguised distaste. "After your discharge, you can take a cab over there." Her crutches positioned, Lizzie paused, almost as if making up her mind to say something more.

But, "Good-bye, Con," was all she said.

In the way of all tribal villages, the news of his marriage's demise must have spread through the ward in a fevered drumbeat of gossip. Compared to previous times, it seemed to Con that the nurse who came to take his vital signs later on that afternoon was more solicitous than usual.

"Anything at all I can do for you, Mr. Costello?" The dark-skinned, trim RN in pink flower-patterned scrubs sounded warmly sympathetic. She stripped the blood pressure cuff from his arm with a quick rip of Velcro. "Some juice? I think we have some Cran-Grape down at the nurses' station. Everybody likes Cran-Grape."

What Con really wanted was a big scotch, but he stretched his mouth in a pale imitation of his trademark smile. "No thanks, but I could use another couple of tabs of Demerol." He was sure he was due. Even if he wasn't, the hand was hurting like a bastard. "And a cup of coffee, if I'm allowed. I've got some arrangements to make, and I'm going to need the caffeine." He shifted in his bed, trying to rearrange his pillows one-handed, but one of them slipped from his grasp and fell with a soft thump onto the linoleum.

"Damn. This is going to take some getting used to," Con said ruefully, a latent flicker of the old talent in his voice.

The nurse reached for the pillow. "Let me do that, Mr. Costello."

Con sat up in the bed and the nurse fluffed the pillow, settling it behind his head. "I'll see about your medication and the coffee," she said. "Be right back, okay?"

Twenty minutes later, thanks to the dose of Demerol, the throbbing was reduced to a distant ache and the world was rosier, softer-edged, and kind in comparison. Con hoped he'd depart the hospital with a generous prescription for something strong, like Vicodin. Binnings had said the hand—it was easier to think of it as "the hand" than as *his* hand—would hurt for a long time. Nearly a week had passed since the moment Snowball had eaten half of it, but the pain was as bad as ever. Living with that pain would call for serious medication, a lot of it.

Con reached for the Styrofoam cup of lukewarm coffee and took an awkward sip, knowing he shouldn't put off any longer the extensive list of things that had to be done. All he wanted to do at the moment was to slip back into his doze, but his new reality awaited. It was time to make some necessary calls.

Time to get his own lawyer. Time to start looking for a new place to live. Con knew he'd be miserable at the residence hotel where his soon-to-be-ex-wife had banished him, as efficiently as though he were an old couch headed to the consignment shop. Finding a house or an apartment to rent in Covington would require the services of a realtor. He'd need his clothes, a coffeepot. Perhaps Liz could be persuaded to share some of the house on the golf course's furnishings, but remembering the greedy gleam he'd seen in her eyes, he doubted it. Con needed to get a new cell phone, too, since his old one was at the bottom of the retention pond. When he returned to work at the farm on Monday, he'd ask Lireinne to go get him one in town.

Lireinne.

In spite of his determination not to think of her, there she was again. Con dreaded facing Lireinne, sick inside at the questions that any thought of her ruthlessly raised. What if she was as repulsed by his hand as Liz was; what if he couldn't bear to see that same look of distaste in her green eyes? Best not approach that question yet, he told himself grimly. Monday would come soon enough. He could wait until then to learn just how bad life was going to be from now on.

And now for those calls. One-handed, Con dragged the hospital phone from the bedside table to his lap. He was in the process of dialing directory assistance when there was a hesitant knock at the half-open door to his room.

"Mr. Con?"

Lireinne. Although low-pitched, that voice was like a remembered song.

But *God,* he wasn't prepared for this, not now. In that heart-pounding, despairing instant, Con thought of pretending he was asleep.

"Mr. Con?" She tapped again, opening the door another shy few inches. She'd be peeking inside before he could stop her.

Con slammed the phone's receiver down, grabbed the edge of the blanket, and draped it over his bandaged hand. He smoothed his hair and arranged a welcoming smile on his be-whiskered face.

"Come in," Con called. He did his best to fill his voice with confidence, but his gut was hot and loose with apprehension. He wasn't going to have the luxury of putting this off until Monday, Con thought, fighting to master his panic. Ready or not, now he would know the worst.

Wait.

Lireinne entered the room as though she were a woodland creature—light-footed and uncertain, as though she could bolt at any moment. She carried a cheesy, plastic-wrapped cone of blue-dyed carnations, but she was wearing his favorite sweater and a slim gray skirt. Con's pulse skyrocketed as Lireinne's wary expression started to turn into a smile, but then her gaze dropped to the lump under the blanket.

Ah, goddamn it, damn it all to *hell.* The appalled horror dawning in her wide green eyes burned like battery acid.

"Oh, *no,*" Lireinne breathed. She raised her hand to her lips, the lips that Con had dreamed of owning, anticipating their taste, their softness, her surrender. That dream was ash. He was right to have been afraid: she pitied him. The beast reached for him then, reality had him by the throat. It would rip his heart out if he didn't fight it off.

And he *must* fight this reality. He dared not give in to it. With the suddenness of a thrown light switch, Con blazed an animal determination to *fix this.* He'd make his own goddamned reality. She would not feel sorry for him—before God, he swore it.

She. Would. Not.

The return of Obi-Wan came like a far-off cavalry bugle. The Jedi Knight was on the ground now, arriving only in the nick of time. With a glad sense of the battle being joined, Con smiled, confronting the pity in Lireinne's eyes.

"Lireinne!" he said, kindling all the warmth he could summon. "It's great to see you. Sit down." With his good hand, he gestured at the chair from where, a mere two hours ago, Lizzie had lowered the boom.

Lireinne blushed, a soft pink suffusing the delicious, poreless white skin of her heart-shaped face. "I had to come," she said, her voice grave and quiet, as though she spoke to someone on his deathbed. "I just had to come . . . to see if you're making out okay." Ignoring his offer of the chair, she took a few steps closer, almost close enough to touch.

"Oh, Lireinne." Con was unsure how to answer her, how to play this.

"Are you *really* okay?" Lireinne asked. Her question was oddly intense. Her hands twisted the stems of the blue-dyed carnations until the plastic wrapper split with a crackle. "I've been, like, so *worried.*"

Touched, Con sat up in the bed, making a gesture of resignation—a half-shrug, a tilting of his right hand that suggested he was maybe not so good, but not so bad either. That had been the way to answer her, he thought as he read Lireinne's face. It now betrayed a cautious hope.

"I'm going to be fine, Lireinne." And that came out just the way he meant it to: not totally convinced, but brave-sounding. Stoic, even. "This could have been so much worse." The irony of that statement wasn't lost on Con, but he added, "It could just as easily have been my head that Snowball had for lunch, after all."

"True that," Lireinne said with a hesitant, tremulous smile.

Taking fresh courage from that smile, Con drew his bandaged left hand from under the blanket, resting it almost casually beside him on the bed. There. Let her look. He'd take this moment on the chin because he didn't have a choice.

Lireinne stiffened. "Oh, no," she breathed. "Everybody said it was bad, but . . ."

Her eyes pooled, seawater droplets slipping free to trace silvery tracks down her cheeks to the corner of her mouth. With a divine un-self-consciousness, Lireinne slipped the tip of her tongue between her rose-leaf lips and captured a tear.

That tear swept Con past all doubt. In the trackless wilds where Con's lost sense of himself had wandered since his accident, a flame burned, a fire beckoned from the hearth of home.

It wasn't pity she felt, Con realized with a growing wonder. This was *compassion.* Had anyone ever felt that for him? Had anyone in his entire life actually felt *for* him? No, no one ever had, not even Emma. Being Con Costello had always been a lonely job. It meant being larger than life, as strong as his namesake, Hercules, and twice as invulnerable. This miracle of a girl, Con knew with astonished joy, was the one he'd been waiting for all along.

The love of his life.

"I'm so, so sorry," the love of his life sobbed. "I'm so sorry about this."

Con's smile was more intimate than a kiss. "Don't, Lireinne. I'm going to be fine."

But Lireinne shook her head and cried, "No, really! It's my . . . no . . . I mean, I'm *sorry.* Really, really sorry." Her slim shoulders heaving, she covered her face with her hands, awash with tears.

I'm alive, Con thought, fierce in his consuming happiness, his triumph. I'm still goddamned alive and I love her. Almost, he reached for Lireinne then, to touch her shining black hair, to cup her exquisite cheek in the palm of his right hand and pull her to him. But Con waited, reluctant to trust this perfect moment to chance. This wasn't the place or the time. Knowing now that he had more than enough time to love her, all the time in the world, with infinite tenderness Con gazed upon the beautiful girl who'd shown him the meaning of mercy. Ah, at last. I've won her.

"There now, honey," he murmured soothingly. "It's going to be all right." He stroked her arm, and thrilled to the feel of her fine bones under his good hand.

Lireinne looked up at his touch, her eyes still streaming. "Are you sure?"

At that moment, with an abrupt knock, Binnings walked into Con's hospital room.

"Sorry to interrupt." The surgeon's voice was flat. There was no mistaking the contempt in his gaze as he took in the scene in front of him—the teary-eyed girl, Con's possessive caress.

"I'm going to need to check those sutures now, Mr. Costello. And you, miss," Binnings said, turning to Lireinne, "you'll need to . . . *visit* . . . another time."

CHAPTER 16

After the recent rains, the newborn seedlings had grown into an earthbound, pale-green mist, a low cloud of life in the rows of Emma's garden.

It was Saturday afternoon, nearly a month since she'd last seen Lireinne. Since it was early days after planting, there wasn't any weeding to be done yet and the chickens had already made their morning constitutional. The breakfast dishes were washed, her bed-clothes changed. The laundry basket was empty and the house was spotless. Procrastinating until well after lunch, Emma had run out of things to do before she finally took a shower. She dressed afterward in jeans, her Top-Siders, and a long-sleeved, blue-striped T-shirt to cover the long, still angry-looking cut on the inside of her arm. She brushed her hair until it gleamed like heirloom silver, lastly strapping on her watch.

There was absolutely nothing left to do now—nothing except what Emma knew waited for her on Million Dollar Road. She locked the front door, checked it again, and paused uncertainly on the porch. Emma's ambivalence wasn't going to win, though: am-bivalence, as Sarah would say, was bullshit. Holding equal parts hope and doubt in her heart, Emma climbed in her truck. Biting her lower lip, she started the diesel engine. "Here goes," she muttered.

"Be good!" she called to Sheba through the truck's open window. Since her return, the hound had kept close to the front porch and garden. Her hunting days, it seemed, were done. Emma was grateful for that. She had never wanted to confine Sheba to the house when she wasn't home, and so the dog's reluctance to wander was a real blessing.

Truly, Emma thought as she drove down the gravel road, cultivating gratitude was a lot easier when you had something to be grateful for. She could work with that understanding in the future.

In the ditches beside the highway, the wild asters and coreopsis bloomed beneath the loblolly pines in miles-long, starry riots of blue and yellow. It was a glorious, high-ceilinged day, cool for the end of September, the air as clean as if it had been washed, rinsed, and hung out to dry.

Yet Emma's mood was sober as she turned over her plan. She hadn't been able to make herself phone first, apprehensive that Lireinne might not even want to accept the call after Emma's weeks-long silence. No, she thought as she made the turn off the highway onto Million Dollar Road, doing this in person was the best way to go about it. Emma had never been good on the phone in any case—small talk had always been agonizingly awkward for her even when she wasn't in the wrong—and so she'd made up her mind to take a chance on an unannounced visit to the Hootens' trailer.

And if Lireinne wasn't home this afternoon, then she'd leave a note. Beset by anxiety, Emma almost hoped this trip would come to that, but long before she was ready there was the mailbox, the weathered letters, HOOTEN, glued to its side. She stopped the truck at the head of the shell drive. The house trailer was barely visible, half hidden in the grove of centuries-old oak trees.

"Do it," Emma muttered, ashamed at her cowardice. "Just go *on,* dammit." What was the worst that could happen, after all?

Well, there was the strong possibility that Lireinne would slam the door in her face. That rejection might be what Emma deserved, but it would be bad. Not as hard to take as discovering that her fears were true, that Lireinne had succumbed to Con's attentions, but hard enough. But there was also the possibility, Emma argued, attempting hopefulness, that the girl might be glad to see her. It was also possible that nothing had happened between Lireinne and Emma's ex-husband. It was possible. Perhaps what awaited her lay in between, something unanticipated.

One thing was certain, though: she'd never find out unless she was brave enough to knock on the door.

And so Emma squared her shoulders, sat up straighter on the front seat of the truck, and drove onto the jouncing, potholed road before she could talk herself out of it. The trailer soon came into dispiriting view. The white, algae-streaked double-wide sat in the midst of the same collection of old tires, random junk, and tree stumps that had been moldering there on her previous visit. A rusted red truck, its rear end sagging, was parked next to the minivan on blocks, but there wasn't another car in sight. Except for the crow perched on the chain saw stuck in the oak stump, the place seemed to be deserted. At her approach, the crow took flight.

Emma stopped, put the truck in park, and shut off the engine. She'd made it to the trailer at least. Now she'd get out and go knock on the door. If Lireinne wasn't home after all, Emma could leave the note she'd written out last night after several attempts, working at getting it right until she'd finally realized she was procrastinating again.

Dear Lireinne,

I'm so sorry not to have been in touch sooner. I came out to ask if you wanted to get together sometime?
I've missed you.
Your friend,

Emma Favreaux

Her hands were trembling when Emma took the note out of her purse and looked it over one last time. It seemed a poor thing, but she couldn't write another one now. She slipped it into the back pocket of her jeans before she got out of the truck. Resolute in her determination to see this through, Emma picked her way through the old engine parts and assorted debris littering the weedy front yard. As on her last visit, the distinct odor of septic tank lay over the good scent of the oaks and faint traces of motor oil, but her heart was hammering now, Emma's mouth was dry, and so her senses barely registered the musty, slightly spoiled smell.

At the top of the cement steps, she knocked a quick light rap. Immediately from the other side of the door came the yapping of a small dog, high-pitched above an odd rumbling noise like a constant, distant thunder. The shrill barks grew louder and more frantic as she waited, and still nobody came to the door.

Emma hesitated before knocking again, debating whether she shouldn't just slip her note under the sill, get back in her truck, and leave, but with a shriek of rusted metal the knob turned.

The door opened, and an almost physical blast from a television assaulted her ears when a big, barefooted man stepped out of the trailer. Quickly, he shut the door behind him before she could see inside. The man was as bald as the tires in the yard and heavily muscled, his strong forearms covered in tattoos. Cradled in one of those arms was the source of the yapping: a tiny white puppy. They were an incongruous pair—the tall, burly man, the toy dog—and despite her dry mouth and runaway heartbeat, Emma's lips turned up in a smile.

The puppy wriggled in a determined attempt to get down, barking at her with vigorous intent. *Intruder!* And the man looked sleepy, as if he'd just woken up, although he was fully dressed in a blue plaid flannel shirt and worn jeans. Emma couldn't help thinking that if this was the Bud Hooten Sarah had described, he really ought to get out of bed before one o'clock in the afternoon if he wanted to get ahead in his luckless life.

"Can I help you?" the man asked in a pleasant baritone. He glanced down at the shrill ball of barking fluff under one arm. "Sorry about the pup—he's a regular ol' watchdog. Hush up, Lunchmeat."

Friendly brown eyes met Emma's as the big man said with a rueful grin, "I know. Hell of a name for such a cute lil dog, but that's what my girl calls him. Now, what can I do for you?"

He waited for her reply, his broad shoulders relaxed. The dog under his arm quieted, sniffing the air as if to catch Emma's scent over the ripe odor of eau-de-septic-tank.

Emma attempted a smile, even as the tide of her shyness threatened to swallow her up into an ocean of embarrassment. "I'm . . . looking for Lireinne," she said hesitantly. "Is she here?"

The man shook his head in regret. "'Fraid you just missed her. She's gone to town, visiting down to the hospital. Won't be back for a couple of hours yet, but you never know. Want to wait for a bit?"

Emma was ready to tell him that she'd just leave a note, thanks, when the man held out a big-knuckled hand.

"I'm Bud," he said. "Lireinne's dad. Well, stepdad, anyway. Nice truck you got there. Me, I'm partial to a Ford, too."

Swallowing her reticence, Emma took his offered hand. Her own disappeared in his warm, calloused grip. "Oh . . . right. It's nice, it's nice to meet you," she faltered. "I'm Emma Favreaux, um . . . a friend of Lireinne's."

"Sure nice to meet you," Bud said, nodding. "Lireinne's talked about you before."

"She has?" Emma asked cautiously.

"Yes, ma'am." Bud's face wasn't giving anything away. "Sure has. Don't you want to wait on Lireinne a little while? Seems a shame, you coming all the way out here, only to miss her."

She couldn't run the risk of offending this man, Emma thought with a mental wringing of her hands. She didn't want him to think she was unfriendly, for she'd no idea what Lireinne had said about her. It might not be good. Emma paused in helpless indecision. Unless she wanted him to assume the worst, though, she had no choice, not really. She was going to brave this out if only to prove that she wasn't the kind of ridiculous, overly fastidious woman who was squeamish about house trailers and unpleasant smells. She *needed* to do this, Emma reminded herself, because it was right. She'd just have to wait until she could decently leave.

"Uh, okay? Sure. Just for a few minutes, but . . . sure."

"Great! Get you something to drink?"

"Maybe a glass of water?" Emma said. Her heart had slowed but her mouth still felt dry as old newspapers.

"Water it is," Bud said with a smile.

Opening the door a crack, he looked into the trailer's interior before he shut the door again. Bud shook his head, a resigned expression on his stubbled face.

"I'd ask you in," he said, "but the place's kind of a wreck and my boy's camped out in front of the dang TV. I got home last night late, haven't had a chance to pick up the front room yet. This is the first Saturday in six months I'm not off workin', so tell you what—I'm enjoying having a day with nothing much to do. Let me go get us a couple of folding chairs. We can set out in the yard while we wait. It's a nice day for settin' in the sun, don't you think?"

The tiny dog whined, struggling in Bud Hooten's arm. It clearly wanted to get down.

Emma said, "That would be fine. I'd like that."

"Good." With a grin Bud lowered the puppy to the steps, next to Emma's feet. "Hasn't been here a week and already this little feller runs the show. If you don't mind," he said, "just watch Lunchmeat here and I'll go round up those chairs, get a glass of ice water. Be right back."

Bud disappeared inside the trailer, shutting the door firmly behind him, leaving Emma on the steps with the puppy. Lunchmeat began sniffing Emma's Top-Siders, undoubtedly eaten up with curiosity at the smell of Sheba.

If Emma had entertained any thoughts of taking off while Bud Hooten was otherwise occupied, she gave them up then and there. Of course she could drink a glass of water and then . . . and then after a polite half hour she could leave. Besides, she was in charge of looking after the puppy until Bud came back. Done with inspecting Emma's shoes, he'd already clambered down the steps and was headed for a big pile of dangerous-looking, rusted machinery.

"Oh, no you don't," Emma declared. Hurrying, she scooped

Lunchmeat up before he could go exploring underneath the trailer. No telling what was under there, she thought, looking around the littered yard with a small shudder.

"You're going to be right here when your daddy gets back." Emma lifted the puppy so that she looked into his precious, panting little face.

"Tell me," she whispered. "Is he a nice man? Or am I going to get butchered with that chain saw over there?" The puppy licked her nose with a pink tongue the size of her fingernail. Emma couldn't help but laugh.

"No massacre today, hmm?" she murmured, brushing her lips on the top of the dog's fluffy head.

Well, why not? The sun was warm on Emma's shoulders, she had nowhere else to go this afternoon, and really, it *was* a perfect day for sitting outside.

The ice water turned into a beer before Lireinne returned.

To Emma's relief, the time had flown by. They'd talked and talked, at first about Lireinne and her promotion and how proud Bud was of her. Emma was inwardly amazed to find that she could listen to Bud's account of Lireinne's new boss, "Mr. Con," without feeling as though her world were flying apart, an entire planet in crisis. In fact, it was almost as though Bud was talking about a mutual acquaintance, one she didn't know all that well. It was a disorienting notion that was nonetheless oddly freeing—thinking of Con as just another man. Emma was still trying that idea on for size when Bud shared some more recent news.

"Lireinne says the word at the farm's that he had himself some kind of run-in with a gator just this past week," he said. "Lost a chunk of his left hand. Big ol' she-gator just et it right off him. Been in the hospital ever since, 'bout five days."

"I hadn't heard," Emma murmured. Her heart lurched out of its previously calmed rhythm into a steady gallop. Oh, Con—what's happened to you? The conceit of him being just another man collapsed into a deep concern, even though she knew all too well that

Con had a new wife to look after him now. He didn't need her anymore; he hadn't for two years. This thought brought its own remembered pain, and Emma struggled to maintain her composure as she
absorbed this information.

"Sounded bad, from what Lireinne told me," Bud went on,
stroking the puppy resting in his lap. "That Mr. Con's sure done right
by my girl, and I wish him well. Sounds like a good man, from what
Lireinne tells me."

"He's my . . . ex-husband," Emma said, keeping her voice even
with an effort. She could hardly deny it. Still, there were those
pounding hoofbeats inside her chest until she saw the shrewd light in
Bud's honest eyes.

"Yes," she said, more strongly now. "I hope he's going to be
okay, too. And maybe . . . well, yes, Con can be a good man. Most
of the time, I guess."

"Most of the time's a pretty fair average, in my experience."

You have no idea, Emma thought, and if you did, you wouldn't
take Lireinne's word for anything you hear about Con. But she only
forced a tight smile, hoping her face wouldn't betray her. She didn't
say anything more, but that smile must have said it all because that's
when Bud offered her the beer.

With an exhilarated sense of having surmounted a Kilimanjaro of
a challenge, Emma felt like celebrating. "Thank you, I'd love one."

Congratulations to me, she thought, alone as Bud went back inside. I just talked about Con and didn't have a damned panic attack.
And a beer sounded like a great idea. Though it had been years since
she'd had one in the afternoon, it was a gorgeous day and she was enjoying Bud's conversation. Upon his return, the cold Pabst tasted
wonderful. To her mild surprise, Emma discovered she didn't even
smell the septic tank anymore. Clinking their cans together in a silent
toast, Emma and Bud's talk turned to other things—the vagaries of
dogs, Lireinne's old horse, Mose, and his new life, Sarah Fortune's
bossiness, and organic farming.

"Got no idea how you go 'bout that," Bud said, scratching his bald head. "Me, I can't hardly even grow hair, let alone grow a garden. I hear organic's supposed to be good for you, but it's a lot of work, ain't it?"

"It definitely is," Emma agreed.

"Must be why that stuff's so danged expensive, then." Bud's face was open, his eyes interested.

That friendly interest was all it took: Emma found herself telling him a lot more than she meant to about gardening, her life on the farm, and her recent resolution to get to know her neighbors. This felt *nice,* she realized happily. The beer helped, too, so like a flower unfurling its petals in the soft-shining afternoon sun, Emma felt herself opening up to the day, to the easy talk, to the man sitting beside her in a rump-sprung lawn chair with the sleeping white puppy on his lap.

After some time, though, with a glance at her watch, Emma knew she had to leave. She'd lost track of how long they'd been talking, but the beer had caught up with her and she didn't want to ask to go inside the trailer to use their bathroom. Both Bud and Lireinne had seemed more than determined to keep her out of the double-wide, so the state of things in there must be pretty chaotic. Emma didn't want to mar this newfound . . . whatever this was, by intruding.

"Thanks so much for the beer. It's been great, getting to know you," she said, discovering to her pleasure that it was true. "But I'd better get home."

"You sure?"

"Chickens and a dog to be fed, farm chores—you know how it goes." Feeling a genuine reluctance to leave, Emma got out of the folding chair and stood with a quick stretch. She walked over to her truck and opened the door. "Thanks again. Please tell Lireinne that I'm sorry to have missed her."

Still cradling the sleeping puppy, Bud stood, too. "Tell her yourself," he said. "That's her car right now." Down the drive, a dark green Explorer was turning onto the shell road leading to the trailer.

Emma's mouth was suddenly arid once more. She tried to swallow past the lump in her throat, watching the car rolling toward her. Emma turned and met Bud's earnest gaze. His face flushed as he cleared his throat.

"Yeah. Y'know, I, uh, I enjoyed this, too," Bud said. His voice was diffident, almost shy. "Maybe sometime you could come back. We could maybe . . ."

But with a screech of worn brake pads, the Explorer jolted to a stop in the weeds across from Emma's truck. Lireinne threw herself out of the dusty green car and slammed the door. Her face was tight with anger, her eyes puffy and red as though she'd been crying.

"What the hell are *you* doing here?" Lireinne demanded. Not waiting for an answer, she stalked past them and took the puppy from her stepfather's arms before she turned to glare at Emma, her green eyes as narrow and cold as a sniper's on a target.

Here it was, the worst-case scenario. Engulfed in a smothering wave of mingled shame and suspicion, Emma had to force herself to meet that accusing stare.

"I'm so, so sorry," Emma faltered. "But . . ."

Lireinne raised a scarred eyebrow. "Sorry, huh? Sorry *shit*. You come out here on another freaking field trip? Want to see how people who have to work for a living get on? Well, look around! Get an eyeful and then get your ass in your freaking fancy truck and go. Nobody wants you here."

Emma's halting words deserted her. Facing Lireinne's scorn, she couldn't begin to find the courage to speak. Her eyes tearing, her mouth trembled.

"Lireinne." Bud's deep voice was quiet. "Ease down, girl. Emma's a guest."

His admonition only appeared to enflame the girl further. "No freaking way! You hear me, bitch? Go someplace else with your fake shit," Lireinne practically spit. Clutching a wide-awake Lunchmeat to her chest, she turned on her heel and ran up the steps to the trailer. As she yanked the door open, thundering armies and the sounds of mortal combat poured out into the yard. Lireinne slammed the old, warped door, but it flew open again, rebounding with a bang against the side of the trailer.

"Hey, I said *leave*." Lireinne stuck her head outside, her lovely face hard as carved white stone. She grabbed the doorknob. "Go away!"

This time the slammed door stayed shut.

Shattered, Emma's tears blurred her vision, making it hard to see her fingers frantically fumbling at the handle of her truck. The day's golden light dimmed as though a cloud had passed overhead in the clear sky above her.

"I really am . . . sorry," she said to Bud, her voice breaking. "But I should never have come out here. I'll go now." She turned her back on him to climb in the truck, to start the engine, drive away, and not come back. Ever.

Oh dear God, what if what she'd been fearing was true? Had it already happened? Was Lireinne this furious because she and Con were together? No, Emma acknowledged with a sinking sense of shame, all this explosive anger was bound to be directed at her alone. She'd hurt the girl, hurt her desperately. She couldn't blame Con. She was the one who owned this.

But did any of it matter anymore?

Before Emma could climb into the front seat of the Ford, though, a big hand came to rest lightly on her shoulder. Wiping her eyes with the back of her hand, she looked up into Bud's worried face.

"Don't take that talk of hers much to heart," he said, his tone mild and level. "Girl's too quick to judge, 'specially when it comes to people she's come to care about. Her mother up and leaving her when she was just a little thing made her that way, I think. Lireinne hasn't ever got over it—made her untrusting-like, always too quick to think the worst."

"I . . . heard about her mother. Sarah told me." Emma sniffled, her eyes streaming. "Oh, Bud, I should have *known* better." She shook her head. "I did everything wrong."

"Here." Bud Hooten reached into the back pocket of his worn

jeans and extracted a folded red bandanna. "Dry your eyes, now, and blow your nose. Sometimes she goes at me like that, you know. It can be a hurtful thing, but she don't really mean it. When Lireinne don't care, she won't have a word for you. Shuts you out forever. At least she talked to you. Lireinne won't even talk *about* her mom. If she goes and gets mad at you, it means she still gives a damn."

"So you're saying I shouldn't give up." Emma dabbed at her eyes with the bandanna.

"It's just my opinion, but . . . yup. That's about it," Bud said. "I figure you still count somehow. You know, Lireinne's mom was kinda restless. Thinking back on it now, I don't know that she ever did want a damned thing to do with her own kids. Sure took off like she never meant to see 'em again. Ain't heard hide nor hair from the woman in eleven years. It was harder on Lireinne than Wolf, 'cause she was old enough to know her own mother didn't give a damn about her and Wolf was too young to remember much about it. For a while after her mom cut out—months, maybe—Lireinne used to stay by the window all the time, always lookin' out into the yard, waiting. 'Maybe she'll come back today,' she'd say. But then one day she just quit waiting. Never asked after her mother again." Bud's voice was deep with regret, weighted with this recollection. "Can't say as how I blame her for that, but it's just the way she is now."

"Poor, poor child." Emma swallowed hard, thinking of the pain she'd unwittingly caused. "I guess that's why when I didn't call or come to see her for so long, she took it so badly. I didn't realize I was . . . hitting her where it hurt the most, but I *ought* to have known."

"She'll come around. Just give her a little time." Bud's words were confident and somehow Emma found a watery smile.

"Thank you," she said, grateful for this kindness. "I had my own damage to deal with, but still—that was no excuse for what I did." Her self-involvement had caused enough misery, her own and others', however unintentional it might have been. Emma admitted this to herself with a shaky understanding.

Sarah had been right again: grow the fuck up. Quit living in the past. *Change.*

"Yep, I figured it had to be something like that." Nodding, Bud's tone was regretful. "I could tell she'd taken a real shine to you, though. Talked for days about what a nice lady you were, how glad she was, you being her friend. When Lireinne didn't hear from you . . . well, it was a bad time."

He hesitated before putting one big, heavy arm around Emma's shoulders in a brief hug. Up close, Bud smelled of sun-warmed flannel, a pleasant, faint trace of beer, and clean man. "But don't give up on her now, will you?" he said.

"You heard her. She told me to go away, to leave her alone. And she sounded pretty positive about it, too." Emma's short laugh was unhappy.

Bud Hooten smiled down into her despairing, gold-flecked eyes. "And she's only eighteen. And she'll get past this sooner than you think. Tell you what, why don't you ask her over to your place sometime? I could come, too, if you want," he offered.

Emma found a weak smile, filled once more with doubt and hope. "Really? You'd do that? You seriously think she'll be willing to talk to me again?" With a last dab at her eyes, she handed Bud's bandanna back to him.

The big man shrugged. "Maybe. Maybe not. Anyways, all she can say's no. I think you could live with it if she does, but she might say yes. Be a start, at least, and who knows? Could be good for you and her, getting past this."

Emma fell silent, mulling over Bud's suggestion.

Be here now.

"You're right," Emma said after a minute. "I'll ask her. And yes, *you* should definitely come. Somehow I think that if I invite all of you—you, your son, and Lireinne—she'd be more likely to say yes. She wouldn't feel so defensive if you were there."

Bud was folding his bandanna, stuffing it back into his hip pocket. His glance was questioning. "You want us over for dinner? Something like that?"

Emma answered him with a vigorous nod, though that really wasn't what she'd meant, not at first. She'd been thinking of something more low-key, like having coffee one afternoon. It had been more than two years since she'd had people over for dinner. Almost always Con's clients back then: large, important business affairs with people she didn't know very well, Irish crystal and the Limoges, her family silver and hours of meaningless conversation. During those dinners, Emma had been content to stay in the kitchen, seeing to the cooking and avoiding the heavy-going of small talk, even though Con had been so very impatient with her shyness. Since then she'd grown accustomed to eating alone every night, except for Sheba.

But this time would be different, Emma told herself. This would be *her* idea now, not Con's. She was a better than good cook, she could try again with Lireinne. *Be here now*. All right, Emma thought. She was here; she'd made it out to Million Dollar Road and had faced her fears at last. She wasn't turning away from this girl again, not without another solid try to repair some of the harm she knew she'd caused her.

"Yes," Emma said firmly. "Dinner at my place."

Certain that she should get to it as soon as possible, she knew her own nature well enough to understand that if she didn't commit to a time and a date, she might never find the nerve to try again. Once at home, safe in her "organic womb," as Sarah called it, she could find a thousand reasons to put this dinner off until it was too late.

"How about tomorrow night then, say seven o'clock?" Emma soldiered on, a part of her halfway hoping Bud would say no, thanks, he had a previous engagement.

But Bud smiled widely, his sunburned face beaming.

"Lady, you got yourself at least one taker. And thank you kindly for letting me invite myself to dinner."

CHAPTER 17

Lireinne stormed through the wizard-and-orc battle Wolf was waging in the front room without a single glance. Sitting cross-legged on the floor in front of the TV, her younger brother's thin face was openmouthed with curiosity, his fingers still on the control pad for once.

"Hey, sis," Wolf asked. "What's up with that lady hanging out all afternoon in the yard with Dad? What the hell were you hollerin' for, anyways?"

"Shut up," Lireinne retorted with a glare over her shoulder. "It's none of your damned business."

Once in the privacy of her room, she threw herself on her bed with the puppy, staring unseeing at the posters of Paris and Oslo above her on the wall, brown-streaked from a leak in the roof. The dog formerly known as Lima Bean, now called Lunchmeat, stretched his puppy-length on the bed next to her. He nudged her hand for a cuddle and she stroked his white fur in an absentminded caress. After her upsetting trip to the hospital, Lireinne was already worn out from her afternoon, beat to death by the turns it had taken. Coming home to Emma Freakin' Favreaux in the front yard after going through that was just too damned much to take for one day.

Earlier she'd made herself go visit Mr. Con in the hospital to see if the talk at the alligator farm was even close to true, but once there she'd been stunned to horror all over again at the enormity of the consequences of her single rash act. Lireinne hated to cry, she almost never did, but the sight of his gauze-wrapped hand had brought her to tears because once she'd seen it, she couldn't escape the knowledge that everything that had happened to him, all of it, was *her fault*.

If Lireinne hadn't taken the boys out to the alligator farm that night, then Snowball wouldn't have gotten loose and eaten Mr. Con's hand. Never mind that no one was ever going to find out—*she* was always going to know. Well, Bolt and Wolf might know about it, too, but when they were fleeing the farm in the Explorer, she'd threatened them, making sure they'd understand that they could all go to jail for trespassing if anybody opened their big mouth. The boys, still freaked after their wild night, had been so scared they'd sworn they'd never tell a soul.

Probably, she could count on them to keep the story under wraps for a couple of months, if she was lucky. Chances were the word would never get back to the farm anyway.

Still, Lireinne was positive she'd have trouble sleeping tonight, remembering how sad, how brave Mr. Con had been. He'd been in a lot of pain, too, she just knew it, even though he was trying so hard to act like he wasn't. During that visit it had been all Lireinne could do not to cry out, *It was me—I did it!* Now she felt like a really bad person for having thought he was just an old toucher. He wasn't an animal about it or anything. Being handsy was probably like a reflex or something, just a bad habit.

Beside her the dog rolled onto his back, begging for a tummy rub. Lord, then there was Lunchmeat, Lireinne thought, her guilt about the puppy an uneasy rock in her stomach. She hadn't just rescued Mr. Con's wife's little dog, she'd, well . . . basically *stolen* him.

Uncomfortable at that thought, Lireinne shifted on the bed, remembering the lies she'd told Bud and Wolf about finding Lunchmeat on the side of the road. But I'd do it again, she vowed.

The poor thing had been cowering in the grove of willow trees, covered in mud and trembling like he was freezing to death. Unscathed except for a bald spot on his little plume of a tail, he was frantic to jump into her arms to safety. The Sykes twins were capturing Snowball while Mr. Con staggered away from the pond, leaning on a wailing Tina, and those two women were screaming as loudly as the peacocks when they saw him covered in blood. In the midst of the chaos, no one had noticed when, desperate to save *somebody*, Lireinne had tucked the puppy under her sweater. She'd sneaked behind the willow trees and run for her car the long way, back behind the barns, and the next morning at work she discovered to her immense relief that nobody believed Lunchmeat had survived the gator's attack. Everyone was still talking about how Snowball had eaten both Mr. Con's hand *and* the little dog.

Well, Lireinne thought, she had no choice but to keep Lunchmeat. Now that she'd stolen him, she couldn't take him back. Moreover, Lireinne was positive that woman, Mr. Con's wife, wasn't capable of looking after a puppy—for shit's sake, she'd brought him out to the alligator farm, of all places! He wasn't even on a *leash*.

As for Jennifer-whoever, Lireinne didn't give a damn, although Mrs. Costello had sure been mad about her, mad enough to whack Mr. Con with her crutch. Huh, Lireinne thought. It was obvious that her poor boss was married to another one of those nose-in-the-air bitches, somebody who treated her precious puppy like a purse, a hat, an . . . accessory.

And besides, Lima Bean was a ridiculous name for a dog that'd narrowly escaped becoming Snowball's next meal. Lunchmeat was much more like it.

Lireinne planted a possessive kiss on the puppy's little white head. "Good dog," she whispered into his floppy ear. "You're *mine* now, not hers."

But what the hell was Bud thinking, hanging out with Emma? When she'd driven up, she hadn't been too angry to notice that they'd been standing awfully close to each other. Lireinne ran her hand through her hair, expelling a perplexed breath full of wordless irritation. Was Bud just being polite? For sure, her stepfather was supernice to everybody, no matter who they were—including stuck-up fakes like Emma. Hell, he was even friendly with process servers and bill collectors.

But what if there was something else going on, like maybe Bud having a, a . . . *thing* for Emma? Lireinne wondered doubtfully. It had been a long time since Bud had had a girlfriend.

No way, she told herself in firm denial. That was plain impossible. Her stepfather wouldn't have been so easy to fool, would he? Surely he could figure out on his own that Emma wasn't worth talking to. Couldn't he see how stupid she looked, looking as stiff and empty-headed as a Banana Republic mannequin in the middle of all the crap in the front yard? How snobby she was, traipsing out to the trailer in those expensive shoes and designer jeans?

No, Lireinne sighed again, positive she knew Bud better than that. He was only being himself. Bud never had a mean word to say to anyone, not even someone who'd . . .

There was a soft knock at her door.

"Lireinne, honey? You gonna let me in?"

"Why?" She didn't want to listen to Bud, not while she was still so upset and confused.

Bud didn't take the hint. "Just want to talk to you, babe. C'mon—open the door for me, now."

With a loud groan, Lireinne got off the bed. She unlocked and opened the door to find her stepfather giving her that *look,* the one that told her she'd assed up.

"What do you want?" Lireinne said, her face sullen. She knew full well he was going to give her a hard time for being rude to a guest.

It was an ironclad rule in the Hooten household, being polite to anybody who knocked on the trailer's old door—even the Parish enforcement officials come to serve notice that the septic tank wasn't up to code, the fat Social Services man who'd wanted to know why Wolf had missed the first week of school, or the cable guy when he came to disconnect the pirated line. According to Bud, those people were only doing their jobs and so there wasn't any need to go off on them, but being nice to Emma Favreaux, in Lireinne's opinion, was just asking to get treated like dirt. Anyway, Lireinne hadn't been rude to her, just *honest*.

Trying to act as though she was indifferent to the look Bud was giving her, Lireinne folded her arms, certain she was holding the high ground in this exchange.

"I think you kinda overreacted out there," Bud said. He scratched his bald head, his eyes full of mild accusation. "Seems to me, you didn't have a call to act like that, no matter how bad that lady hurt your feelins before."

Of course he'd say that. Rolling her eyes, Lireinne turned her back on Bud and flounced across the room to her bed. "She didn't hurt my damned *feelings*. I just don't want her being here at the house—that's all." She collapsed on the edge of the mattress, not looking at her stepfather, wishing he'd let it go, even though she knew he wouldn't. Not yet. Bud could be so freaking stubborn.

"I hear what you're sayin', but she's a nice lady . . ."

"No!" Lireinne was adamant. "She's nothing but a lying bitch. We don't need her for a damned thing." So there, she thought. Still, she couldn't help feeling as though she was letting Bud down somehow, and that made her angrier than ever. Emma was the one who was wrong here, not her.

Bud wasn't ready to drop it, though, because he came in her room. He sat down on the bed next to her, the old mattress sagging under his weight. Lunchmeat crawled into his lap, little tail wagging, and commenced chewing at a button on his plaid flannel shirt.

"Everbody makes themselves a mistake now and then." Bud's big hand, as tough, scarred, and calloused as an old work boot, gently disengaged the puppy's teeth from the button. "It's like this here little dog. He don't have any idea he's doing wrong when he gets into something—like your flip-flops. Remember how you handled that, him chewing on 'em? Like he just needed to learn better? I think this lady's got her heart in the right place. She didn't mean nothing harmful by it. Emma's been through hell, I figure. I believe she's trying, too. Trying real hard, 'cause you sure weren't cutting her any slack out there."

Lireinne barked a bitter laugh, amazed at Bud's naïveté. "Yeah? Then she should try harder at minding her own business. I *hate* her." She retrieved Lunchmeat from Bud's lap, knowing she'd sounded like a little kid but not caring. She shouldn't have to listen to this talk of being nice to Emma.

"I hope to hell I never see her ass again," Lireinne added vehemently.

"Uh, that's a 'nother thing I want to talk to you about," Bud said with some deliberateness. He rubbed his big hand over his head as he gave her a long look. "See, Emma's invited us all over for dinner tomorrow night and I hope you'll go. Give her another chance, Lireinne. I think it took a lot of guts for her to come out here to see you, so you know she's not just yankin' your chain, darlin'. C'mon, say yes. Be the bigger person."

"I'd rather . . ." Lireinne paused, trying to think of the most stupidly heinous act in the world. "I'd rather swim with *Snowball*. And, and I'm a plenty big enough person already!"

"You sure 'bout that?"

Lireinne couldn't believe he'd just said that. Worse, she couldn't think of a thing to say back to him in self-defense. Still, after Bud left her room and shut the door behind him, she was filled with a disgruntled speculation. Why on earth would Emma have invited the Hootens over for dinner?

What was in it for that high-toned heifer?

The rest of the day passed while Lireinne moped around the trailer in a state of low-level piss-off, holding out and not talking much to anyone. She retired to her room to eat the dinner Bud cooked that night—canned beans, canned corn, and canned ham—with only the TV for company. Without having to say a word, her stepfather had managed to communicate his disappointment with her, but she wasn't about to give in and accept Emma's invitation. Even talking about it would only encourage him.

The next day, Sunday, was much the same. That afternoon, fed up and restless, Lireinne got in the car and drove up to Folsom to see Mose. *He* wasn't going to give her a hard time over Emma and her stupid "please-like-me-again" dinner party. She spent the afternoon hanging out with the old Thoroughbred and a couple of the handicapped kids, teaching them how to groom Mose the way he liked best. To Lireinne's satisfaction it was a good afternoon, an experience she'd like to have again. Maybe she'd volunteer here, she thought as she drove away from the center. It'd been pretty cool, the way those kids looked up to her, just like she really knew what she was talking about.

When Lireinne got home late in the day, she found the trailer empty and quiet. Bud and Wolf were at Emma's house, she supposed. No freaking problem. It would be good to have the place to herself for a change—no stupid Xbox, no stepfather giving her that *look*— but the rest of the afternoon rolled on as slowly as a car with a flat tire. It was well after dark when Bud and Wolf finally returned. At the sound of the truck coming down the drive, Lireinne made sure she was holed up in her room so she wouldn't have to deal with them.

But even through her locked door, she found she couldn't escape Bud and Wolf's good-humored conversation as they came inside the trailer's front room. She raised the volume on the television. Lireinne didn't need the aggravation, hearing about what kind of a time they'd had, didn't want to know what they'd eaten or what Emma's place was like. She and Lunchmeat were doing great all on their own, Lireinne told herself stoutly. She had the TV for company and the puppy was gnawing the rawhide chew toy she'd bought for him at the Dollar General. He was happy, her flip-flops were safe, and she didn't feel the least bit left out.

Lireinne was having a hard time ignoring Bud's and Wolf's voices in the front room, though. She rolled onto her side in her bed and stuffed the pillow over her head. The trailer walls were so thin she couldn't help but overhear, though, and, she suspected grumpily, Bud was pitching his voice louder than his usual soft-spoken rumble so she *would* overhear.

"Can't remember the last time I had a home-cooked meal I didn't make myself," Bud boomed. "We ate good tonight, huh, Wolf? That French stuff turned out better than I'd-a thought. Never had beef stew so fine before, what with the wine in it and all. Mighty nice."

Not as loudly, but still too audible for Lireinne's comfort, Wolf asked, "What was that we had for dessert? That shit was awesome."

Bud laughed. "Well, I don't know 'xactly, but it weren't shit, son. Emma said it was a, a *clafouti*? Yeah, that was it. Seemed like some kind of cherry pudding to me, but man oh man! Sure was tasty. You had seconds, didn't you?"

Lireinne didn't have to listen to Wolf's reply because he'd turned on his Xbox. The familiar EverQuest theme music drowned his voice in a strident skirling of trumpets, bagpipes, and drums.

"You did fine, son." Bud had raised his voice above the noise. He was being *so* obvious. "You don't need to worry what a nice lady like that might think of your manners. You did just great. Yup, 'bout the best meal I've had in a long, long time. Good food, good company." The trailer rocked under Bud's heavy footsteps until they stopped at the other side of her door. Her head buried under the pillow, Lireinne groaned in vexation.

Bud knocked. "Lireinne, honey? You still awake?"

Giving up on pretending she was asleep, Lireinne removed the pillow and rolled over onto her back. "Yeah," she called, her voice raised, determined to communicate how irritated she was. "Who could sleep with all that loud-ass jabber out there? I have to get up early for work tomorrow, you know."

Bud was quiet for a moment. He said, "Yeah, don't we all. You missed a real nice time, honey. Emma was sorry you weren't feeling well."

"Why'd you tell her *that*? I'm not sick. You should have said I told her to go to hell!"

Bud ignored that. "She sent home a plate for you, if you're hungry."

"I'm not hungry," Lireinne said, even though she hadn't had any dinner. Nothing had appealed to her earlier, the leftover canned supper in the fridge promising to be as unappetizing and tasteless tonight as it had been the night before.

On the other side of the door, Bud said, "You sure? This's some kind of good—different, but real good. Beats the hell out of beans and fried Spam."

"I don't want any freaking food," Lireinne said angrily, sick of talking to him. She didn't want *anything* from that woman.

"Okay, Lireinne. But if you change your mind later, I left that plate in the fridge for you, darlin'. Night." His footsteps receded down the hall before he shut the door to his room.

As if, she thought. Like she'd eat anything from that woman's hands, no matter how much Bud praised her cooking. She'd rather starve.

And yet there had been an unfamiliar note in Bud's voice. He'd sounded . . . well, relaxed in a way Lireinne hardly ever heard him, like for once he wasn't bone-tired, like he'd had a really good night for a change. Yeah, he'd sounded relaxed, but *happy*, too. She couldn't remember the last time Bud had seemed happy over something as ordinary as food. Except . . . she did remember. Ambushed by a bittersweet, melancholy memory, Lireinne hugged Lunchmeat to her chest, rocking him in her arms.

When she'd been little, before Wolf was born, sometimes Bud had come home from work early, and her mother would have made dinner for once. Then the three of them would sit around the table, eating together like a real family. The food, rarely anything but barely passable, had never tasted better than those times. Bud had still smoked then, and after supper he'd light up and beam with contentment, tapping his ashes in an old chipped saucer as the blue smoke rose in a fragrant cloud around his head.

He'd seemed really happy on those nights, for sure, almost as happy as Lireinne had been. He didn't seem to mind the washing up when Lireinne's mother declared she wasn't going to do it, that she was too tired since she'd been running around behind the kid all day. No, when Bud did the dishes, he'd tie a towel around Lireinne's waist and they'd wash plates together, talking and laughing. Her mother would just sit in front of the TV and smoke her own cigarettes until she was ready to go to sleep. Sometimes, she said good night to Lireinne. More often than not, though, she didn't, just stalked down the short hall to the bathroom where she spent a long time with all her soaps, creams, and lotions before she went to bed. Bud would tuck Lireinne in on those nights, making a shadow-puppet show on the wall with his hands and inventing the story as he went along. Sometimes he'd fall asleep in the middle of it, he was so tired, but Lireinne didn't mind. Being tucked into bed was a rare and precious thing to her, something her mother never did at all.

Putting Lunchmeat down on the bed beside her, Lireinne was plenty sure that an indifferent dinner, prepared by a woman who hadn't wanted to make it, wasn't the way tonight's meal had gone down at Emma's house. She didn't know what to think about this unsettling development. She sure as hell wasn't pleased, knowing Bud had been sucked in again by another woman who thought lying to people was okay.

What was the story with Emma Favreaux, anyway? So Bud thought she could cook. Big whup, it was just *food*. Since she'd dropped all that weight this past year, it wasn't like Lireinne was all that into eating anymore. Food, as she now saw it, was just like gasoline, fuel that ran the engine of her body. Only little kids and fat people thought it was anything else. Like those suppers her mother would throw together—Hamburger Helper, Tater-Tot casserole, once some fried chicken she'd burned to a blackened, inedible mess, almost setting the trailer on fire—fuel, all of it. Lireinne had gained some perspective on food since her weight loss: she'd been a pudgy kid and then a fat chick because she'd mistaken an over-full sensation with somebody's giving a damn about her. Well, not anymore. She was over food the same way she was over Emma. For good.

Lireinne propped herself up on her pillows and lifted the now-snoring puppy from his place on the bed, snuggling his warm, sleepy body under her chin.

"Beef stew, huh? Sounds like breakfast for you, Lunchmeat," she murmured. She gave him a soft kiss on the top of his tiny head. "Beef stew, my *ass*."

Wolf quit the Xbox sometime after ten and shuffled past Lireinne's bedroom door on his way to the bathroom. The water ran for a few minutes and then he came out.

"Night, sis," he called, his jaw cracking in a yawn loud enough to hear through the closed hollow-core door. The night drew on and soon it was time to go to bed herself, so Lireinne undressed, put on her nightgown, and got under the covers. She turned off the light, but left the TV on so she wouldn't feel so alone in the silent trailer.

An hour later, the flickering *Friends* rerun on the only station she could get tonight turned into an unbelievably boring hair-restoring infomercial. Lireinne wasn't a bit sleepy. Her clock said it was after midnight. Due to Mose's departure, she could have an extra half hour of sleep, but seven a.m. was going to come over the horizon long before she was ready for it. She needed to get to sleep soon or else she'd be wrecked at work in the morning. Lireinne thumped her pillow and tried to empty her mind, but her thoughts were scurrying through her head like unseen mice in a dark room. Right about the time she'd start to ease down into sleep, the memory of Bud and Emma in the front yard would sneak around the corner, as impossible to dismiss as the thought of her stepfather and Wolf sitting down to eat with the woman she'd made up her mind to hate.

Hating Emma, Lireinne thought with a resigned sigh, was turning into a lot of work. She turned over and lay flat on her back, brooding in the wavering light from the TV. She got up and turned it off, but that didn't help. Now all that kept her company was Lunchmeat and the crickets singing outside her window in the moonlight.

Finally, at one o'clock in the morning, Lireinne had to admit she was hungry. Really hungry. Maybe if she ate, she could get to sleep. She threw back the covers, got out of bed, and eased the door open.

Tiptoeing down the hall's worn carpet into the front room, she paused. The trailer was dark and soundless except for the muffled, occasional snore coming from behind Bud's closed bedroom door. Sprawled on the sectional like a dropped bicycle, Wolf turned over, one arm hanging off the couch. He muttered in his sleep.

Lireinne tiptoed into the kitchen and opened the refrigerator door a crack, trying not to let the light escape because it might wake her brother. She didn't feel like explaining what she was up to: it was none of his business anyway. Inside on the top shelf of the fridge was a plate—a real china plate, not a paper one—covered in aluminum foil.

"Hmph," Lireinne snorted under her breath. Too good for paper plates, was she? Either that, or Emma seemed to think she'd be getting that plate back soon. With a glance at Wolf on the sectional, she grabbed it off the shelf and hooked a spoon from the drain board by the sink. Lireinne carefully made her way back down the hall to her room, feeling both sneaky and elated, as though she'd just stolen something from Emma and gotten away with it. That was a stupid way to feel, though, because this was only fuel and she was totally starving.

After easing her door shut, Lireinne sat cross-legged on the bed next to a very intrigued Lunchmeat, peeled back the plate's foil, and took a small bite. Even though the food was cold, she had to concede that Bud had been right. This beef stew (*boeuf bourguignon,* her memories from French class reminded her) was the best she'd ever tasted. That spoonful filled her mouth with a delicious mélange of flavors—succulent mushrooms, tender beef, and sweet, mellow pearl onions. The richness of the deep brown braising liquid was so complex and satisfying that she hated for it to end. Lireinne saved a tiny bite of beef for Lunchmeat, but too soon she was scraping up the last of Emma's stew and wishing there was more.

Okay, who knew the snobby cow could cook like that, she thought. Big deal, right?

But now she felt like she could sleep. With a big yawn, Lireinne got up to put the plate on her dresser, her stomach telling her that it was satisfied, as though it had been well taken care of instead of merely fueled. Lunchmeat jumped off the bed and dived into her closet, probably looking for a flip-flop to chew.

"Hey, come back here!" Reaching into the closet, Lireinne scooped him into her arms. Before she shut the door, though, her eyes stopped for an instant, arrested.

There, hanging among the other clothes from Banana Republic, was the sea-foam-colored dress. Emma had bought it for her that day back in September and she'd never worn it. The puppy tucked under one arm, Lireinne ran her hand down the dress's smooth length, fingering the silk, remembering the magical shopping trip to the mall. Lireinne had to admit that it had been a good time, being with Emma, someone she'd allowed herself, however stupid she might have been, to think of as a friend.

"Please." Emma had looked wistful. "It'd make me happy to buy it for you."

"You mean it?" Lireinne asked incredulously. She adored how it fit, the way the pale green silk turned her eyes to emeralds. She was already in love with this amazing dress. She'd never owned anything like it. "But, like, where am I going to wear this?"

"Why not Paris?"

"*Paris*? No way." Lireinne dismissed the suggestion, but gazing at her reflection in the mirror, suddenly she could see herself wearing this dress, this perfect dress, as she strolled down the Champs-Élysées. She would be so cool, just like the *Vogue* models—elegant, confident, and free.

Forget it, though. She wasn't so crazy as to think *that* was ever going to happen.

"Nope. I'm never gonna get to Paris," Lireinne had said in dismissal.

"You never know," Emma murmured.

CHAPTER 18

"Paris?"

The phone wedged into the hollow between his shoulder and his neck, Con shook two Vicodin tablets onto his desk. He hesitated, picked them up, and dry-swallowed them with a grimace. Still a gauze-swathed lump, his left hand rested in his lap while the right one struggled uselessly to get the cap back on the plastic vial.

It was a sunny Monday morning in October, a week after his discharge from the hospital, and Con was still trying to dig himself out from under the avalanche of paperwork that had piled up in his absence. It was proving to be an even more arduous job than he'd expected because he was having some trouble concentrating these days.

"Hell yes, I'm up for Paris," Con said, trying to sound alert and on top of things. "I'm good to go." The pill cap twisted out of his fingers, flew across the desk, and landed on the floor beside his feet.

On the other end of the phone, Roger didn't sound convinced.

"You sure, ol' son? I mean, this here BFG deal's headin' west on us. Need to have someone on the ground over there makin' sure we get what's owed us fair and square. You gotta be a hunnert and ten percent, Con, but I gotta tell you, seems like you're woolgatherin' some lately. If there was someone else to cover it, I'd ask 'em. Hail, if I was half the negotiator you are, I'd go myself, but you know how those frogs get my fur up. Prob'ly make things worse and we cain't afford nothing like *that* right now, if you follow me."

Con's good right hand clenched on the desk. Roger was alluding to the EPA matter: last week Hannigan had been summoned to Washington to answer the agency's charges regarding the farm's illegal dumping of toxic materials—the watered-down blood and feces from 250,000 alligators. The senator wasn't returning Con's calls, the EPA was charging unstoppably as a maddened bull for court, and Roger's fifty-thousand-dollar campaign contribution was as surely down the drain as the problematic wastewater. The French deal couldn't get turned around fast enough.

Con's reply was muffled as he groped around on the floor for the pill cap. "I said I've got it, Rog." His prize captured, he sighed with relief. He'd get Lireinne to put the cap back on the vial later. Damned things were a bitch to get on and off under normal circumstances. It was next to impossible with one hand.

With a gusty, dubious-sounding exhalation, Roger said, "Okey-doke. Bring these French sons-of-bitches back to the table. There's a lot riding on this deal, I mean to tell you—cash flow's hanging fire and we got bills to pay. Feed, natural gas, insurance, quarterly taxes. Cain't have 'em blowin' hot and cold. Nail it down, Con. Get your ass to Paris by Thursday and get her done, whatever it takes."

Roger hung up without saying good-bye.

Whatever it takes. Con slumped in his chair, thinking about that. He was a long way from feeling as certain he could pull this off as he'd assured Roger he was. He was afraid he'd lost his edge somewhere in the hospital. A week out from his discharge, Con was still dosing himself liberally with painkillers. At least Binnings, that little snake, had come through with a generous prescription, but that was only right, especially in light of the fact that he was surely plotting to make time with Con's not-yet-ex-wife.

Con had called Liz only once since the scene in the hospital and that call had been difficult enough. He'd been told in no uncertain terms that he was to leave her the hell alone. Beyond a cold reference to the impending divorce, she refused to discuss her plans for the future, and when Con had mentioned the baby, she'd cut him off and ended the call. He didn't know how he was supposed to feel after that. Wistfulness and regret were emotions he normally had little time for, but Con was pretty sure that these were the feelings he experienced whenever he allowed himself to think of how his latest marriage was ending. Aside from leaving him flat and as close to broke as possible, what was Lizzie going to do next?

And now Paris. Con wondered if he was up to it at all.

Waiting for the pills to take effect, his left hand throbbing, Con remembered the French tanners from his last visit to Paris six months ago—a slippery, smiling people, cunning as Arab emirs looking for an advantage in the oil markets. He knew he wasn't in the best shape to take them on. Even if Con merely adequately drugged himself, there was a strong likelihood that those sharp-dressed, urbane thieves would steal the BFG skins away from him with a smirk and a Gallic shrug and he might not be alert enough to notice.

Where was his A game now, where was that old Jedi, Obi-Wan? Somewhere in the bottom of the vial of Vicodin, Con suspected. He was sure Roger would take a dim view of the extent of his self-medicating, but Roger didn't have to cope with the ever-present pain. As soon as the pills began to work, Con hoped he'd be able to concentrate on the westward-headed French deal. He had to: his future with the company might be riding on this one hugely important sales meeting in Paris.

This pressure aside, traveling out of the country also loomed as a trial by fire. There'd be bags to carry, terminals to negotiate, immigration to get through: all this, one-handed and doped to the eyeballs. Con's mouth tightened while his left hand continued to throb an insistent drumbeat, deep and unrelenting. He was trying to stretch the interval between doses as far as he could stand it. He'd craved his medication a half hour ago, but had wanted to be sharp for Roger's call. No, that conversation had been an agony, but at least it'd been a coherent agony. Hurry, Vicodin, Con thought grimly.

"Is everything okay, Mr. Con?"

During the phone call, Lireinne had looked up from the pile of papers she was working on over at the conference table. In spite of his aching hand, Con basked in the concern he was certain he heard in her question.

Ah, Lireinne.

She'd been so very attentive to him since his return to work, so much so that he sent the home-help nurse packing after the first day. Every morning since his discharge, Lireinne had picked him up from the new apartment so he wouldn't have to drive. She had his newspaper and a cup of coffee ready and waiting, and during this stolen time in the car Con had come to appreciate that she was more free with him when they were out of the office. While Lireinne was behind the wheel, he greedily ate up her young, artless chatter, thinking that her unself-conscious beauty was sweeter than any drug. These hours alone together had become necessary to him, and it seemed to Con that she genuinely enjoyed being with him as well. Whatever Lizzie's plans might be, day by precious day, his relationship with Lireinne was growing into something he'd never imagined feeling for a woman before.

With a self-deprecating smile, Con handed Lireinne the cap to the pill vial. "Can you help me with this?"

Soon enough the bandages would have to come off, but he had no fear now she'd be repulsed by his mangled hand. Lireinne's compassion was a comforting flame he turned to again and again, a welcome antidote to Liz's antagonism and disgust.

She replaced the top and handed him back the Vicodin, but Lireinne's grave, green eyes were easy to read. Although she hadn't actually said anything yet, Con had perceived for some time that she was worried about the narcotic he was taking.

This morning Lireinne's doubtful expression tugged at his heart, but Con was in the habit of telling himself every four hours—after he'd had a dose—that he had this shit under control. Well, maybe he was becoming somewhat concerned about his escalating need for the drug, but what else could he do? Even now the slow, languorous ease approached on stealthy feet. Soon the narcotic would soothe his hand's damnable throbbing, giving it a junkie's kiss to make it all better. Anticipating the Vicodin's warm embrace, Con almost groaned, hungering for its promise of relief.

"You want me to get you some coffee?" Lireinne asked helpfully.

"That would be great, Lireinne."

Today of all days, he was going to need plenty of caffeine. He needed to keep his edge keen while he worked his way through the daunting backlog piled on the desk in front of him. Con didn't want to have to leave for Paris without being as prepared as possible before meeting with the tanners.

"Be right back, then." Lireinne's tentative smile was uneasy, but Con was wading into the sweet, seductive pool of the Vicodin by now and so didn't mind very much.

Heading to the kitchen to fetch his coffee, as she walked away Lireinne smoothed her skirt over her hips, an unconscious lure, and those exquisite, swaying hips called Con's name.

The coffee helped somewhat. Still, it wasn't until after he'd asked Lireinne to call United for a round-trip flight—for Wednesday, New Orleans to De Gaulle, First Class, bulkhead window seat—that Con came to an elegant solution to his travel dilemma. It was classic, it was obvious, and more importantly, it solved another problem as well.

"Lireinne," he said, his voice full of renewed cheer, "could you get away for a few days? I'm going to need you to go with me on the trip to Paris." Oh, this was a *great* idea, the best he'd had in a long time.

Seated at the conference table, Lireinne looked up from the EPA documents she was collating for the litigation. Her full lips parted, her eyes widened to shining green stars.

"Really?" she gasped. "Me? *Paris?*"

Con grinned at her breathless questions. God, she was such a sweetheart. "Paris. As in Paris, France. Can you go? I really need your help."

Lireinne sagged against the back of the chair, her long-fingered hand at her half-open mouth. "Oh, Mr. Con. I've wanted to go there, God, like my whole *life*. Do you really mean it?"

"Of course I mean it, honey." Con lifted his bandaged hand. "You see how it is for me right now. Notwithstanding your lovely presence, I'm going to need an assistant to help me get around. That would be your job, right? We've only got a couple of days, so we'll need to get you an expedited passport, but Jackie's done that before. I'll put her on it before lunch and you can drive to New Orleans to pick it up tomorrow."

Yes sir, Obi-Wan had come through again, Con thought in happy complacence. Lireinne would be a godsend for the travel problems he might face on this trip, and what better place to make love to her the first time than Paris? Vastly pleased with himself for this offing of two birds with a single rock, Con reached for a cigar from the humidor on his desk, struggling to get the cellophane wrapper off one-handed.

"Here. Let me help with that, Mr. Con." With alacrity, Lireinne leapt up from her chair. She leaned over his desk, proffering the cut-crystal lighter, and he glimpsed the white swell of her breasts, revealed in all their splendor under her dark blue shirt.

"Thanks, Lireinne," Con said, drawing on his cigar and feeling like a sultan. "Now call United back and make a reservation for yourself, too. Oh, and you'll need to go get the phone number from Jackie for the Plaza Athénée, too."

"The Plaza Athénée?"

Lireinne's French pronunciation wasn't bad, Con thought in mild surprise. Better than his, for sure. "That's where I stay when I'm in Paris," he said in careless good humor. "They'll have me in their system, so book my regular suite on the fifth floor, the one with a view of the Eiffel Tower."

The Plaza Athénée was one of the most prestigious hotels on the continent, a staggeringly luxurious palace of a hotel with its romantic red awnings and spectacular rooms. The staff there was excellent, too, Con remembered. Once he had a little privacy, he'd call the concierge himself. The man could be trusted to see to it that several of those enormous flower arrangements and a cold bottle of Taittinger champagne would be delivered to the suite before their arrival, perhaps a box of chocolate truffles from Vosges as well. Why not? It was all going to go on the expense account.

Recently, Con had confronted the disagreeable fact that money was becoming even more of a problem than usual. There was the note on the house where Lizzie had staked her claim, Emma's alimony, the car payments, insurance, and now the rent on the apartment down in Covington. All this and a pile of credit card debt was stretching his means like a fraying rubber band. Yes, this fortuitous trip, underwritten by Sauvage Global Enterprises and Roger Hannigan, was the answer to the question of Lireinne and their all-important first time together. The apartment, while a marginal improvement over the dismal suite at the Marriott where he'd spent a single night, was largely bare of furniture and depressing as only rented, anonymous rooms in a sprawling complex could be. It was no place at all for the night he'd schemed to bring about for so long. A local hotel room, even one in New Orleans, would be nothing more than . . . tawdry, a place of assignation, and he wanted only the best for Lireinne.

First, Con decided with a Vicodin-inspired optimism, he'd get on the plane. He'd fix this gone-to-hell deal by Friday, by God, and then he'd have the rest of the long weekend to spend with Lireinne, showing her the best of Paris. The timing, the place, the season—his plan was falling into place. A perfect trip for the perfect girl.

"Go on, see Jackie about that number and your passport," Con reminded her. Lireinne hadn't moved an inch, visibly glowing with excitement.

"I'll get to it right away, Mr. Con." She hurried down the hall. Con grinned, smoking with more pleasure than a cigar usually afforded. He glanced at his watch: it told him the four-hour window between Vicodin doses was a good hour down the road. He really should wait.

"Oh, to hell with it," Con muttered.

He could afford to cut himself some slack today. He'd gotten through that phone call with Roger, hadn't he? He didn't want the hand distracting him now, didn't want the pain to sneak up on him again.

Besides, he'd earned it. Opening the bottle was always easier than closing it anyway, and so Con did just that, shaking another two tablets onto the desk and washing them down with the cold coffee.

Leaning back in his chair, Con closed his eyes, envisioning the end of the long game he'd been playing, the true beginning of his life with Lireinne. He was thinking about the Plaza Athénée's huge marble bathrooms that were the size of an ordinary suburban bedroom, those deep soaking tubs you could almost swim in, the floor-to-ceiling, gilt-framed mirrors everywhere, the towels thick and soft as fox-fur coats from Norway. He was imagining Lireinne in one of those bathtubs, clothed only in a fragrant cloud of bubbles, blowing him a kiss and sipping the Taittinger from a crystal flute. "Happy, my love?" he'd ask. Not stopping to wrap herself in a towel, Lireinne slipped out of the tub and into his embrace, her lithe body warm and wet and real next to his skin.

It was an erotic, blissful image, and that image and the Vicodin coursing through his veins delivered Con into sleep's arms instead of Lireinne's. His mouth going slack, his head lolled in loose abandon against the back of the chair.

When Lireinne returned to the office, he was past nodding and deep in slumber, his red hair rumpled, his bandaged left hand dangling between his knees. The bottle of Vicodin was open and lying on its side, a scatter of white tablets strewn across the papers on his desk.

"Lireinne," Con mumbled, lost in his dream.

"Lireinne."

At first, Lireinne wasn't sure what it was Mr. Con had said. Her boss was asleep in his chair again, something that was happening with an alarming frequency since he'd come back from the hospital. His un-pressed shirt was pulled halfway out of his khakis, he'd forgotten his socks again, and he needed a shave.

It seemed like Mr. Con was taking a *lot* of those pills, Lireinne worried. They made him drift off like a tired child who'd stayed up past his bedtime, and while she didn't have any real experience with painkillers, Lireinne knew it couldn't be good for him to take so many, not with all the pressure he was under. Though he was trying hard not to let on, she could tell Mr. Con was way behind on his work, and while he never complained about his hand, he must be hurting a lot. It was because of the pain, his taking too many drugs. That woman he was married to should be looking after him. Lireinne pursed her lips in disapproval. But Mrs. Costello had thrown him out of the house and now he was all alone at that humongous apartment complex down on the highway with nobody to care about him—nobody but her.

If Lireinne hadn't felt responsible for Mr. Con's accident, she wouldn't have cared so much about his drug use, except . . . once Bud had told her about a man on the loading dock who'd gotten hurt on the job. He'd ended up addicted to drugs just like these, hooked like any other pill-freak. But come on, be real, Lireinne told herself uneasily. Mr. Con wasn't going to end up like that friend of Bud's, serving three years when he'd tried to buy his dope from an under-cover cop. Rich people like Mr. Con always went to rehab instead of jail, didn't they?

Her boss snored abruptly, again muttering something she couldn't quite make out. Disquieted, Lireinne sat at the table and tried to get back to work on the EPA documents, but a couple of minutes later he spoke once more. There couldn't be any doubt about what he said this time.

"Lireinne, honey." Mr. Con sighed deeply, smiling in his sleep.

She gasped, her mouth falling open. No way she'd really heard him say that, did she? God, like she was in his *dreams*?

All those times Lireinne had looked up to find him watching her when he was supposed to be working, all the times he'd touched her that she'd tried to convince herself were no big deal—all of it had been in his eyes since the very beginning. She'd been a moron for try-ing to make all that other than what it really was. Lireinne couldn't deny what she knew to be true any longer.

Mr. Con had a . . . *thing* for her. It was the reason he had given her the job, it was the reason for the money, the car, and the prom-ise of a trip to Paris. He might not have grabbed at her like Harlan had, but that was the only difference between Mr. Con and every other creep who wanted to get in her pants.

Rubbing the scar at her eyebrow, Lireinne slumped in her chair, overwhelmed. *Now* freaking what? She crushed a stray piece of pa-per into a wadded ball. So what in the hell was she supposed to do with this unwelcome, dangerous knowledge? So what was the big plan now, huh?

So there wasn't a question about it, a newborn determination told her in a voice as cold and hard as arctic ice. Get a grip, it said. There'd never be another chance for her to get to Paris, and nobody, not even Mr. Con and his . . . his wanting her that way, was going to stop her from taking this trip. Nothing was going to stop her. *Noth-ing.* It was a conscious decision, narrow-eyed and calculating, herald-ing a sudden change within on a level deeper than she'd ever felt in her life.

And with this decision came the understanding of what a narrow, careful line she was going to have to walk. No way, Lireinne thought, there was no way she'd ever sleep with him—God, no—but Mr. Con didn't have to know that. Not yet. She'd go to Paris and then . . . manage the situation. Somehow, anyhow, she'd make it happen be-cause she'd never wanted *anything* as much as this trip.

Setting her jaw, swallowing past the dry lump in her throat, Lireinne picked up the phone and dialed the Plaza Athénée's num-ber. She waited through the series of transatlantic beeps, twisting the phone cord in her nervous, trembling fingers. It seemed to take a long time before she was connected.

"*Bonjour, la Plaza Athénée.*"

Paris. The hotel operator's banal greeting in her ear shivered a fierce thrill of joy through Lireinne's entire body. A real, live French person was talking to her! Stealing a glance at Mr. Con sleeping at his desk, Lireinne cleared her throat, forcing her lowered voice to be calm and weighted with an authority she didn't really feel.

"*Bonjour.* I need to make a reservation, *s'il vous plaît,* for Monsieur Con Costello."

The operator smoothly transitioned from French to English. "Of course—his usual suite, *mademoiselle?*"

"No sir, on this trip Monsieur Costello will need a suite with *two* bedrooms."

There was bound to be a lock on the door, and Lireinne planned to use it.

Five minutes later, the reservation confirmed, she got up from the conference table, girding herself to go down the hall to accounting to remind that bitch Jackie to arrange her expedited passport, whatever that was, before Wednesday. Lireinne was taking no chances. Let Jackie think whatever she wanted about her going with Mr. Con on a business trip to Paris; let her tell the whole damned farm if that would make her miserable ass happy.

Lireinne's step was light as she walked down the hall, but her mouth was set in an uncompromising line, her backbone straightened with a resolve like forged Swedish steel.

Paris.

CHAPTER 19

Lizzie couldn't deny it: when she turned sideways, she was positive she could detect a thickening of her waistline in the long mirror's reflection.

"Oh, hell!" she exclaimed. She turned again, running her hand over the front of her silk tunic. Even though she was only two months along, she could *see* it, the pregnancy, a half-imagined, intrusive presence lurking like a feral cat under the house. A couple of hours from now on this Monday afternoon, Liz would be having her first dinner date with Skip Binnings. Tonight was the first night in ten days that Skip hadn't been on call and he'd wasted no time asking her out. Gratified by this evidence of his determined pursuit, she was ransacking her closet for clothes that could disguise the almost invisible bulge besieging her previously flat-stomached, high-waisted figure. This loose-fitting ivory charmeuse tunic from the back of her closet hadn't done a thing to flatter her before she was pregnant, Lizzie thought in heavy discouragement, much less *now*.

And these days, instead of the constant nausea of morning sickness, she was so hungry all the time she couldn't seem to stop eating her head off. This raging appetite wasn't helping her waistline either, that was for damned sure.

Heaped clothing draped the armchair in the bedroom; another pile of discards was piled in a mound of expensive, lush fabric on the bed. Lizzie impatiently shrugged out of the tunic, tossed it on the chair, and headed back to the closet—roomier now, thanks to Con's departure—to continue the hunt. First dates were so important and this dinner with Skip was going to be *major*. What kind of impression would she make? Liz fretted as she limped out of the bedroom.

At least she was in a walking cast now, and good riddance to the crutches consigned to the back of the garage with the rest of the crap she and Con had managed to amass over the past two years: snow skis, water skis, life-preservers, croquet mallets, pool toys, tennis rackets, a kayak, the lawn furniture too beat-up to leave out on the patio, the collection of ice chests, a big cardboard box full of Mardi Gras beads, and poor Lima Bean's crate. The new black Kevlar boot wasn't much of an improvement over her plaster cast, fashionwise, but it was one hell of a lot better than stumping around on crutches, and Lord, it was heaven to be able to shower again like a normal person. The orthopedic surgeon had told her she was healing beautifully, that she'd be free of the walking cast in another three weeks. Once that was out of the way, Liz thought, she'd finally be herself again.

Except for being pregnant.

Lizzie had been forced to admit that this inconvenient situation wasn't going to go away on its own, but every time she picked up the phone to dial her gynecologist for an appointment to discuss . . . the alternative, she found herself putting it down again, unable to make that call.

And why was that? Liz wondered, impatient with this inexplicable, uncharacteristic procrastination. It wasn't like she was actually going to *have* this baby, she thought as she pawed through her sweater drawer, looking for the black silk-blend Ralph Lauren. Of all the times to be pregnant, if ever there was one, this most certainly was not it. Lizzie yanked the sweater over her head and returned to the bedroom mirror. Really, it was just one little procedure and then she'd be shut of Con for good—except for the settlement and alimony, of course. The very idea of being a single mother, *plus* having to continue to put up with him and his shit, wasn't merely absurd: it was out of the question.

A baby, Lizzie thought, would only make her miserable. She was sick of being miserable.

She smoothed the sweater over her hips. This combination would do, Liz decided, as she revolved in front of the mirror, looking at herself from all angles. Black, at least, was slimming, and coupled with the pair of charcoal skinny pants she'd managed to squeeze into, she looked better than she'd dared hope. Maybe not up to her usual standards, but still damned good. This sweater had always been a favorite, playing up the caramel and gold lights in her hair, accenting her natural high color. Lizzie put on her diamond earrings, too. Their sparkle would draw Skip's admiring gaze to her face, away from the unwelcome roundness at her middle and the cumbersome walking cast. In any case, it was the best she could do with what she had to work with.

Tonight's outfit seen to, Lizzie scooped up the discards and piled them all on the floor of the closet for Consuelo to put away when she came in tomorrow. The arrangement with CoCo Hannigan had dwindled to the maid's coming in every other day, but Liz felt sure she'd have one of her own soon. Con was in no position to insist on her keeping the house, not anymore, and so there was no reason not to do that for herself. After she got in touch with her gynecologist and . . . took care of things, Lizzie planned to return to work. Her old associate's salary, added to the cash she'd get out of Con, would ensure plenty of money for whatever she wanted.

Finally free of housework and all that damned cooking, Liz would be happy if she never saw a copper pot again. As if in answer to that thought, her stomach growled like a pit bull. Suddenly, she was almost faint with hunger. She couldn't *wait* for dinner.

That was probably because she was eating for two.

It was another disconcerting thought, so Lizzie dismissed it in a hurry. Okay, rather than having a big meal tonight, she'd give in and have something to eat beforehand. A little snack now, and she'd be able to order just an appetizer and a salad later tonight. That would be a dainty meal, consistent with the way she wanted Skip to view her, a glamorous, ethereal creature living on small, exquisite plates and heirloom lettuce leaves. Cheering up at the thought of food, even lettuce, Liz decided she'd have a glass of wine or two with dinner—since she was going to make that appointment soon. With a last critical glance at her reflection in the bedroom's long mirror, Lizzie went into the kitchen to find something to appease her stomach's insistent grumbling.

The big stainless-steel refrigerator reflected Con's absence in much the same way the closet did: its insides were largely bare. Liz hadn't gone grocery shopping or made a meal in many weeks. Consuelo's dinners might be pretty basic, but they definitely beat having to cook. Too bad there weren't any leftovers, Liz thought as she glumly surveyed the empty fridge. Right now the lack of groceries on hand was damned inconvenient. She could hardly make a meal out of a can of Diet Coke and a loaf of stale bread. There wasn't anything to make a sandwich with either, only a head of cabbage in the vegetable crisper and a handful of elderly carrots. Liz shook her head, disgusted at the state of affairs in her refrigerator. What could she do with just cabbage and carrots?

Coleslaw! her gnawing hunger promptly responded. Lizzie had always been fond of coleslaw. Her mother, not much of a cook herself and given to homely staples like meat loaf and tuna casserole when feeding her large, always-hungry family, had nevertheless made a great coleslaw. Now, where was the mayonnaise?

Gathering the ingredients, Liz got down to business with the chef's knife on the expansive marble island's cutting board, slicing the cabbage into a chiffonade, scraping the carrots and slicing them into slivers, and then mixed it all together in a big blue mixing bowl with half a jar of mayonnaise. As a crowning touch, she seasoned the mixture lavishly with basil, fresh-ground black pepper, and salt. During the preparations, Lizzie's mouth watered. Feeling as though she would perish of hunger before she could taste the first generous spoonful, she wanted coleslaw now with an almost mindless yearning for all that creamy, green crunchiness.

Done stirring, with happy anticipation Liz pulled up a bar stool to the island and sat down with the blue bowl, a big spoon, and draped a dish towel around her neck to protect her black sweater. And then, methodically as a backhoe, she set to work.

Lizzie ate to the point where she had to unbutton the waistband of her skinny pants. She ate until the bowl was nearly empty, leaving just a bare cup of cabbage swimming in the watery dregs of mayonnaise, flecks of pepper, and basil at the bottom of it. Now that she was uncomfortably sated, she couldn't remember ever having been so famished. She'd eaten *so much*. Coleslaw, of all things. What the hell had gotten into her?

Lizzie slumped against the back of the bar stool, confounded and more than a little dismayed. She never ate like that, never. She'd been obsessive about her weight ever since she'd gained that damned freshman fifteen, back at LSU. It had taken what seemed like a thousand hours on the treadmill in the gym and months of calorie-counting to lose the pudge encircling her hips and thighs. After all that grinding torture, Liz had sworn she'd never gain a pound again, knowing even then that the kind of man she'd been determined to marry—whoever he turned out to be—wouldn't want a wife carrying any extra weight at all. They never did. Con certainly hadn't.

But this out-of-control binge was something different from those midnight forays to the vending machines, scarfing bags of corn chips, cookies, and guzzling chocolate Yoo-hoos. This binge had been almost, well, like a crazy sickness.

No, not a sickness. With a shiver of dread, Liz understood that this had to have been a . . . a . . . *craving*. Pregnant women got cravings. Abruptly humiliated by her own gluttony, she hurried the rest of the bowl of coleslaw to the sink, stuffed the remains down the garbage disposal, and flipped the switch to get rid of the evidence. She left the bowl in the sink for Consuelo to wash the next day.

There was a sliver of carrot and a dribble of mayonnaise on the soft black sleeve of her sweater, and she'd need to redo her mouth before Skip arrived in thirty minutes. Liz rubbed her lips roughly on the dish towel. What if Skip had seen her chowing down like that?

He'd have thought she was insane, or worse, a woman who'd turn into a hog on a moment's notice. She hadn't told him about her pregnancy, sure it would spell the end of the attraction she hoped he felt for her. What kind of man would be so infatuated he'd be okay with taking *that* on?

The coleslaw episode confirmed it. Lizzie was going to call her gynecologist tomorrow, no matter what.

By the time Skip Binnings arrived at the front door, Liz had won the struggle to get her skinny pants zipped again and, as the faithful mirror informed her, she'd cleaned up better than any woman who'd just consumed practically an entire bowl of coleslaw had any right to expect.

And the admiration in her date's eyes was a flattering confirmation. "Lord, Lizzie," Skip said, taking her in with a sweeping glance, from her shining hair to her ballet-slippered toe. "I never knew any woman who could carry off a walking cast like you do. You're positively gorgeous."

That reassuring compliment eased her mind. It was a good thing she had to wear a flat shoe anyway, Liz thought. The top of this man's head barely came to her shoulder as it was, but at least he had good hair—thick, dark, and sleek as sheared mink. She stepped out onto the porch, shutting the front door behind her, and slipped her arm in Skip's.

"You're not so bad yourself," she said with a big smile. Skip, wearing a blue sport coat, a pinstriped shirt, and a pair of dark jeans, grinned in return.

"Shall we go?" he asked.

"Let's," Liz replied, giving his wide shoulders a discreet glance of approval. They walked together down the steps to Skip's car, a Mercedes S-Class coupe. Nice car, but nothing less than she'd expected: plastic surgeons had piles of money, everybody knew that. He had good taste in music, too, for when Skip started the car the tenor sax of a light jazz arrangement surrounded them, pouring through the Mercedes's impressive sound system.

"I thought I'd take you to the Lemon Tree," Skip said. "If that's okay with you. We can go anywhere you want, but Covington isn't exactly New Orleans. If you want a decent meal without crossing the lake, our choices are pretty limited." He glanced at her in the passenger seat. "I might be rushing things a bit, but I'd like to make sure you have a good time tonight."

Oh, *great,* Liz thought, not the Lemon Tree again. But she smiled and said, "That sounds wonderful. I love the food there." Actually, Lizzie hadn't been back to the restaurant since that night, nearly two months ago, when she'd thrown champagne in Con's face. Since her accident she hadn't been remotely interested in going out to dinner, not on those damned crutches, and especially since she couldn't have a drink.

"That's good," Skip said. "They do a pretty respectable filet there, and a fantastic crème bruleé."

As soon as the words *crème brûlée* came out of his mouth, though, a dull knot twisted in Liz's stomach, just above the bulge. Her hand went involuntarily to her waist, pressing against that roiling sensation. She stifled an impressive belch.

That damned coleslaw, Liz thought uneasily. God knows she'd bolted it like a starving horse. She belched again.

"How's the plastic surgery business going?" she asked, trying to deflect her date's attention. It was almost always a successful gambit to ask a man about his work, and Skip proved no exception. During the drive to the restaurant, he told her a great deal more about plastic surgery than she'd ever had any desire to know. And, too, Lizzie's increasingly querulous stomach was proving to be a major distraction, making it tough going to feign an interest in his current cases— nose jobs, boob jobs, face-lifts, and the odd trauma patient like Con. Summoning a grim determination to master her gut's loud complaints, she maintained a rapt attention, keeping the conversation lively to cover the growls coming from her midsection.

But by the time Skip opened the large front door of the Lemon Tree for her, Liz's agitated digestion was in full cry, bloated and distressed by the burden of nearly a whole head of cabbage. Hang on,

she commanded herself. You can do this. No matter what, Liz meant
to carry off this evening with her customary, well-honed dating skills,
even though she felt as though there were an Asian land war going
on inside her stomach. A glass of pinot grigio might settle things
down in there, Liz hoped, amid her growing agitation.

"Reservation for Binnings," Skip said to the long-waisted blond
girl in the black dress behind the hostess's desk.

Despite her insides' near-revolt, Lizzie was instantly watchful. As
though it was yesterday, she recalled the hostess from her previous
visit to the Lemon Tree, how that night she'd seemed much too familiar with Con, in Liz's opinion. He'd called the hostess by name,
too. What was it? Liz couldn't remember.

The blond girl smiled a charming welcome. Gathering a couple
of menus, she gestured at the dining room's entrance.

"Right this way, Dr. Binnings."

It was the same saccharine, little-girl lilt of Con's infamous voice
mail. This was *Jennifer,* naughty-underwear-from-Victoria's-Secret
Jennifer, this was the girl Con had been doing behind her back! Eyes
narrowed into slits, Lizzie's throat swelled, her face and chest flushed,
and her hands clenched into fists. *Jennifer.*

But in the same instant of Liz's swift, inarticulate fury, a hot sheen
of perspiration broke on her forehead. In awful certainty her stomach announced that things had gone too far, that enough was enough.
It was *done* with all that indigestible coleslaw.

Torn between the furious desire to slap this blond bitch, her hope
to acquire Skip Binnings's very necessary approval, and the more
pressing, immediate imperative to find the bathroom—fast—Liz called
up every ounce of self-control she possessed.

"Excuse me, Skip," she managed, queasily swallowing the bile in
her throat. "I, I need to find the ladies' room."

Jennifer barely had time to point to a door christened *Femmes* before Lizzie made an awkward, limping beeline for the bathroom,
leaving confused Skip Binnings behind.

"Are you all right?" he called. "Lizzie?"

But Liz was shoving open the door to the marble-tiled ladies' room, frantic to get to the toilet before she threw up all over the floor. She pushed inside a stall at the last possible moment, only just able to slam and latch the door before the inevitable happened. And happened.

And happened.

Several minutes later, Lizzie was exhausted and shaking from her ordeal, but the worst was over. Lord, what must Skip be thinking? she wondered as she flushed away the remains of the coleslaw. She'd cut out of there as though she were running from a gun-waving lunatic. *That* was going to take some explaining. Liz was wiping her mouth with a handful of toilet tissue when, outside the stall, the door to the ladies' room opened. A pair of heels tripped briskly across the marble floor and stopped on the other side of the stall.

"Ma'am?"

Jennifer. Her hand itching to yank the hostess's yellow hair off her head, Liz was filled with loathing at the sound of that childish, tinkling syllable.

"Ma'am, are you okay?" Jennifer's tone was solicitous, exactly as any employee's in a good restaurant ought to have been. Under other circumstances, Liz would've approved. "Can I get you something? A little sparkling water from the bar?"

"No," Lizzie snapped, brusque and short. Just get the hell *out* of here, you stupid slut, she thought. Liz had no intention of leaving this stall until she was thoroughly composed, and Jennifer was the last person on earth she wanted to see her like this—the last person she wanted to see, period.

"Are you sure?" Jennifer, that skank, wasn't getting the hint. Her question was plaintive, just like the one in that infamous goddamned voice mail. *Why haven't you called me?*

Goaded beyond endurance, nevertheless Lizzie surprised herself when she snarled, "Do you even know who I *am,* you ignorant whore?"

A shocked silence filled the lavender-scented air of the bathroom. Liz coughed and wiped her mouth again. Whatever was this idiot girl's problem?

"Ma'am?" the hostess finally squeaked. She sounded terrified.

Lizzie ran her fingers through her taffy hair, praying she wouldn't lose it. Wouldn't that be a scandal? A catfight in the ladies' room at the Lemon Tree? How people would love to spread *that* juicy story around town.

"Excuse me?" Jennifer quavered.

"Shut up. *I'm Con Costello's wife,*" Liz grated. "Now get the hell out of this bathroom before I take you apart."

"Con's . . . wife?"

"Didn't you hear what I said? Get the hell out of here!"

Jennifer mumbled something inaudible, something that could've been "I'm sorry," but then she got the hell out of there. What had Con seen in that vacuous fool? Liz thought. What had he gotten from someone so . . . *ordinary* that it was worth risking his marriage to her?

Alone in the ladies' room, exhausted and trembling, Lizzie realized she needed to pee before she had to go back out there and face what was turning out to be a perfectly disastrous first date. As she unzipped her skinny pants and sat on the toilet, she refused to cry because tears would leave her with raccoon eyes of melted mascara. She wasn't going to risk *that* particular humiliation. The evening might still be salvageable, although at this point it seemed such an uphill battle, she wasn't sure she was equal to resurrecting this date.

Her thoughts turning to possible explanations to offer Skip, Liz's eyes fell, noticing a bright carmine stain on the white silk of her underwear. Great, she thought. On top of all this, what a time to be getting my period. But then Lizzie remembered. That single spot of red, the size of a quarter, took on an ominous, terrible significance.

She was losing the baby because she'd nearly vomited herself to death.

"No." Lizzie moaned. "Ah, God—no!"

Blindsided by the implacable reality of this spot of blood and what it meant, Liz was utterly unprepared for the grief that slammed her like a bone-shattering gale. Heedless of her eye makeup now, she sobbed with a desolation she'd never known could have existed within her, not until now.

Losing Lima Bean had been awful, but this was a bewildering agony. Lizzie bent over her knees, covered her head with her arms, and wept inconsolably for the child dying inside her. The child who, until that scarlet stain, she hadn't known she'd wanted all along.

Liz had done the best she could to repair her face, but there was going to be no denying her reddened eyes had been flooding like a broken water main. At the sink, she rubbed the melted mascara off with a tissue, rinsed her mouth out one last time, and dispassionately reapplied her lipstick. Nothing, least of all her makeup, seemed to matter anymore.

"You," Liz said to her pasty reflection in the mirror with weary indifference, "are a fright. No man's going to want you looking like this." It was a statement Lizzie believed to be a cold fact, but found she hardly cared. She pressed her hand to her stomach and closed her eyes. Oh, the baby, she mourned.

She was losing the baby.

Sure there was nothing she could do to stop the miscarriage, Liz had to stop thinking about it or she'd be lost to her grief, however incomprehensible it was. She had to leave the bathroom, go out and face what was bound to be an impatient Skip Binnings, since she'd been in here for over twenty minutes. At least it was Monday, a normally quiet night for dinner in Covington, and so she'd been alone in here with her sorrow—except for the ridiculous blonde who'd slept with Con.

At that thought, Lizzie found a little pride. She set her jaw and exited the bathroom, emerging into the reception area where Skip was waiting for her on the long padded bench by the entry. The hostess was nowhere in sight. Thank God for small favors, she thought with a sniffle.

Don't cry, Liz ordered herself. Don't you dare cry. She attempted a confident smile, except that smile was trembling on her tear-ravaged face, and in that instant, more than anything on earth, she wanted to go home. Before the night was over, she and the baby would be in the hospital, and after the miscarriage was over, she'd be leaving alone. Skip would never call her again, that was for damned sure.

But to Lizzie's amazement Skip was rising from the bench and hurrying to her from across the foyer, his hands outstretched. His face calm but concerned, he put his arms around her waist and looked up into her wondering, puffy eyes.

"Let's get you out of here," Skip said. "Come on, I'll take you home."

During the ride back to the house neither of them spoke, but Skip's hand lay in light comfort on Lizzie's knee, squeezing it from time to time. Lizzie was grateful for that and grateful in a way for her exhaustion, too, for now she felt mercifully emptied out and almost numb. For the time being, her tumult, her grief—both were still and quiet as dead things.

Once she and Skip had reached her front porch, Lizzie unlocked the door. She wanted to put a good face on the end of the evening, if such a thing was possible. "Sorry to have made us leave before we even ate," she said. In spite of her attempt to be polite, her voice was leaden. "Thanks for bringing me home." She put her hand on the doorknob, wanting only to go inside, to be alone with her baby a few minutes more, before she called her doctor and went to the hospital.

"May I come in?" Skip asked. "We could still have a drink together. Right now, that might help you feel better."

A drink? God, she'd never needed one more. But remembering the reason she hadn't had a glass of wine in weeks, Liz couldn't suppress a shuddering, wordless sob.

"Are you okay, Liz?"

She'd never be okay again. Lizzie's eyes filled once more with the hot tears, then her mouth fell open, and to her horror, it began to spill all her secrets. Unable to stop if she tried, she told Skip *every-thing*. The coleslaw, Jennifer, losing the baby—Skip listened to it all, not saying anything but stroking her back as though she were a heartbroken child, until this gentle, human touch calmed Lizzie's wild weather at last. She took a deep breath, wiping her nose on the back of her hand.

"Here." Skip reached into the pocket of his jacket and handed her a clean handkerchief.

Oh, wouldn't you know it: he was the wonderful kind of man who carried a handkerchief, her favorite kind of man. Blowing her nose, her tears spent, Lizzie assumed that any minute now wonderful Skip Binnings was bound to take his handkerchief back, walk down the steps, and leave. After her confession, why was he still here? She couldn't think of a single other word to say to him. God knows, she'd said it all already.

"You should have told me before," Skip said.

His handkerchief a damp ball in her hand, with downcast eyes Liz nodded, feeling gray as November rain with fatigue. "I didn't think I was going to keep it," she murmured. "I thought I wouldn't be able to do it, being a single mother. Even then, Con would still have been a part of raising the baby and I didn't want that. God, I thought I was going to call my gynecologist tomorrow for an appointment to . . . you know." She bit her lip. "But then, *this* happened. All of a sudden, I realized I *wanted* this baby." Lizzie raised her eyes from her feet to meet Skip's. "I guess I'm just . . ." She struggled to find the words, gave up, and said with a sigh, "I'm just blown away."

Skip shook his head.

"This doesn't mean you've lost the baby, Lizzie, not necessarily." In the glow of the flickering porch gaslights, his handsome face was reassuring and kind. "Some spotting's not unusual, not in the first trimester." He reached up to stroke her hair, smoothing it off her face. "You ought to get an appointment, though. You need a prenatal checkup."

Lizzie went quiet, stunned by sudden hope. "You mean . . . I could still be pregnant?" she said eventually.

"It's likely you are, so cheer up." Skip drew her into his arms. "Come here, honey."

And Liz melted. Her head drooped, coming to rest on his wide shoulder. She didn't care anymore that he was short. Skip felt so *solid,* so strong.

"Look," he said, his voice soft. "I think you're an incredible, beautiful, brave woman. You can have this baby if you want to."

Liz sobbed again, but this was a sob of pure gratitude for her deliverance, for the warm arms around her. She clasped her hands around Skip, lowering her forehead to his upturned one. "How am I going to do it, raising a child on my own?" she whispered. It seemed impossibly daunting.

Those wonderful arms tightening around her as though he would never, ever let her go, Skip Binnings smiled an intimate smile.

He kissed her, whispering against her lips, "Who says you're going to have to?"

CHAPTER 20

The wind was out of the north this late Tuesday afternoon, a high, cold river of air rushing through the tops of the pecan trees. Their bare branches creaking overhead, dull-gold leaves swirled in the current before drifting down to the brittle, aromatic carpet crackling underneath Emma's boots.

She was in the grove gathering wind-fallen branches for she planned to build a fire this evening, and pecan wood burned bright and clean. Dressed warmly against the wind, Emma was bundled up in jeans, a heavy, cream-colored Irish fisherman's sweater and a knitted cap, her leather gloves and wearing a bright scarf around her neck. Autumn seemed to be coming early this year, but Emma knew that long-anticipated Louisiana season could be fickle, that a cold front like this one could turn humid and mild again overnight. Still, today felt like a promise. A fire would be a good way to welcome this first day of fall's return, Emma thought, bending to pick up another branch. A fire and perhaps a glass of wine to drink while she watched the flames.

And despite the lingering disappointment of Lireinne's rejection of last Sunday's overture, Emma was ready to celebrate the day—the wind, the brilliant, slanting sunlight, and the turning of the year all serving to lift her spirits. *"All the leaves are brown,"* she sang under her breath, but the sky was anything but gray today: it was a layered, translucent blue, deep as a wild ocean, fathomless and wide above her.

Her arms full, Emma returned to the pile of wood at the base of the pecan tree, satisfyingly large and promising a good blaze on the hearth tonight.

"Sheba!" The hound bounded up to meet her from the end of the grove, frisking in the wind like a half-grown pup. Emma reached down to stroke Sheba's head in a quick caress. "Good girl. Let's go home." She stacked as many of the branches in her arms as she could carry on this first trip. She'd need to come back for the rest after she got her load to the house.

Emma trudged past the edge of the garden with her burden. Swaying in the wind from their trellised vines, summer's gourds—warty balloons of striped green, yellow, and orange—hung ready to be harvested. Loving their color and fantastic shapes, she meant to keep a few to decorate her kitchen table in a big pottery bowl. The rest were headed for the farmers' market this Saturday, as well as the bushel basket of her pecans on the front porch. Okra's dubious bounty was done at last, and it would be another week before most of the greens would be ready to cut, bundle, and sell. Pausing to survey her acres stretching to the surrounding trees, windswept and light-limned in the late-afternoon sun, Emma smiled, knowing that she'd been, well, *hungry* for change and here it was.

It was good to be alive.

And this was a good day. Tonight she was going to cook herself a real meal, something to suit the season. Maybe a gratin dauphinois and a salad of baby kale from the garden, a chicken breast browned in butter and then sautéed in white wine with a hint of garlic.

Emma's thoughts turned to the dinner two days ago, to Bud and Wolf. She felt that had been a beginning of something, although what it was, she wasn't sure. Since then she'd fingered the evening in her mind like a rosary, telling remembered moments like beads. How different and yet so sweetly familiar it had been, feeding people other than herself and Sheba. Bud and Wolf had seemed to enjoy themselves and, after she'd gotten past her chagrin that Lireinne hadn't wanted to come—Bud said she wasn't feeling well, but Emma knew that was a kind lie—she'd found herself hungry for both the food and the company. When they'd gone, she couldn't stop smiling as she cleaned the kitchen, reliving the conversation, the warmth.

The wind gusted and under her cap Emma's silver hair lifted in a static-snapping nimbus. Sheba nosed her thigh, a reminder that it was time to go indoors.

"Sorry, girl," Emma said. The dog was surely wondering why her master was hanging around in the yard with a load of wood in her arms when it was more comfortable inside the house. "Let's go home."

Emma had opened the front door when she heard the distant rumble of tires on the gravel road that led to the farmhouse. Turning, she looked to see who would be coming all the way out to visit her this afternoon. It could be Sarah Fortune, although that would be out of the ordinary: she rarely came by this late in the day. But the car wasn't Sarah's noisy Mercedes. The vehicle clattering down the road was a battered red pickup truck.

Bud's truck, memory reminded her. Why had he come? Emma wondered, and was happy to discover that it didn't matter to her in the least. She was glad to see him again, whatever the reason. Her mouth turned up in a welcoming smile as she shifted the firewood in her arms to wave a gloved hand at his approach. The truck rolled to a stop in front of the house with a dieseling, dying rattle. The driver's door creaked loudly as Bud got out.

"Here," he said. "Let me get that for you."

Emma looked down at the pile of wood she was carrying. "Oh," she said. "I'm stronger than I look. I've got this. Just give me a minute to carry it in the house."

But Bud hurried up the front steps anyway, his arms reaching, his expression determined, so Emma surrendered her load with a breathless laugh. "Well, thanks! Come on inside, get out of this wind," she said, opening the front door.

Bud wiped his work boots on the mat before he came into the hallway. "You want this by the fireplace?" he asked. His blunt features reddened by the wind, he was wearing an old tan Carhartt jacket, faded jeans, and a felt fedora with a crushed crown.

"That would be great," Emma said, leading him into the front room. Bud followed, carefully stacking the wood on the brick hearth in a neat pile.

"You got any more?" he said. "Don't look like this here's enough to see you through the evenin'."

"The rest of it's out in the grove, but please don't bother."

"No trouble a-tall." Bud swept off his hat. "Sorry, my old mother always used to say a real gentleman takes his hat off indoors, 'specially in the presence of a lady."

Emma blushed. "I thank you kindly, Bud Hooten." Lord, she sounded as prim as an old maid with a row of straight pins between her lips. "Why don't I make us some coffee? It won't take a minute."

"I'm going to bring in the rest of your wood," Bud said. "But a cup of coffee sounds good to me. Be back directly."

Ten minutes later the wood was beside the hearth and the coffee was made, filling the kitchen with its genial welcoming aroma. The air in the house had seemed almost hot after being outside in the wind, and so Emma had changed out of her heavy sweater, pulling a soft cashmere cardigan on over her knitted thermal shirt. Bud shrugged out of his jacket and hung it and his hat on the back of a chair, Emma poured the coffee, and they sat down across from each other at the old scrubbed pine table.

"Feels good in here," Bud said, reaching for his cup.

"Thanks for bringing all that wood inside," Emma said with a grateful smile.

But although Bud smiled in return, it was just a preoccupied, quick stretch of his mouth. "Happy to do it," he said. He didn't drink from his cup right away either, only turning it in a tight circle on the tabletop. His eyes were lowered, his broad shoulders hunched. Emma took a nervous sip of coffee, wondering what was on Bud's mind, what had brought him out here at the end of what she knew had to have been another brutal day on the loading dock.

Still keeping his eyes fixed on his cup, Bud said, "Hope it's okay with you that I dropped in so late, but after work I got to thinking. I could sure use your take on something."

"Me?" Emma said with a surprised laugh. He looked up at that, his face wearing a guarded expression she couldn't read. "I mean," she went on, "I'm not exactly a poster child for useful advice. Even on my good days, I'm still kind of a recovering mess."

"Don't know 'bout that. You sure seem like a lady who's got her act together to me." Bud sighed and looked away again, obviously working up to the point of his visit. A minute passed and Emma's curiosity was growing.

"It's Lireinne," Bud finally said. "Tomorrow she's getting on a plane to go to Paris, France." He raised his eyes to look at her. "With your ex-husband."

It was a body blow. Her head reeling, Emma was suddenly unable to draw a breath.

Her *heart*. Oh my God, her *heart*. Unthinking, she gripped her coffee cup in both hands, so tightly it seemed as though she could shatter it. The revelation Emma had been dreading all along hung in the air between them, loaded with the threat of her disappearing into nothing, into smoke. And Bud—he continued to gaze at her, an awful expectancy suffusing his honest face. She gasped a deep, frantic breath, then another, snatching at the air to bring it into her lungs.

You don't have to listen to this, Emma thought wildly. Raise your walls, raise them high! Tell Bud you're sorry but you can't help, get him out the door. *Then* you can fall apart.

And yet, even as panic screamed across the windy plains of Breakdown Country, Emma heard herself saying, "Oh, no, Bud." It was all her faltering tongue could manage. "Oh, no."

Bud ducked his head between his broad shoulders. "Yep. I'm 'fraid you heard right. Sorry to bring you trouble like this." He sounded miserable and almost ashamed. "I wish it weren't so, but she's set on going and won't listen to me."

"No." Emma's voice was faint as she struggled to breathe again. "No, she won't listen to anyone."

She couldn't forget that night in the truck on the way back from the mall. She could still hear Lireinne, swearing with all the passion her young heart possessed that she'd give *anything* to go to Paris. Emma, fighting to keep her head above the girl's river of wounding words, could only half listen, but still, there'd been no missing the naked desire, the longing, as Lireinne told her about the city of her dreams, a place she knew only from pictures in her French book, fashion magazines, and her posters. Con had to have known that this was the perfect bait to dangle, but how?

I'd give anything *to go. Anything.*

"It ain't good, Emma," Bud said, shaking his head. "She calls it some kind of business trip, but I don't like the look in her eyes—like she knows she's doing something wrong but ain't gonna own up to it." He sighed. "Look, the reason I come over is . . . I got to ask if your ex-husband is the kinda man to, to . . . to take advantage of a young girl. If you say he is, I mean to drive all night if I got to. Find him wherever he's at, tell him he better leave my little girl be."

Bud's big work-roughened hand spasmodically opened and closed in a fist. His square jaw taut, he seemed to wrestle with himself for a few moments. In a sudden, violent move he pounded the table, startling Emma out of her private panic.

"Can you tell me, Emma? *Is* he that kind of man? Tell me, 'cause I'm afraid for her. Please, help me out here."

Before she knew she was doing it, Emma reached across the table and placed her hand over his tightly closed one, wanting only for him to stop speaking because he was hurting her. He didn't intend to, he couldn't know, but this was too much, far too much. Con, with Lireinne. She still couldn't bring herself to face it, not completely. She wanted to get up, to leave the room and take a tranquilizer, before she remembered she'd swept them up and thrown them away weeks ago.

But Bud opened his fist and gripped her hand. She wished then he hadn't come, wishing, too, that she were capable of being equal to this. She wished for words to comfort him.

But there weren't any, and so her silence answered his question. *Is he that kind of man?*

★ ★ ★

Emma and Bud stayed at the table for another half hour, wordlessly drinking coffee. The unsaid—*yes, he is*—lay between them like a corpse until, finally, Bud put his hands over his face and rubbed his stubbled cheeks. "Oh, hell," he muttered, knuckling his eyes. He seemed so tired, so defeated.

"If only I could help," Emma said softly. In the quiet space between them, her panic had gradually passed without resorting to Xanax. She'd fought her way through the steadily ticking minutes one breath at a time, somehow arriving on the other side filled with concern for Bud's anguish and a deep, restless worry for Lireinne. "I'm so sorry."

"Not your fault." Bud said, his voice resigned. "But it wouldn't do any good, would it. Going to talk to your ex-husband, I mean." It wasn't a question.

"No." In truth, nothing would do any good.

"I'm gonna have to let my little girl go," Bud said heavily. "I got to pray she don't come to harm by him."

"That's hard," Emma said. "She's your child."

Bud tried to smile. "Lireinne's been my own kid since she was four years old, a scrappy little thing, and wild as Tiger Branch after a big rain. Always was a good girl, though, and didn't she grow up to be a real beauty?" His face turned somber. "When I couldn't talk her out of quitting school, that near 'bout broke me up inside—smart girl like that, giving up on her education. This is worse. I'd kinda hoped that her *Mr. Con* was just giving her a hand up like she said, but now I see I was mistaken. She went to New Orleans today, picking up her passport and buying herself a new winter coat. Says it's cold over there in France and she wants to look good."

"I imagine she does." Oh, Con, Emma thought sadly. So many women in the world you could have trained your attentions on, so many other girls you could have had. Couldn't you have let this one alone?

"Well, thanks for the coffee, and for listening to me." Bud got up from his chair and reached for his hat. "Guess I'll be headin' out," he

said. "Took up too much of your time already." He smiled a half-
smile for Emma then, his eyes meeting hers and lingering for a
moment. Though his shoulders were slumped, his mouth a tired, discouraged line, to Emma Bud somehow filled the room with his solid
strength: a good man, carrying a terrible burden of love and fear. She
didn't want him to leave. Not now, not like this.

"Can you stay for dinner?" Emma asked, struck by an impulse.
She had no advice for him, but she could offer the comfort of this
one thing. "Wolf's invited, too," she added quickly.

Bud smiled, shook his head, and picked up his old jacket. "Dang,
Emma. I invited myself over here this past Sunday, and you fed me
and my boy like kings. Don't mean to overstep again."

Emma rose, too, and put her hand on his arm. "Please, it's no
trouble. I'm cooking for myself anyway and . . . I'd love the company." Blushing at her unusual forwardness, still Emma knew without question that she needed to feed this man tonight—for her own
sake perhaps, if not for his. She wasn't ready to be alone again, she
thought with a shiver.

With what Emma hoped was a winsome smile, she asked,
"Please?"

"Well," Bud said slowly, "Wolf's over to his friend Bolt's house,
some kind of video-game throw-down goin' on tonight. Was looking at eating alone anyhow. Usually don't cook when it's just me, seeing as how I'm not worth much in the kitchen." This new smile
seemed to come from behind the clouds in his eyes, a hesitant, stray
beam of good humor. "Getting kinda tired of Spam."

"I can have everything ready in an hour. It's just chicken. Please,
say you'll stay."

Bud's smile broadened until he chuckled. "Lord knows you can
flat cook, Emma. Can't imagine anything you'd fix would be 'just
chicken.' I'd be pleased to join you, but you got to let me help out
some kind of way."

"Oh, wonderful!" Emma said. Her return smile brightened her
gray, gold-flecked eyes. "How good are you at peeling potatoes?"

★   ★   ★

"I don't have any beer, I'm afraid, but would you like a glass of wine while we wait?"

Walking into the front room, Emma flourished the opened bottle of chardonnay: there was plenty left over after putting the chicken to braising in garlic, butter, and wine. She put the bottle and two glasses on the low wooden blanket chest that served as her coffee table.

The chicken was simmering, the salad was made, and the gratin was in the oven. Bud had built a fire and now they were sitting on the low couch in front of the flames, enjoying the warmth as the chill retreated to the corners of the bookshelf-lined room.

"Don't know a thing about wine, but I'll try some and thank you," Bud said. With a cautious settling of his wide shoulders, he relaxed deeper into the soft cushions.

"Great. Here." Emma poured the golden chardonnay into both glasses and handed one to him. She raised her own glass and tapped it gently against Bud's with a clear *ting* of crystal. "Cheers," she said. "To . . . better times?"

"I'll drink to that." Bud took a bare taste and nodded in appreciation. "That's good," he said. "Nice change from beer—not that I'm much of a drinker, anyhow. Had me a wild youth, tore up this town like all kids do when they ain't responsible for much. I cut way back on the booze when I married Lireinne's mother and there was kids in the house. These days, a six-pack lasts me a week or more." Bud had another sip of wine.

Emma curled up on the other end of the couch, drawing her long legs underneath her. "I'm not much of a drinker myself," she confessed. "Back when I was married, Con drank enough for both of us and then, after the . . . the divorce, I was such a head case I was afraid I'd end up a raving drunk in detox, if I wasn't careful." She was silent a moment, remembering those days, but then Emma shook her head impatiently. *Be here now.* Be here now with Bud, enjoy this good feeling, and let the past lie quiet for once.

"It was a bad time for you, wasn't it," Bud said neutrally. His eyes were a deep brown, accepting as the earth of her garden.

Startled by his observation, Emma paused to think before she answered. She took a gulp of the crisp, cold wine. "You could say that," she said. "That time was, almost literally, the end of the world for me."

"You must have loved him a whole lot."

With a deep breath, Emma nodded. "I did." It was a painful admission, but at least it felt honest and clean. "Con was the world to me. When I found out who he'd really become—a serial, no, a *successful* philanderer—when he told me we were through, it was like that *Superman* movie, you know? That scene where Krypton's gravity fails, it cracks apart, and the pieces fly off into the universe in slow motion? I guess I was like that planet, orbiting around a red sun until it died." She'd never thought about it in quite that way before, but floored by the heart-striking truth of that unlikely metaphor, Emma fell silent again.

At the other end of the sofa Bud leaned forward, his arms on his knees, his wineglass cradled in both of his big hands. "You don't strike me as the kind of woman who'd love like that without a good reason," he said. "You're smart, Emma. Real smart. Educated, too. Not like me. I can be foolish sometimes. I mean, I knew Lireinne's mom had a hell of a past before she met me, but I thought if I loved her enough she'd be different, that she'd be happy being my wife. I was wrong as a man can be." He stared at his wine, seemingly lost in thought.

After a moment, Bud went on, his expression faraway. "I remember she was the prettiest girl at the Parish fair that year," he said softly. "Not even twenty-one yet, and high-spirited as a, a unbroke filly. She was laughing at everyone and everything. Seemed like a hundred fellas following her around, buying her whatever carnie crap she set her eye on. She'd already had Lireinne then, but only saw her when she had to go home to drop her off at a different relative's house. She could do what she liked then, without being held down by her own kid. I didn't know about that side of her when I decided to marry that girl or die tryin', but I was only twenty-two myself, too young and ignorant about women to know better.

"Three years later when she up and left, I come home from work to find Lireinne by herself and takin' care of her baby brother. She was only seven years old, Emma. 'Mommy's gone,' was all she said. There wasn't even a note. Finally heard from my wife's people up in Mississippi. They said she'd gone to the coast with her old boyfriend and wasn't coming back. Those folks told me I was on my own with the kids. Seems they had their hands full already and they was done with having Lireinne underfoot, much less her brother. My wife's own mother told me maybe the boy wasn't even mine, since everybody knew she'd been steppin' out on me for years. I'd been so blind in love with her I never suspected a thing. I swear I don't know what I did to that woman to make her leave, but she's gone and Lireinne and Wolf turned out to be the best part of the deal."

Emma remembered Bud's talking about his ex-wife's desertion before, and Sarah's telling her that he'd married a "trashy piece from Tylertown." That description didn't do Lireinne's mother a remote justice, she thought. Even cats didn't walk away from their kittens until they were old enough to fend for themselves.

"How did Lireinne get the scar on her eyebrow?" Emma asked. She was wondering if Bud's ex-wife had been abusive as well as desperately irresponsible, but didn't want to ask outright.

Bud looked ashamed, but he met her eyes steadily. "That was my fault. The neighbor woman who was watching the kids for me let her fall down the steps to the trailer. By the time I got home from work and drove her to the emergency room, the doctor told me there wasn't much he could do, said she was gonna need plastic surgery. Couldn't afford that. I always feel bad, lookin' at that scar. I hope Lireinne don't care about it too much."

Ah, poor Bud, Emma thought. Poor Lireinne and Wolf. She couldn't imagine how this man had managed on his own with two little children, two abandoned kids who had no one in the world but him. Her heart swelled with pity and a dawning sense that Bud Hooten was a remarkable man who'd always deserved better than what life had handed him.

She was lost in these thoughts until Bud cleared his throat. "Uh, not meaning to tell you your business or nothing, Emma, but I think I smell something burnin'."

The potatoes were browner than Emma would have liked, but Bud ate everything on his plate with a real hunger and insisted on a third helping of the slightly singed gratin.

"Best spuds I ever et," he said, wiping his lips on his napkin with evident satisfaction. "And the chicken was mighty fine, too. Thanks for the meal, Emma. It sure hit the spot."

Emma smiled happily, rose, and began to clear the table. "It was my pleasure," she said. "I'd forgotten how I love feeding a man who can really eat, and you're always such good company. I enjoyed having you here."

Bud put a gentle hand on her arm as she reached for his plate. "Would you mind leaving this for now?" he asked. "Can you do me another favor? Set here and talk with me some more? Just for a bit."

Bemused, Emma put down the plate and sat again. "Of course."

Bud rested his elbows on the table, steepled his big-knuckled fingers, and was quiet for a moment. He took a deep breath and expelled it in a gusty sigh.

"Tell me about your ex-husband," Bud said, returning his hands to the table. "Like I said before, you don't seem like a woman who'd love so hard for no reason. Give me a better idea of him, if you can, if it's not too much trouble for you. That way . . . I can maybe tell myself that he won't hurt my Lireinne."

Emma was confounded by his request. How to explain Con to him, how to explain Con to anyone? Con was a rogue comet, a man as full of contradictions as he was full of hungers. Impulsive, thoughtless and destructive, blazing with a consuming determination to capture and keep anything he wanted to possess. You could get burned when you got too close to Con.

And yet . . . she'd loved him. She'd loved his generous spirit, his unexpected, unseen kindnesses, loved the fire of his trajectory across the domed sky of her earthbound world. She'd been in love with the way he'd never let her retreat from life, but grabbed her hand and pulled her along with him instead. *Come with me, come with me.* Oh, yes—Con burned, but he burned bright, so bright you couldn't help but be drawn to the light he cast.

Would he harm Lireinne? Emma pondered this question. No, he wouldn't, not consciously. She'd finally come to understand that women were like . . . found money to Con. They were the same as hundred-dollar bills lying around in the street, waiting for anyone to pick them up and pocket them. He wouldn't manage his own appetites, and what was worse, he didn't think he should have to. Still, if Emma looked at him with a hard-won dispassion, she knew Con didn't mean to do harm any more than a wildfire did, scorching across a dry marsh.

And he'd never set out to hurt her either. Tonight, Emma could finally make her peace with that remembered pain. It had simply been Con, having his own way, only that. Emma had been so in love with him, she'd never stopped to count the possible cost of loving a nature like his, nor had she known how to stop loving him, even if she could. And yet her heart, she now understood, had in some secret part known the truth about this man all along and loved him anyway. She'd never allowed herself to accept the possibility that, inevitably, she'd be hurt.

But what about Lireinne? Emma thought again of the stony hunger in the girl's voice that night. She'd unconsciously recognized the steel cable of relentless ambition woven through the gauzy fabric of Lireinne's dreams, so like Con in that way Emma couldn't believe she'd missed it. Lireinne was going into this situation with her eyes wide open, Emma suspected, and strange as it might seem, if anyone could take on Con Costello and come out the other side not only unscathed but ahead of the game, that woman just might be eighteen-year-old Lireinne Hooten. She was powerful in her own way, like the deep, invisible current beyond the breakers, a riptide sweeping you out to sea. Emma almost smiled then, imagining Con's fire confronted with that water's power.

Slowly, feeling her way, she said, "I think . . . Con's probably met his match in your daughter. You're right to be concerned—any father would be, and with good reason—but he's not a bad man. Not really. Thoughtless and careless sometimes. A man to take advantage, yes, but . . . it's just that Con's so determined to get what he wants that he forgets someone always ends up paying a price for it. Still, I believe Lireinne's smart enough to figure that out, for all she's so young, even though she's been so damaged. I didn't know her long, but I think she's a resilient girl, one who seems to know exactly where the ground is under her feet."

And she knows exactly what she wants and won't rest until she gets it, but Emma didn't say that. These were private observations, not something Lireinne's father would want to hear.

"So," Bud said, his mouth wry. "You're sayin' my girl's prob'ly got this under control, that I shouldn't go find your ex-husband and beat the living shit out of him?"

Alarmed, Emma shook her head. "Oh, no! That would be a *bad* idea. You'd end up in jail, for one thing. And then, whatever it is that's going on between them, you won't be able to stop it anyway. Your daughter's of age, so unless you lock her up, she can do what she wants to, legally. You're going to have to trust Lireinne to look out for herself, Bud. I know that's hard to hear and even harder to do, but that's all the advice I can give you." And it was good advice for Emma, too, since there was nothing she could do about Con and Lireinne either. There never had been.

With a long look at Emma, Bud nodded.

"Thanks," he said. "I guess it's as good a recommendation as any. Can't afford getting slammed in the Parish lockup. That would purely play hell with everything, wouldn't it? And maybe you're right about Lireinne. Not to make a bad joke at his expense, but it might be ol' Mr. Con's gone and bit off a mite more than he can chew *this* time." He picked up his plate and reached for hers. "Here, let me do these dishes."

"Oh, no," Emma said, laughing. "I don't know you nearly well enough for that, Bud Hooten."

Bud frowned. "Don't seem right, you doing all the cookin' and cleaning up, too."

"I'm a stubborn woman. Sarah Fortune says so." Emma lifted an eyebrow in mock imperiousness. "I'll have you know I mean to get my way in this."

With a look of amused alarm, Bud raised his hands in surrender. "Yes, ma'am. I make it a point to let a woman have her own way no matter what, being a peaceable man by nature." He pushed back from the table. "Guess I'll be goin' then, give you your evening back. Time to head home. Four a.m. and the loading dock's going to come plenty early enough, I guess."

Seeing he meant to leave, Emma nodded with real regret, understanding that time and Walmart waited for no man. They walked out of the kitchen and into the front room where the fire had fallen into glowing embers and ash. Bud put on his jacket and picked up his hat.

"Thanks for another fine meal, Emma," he said. "And thanks for listening. I'll take what you said to heart."

Emma had to ask. "What are you going to do?"

"Love her." Bud opened the front door, and the cold north wind swept the woodsmoke's incense into the hallway. "Just love her."

Hearing that, her heart suddenly too full to contain what she felt for him, Emma shed her last inhibition. She slipped her arms under Bud's jacket, around the wide, solid warmth of his back in its flannel shirt, clasped her hands together, and held him close.

"I think you need a hug," she murmured shyly into the front of his coat.

Bud was as still as though he'd been struck with a stone. But with a low exhalation, he cupped her jaw in his hand. Lifting it gently, his brown eyes searched hers.

"Woman," he said, his voice husky. "I think you need a kiss."

Emma nodded, mute but sure of this. For once she was sure of something: she was sure she wanted Bud's kiss. The first touch of his lips told her he was a careful man, that this kiss would be sweet and chaste, but his mouth was saying something more. Emma tightened her arms around him, pressing her narrow hips to his.

"More," she sighed against his stubbled cheek. "Please, more."

And then it was. Bud's mouth covered hers again, his big hands tightening on her waist. Emma wound her arms around his neck and returned his kiss, swaying with the startling discovery of him, of her own unlooked-for desire, until Bud's hand found her breast. Her knees sagged. That intimate caress, the first time any man other than Con had touched her there, jolted her senses.

"Oh!" Emma pulled away, her eyes huge.

Bud's face reddened. "Sorry," he muttered. "Didn't mean to . . ."

Emma put a finger to his lips. "Shh. You're a very attractive man, Bud Hooten, a wonderful man. I'm hoping to see you again. Soon. I'm just not quite ready for this, not yet. I, I need to take things a bit slower, okay?" she asked softly.

His worried expression easing, Bud said, "Emma, you can see me whenever you want." He pulled her to him again, but this time his lips pressed her forehead firmly before he released her. "And now I'm going to take my leave."

Later Emma lay in her bed, alone, thinking about the evening. Con and Lireinne seemed somehow . . . not the threat she'd been so sure they were. Whatever happened, whatever regrets she might have, they were their own people and would do as they would.

Remembering Bud was better. Whenever you want. Emma smiled and turned over, settling herself for a sleep she knew would be deep and without dreams.

Whenever you want.

CHAPTER 21

In the First Class cabin, the captain announced it was 8:30 Thursday morning, Paris time. As though the air were a staircase, the big 767 was descending through zero-visibility white clouds. So thick was the fog, Lireinne's first glimpse of France was of the impossibly green grass of the airfields rushing up to greet her.

And then as the plane continued to descend, my God, look at the *rabbits,* she thought in amazement. She could hardly believe what she was seeing. There were hundreds of rabbits, many hundreds, bounding madly through that emerald sea of grass, starling-like in their sweeping patterns. But then the airport appeared in all its massiveness and Lireinne forgot the rabbits. So many planes, so many buildings! Like JFK, De Gaulle was way too big to take in at a single glance.

"Thank God, we made it," she murmured. She rubbed her gritty eyes, exhausted from the long hours of travel. She hadn't slept at all, positive that if she closed her eyes the plane would fall out of the sky. Lireinne turned to her boss in the seat beside her.

"Mr. Con, we made it!"

But just as he had been for the past several hours of the transatlantic flight, Mr. Con was passed out, snoring even as the wheels grabbed the ground with a rough thud and the plane shuddered with a *whoosh* of reversed engines. The white-bandaged hand rested in his lap. How could he sleep through this? Lireinne marveled. Although it was the second landing of her life, and somehow she'd survived the first one, she braced herself against the back of the roomy seat, gripping the armrests like floating spars in a rough sea. Her entire body was held rigid and tensed against the g-force of deceleration. What if the plane didn't stop? What if it slammed into some wall somewhere and everybody on board died in a fireball?

But just as the first plane had done on their flight from New Orleans to JFK, this plane was slowing now; the landing had gone without a hitch. Lireinne let go of the armrests, rubbing her cramped hands. She was alive, she'd be in Paris soon, and the confusing, anxious sixteen hours of travel to get here had been worth every minute.

While the plane taxied to the terminal, all the passengers began to stir in the First Class cabin and started gathering their belongings— all except for Lireinne and her boss. She didn't want to try to wake him in front of all these high rollers in this exclusive section of the plane, unsure what he'd be like after he'd been unconscious for so long. Mr. Con had taken two of his pills just a few hours ago and washed them down with a double scotch. This was on top of the previous pills and scotches at the Red Carpet Club in the United terminal during their layover. Lireinne had been unhappy about that, sure that she wouldn't be able to navigate their passage to the gate by herself if he got any more messed up than he already was, but somehow Mr. Con had pulled himself together. He seemed to sleepwalk through the boarding process and onto the plane in time for takeoff. As soon as the plane was in the air, though, he'd started drinking again.

"Champagne, Lireinne?" he'd asked her when the stewardess came for their drink order. "It'll help you relax. Maybe you can get some sleep on the flight." His eyes were sweet and a little unfocused as he patted her knee. "It's the best way to pass the time, unless you like watching movies on a small screen."

Trembling from the stress of another takeoff, Lireinne accepted a foaming glass of champagne from the flight attendant and finished it in about three big gulps. She was surprised to find out he was right:

it did help. So when Mr. Con began to nod off, Lireinne figured out how to select a film from the menu and watched it happily until their dinner came: some kind of fish the stewardess told her was sea bass and tiny baby vegetables in a savory, buttery sauce. Mr. Con slept through the movie and the meal. He woke up somewhere over the Atlantic, asked Lireinne to get him another double scotch and took some more pills, saying his hand hurt. He slept through the breakfast of a croissant and coffee, too.

The plane was docking now, all the other people were lining up to get off the plane, and still he slept. They were the last seated passengers in the First Class section. Lireinne bit her lip and shook his shoulder timidly.

"Mr. Con?" she whispered. "You have to wake up now. We're here."

He opened one sea-blue, bloodshot eye. "Lireinne," he said, his voice soft and slurred. "Y'ready to get off this dam' plane, honey?" With a big yawn reeking of stale whiskey, he fumbled at his seat belt with his right hand. "Got th' yella cards?"

Relieved, Lireinne nodded. He'd snored through the part about the cards. She'd filled out both of their embarkation forms with some help from one of the attendants since she was terrified that she was going to make a mistake and then wouldn't be allowed off the plane, but had soon realized it wasn't that difficult anyway. Names, addresses, reason for coming to France: that was all there was to it.

Gathering her purse and passport, she stood now, reached into the overhead bin, and pulled down their bags and Mr. Con's briefcase. She put on her new coat and tucked the First Class envelope of travel-sized toiletries carefully inside her purse. They were free.

Mr. Con rubbed his face. "'Kay," he said with another big yawn. He staggered to his feet. "Less do this." Taking his briefcase from her with his right hand, he almost dropped it on the floor of the plane. "Whoops."

Watching him weave unsteadily down the aisle behind the last First Class passenger, Lireinne worried that he might not make it off the plane after all before he fell down or lost his luggage. With a determined frown, she grabbed their bags and hurried to take his case, too.

"Let me carry that," she said. "You're tired, and I bet your hand's hurting."

His briefcase safely in hand, Lireinne slung her carry-on and his suit bag over her shoulder and gripped Mr. Con's elbow to help steady him. She ignored the raised eyebrows of the flight attendants waiting for them at the door to the plane.

"This way, Mr. Con," Lireinne muttered firmly as he bumped into the bulkhead.

After emerging from the tunnel into the immigration area, Mr. Con's balance seemed to get a little better as he walked, although she almost lost him several times in the dense, shuffling crowds waiting in the long immigration lines.

As wiped out as she was, Lireinne's heart pounded at the press of humanity massed around her. Weighed down by the luggage, she held tight to Mr. Con's coat sleeve, intimidated by everybody. Those must be women underneath those dark bedsheets—shapeless, ambulatory bundles of fabric with only their kohl-rimmed eyes and tennis shoes showing. Like herds of obedient goats, these silent, alien females followed a step behind bearded men in patterned headscarves, black suits, and tons of gold jewelry. And just like her, the women were carrying the luggage even though the men seemed perfectly fine to Lireinne. It must be a foreign custom, she thought.

Foreign was everywhere. Lireinne averted her eyes, trying not to gape at the tall, dark-skinned couple in long, bright-colored robes and ropes of stone beads, a proud man and woman with aquiline features who looked nothing like the few black people she'd seen around town back home. It wasn't like there weren't any black folks there, but in Covington they had their own neighborhoods and stores. These people seemed like some kind of aloof African royalty. And were those Russians? Lireinne couldn't stop staring at the burly men bundled into fur coats and big wolf-skin hats. There were a thousand other strangers: strange clothes, strange faces, speaking strange languages and smelling of strange, exotic lands, all of them waiting in varying degrees of patience for their turns at the Plexiglas booths of the immigration officers.

Mr. Con weaved through this milling crush as though he were pushed along by the crowd, but he mumbled answers to the busy officer's questions and got their passports stamped. Somehow he got them through the nothing-to-declare line at Customs as well, and Lireinne was desperately grateful when they finally passed into the United Airlines hub—grateful until Mr. Con suddenly stopped. They were in the midst of the sea of hurrying people, those loaded with suitcases, those pushing carts piled with cartons of TVs, microwaves, and other improbable burdens. Dozens of men holding cardboard signs with important-looking names written on them, arriving passengers, departing passengers, and briskly moving airline personnel dragging their wheeled bags behind them like fat, lazy dogs—everybody was moving through the terminal purposefully, except for them.

Mr. Con reached into his coat pocket for his vial of pills, a new one that was easier to open and close, and shook it.

"Gotta take care a business, swee'heart," he mumbled. "Wait, uh, here." With a vague wave of his bandaged hand, he wandered away before he disappeared into the crowds.

Couldn't he have waited for his pills for once? Lireinne wondered in a fresh panic. Where had he gone? She was alone now, no longer in America where everybody spoke English. Lireinne had never known she could feel so alone, so freaked, not even on the first day of high school when she'd gotten lost in the unfamiliar building, tons bigger and so much more confusing than middle school had been. She pushed her hair out of her eyes with a shaking hand. Mr. Con's suit bag and her own carry-on were parked at her feet on the grimy floor because her shoulders were aching. Lireinne didn't dare leave the luggage to go in search of him, the only person she knew in this vast place. Paris was full of thieves. Mr. Con had warned her about them back in the Red Carpet Club, back when he was still making sense. For long, tense minutes, Lireinne waited in intimidated silence, praying her boss would come back soon.

Wait—there he was! Mr. Con was wandering toward her through the throngs, looking a little better. His head was up at least, and his smile was confident. Sometimes the pills worked that way. He'd act more like himself for a while, but Lireinne had learned to her exasperation that this seeming lucidity wouldn't last for long.

"Taxi." Mr. Con said only that as he rejoined her, as though speaking was an effort. His gaze was as glassy as a blue-tinted windshield. "Gotta get a taxi outside."

As if he'd overheard that mumbled observation, an olive-skinned man with broken teeth approached them as they walked to the big doors leading to the sidewalk outside of the terminal. "Taxi?" he said. "You want taxi, I got taxi." He reached to grab their bags, but Mr. Con waggled his finger at the man in admonishment.

"No, no." That was all he said, but immediately the man rushed off to ambush another confused-looking couple, two of the few people in this place who looked like they might be Americans to Lireinne.

"We go now, you bet!" The olive-skinned man tried to grab their luggage, too. Maybe he was trying to steal it from them? Afraid to take her eyes away from him, Lireinne held her carry-on, Mr. Con's suit bag, and his briefcase close to her. She wondered if she could fight the man off if he came back, but the American couple was following him now, their luggage in his hands. She hoped they'd be okay.

"Damn Algerian gypsy cab, can't take one a *them*," Mr. Con said owlishly. "Thieves. Take you t'hell n'back." Lireinne wondered if he meant the man was a real Gypsy like the ones back home who stole stuff from the front yard when no one was home, but Mr. Con was moving again. "C'mon, baby," he said. With a helpless shake of her head, like a laden burro Lireinne followed his wandering back to the doors marked *Sortie*.

Outside the airport the air smelled different, it smelled . . . it smelled of jet fuel and bus exhaust and cigarettes—everyone, it seemed, was smoking—but none of these familiar odors were exactly it. The cold, damp air was different in a way Lireinne would have been hard-pressed to explain, but for sure it was nothing like the air back home. French air, she thought, a surge of elation dispelling her fatigue. Waiting in line at the taxi stand in the diffuse yet crystalline sunlight of a northern latitude in October, she inhaled deeply and often, wanting to fix this moment in her mind for forever. Lireinne knew she would never forget this if she lived a hundred years. When she was an old woman, she'd remember the intoxicating scent of her first breath of France.

It smelled like . . . adventure.

Once in the taxi, Mr. Con slept the whole way into Paris.

It took nearly an hour to pass beyond the city's bleak industrial outskirts, all the unfamiliar white French road signs flashing past before Lireinne could manage to read them through the grimy window. It seemed to her then that the Paris of her dreams was merely a made-up story, a lie. These gray tower apartment buildings with the laundry hanging from their windows, these smoke-belching factories and warehouses: as far as she could see, all was grim and forbidding, nothing like the pictures she'd pored over for years. Right before Lireinne began to despair of ever seeing the real Paris, with no warning the wordless cab driver muscled the cab across four lanes of terrifying traffic, swooped down a ramp, and they were off the Périphérique and onto a busy Paris street.

The driver turned soon and with a thrill Lireinne recognized the tree-lined, cobblestoned streets of the Champs-Élysées from the *Vogue* photo shoot on the wall of her bedroom back home. It *is* real, she thought, awed. The taxi hurtled down the bumpy surface too fast for her to take it all in—the well-dressed people hurrying to work, people walking dogs, people on bicycles, people carrying shopping bags and briefcases and bunches of flowers and cups of coffee— just another Thursday morning for them, but they were *Parisians*. Lireinne stared at these incredibly lucky folks, enrapt with fascination and trying to imagine their lives.

But there, up ahead—l'Arc de Triomphe! Her face pressed to the window, Lireinne's sleep-deprived eyes widened at the majesty of the

high stone arch while the cab rattled around the Arc's immense traffic circle, a fast-moving steel whirlpool of at least two hundred other
cars. Horns blared; a police car's siren wailed a repetitive klaxon. A
couple on a motorcycle cut in front of the taxi so narrowly that it
seemed the young biker had a death wish for himself and the pretty
girl riding pillion behind him.

The taxi driver muttered some foreign curse and laid on his horn
just as he spun out of the circle, turning left onto another beautiful,
tree-lined street. Lireinne almost missed the small blue street sign on
the stone building on the corner. They were on the Avenue Montaigne.

In the backseat of the taxi, the names on the shops lining the
avenue—Prada, Gucci, Jimmy Choo, and Fendi—appeared and were
gone, almost too quickly for Lireinne to recognize. But, she thought,
these were the real stores, not just pages in a magazine. In the icy
early-morning light, people were rolling up security gates and rolling
down awnings, getting ready to start their day selling fabulous things
to fabulous people, and she, Lireinne Hooten, high-school dropout
and ex-hoser, was *here*.

In the next block, an elegant granite building with red awnings
was coming up on their left. The taxi slowed, rolling to a stop with
a screech of worn brakes in front of an ornate glass-canopied entrance. Peering through the fogged window of the cab, Lireinne
stared openmouthed at the flower boxes overflowing with masses of
scarlet geraniums, the lacy black wrought-iron balconies, and flutter-
ing flags. Could *this* be their hotel? It looked like something out of
one of Miss Penny's fairy tales, a palace.

"Voilà la Plaza Athénée," the cab driver announced, turning off
the meter. *"Cent dix euros."*

Euros? She remembered enough French to understand how
much money the driver wanted, but Lireinne had no idea what a
euro was or where to get any. Since Mr. Con was still sleeping, she
nudged him until his eyes opened.

"Mr. Con, the driver wants a hundred and ten euros."

With a snort, Mr. Con sat up straighter on the backseat, blinking. "Whazzis? A hunnerd and ten?" He patted his jacket's breast pocket and swore. "Dammit, forgot to change money at th' airport."

The taxi driver stared through the windshield as though he were deaf. He didn't turn around, ignoring Mr. Con, who was unsuccessfully trying to use a credit card.

"*Cent dix euros,*" the man repeated loudly. It didn't seem that a credit card was going to be an option and, in the middle of this going-nowhere exchange, Lireinne's door opened. A hot-looking guy in a smart gray uniform bowed in welcome. With a finger to the brim of his gold-braided black hat, he held the door open for her.

"*Bienvenue á la Plaza Athénée, mademoiselle.*"

"*Bonjour.*" Oh, wow—she was speaking French to a Parisian person! Lireinne's smile was luminous as she climbed out of the taxi.

When he rose from his bow and subtly studied her, the uniformed young man raised one eyebrow. Giving her a respectful glance, he nodded his head once in obvious approval. Lireinne was pleased to discover that she'd been right to wear her nicest work clothes—the gray skirt, white blouse, black stockings, and a new pair of heels—for the trip, no matter that Mr. Con had told her she could wear jeans.

"Is it that the young lady is visiting Paris? You are American, yes?"

Beginning to feel uncomfortable under his scrutiny, Lireinne tried not to blush because the hot guy's appraisal seemed to calculate down to the dime how much she'd paid for the black wool coat with the princess seams from Banana Republic (on sale, of course) and her new black suede pumps. Now she wished she'd bought a new purse, too, because she'd owned this battered old shoulder bag since high school. Still, the uniformed man was smiling so she must have just passed some kind of French test.

And then Mr. Con half fell out of the backseat and staggered onto the sidewalk. The hot guy's expression changed almost imperceptibly, his solicitous smile turning into a suggestion of a leer.

"*Bienvenue, m'sieur.* You and . . . the young *lady* are guests of the Plaza Athénée, no?"

Sounding distracted, Mr. Con muttered, *"Oui."* He turned to Lireinne and shook his head. "Gotta change money inside, 'kay? Wait here with th' valet. Be right back." He lurched up the stairs and through the shining glass-and-brass doors of the hotel, leaving her alone outside with the now openly smirking valet while the taxi driver unloaded their bags from the trunk.

The driver dropped the luggage at her feet before he and the uniformed man exchanged complicit smiles. The two of them rattled off a stream of French that Lireinne found impossible to follow. They both glanced at her with oily grins, as if they knew something she didn't.

"What?" Lireinne demanded, feeling more uncomfortable than ever.

"The young lady, she is an *escort,* is she not?" This time the valet's eyes were like fingers, roaming her body through her coat. In spite of being determined to maintain her tenuous poise, Lireinne colored, creeped out by both his change of attitude and his incomprehensible question.

"Non," she replied haughtily. An escort? What the hell did he mean by that? But before she could think of the words to explain in her halting French that she was in Paris on important business, that she was here with her *boss,* Mr. Con pushed through the doors and hurried down the stairs.

"Voilà," he said to the cab driver as he handed him a bunch of bills. To the young man in the gray uniform, he said, *"Merci,"* and as if it were the most natural thing in the world, he took Lireinne by the elbow. "C'mon, sweetheart." She allowed him to lead her up the steps into the hotel, but in the doorway she looked back over her shoulder, down at the young man on the sidewalk.

Now there could be no mistaking the superior, knowing glint in his eyes: the valet, like the women at the alligator farm, had assumed she was Mr. Con's whore. Lireinne raised her chin and coldly narrowed her eyes at him, but she broke into a light sweat walking into the reception area of the Plaza Athénée on Con Costello's arm. The immense flower arrangements—thousands of breathtaking blossoms in old-looking silver urns—the echoing marble floors, deep-pile carpets, and cascading chandeliers of brilliant prisms greeted her, but Lireinne, her heart a stone inside her chest, stood in the middle of this incredible luxury without seeing it.

Why did everyone always seem to think that about her? Why?

Mr. Con was at the reception desk, checking them in. Lireinne waited for him, wondering if she'd made a terrible mistake in coming here. Home was across a whole ocean, and suddenly, even though they hadn't parted on the best of terms, she desperately wanted the comfort of Bud's voice telling her that she was doing fine, honey. But Bud wasn't here: he didn't know how it felt.

So get over it, she told herself with an inward shake of her shoulders. She was in *Paris*. It doesn't matter what the asshole car-park guy thought about her any more than what those bitches at the farm thought.

But somehow . . . it did matter.

It always had.

A cold bottle of champagne was waiting for them in the flower-filled suite, as well as a silver tray laden with a small urn of steaming coffee, a pot of hot milk, and a plate of pastries. Lireinne didn't want any of it. She was still thinking about the scene with the valet, her stomach hollow with the memory of her humiliation, but Mr. Con slugged back two cups of coffee while waiting on the bellman to deliver their luggage.

During the time he was on the phone with somebody named Julien, Lireinne wandered the suite for a few minutes, then unpacked and put her clothes away in the smaller of the two lavishly appointed bedrooms. The delicate gilded armchair and even the walls were upholstered in a soft peach silk, the sage-green curtains at the window drawn open to the morning. Lireinne found herself smiling as she explored the separate bathroom in giddy wonder, touching the super-soft white towels piled on the edge of the deep soaking tub. Her old toothbrush and few Dollar General cosmetics looked out of place and forlorn on the marble sink's edge, but Lireinne didn't mind. For the next four days, this crazy-rich space was for her, just her, and she could lock her door, just as she'd planned. Cheered, she went back out into the sitting room.

To her relief, Lireinne found that the coffee seemed to have woken Mr. Con up some. His eyes were sharper, he wasn't slurring his words anymore, and if he'd been displeased at not being in his regular suite, if he was unhappy about the second bedroom, he didn't mention it. Maybe he'd misspoken, maybe he'd always meant for her to have her own bed. Lireinne hoped that was true.

If not, well, there was that lock on the door.

"Champagne?" Mr. Con said. "You'll need to open it, honey." He waved his left hand. "Some things are still beyond me, I'm afraid."

Champagne sounded like a good idea, Lireinne thought, remembering how it had calmed her nerves on the plane. "Sure, Mr. Con. I'll get it." Stripping off the bottle's foil was easy. How to get it open was something of a mystery at first, but soon she figured out how to twist the cork free with a muted pop and a spill of effervescent champagne, just the way they did it on TV.

"I'll pour." Mr. Con took the bottle from her and filled both their glasses. "Coffee and champagne. Best cure for jet lag in the free world." He handed Lireinne the crystal flute and said, "Welcome to Paris, darling."

Darling. Honey. Sweetheart.

Lireinne drained her glass, barely tasting it.

"Here. Have another." Mr. Con took her glass and refilled it.

After a moment's hesitation—was he trying to get her drunk?— she took it from him. The bubbles tickled the inside of her nose as she took a small swallow, and maybe it was just the effects of the champagne, but Lireinne's apprehension retreated for the moment as she savored the smooth taste of the Taittinger on her tongue.

It was just after ten in the morning and she was drinking champagne in a suite that astounded her with its comfort and luxury wherever she turned. Whatever happened next, Lireinne told herself, she'd find a way to make this trip work somehow. Like, what was the worst Mr. Con could do if she had to refuse to sleep with him? Send her home? Lireinne took another sip of champagne, wondering if he'd do that. To be in Paris at last, and then to lose all this would be so much worse than never having come at all. She didn't know if she'd ever get over the disappointment. With that thought, suddenly, Lireinne was dying to go out into the city and explore, to snatch as much of Paris as she could before it might be lost to her.

"Hey, sugar," Mr. Con said. "Come on out. You're going to love this." He opened the long glass doors onto the small balcony over-looking the bustling Avenue Montaigne below.

Oh, *yes*. Putting her concerns aside, Lireinne joined him. If she leaned over the slender ironwork railing, she could just make out the black silhouette of the Eiffel Tower in the distance. Between the sight of that faraway, evocative structure and the lack of sleep, the whirl-wind of change she'd experienced within the last twenty hours and the champagne, it seemed as though Lireinne was in the middle of some fantastic, please-don't-wake-me-up kind of dream. But she was really here, this was no dream, this was no picture in a magazine. It was like hearing the joyous, first notes of a symphony, thrumming deep in her bones, calling to her with love.

And it was then that Lireinne fell forever in love with Paris, her heart opening wide to the city with a wondering adoration. Months later she would learn this life-changing instant was what the French called a *coup de foudre*—a thunderclap—but this morning she was stricken silent.

"Gorgeous view, isn't it?" Mr. Con slipped his arm around her waist, his right hand resting lightly on her hip. Lireinne froze. Please don't ruin it, she begged silently. Trying not to be obvious, she slipped away, moving as far from him as she could on the tiny balcony with-out backing herself into a corner.

"You all right?" Mr. Con asked. He gave her a concerned look.

Lireinne wished she were older and more experienced, that she knew how to deflect this alarming attention. "I guess I can't believe I'm really here yet," she said, thinking quickly.

Mr. Con's handsome face relaxed, softening into an easy smile. "Oh, that's just the jet lag. Look, I've got a meeting over on the Rue

Saint-Honoré in about forty-five minutes. Why don't you try to take a nap while I'm gone? Later on, after you wake up, you might want to go out and do some shopping, but I'll be back for you around six this evening. We'll go to dinner at eight. Hope you like oysters. There's a great place not far from here where the *fines declaires* are the best in the whole damned city." Mr. Con reached into the breast pocket of his jacket and got out his wallet. "Here."

To Lireinne's surprise, he pressed a handful of brightly colored notes into her hand. It was funny-looking money with colorful pictures on it, oddly insubstantial to the touch. It felt nothing like the almost greasy heft of dollar bills.

"That's seven hundred euros, about five hundred bucks or so," Mr. Con said. "Why don't you head down to the Avenue after your nap, go shopping." He finished his glass of champagne with a grin and a flourish. "And now I'm off to shave and change." He took a confident step toward Lireinne, and before she'd realized what he was doing, he pressed a quick kiss to the scar on her forehead.

"You're so pretty this morning. Rest up, baby. See you later."

Mr. Con was whistling when he went back inside the suite.

Feeling as though she'd gotten a Get Out of Jail Free card, Lireinne stayed behind on the balcony, thrilled to be alone at last with Paris. The Eiffel Tower was still there; in the street below the cars flowed and a man called out a greeting to someone. *Bonjour!* Lireinne breathed a huge sigh of contented fulfillment. She leaned her elbows on the railing, her empty glass clasped loosely in her fingers, and lifted her face to the day.

Champagne, this totally amazing suite, and all of Paris at her feet—despite having crossed an ocean only to find that the word whore had followed her here, despite Mr. Con's insane and deeply worrisome *thing* for her, Lireinne's spirits soared as high as the flock of burbling pigeons over her head.

CHAPTER 22

"That's bullshit, Julien, and you know it," Con said, doing his best not to give up and just throw something. He'd been at this for hours and he needed another dose of Vicodin. Soon.

In the wide-windowed atelier, the burlap-covered walls glowed with the tannery's collection of exotic skins. They were dyed every color imaginable: viridian-green ostrich, cerise python, lemon-yellow crocodile, fine-scaled lizard in Phoenician purple and shining gold, stingray in a lucent, starry ebony. The twelve-foot cerulean-blue alligator skin, though, lying across the immense mahogany conference table, dominated the room with an elegant, stupendous savagery.

Julien snorted Gallic derision. "Bullshit, eh? I think not."

Up till now the negotiations had been going better than Con had dared hope, but the devil, as they say, was in the details. Contrary to their reputation as surrender monkeys, the French were sticking to their guns: the last shipment of flawless alligator hides had been, in fact, less than flawless, and Julien, that sly bastard, was using that unfortunate shipment as leverage to drive down the current deal. Predictably, Roger had been furious when Con called him during a break in the meeting to bring him up to date—"Tell 'em I said *hail* no!"—

so it was back to the salt mines of guile and argument for the rest of the afternoon.

Although his left hand muttered and growled, Con hadn't taken any more Vicodin since earlier that morning because he needed every ounce of wit and Obi-Wan skills at his disposal so he wouldn't get skinned alive. He needed this deal to happen *today*.

"Give me a fucking break, Julien."

Looking as smug as though the cards in his hand were all aces, Julien raised his eyebrow and wagged a finger at Con. "Hah! I am thinking you are the one with the bullshit, Costello. What do you call that last lot of crap?" The skepticism on his long-nosed, saturnine face turned to amused contempt. "Twenty percent of the shipment was not of the premiere grade and had to be sold to the Japanese for a loss. That, *mon ami,* is the bullshit."

Although privately Con had to admit Julien had a legitimate complaint, he wasn't going to give anything away. He couldn't. It was coming down to that inevitable crossroads, the crux of the deal, and Con was going to have to bring it home without consulting his boss. Drumming the fingers of his right hand on the conference table, he realized the moment had come. Roger was going to hate what he'd have to do to make the transaction happen, he knew it.

But ol' Rog wasn't here.

After a long, tension-filled minute, Con made his own move. "Look," he said. "I've got my instructions from Mr. Hannigan. He's not going to budge an inch. There's no room for a discount, not on this deal. *But,*" Con emphasized, playing his hole card, "if you agree to buy another twenty thousand eight-foot skins before the end of the year, I can offer you a small reduction on the price per centimeter— say, three percent?"

Con had the fingers of his good right hand crossed, praying that Julien would fold his own cards and take the offer. It wasn't an ideal solution, but Roger would just have to live with it: this French tannery *was* the market for eight-foot hides. It wasn't like SGE would do any better trying to sell them someplace else, and would probably take a loss. The taut atmosphere in the room held its breath as Julien gazed out the wide windows of the atelier, tapping his aquiline beak of a nose with a manicured forefinger.

Con was beginning to sweat, but he was determined to remain outwardly unperturbed. This was the moment, the precise circumstances, where his talent excelled. This was the kill. Julien's silence might be hell on his nerves, but sometimes silence was an ally. When you're holding a pair of nines, Con reminded himself, you play it like you've got four queens. Better yet, five queens. Certainly Julien didn't have all the aces: Con had one of his own. This morning on the way to the meeting, he'd done his homework, making some discreet calls to his contacts in Italy. The word in the industry was that just days before, the tannery had signed a contract with Luigi Spada, a brash and sometimes outré Italian designer. Young Spada needed a boatload of eight-foot hides for his new line of motorcycle jackets, thigh-high boots, and trench coats. There was even a rumor of an alligator-skin wedding gown, the centerpiece of the new collection. Julien would have to purchase a whole warehouse of new inventory to honor *that* contract.

Con craved his pills, couldn't wait for them much longer, but at this point in the negotiations it was necessary to give his opponent enough time to weigh the lucrative Spada deal against the tannery's recent loss. In his coat pocket, the Vicodin wheedled promises of relief, but he endured the pain with a stoicism that was beginning to feel heroic.

Finally, after an interminable minute more, Julien swiveled his chair back to the table, facing Con. Lighting a cigarette, he gave him the big nod.

"Done, then," Julien acknowledged. "Done, you skin-dealing thief, but this means I must eat some shit with my boss. You owe me one, as you say." He extended his hand. "*Enfin,* it's after four and the day is finished. Let us shake on this deal and go get *un verre,* a drink, before I take you to dinner, yes?"

Con grasped Julien's hand and pumped it once. He'd pulled it off, the Jedi Knight had come through again, and pain be damned. Ready to crow his victory to the adjacent Saint-Honoré slate rooftops and swallow his pills besides, Con found an easy smile instead.

"A drink sounds good, but I've already got dinner plans. Maybe another time?" Even if Con hadn't already made the reservation at Marius et Janette, a world-class seafood restaurant on the Avenue George V, he didn't want to share Lireinne with anyone tonight. For Julien's part, it wasn't as though he would object to the company of a *petite amie*. Like so many French power players, he'd accept Con's girlfriend as a charming addition to the evening, although he never brought a woman of his own to an after-hours business dinner. This was unusual, sufficiently so that Con had speculated perhaps Julien wasn't into girls—that, or else Julien was damned discreet. Throughout the two years Con had known him, he'd never once discussed his love life, and in the male-dominated skin business this reticence alone made Julien something of an odd bird.

Odd bird or not, dinner with Julien would keep. Tonight Con meant to celebrate a much more special event than the mere successful conclusion of a huge deal. Tonight would be waiters in white aprons bearing great silver trays of oysters. It would be Iranian caviar and blinis, flaming desserts and cold champagne. Con would command anything, however costly, to delight Lireinne's senses, for dinner would be a prelude to love. Afterward, they'd return to the privacy of the hotel suite. There, the rest of the night was going to be all he'd dreamed of and more. So much more.

The two men rose, buttoning their coats, and gathered the papers scattered across the brilliant blue monster-hide on the conference table.

Julien said, "I have heard of your misadventure, Costello. What a terrible thing! How goes it with your . . ." He gestured at Con's bandaged hand with a sympathy unusual for him.

"The skin business is a small world, I suppose," Con said. He'd known people were going to spread his grim story throughout the industry, but that didn't mean he had to like it. "It goes as it goes, you know?" He shoved his left hand in his trouser pocket, out of sight.

"You will be better soon, yes?"

Con grinned, thinking of the girl waiting for him back at the Plaza Athénée. "Much better, my friend. Soon I shall be very much better indeed."

"*Bon.* Let us go find that drink. We finish our business tomorrow, yes?"

After a round of double scotches with Julien at the bar in the Hôtel de Crillon (and a couple of Vicodin in the men's room), Con paid the bill, shrugged into his overcoat, and went outside into the cold, pale-violet air of the Place Vendôme.

During his latest appointment with that little son-of-a-bitch Binnings, the plastic surgeon had declared the operations had been as much of a success as could be hoped. Con was healing, although the deformed hand was every bit as hideous as he'd feared it would be— a grotesque claw. Lireinne was made of more compassionate stuff than Liz, though. She wouldn't be sickened by him. Not my Lireinne, Con thought with a confident smile.

It was time for that victory cigar. The fresh bandage on his left hand was considerably less bulky, freeing his thumb and index finger, and so with only a little trouble Con unwrapped the cigar and lit it. Shoving his left hand back out of sight into his overcoat pocket, he set out on his solitary walk back to the Plaza Athénée.

This late Thursday afternoon the Place Vendôme was filled with throngs of soignée shoppers, all hurrying home from the Rue Saint-Honoré, all carrying glossy, tastefully appointed bags of designer swag. The Arabs were out in force, too, roaming like well-heeled Armani-suited nomads across the vast stone space. There were the ubiquitous bundled-up tourists wearing fanny packs with their maps and cameras in hand, and the pretty shopgirls in fur-trimmed coats and stilettos heading to their shared one-room apartments at the end of their working day. Con paused beneath the obelisk to admire them, the long-legged beauties passing him in pairs, chattering in rapid French.

The thin, lavender-tinted light was just beginning to fade into indigo dusk. Glowing lights from the ground-floor shop windows fell onto the cobblestones in pools of yellow. Con sauntered the perimeter of the Place enjoying his cigar, gray smoke a thin, acrid plume trailing behind him. The excellent scotch and his pills had filled him with a crackling-warm sense of well-being, further fueled by the satisfaction of having prevailed. Like an alchemist, once again he'd effected a miracle: what had been dross metal had come out of the crucible as gold. As was the case in most negotiations, it was true that nobody was getting a hundred percent of what they wanted. Without a doubt Roger would be less than ecstatic about the terms of the new skin contract. But a deal, Con thought, was still a deal.

As Julien had put it over their second drink at the Crillon, "When the foxes quarrel over the chicken, the farmer still has the shotgun, eh, Costello?"

The October evening was turning colder. There might be frost on the statues, a thin rime of ice edging the fountains' basins by to-morrow morning. The last of the daylight had disappeared behind the roofs of the surrounding tall stone buildings when Con stopped in front of the display window at Chopard. The venerable store was an undisputed icon of opulence even among the exclusive ground-floor jewelers of the Place Vendôme. Last spring in Paris, Con had bought Liz her diamond solitaire earrings at Chopard, and this eve-ning the gold watches, emerald rings, ruby bracelets, and the magnif-icent necklace of tawny topaz and rich amethysts caught both his eye and his imagination.

On the other side of the window, the saleswoman in her severely chic black dress and smooth chignon was removing the displayed merchandise, preparing for the store's closing. Con tapped at the window to get her attention.

Startled, the saleswoman looked up from the gray velvet tray of jewelry. One impeccably drawn eyebrow arched in a silent question. *"Oui?"* her crimson lips mouthed. Con pointed to the canopied en-trance where another saleswoman was in the process of locking the doors, then pointed to himself with a quizzical tilt of his head.

"S'il vous plaît?" His cigar between his teeth, with a charming smile he gestured at the doors, the fingers of his right hand miming

walking inside. The saleswoman seemed uncertain. Con kissed the tips of his fingers with an admiring nod for the older woman, trusting his talent to do the rest.

With a slowly dawning smile, she nodded in emphatic agreement. *Mais oui!* Grinning, Con stubbed his cigar out in one of the ilex-planted stone urns flanking the entrance and strolled into Chopard, a conquering prince ready to take the spoils of war.

When Con returned to the suite, Lireinne wasn't there.

Night had fallen and he'd expected her to be waiting for him. He wasn't truly worried, though, not yet. She was only eighteen and on her own in Paris, a huge, confusing city, but she was probably still out shopping on the Avenue Montaigne. Lireinne would return soon.

But thirty minutes passed and so, killing time, Con called down to room service for another bottle of Taittinger to settle his growing unease. While he waited, he paced the sitting room, fingering the bottle in his pocket like a plastic talisman. Con managed to resist the Vicodin's seductive call, telling himself he could hold out against it. The quiet in the suite became increasingly oppressive, though, so he turned on the radio to keep him company: he'd always found French TV to be, for the most part, incomprehensible.

At 6:15, the waiter had delivered the champagne and was opening it when Lireinne came back. Hearing the click of her key in the lock, Con's rigidly held shoulders sagged, releasing a tension that had been growing more unbearable the longer he waited for her return. His girl was home, unscathed. But to Con's surprise, when Lireinne walked inside the sitting room she wasn't carrying the armfuls of shopping bags he'd expected—or anything else, for that matter. Only her old purse was in her hand. But her green eyes were shining, her hair was windblown, and her creamy cheeks were flushed pink from the cold.

"Where've you been, sweetheart?" Con said. "I was getting worried." He tipped the waiter, whose eyes had widened in appreciation when Lireinne entered the room.

"Merci, m'sieur." The older man sneaked another glance at

Lireinne on his way out. *"Bonsoir, mademoiselle."* With a suggestion of a bow, the waiter backed out of the door to the suite and shut it behind him.

"Is it late? I didn't notice, but oh, Mr. Con!" Lireinne's face was radiant as she slipped her black coat off her shoulders. "I gotta tell you. The taxi driver was, like, *so* freaking funny. When I tried to tell him I wanted to see the Eiffel Tower, I used the wrong verb—*voler,* to steal, and not *voyer,* to see—and he, like, totally lost it." Lireinne's helpless laugh was as welcome as well-loved music to Con's overstretched nerves.

"How so?" He couldn't take his eyes off her, making a mental note to speak to her about being out after dark in Paris, how dangerous it could be for a young girl, alone.

Lireinne explained, "I'd said I wanted to steal the Eiffel Tower! So, this cab driver says, 'Mademoiselle will need a much bigger bag to hide it in.' I had to crack up, too, 'cause that was a stupid mistake. Anyway, when we both stopped laughing he took me there. Oh my God, Mr. Con—it was, like, so fantastic. You can see all of Paris from up there, for miles and miles."

"You went to the Eiffel Tower by yourself?" Con was more than a little impressed at her audacity and initiative. Parisian taxi drivers were infamous for their impatience and borderline rudeness. He hadn't known she spoke enough French to be able to order lunch at a bistro, much less take on one of those snide semi-gangsters and come away laughing.

Lireinne draped her coat over the back of a gray silk-brocade armchair. "Well, yeah—I always wanted to get to the top of it one day. But that was just this morning. When I saw the bridge, the Pont de L'Alma, I decided to walk back to the hotel along the Seine and it took, like, forever. And you wouldn't *believe* how much dog crap there was on the sidewalks—I had to watch my step or my shoes would've been toast." She accepted the glass of champagne Con offered her and drained half of it, the smooth muscles of her long throat working. "Thanks. I didn't realize I was so thirsty."

That was a long walk, about four kilometers. Forgetting that until just a few weeks ago, Lireinne had walked two miles a day to work and home again, Con marveled at her stamina.

"I thought for sure you'd go shopping today," he said, his thoughts going fleetingly to Liz as he topped off her glass. There'd have been no Eiffel Tower stopping *her* from hitting the stores. "Hell, Lireinne, the Avenue Montaigne is designer nirvana, but I'm glad you had a good afternoon sightseeing. Why didn't you take a cab back to the hotel?"

Lireinne shrugged. "I wanted to see as much of Paris as I could up close, you know, so I bought a map at the gift shop." She sank into the deep, down-filled cushions of the settee with a groan of relief. Kicking off her suede pumps, she rubbed her narrow, black-stockinged feet, saying, "That's better. These heels really sucked for walking. My feet are, like, *killing* me."

"I bet they are." Con took a sip of champagne. "That's one bitch of a hike. You're not too tired to go to dinner, are you? I've made us reservations at—"

Lireinne interrupted him. "Oh, hold on. I almost forgot." She rose from the settee with a pretty grimace at her feet. "Ouch. Look, I didn't use hardly any of the money you gave me. After paying for the taxi and buying the map, there's six hundred and eighty-two euros left over." Crossing the suite in her stocking feet, she went to her purse on the gilt table by the door, dug around inside it, and found a crumpled handful of money.

"Here." Lireinne hurried back to him, proudly presenting the wad of bills.

She had to have seen a thousand things she'd wanted to buy today, Con thought, full of tenderness at this evidence of her sweet frugality. Lizzie would have spent every nickel in the first store she walked into before demanding another infusion of cash. What an amazing, incredible girl she was. How lucky could one beat-up skin dealer get? Con wondered.

"Darling, that's just walking-around money," he said with an indulgent smile. "Keep it. Buy yourself something pretty." Con was thinking of the small, dark-blue leather box from Chopard in his coat pocket and the pair of earrings inside it—perfect sprays of dangling droplets, a rain of green tourmalines and tiny diamonds. The unusual green stones were the precise color of Lireinne's eyes and he planned to give them to her at dinner tonight. And then, once he brought this glorious girl to bed, those earrings would shimmer like green fires in the dark, silken forest of her hair when it was spread across his pillow.

He couldn't resist. Ignoring the money she was holding, Con closed his hand around Lireinne's possessively. He tightened his fingers, drawing her closer.

Her eyes shifted, her face fell. Yanking her hand free of his, Lireinne took a hasty step backward. "Oh, no! I can't take all that money. It's, it's not right. I should have used my own, really." She dropped the bills on the carved pear-wood coffee table as though the notes were burning her fingers. With a nervous-sounding laugh, Lireinne shook her head in vehement denial.

"I mean, you don't have to do that, Mr. Con."

"But I want to," Con said. Grinning, he took a confident step and captured her hand again. "And come on, baby—don't you think it's about time you stopped calling me '*Mr.* Con'? Call me by my name, Lireinne. Please."

In the sudden silence that fell in the sitting room, the measured, calm voice of the BBC announcer on the radio seemed too loud. Except for her stricken eyes, Lireinne's heart-shaped face was expressionless. Her hand was limp in his. Con was forced to let go of it when she backed away from him and turned around to face the long windows. As if she felt a chill in the warm air of the suite, Lireinne crossed her arms tightly to her chest, staring at the lights of Paris outside the window, glowing like stars and bright nebulas in the black vault of the night.

What was *this* about? Con wondered. Was she upset? He'd only wanted to hear his name on her lips. No, that "Mr. Con" business was a relic of before, and he was more than sure that even if she wasn't ready to love him yet, Lireinne had to feel *something* for him. The past weeks proved it. She'd agreed to come on this trip, after all, and it wasn't like he'd been keeping his feelings for her to himself. Puzzled at her reaction, Con waited for Lireinne to talk to him, to explain, but she said nothing.

Unable to bear the apprehension her silence provoked, Con pressed her. "Are you okay, sweetheart?"

Her back still turned, Lireinne ran her fingers through her hair and sighed. Her slim shoulders drooped. "I think . . . I'm just tired. It was a big old walk. I hardly slept at all on the flight, too. I guess I was too wired to take that nap like you said I should."

So that was it, Con thought, his apprehension dispelled. The silly, darling girl had been on her feet for miles and she was exhausted.

"Do you still want to go to dinner, honey? We could order up room service, stay in for the night instead."

Since she was so tired, that could be a better plan for them than the romantic dinner he'd arranged at Marius et Janette. Con's breath caught, imagining Lireinne wrapped in the hotel's sumptuous terrycloth robe, naked underneath its soft white folds. Oysters and caviar would still be there tomorrow night, and suddenly all he wanted was to hold her.

"Oh, no—not room service." Lireinne glanced back at him over her shoulder with a forced-looking smile. "I mean, going out sounds like a great idea to me. I was having such a fantastic time I forgot to eat anything today, so I'm, like, *starving*, okay? I think I'll just have a quick shower and get dressed up. I bet we're going to a real fancy place." She turned her head away from him, facing the windows again.

"You're so beautiful," Con said. It felt like a staggering understatement.

She didn't reply.

He tried again. "Lireinne, sweetheart. You'll be the most fabulous girl in the room, no matter what you wear."

Con couldn't continue merely watching her anymore. He put his empty champagne glass down and went to Lireinne. Her slim back to him still, he encircled his right arm around her slender waist, pulling her tight to his chest. He pressed his lips to the dark crown of her head and inhaled deeply of her hair, scented with the cold night air of Paris and her own subtle perfume. Except for the rigidity of her back and shoulders, she fit perfectly into his embrace. Closing his eyes at the intensity of his sudden arousal, Con's breath left his body in a long sigh that was almost a groan, as if it had been living at the bottom of his lungs for months, waiting for this moment to be freed.

At last. Con's previous concern evaporated at this long-awaited intimate contact with Lireinne, his heart and mind and body united and at peace for once. At last, she's mine, he thought. I'm holding her and I'll never let her go. His hand tightened on her waist, and loving the lyre curve of it, Con lowered his flame-red head to kiss the point of her left shoulder, the hollow where her shoulder met her neck, the corner of her jaw. The hard length of his erection pressed against Lireinne insisted that he cancel the dinner reservation.

"Look, I . . ."

Lost in his need, Con almost didn't hear what she was saying.

"What's that?" he murmured.

"I need to get ready now." Lireinne's low voice was curiously flat. "I don't want to make us late."

"Relax. We can be late." Con buried his face in her hair, glorying in the feel of it against his lips.

"Look, I need to *change,*" she said urgently.

She must really want to go out, Con thought. Lireinne must have been looking forward to a night on the town in Paris for a long time. She'd probably never traveled far from Covington, he realized. With strong reluctance, Con dropped his arm from her waist.

"Well . . . sure, darling. We'll go out. Whatever you want."

Lireinne turned to look at him then, her lovely face unreadable and closed. "Thanks. That is what I want." Without another word or a backward glance, she crossed the suite and picked up her shoes and her purse. She went in her room and shut the door firmly behind her, leaving Con alone with his still-insistent erection. He shook his head, perplexed by love.

Women, Con thought, shaking his head. Who could figure out what they *really* wanted?

★ ★ ★

While he waited for Lireinne to get ready, Con cracked the long windows, letting the Paris evening into the suite with its sounds of traffic and faraway sirens. Walking outside onto the small balcony, he smoked a cigar while he made the phone call he'd been putting off since this afternoon's meeting with Julien. As he'd expected, Roger wasn't thrilled with the new skin deal, but on the whole Con thought he took the terms better than he'd expected.

"Cash flow, ol' son," Roger said with a weighty sigh. "We need the cash right now, for certain-sure. Got to cut some corners before the end of the year, but I guess it'll all come out some better than I'da thought it would." This was faint praise, although Con hadn't exactly expected Ol' Rog to turn backflips at the news of the discounted skins. "Damn lobbyist's eating up the operatin' capital." Con didn't respond to that: you can only fix one mess at a time, he told himself. It's not like the EPA is going anywhere. It never does, not when you operate on the wrong side of it. SGE could pay to fix the problem, or they could pay the lobbyist: either way, they'd pay.

"By the way," Roger said, "where's that pretty lil gal, Lireinne, at? Tina tells me she's with you."

Roger's question was deceptively mild in its tone, but Con recognized the hard-shell, Baptist deacon disapproval behind it. He'd been anticipating something like this enquiry, certain that Roger wouldn't be happy about his new relationship with Lireinne once he found out about it. Even though he was well on the way to being a free man thanks to Lizzie's coup d'état, his boss would be of the opinion that Con should have waited a decent interval before he embarked on a new liaison—meaning, until he was actually divorced.

No sweat, Con thought, making an effort to shrug off his irritation at this intrusion into his affairs. Roger didn't have to know everything, not right now. "Lireinne's fine," he said casually. "A huge help to me on this trip. Invaluable, really, so it's a good thing she came."

Roger harrumphed. "Glad to hear it, 'cause I mean to tell you I was kinda taken back when I heard she was with you. Don't look right, in my opinion. Now I know you got a world of hurt brewing with the little woman these days, but you oughta be a mite more careful. I'd a hoped you'd think twice about how this kind of thang's gonna look to people."

So who gave a damn besides Roger? Con swallowed a contemptuous snort. "But it's not the way it looks." And even though it was the way it looked, none of this was Ol Rog's business. Lireinne must have misunderstood his instructions about the reservation, but in any case it had turned out for the best, not having to lie to Roger outright.

"This is all on the up-and-up. I booked us two rooms," Con said virtuously.

"I should think so. Cain't imagine why you wouldn't."

Taking a big puff of his cigar, Con paced the balcony. Damn, it was cold out here. "Of course I did. Besides, didn't I just bring this deal back from the dead? Don't worry yourself about a thing, Rog. Please."

"Still, ol' son, you gotta listen up now . . ." Apparently not reassured, Roger opened his book of homespun admonitions and launched a dogged sermon, chapter and verse.

A bored and unrepentant sinner, Con couldn't hang up in the middle of his boss's harangue so he resigned himself to making noncommittal noises in appropriate places. Amen, pass the plate, let's go already! he fumed. Tuning out the annoying drone in his ear, Con checked his watch. It was nearly eight and Lireinne hadn't emerged from her room yet. She'd been in there for over an hour. How long could it take her to shower and change? The night was turning frigid and Con's impatience burned hotter the longer Roger sermonized.

Still, it was more than ten minutes later before the old sermonizer began to run out of both gas and unsolicited opinions. "So think on what I'm sayin', real hard now. Don't want anybody getting the wrong idear, get me?"

"Right. Got it. Talk to you tomorrow." Con snapped his cell phone shut before Roger could find his second wind. He'd have to bring his boss around to the real facts once he returned, but for now

Con had a beautiful girl to take to dinner. Tossing the butt end of his cigar over the balcony railing into the flower box, he went back inside the warm, well-lit suite.

Finding Lireinne's door still shut, he tapped on it lightly.

"Honey?" he called through the door, pitching his voice low. "You ready?" There was no answer, so Con turned the handle and stepped inside.

The room was mostly dark, but the bedside lamp was on, illuminating the sleeping girl lying on the low bed. Her lips slightly parted, Lireinne lay in exquisite abandon across the pink damask bedspread, fully clothed in a clinging, sea-foam-green silk dress, black stockings, and her black suede pumps. One hand was curled under her cheek, the other loosely wrapped around a hairbrush.

She was so tired she must have fallen asleep in the middle of getting dressed, Con thought. He was filled with a tender wonder at her unconscious perfection, rare as a carved ivory pillow doll. Con stood by the bedside, mesmerized by the slow rise and fall of Lireinne's white breasts under the green silk. Should he try to wake her?

No, he sighed. Lireinne needed her sleep, poor kid. So, with mingled regret and affection, he removed the brush from her hand and put it on the table beside the bed. He slid her pumps off her feet, ignoring the impulse to run his thumb across the high, delicate arches, and drew the duvet up and over her shoulders. Con's mouth was gentle when he kissed her forehead, Lireinne's sleeping innocence filling him with an almost painful sense of protectiveness. Of course she'd passed out after nearly twenty hours of travel and her day wandering the city. There hadn't been anything wrong earlier; there was nothing to worry about. She was just jet-lagged.

"Sleep well, darling," Con whispered. He couldn't help it, he had to touch her one last time, so with a fingertip he traced the line of her cheek. Deep in slumber, Lireinne sighed, a half-smile on her dreaming face.

"I love you." Con barely breathed the words, the first time he'd said them out loud.

He turned out the lamp before he tiptoed from her bedroom,

shutting the door with a quiet, final *click* that seemed to punctuate the demise of his plans for this evening. The click echoed in his heart and in that moment it was all he could do not to go back in there and slide into bed beside Lireinne, to wake her with kisses, to tumble her into his arms and claim the splendor of her sleep-soft body as his own.

His hand still closed around the brass knob, Con pressed his forehead to the door, breathing hard and fast. Down, boy, he thought with a roughly amused shake of his head. Let her sleep. You've got a date with the rest of the champagne, a couple of Vicodin, and dinner downstairs, alone.

Sleeping Beauty's prince was going to have to be patient just one night longer.

CHAPTER 23

Where was she? What time was it?

Waking from a deep sleep to the far-off whine of a vacuum cleaner somewhere in the hotel, Lireinne sat bolt upright in her bed, dazed with a confused sense of dislocation. She blinked in the bright sunlight falling on the deep-piled carpet of the room, her hands in her tangled hair. The hotel room. She was at the Plaza Athénée, she was in Paris, and it had to be sometime Friday morning.

Her eyes narrowing, Lireinne ran her hands over the front of the only slightly wrinkled green dress. She must have slept in her clothes, but where were her shoes? They were over there, on the floor in front of the pink silk-upholstered armchair. Frowning, she threw off the goose-down duvet and swung her black-stockinged legs off the edge of the bed. Lireinne rubbed her face, swimming up out of sleep into a spate of questions. What had happened last night? How had she gotten into bed? She recalled showering and dressing to go to dinner, sitting on the bed to brush her hair . . . and then she must have passed right the hell out. But she didn't remember taking her shoes off, and there was something else, she was sure of it. Something, something *bad*.

Oh, God. She remembered now.

Con.

Call me by my name, Lireinne. Please.

Lireinne shuddered at the searing memory of the night before, how Con had put the big move on her. That had been close, she thought, way too close to that confrontation she'd hoped to avoid forever. The minute he'd put his arm around her, Lireinne's heart had plummeted, knowing she wasn't going to get away with pretending she didn't know what Con wanted anymore. No, that big ol' cat's out of the bag now, she thought grimly as she stalked into the marble-lined bathroom to brush her teeth.

A few minutes later, feeling more like herself now that her teeth didn't feel as though they were wearing sweaters, Lireinne tried to calm her racing pulse. She gazed at her reflection in the mirror. "You can do it," she whispered. Whether she was ready or not, it was time to face Con. She needed to be strong enough to be honest and tell him what she *really* thought about his crazy thing for her. Lireinne closed her eyes. "Please," she prayed. "Don't let him take it the wrong way."

Remembering the embrace, all that *kissing,* though, Con's taking it any other way was a long shot—as unlikely as a cat deciding it wanted to live in the ocean, like a fish. Still, she had to do it, and she had to do it now.

Taking a deep breath, Lireinne cracked open the bedroom door and peeked out into the sunlit sitting room.

"Hello?" She despised the way her voice quavered, but no one answered anyway. The dishes and silverware of a solitary breakfast, a strew of newspaper pages, and the faintest trace of Con's cologne greeted her instead. Somewhere the radio was playing a soft, light jazz but otherwise the big, beautifully appointed room was quiet.

He's gone, she thought, relieved at his absence, although she knew it only prolonged the inevitable. The confrontation would come later, rather than sooner.

But wait—there was a folded piece of hotel stationery on the table next to the arrangement of white roses, ferns, and fragrant stock. Barefoot, Lireinne padded across the room and picked it up, recognizing Con's eccentric, spiky handwriting. A pile of euros was lying underneath the note. As she read it, her pulse leapt again with renewed dread.

> *Good morning, darling,*
>
> *One more meeting today but will be back to take you out around seven. Order some breakfast from room service, then go have fun. Spend the money!*
>
> *Love, Con*

Her mouth falling half open, Lireinne looked up from the note to meet her own horrified green gaze in the gilt-framed mirror. "Shit!" she swore. The piece of paper fell out of her hand to the floor, dropped like a discarded murder weapon, as though she were terrified to have her fingerprints on it.

Love, Con.

Everything had gotten out of hand, way out of hand. Lireinne had mistakenly thought she could control the situation if she was careful, but now she realized she'd never had the first clue about what was in Con Costello's head. It was bad enough when she'd thought all he wanted was sex, but *love*?

"*So* not going to happen!" Lireinne passionately declared to her reflection. Her reflection agreed, saying that yes, it would not happen.

But what would she say to him after this? Get lost? Leave me alone, you letch? Hell, if Con was so deluded he thought he was . . . in *love* with her, if he was so crazy he thought she felt anything for him beyond gratitude, when she told him the truth he might get so mad he'd fire her. Having to leave Paris would be the least of her worries then.

The loss of her job loomed like the descending blade of a guillotine. What about Wolf and the money she was supposed to be saving so he could go to LSU, what would she do about that? Lireinne thought, her hands shaking with panic. Get a job at the McDonald's in Covington? Oh, God—she'd lose the car, too, so even that would be out. She'd have no way to get to her new executive position cleaning the fry-o-lator.

Lireinne had always been halfway afraid that the rapid change in her circumstances had been too good to be for real, but refused to let herself think on it much. She'd believed the gray days of hosing were behind her because she'd needed to believe it. Now, after reading Con's note, her newfound security was suddenly revealed as a precarious thing, dependent on one man's whim. All Lireinne could see was an inexorable slide: back to hosing, or something worse.

A real job had turned out to be too much to ask of an indifferent world, and Lireinne hadn't wanted much—no more than what everyone wanted. Steady, respectable work, a real paycheck, and, and . . . Lireinne had also wanted the chance to go to Paris. Since that first day when Con had summoned her to the office, she'd been living a fantasy, one too wonderful to examine as closely as she should have done. Hosers didn't become personal assistants; they never got out of the barns. In Paris, the only place for a hoser was in the boss's bed.

Forced to confront her helplessness, Lireinne's panic was gradually giving way to a familiar resentment. Picking the note off the floor, she tore it in two and crushed the halves into a ball. So she'd schemed to get this trip, but only a little. So for days she'd pretended she wasn't aware of Con's real intentions. She didn't deserve to lose her job because she'd done nothing wrong.

Or . . . had she? After Brett's assault, Lireinne still agonized when she thought about it, even though she knew she wasn't supposed to feel that way. She'd often turned it over in her head, reliving every moment of that night up until the rape. What if, somehow, she'd brought it on herself?

"No freaking way!" Lireinne told her reflection stoutly, but there was doubt in her green eyes now. Remembering the subtle power she'd enjoyed the afternoon she met Con, now Lireinne wasn't as sure. Maybe she should have stopped this before everything got out of control. Maybe she was paying the price for being such a dumb-ass.

So if she wanted to keep her job, what if she'd have to go through with . . . sleeping with him?

"No way!" Lireinne vowed again, knowing she could *never* do that. Ever since Brett, the thought of any man touching her had left her feeling sick, on the verge of vomiting with fright . . . and ready to fight. It had been all she could do not to strike Con's hands away last night.

Besides, even if she could find a way to stand it, then everybody would be vindicated in the hateful things they said about her. She really *would* be a slut.

This was one hell of a tangled mess, but Lireinne was positive about one thing in her short life: she was no slut, no matter what people said. She was poor, a high-school dropout, and—thanks to Brett—damaged goods, but she wasn't a whore. She wouldn't sleep with Con Costello for anything, not even if he paid her a million dollars a year and bought her a goddamned Mercedes.

Bud would just *die.*

Lireinne could hardly bear it, imagining the disappointment in his eyes if he knew she'd contemplated such a thing at all. He would never find out, of course, but in that moment she keenly longed for Bud's steady love, the unselfish care he'd always taken of her. Paris was such a long way from home and she couldn't even call him. For one thing, she wasn't sure how to make an overseas call, but if she did figure it out somehow, he'd know right away that something was wrong. Lireinne had never been able to hide how she felt from Bud, not for long. It didn't matter that she hadn't told him when she'd been raped, or after Harlan had grabbed her. With that Bud-radar of his, despite all her protestations that she was *fine,* she'd often looked up to find him watching her, a grave, unspoken concern in his eyes. It had been hell on earth, hiding her misery from him, but Lireinne hadn't had a choice. Lying to him was the only way to make sure her stepfather didn't go to jail.

Her distracted gaze fell to the stack of euros on the table, a bigger pile of money than Con had given her yesterday. Lireinne counted it, unbelieving, and then counted it again. A thousand euros. That had to be nearly eight hundred dollars. Well, Con might be thinking he could buy her with all that money, but he had another think coming, for sure. After last night, after that *note* this morning, she wouldn't spend another dime that wasn't her own.

But Lireinne was hungry. The last meal she'd had was the crois-sant on the plane. The room service menu lay next to Con's solitary dishes, a leather-bound volume of heavy vellum pages. Lireinne opened it to the breakfast section. Fifty-five euros for *le petit déjeuner Américain* of bacon and eggs, eleven euros for orange juice. Horrified at the prices, she threw the menu down on the coffee table.

Her empty stomach had begun to growl, though, and so even-tually Lireinne gave in, picked up the phone, and ordered the cheap-est thing on the menu: coffee and a brioche for twenty euros. She really needed the caffeine and she'd never had a brioche before, but it must be like a pastry. When breakfast finally arrived, the brioche turned out to be just a sugar-topped roll of bread, but by then Lireinne didn't care. It was too yummy not to eat it all, especially af-ter she'd smeared it with real butter and strawberry jam: she ate even the crumbs. The milk-laced coffee was strong and hot, too. Trying to fill herself, Lireinne drank the whole pot and the glass of water as well.

Fuel, she reminded herself grimly. It's just fuel. If she found her-self on the next flight out of town, Lireinne didn't know if she'd be able to eat again anytime soon. It would be hours before Con came back. She had a long time to wait until she knew how bad her pre-dicament was going to get.

That realization left Lireinne as wired as Wolf's Xbox after a long afternoon of destruction and mayhem. She had to get out of the sud-denly claustrophobic suite, out onto the street, before she lost her mind. Moving quickly, Lireinne washed her face, brushed her hair, and put on her shoes. She didn't stop to change out of the dress she'd slept in but only threw her coat on over it, slinging her purse over her shoulder on the way out the door.

While waiting for the elevator, Lireinne checked to make sure that the hundred dollars she'd brought with her was still in her wallet. She did the math rapidly in her head: a hundred dollars was probably worth something like one hundred and thirty euros. She'd change her money downstairs at the reception desk and then she'd take a walk. Walking helped her think sometimes and she had a lot to think about before Con got back. Maybe she'd head to the Louvre today, although she wasn't sure if her mood was equal to looking at art. She could go to Père Lachaise, the famous cemetery, since according to the map it wasn't too far from the hotel. One of Wolf's heroes, Jim Morrison, was supposed to be buried there and this morning a trip to a graveyard would suit her mood down to the ground.

Money changed at the front desk, Lireinne hurried through the lobby to the front of the hotel, summoning a distant, preoccupied nod for the uniformed doorman.

"Bonjour, mademoiselle." The doorman touched the brim of his cap with a perfectly polite, respectful smile. He could have been greeting somebody who was a big deal—a diplomat, an OPEC minister, a princess on a state visit—instead of a soon-to-be-unemployed ex-hoser. In the middle of all her turmoil, she'd been almost too distracted to have noticed the doorman's smiling salute altogether, but Lireinne was struck by a new thought.

Acting like somebody too important to be nice was something she'd never tried before, although she'd had plenty of role models. In high school, all the popular kids had always ignored her shy attempts to even say hello. They had this attitude, like they were better than everybody else, too cool to be bothered with unimportant people.

Maybe it was high time to grow some of that attitude, Lireinne decided, as she surveyed the traffic-filled Avenue from the top of the hotel's steps. She'd try it out on her nemesis, the valet. His expression was irritatingly expectant, as though he'd been waiting for her to come out this morning and was ready for her.

And so, "Go to hell," she said to the valet in passing, her tone as cold as the Seine in winter. Lireinne noted his startled, red face, and was satisfied. She tossed her hair and set out at a brisk walk.

This is your brain on *attitude,* sugar, Lireinne thought. Time to work on that.

★ ★ ★

Once out on the sidewalk, the sun filtering through the chestnut trees' yellow leaves was bright and warm on her face, the shops were open, and there were lots of people on the street today. A business-suited man, walking a tiny white dog that could have been Lunchmeat's brother, gave her an appreciative nod. Since she wasn't in the mood for any man giving her that kind of look, not today, Lireinne ignored him.

Faced with a long day with nothing much to do but walk, though, why not take a stroll on the Avenue Montaigne to do some serious window-shopping? Lireinne thought. Paris was such an expensive city, now she got it: there was no way she could actually buy anything with her hundred and thirty euros except maybe a pair of pantyhose. But her black mood had begun to lift and the Avenue was alive and bustling on this gorgeous morning. She owned this whole Friday free and clear, didn't she? Lireinne gave that thought an emphatic nod. Con Costello couldn't take *that* away from her.

And the store windows were *amazing,* although most of their clothes and shoes and bags were, as Emma had put it what seemed light-years ago, too old for her—and far beyond her reach, too. Lireinne felt sure she should keep a tight rein on any fantasies this morning. It seemed like spitting in the eye of fate when she had no idea what the evening would have in store for her. Instead of being merely sort of poor, she might be unemployed and flat broke.

Still, Lireinne couldn't help but hungrily eye the lush fabrics at Balmain, the precise detailing on the linen dresses in the window at Hermès, the feathered, rhinestone-studded heels at Jimmy Choo. Banana Republic was never going to seem the same to her again, Lireinne reflected, when she paused in front of the Burberry store, even though Emma had said that for the money, the clothes there were of good quality. Compared to the contents of these windows, Banana Republic seemed so ordinary now.

Unenthused by Burberry's welter of plaid, Lireinne moved on to Prada and immediately forgot her anti-fantasy resolution. Enrapt at the elegant lines, rich fabrics, and muted colors, she imagined the thrill of being able to walk right in the doors, plunk down a pile of money, and buy that drop-dead pair of stilettos. Lireinne's resolve wasn't proof against shoes. After months of shrimp boots and flip-flops, years of making do with Walmart's imitation leather sneakers and ugly knockoffs, she'd always longed for a room full of beautiful shoes like these.

That dream would always be out of reach now, Lireinne thought gloomily. Thanks for nothing, Con Costello. With a lingering glance at those kick-ass shoes and a sigh, she moved on, hoping the next window would lift her spirits again.

And after crossing the street, it did. Lireinne had to stop cold, arrested by the outrageous display in the Luigi Spada windows. An alligator—a real, stuffed four-footer wearing a toothy grin and a fez—lolled on the high seat of a Chinese-red rickshaw. The rickshaw was drawn by three attenuated mannequins in straw coolie hats and clothes made entirely from alligator skin. Unlike the stiff, patent-finished hides she'd seen at the farm's offices, this was a liquid-textured, subtly draped matte leather. It practically begged her to touch those supple, scaled folds.

"Check it *out*," Lireinne breathed.

Her mouth turned up in a grin, thinking that this was where all those gators went after they died. They were transformed into shift dresses and beautifully cut blazers in the deepest blue imaginable; they turned into burnt-orange fringed scarves; exquisitely wrought aubergine skirts and wrist-length olive-green gloves. The manne-quins' gold accessories of earrings and charm bracelets matched the gleaming hardware on the clutch purse and dainty chains on the shoulder bag. A discreet sign in the bottom corner of the window adver-tised, LUIGI SPADA REINTERPRETS THE LADY-LOOK.

And she'd thought the animals at the farm only went for hand-bags, cowboy boots, and belts! So enthralled by the eccentric, mar-velous display, Lireinne didn't immediately notice the three people who burst out of the shop onto the sidewalk—not until they began a loud, contentious discussion.

"But you cawn't be serious!"

Lireinne half turned her head at that English accent. It belonged to a tall man of an uncertain age. Long-legged, long-necked, and long-lashed as an ostrich, his curly hair was a red so violent it had to be dyed. He was wearing skintight black leggings that revealed hairy ankles, a pair of dirty tennis shoes, and an orange-and-black-striped knitted scarf knotted around his spindly neck. The scarf clashed horribly with his orchid-colored alligator-skin motorcycle jacket. Lireinne tried not to gawk at the man's penciled eyebrows, dewy foundation, mascara, and rouge. Attitude was one thing, but she didn't want to be rude to a man too loopy to know he looked like an ugly woman. Quickly, she returned her gaze to the window's display before he caught her staring at him.

"I won't allow you, dearest." The ostrich shook his improbably red curls. Big gold hoops that looked just like the earrings on the mannequins in the window bounced in a jingling chatter of indignation. "It's simply not *done*."

Yesterday Lireinne had encountered some *très* interesting types on her walk along the Seine, so this freakily dressed guy in the makeup didn't strike her as dangerous—for Paris. Back home in Covington he'd be a serious weirdo, but over here it was like some people got up in the morning, put on whatever they wanted, and nobody seemed to give them a second glance.

"*I* will do it," another voice said.

"No, you mustn't!"

Lireinne chanced another peek through the black scrim of her hair at the ostrich's equally odd companions—a youngish, pudgy man and an older woman with white hair styled in a severe buzz cut, so closely cropped her pink scalp glowed in the morning sunlight.

The English-sounding guy was begging the pudgy man, "Please listen to reason, Lu-Lu."

"*Basta!*" Wearing enormous black sunglasses, a black cocktail dress revealing an alarming, wrinkled décolletage, and an identical motorcycle jacket in Nile green, the blade-thin older woman slapped her head with a masculine hand the size of a five-pound flounder.

"*Basta!*" She stamped her black patent-leather stiletto on the grimy sidewalk. "You are not to say that *Lu-Lu*. This is a name that is not a name. My brother is Luigi. Say it! Loo-*ee*-gee." Her deep, rasping accent was heavy, different from the English guy's, maybe Italian.

Hold the phone, Lireinne thought, more curious now than ever. Could that dumpy-looking little man, the one the ostrich had called Lu-Lu, be *the* Luigi Spada? She'd seen his collections in magazines, but had no idea what he looked like. What were the odds of running into a famous designer right here on the street, arguing like a regular person?

Drawing her hair behind her ear and away from the side of her face, Lireinne dared a longer glance. Pale-faced Luigi's hair was gelled as flat as a fantastic coat of dead-black paint, his pouting lips glossed a dark maroon the color of dried blood. Small diamond solitaire earrings, two in his right ear and three marching up the side of his left one, glittered in the pale sun, and he was wearing an alligator motorcycle jacket just like the others. A pure white, Luigi's jacket complemented the too-long, baggy, ivory linen pants puddling around his black rubber flip-flops. Fascinated, openly studying him now, Lireinne couldn't help but notice he was shirtless underneath the jacket, although the morning air was wicked cold.

Throwing up his hands, Lu-Lu/Luigi expelled a dramatic sigh that would've shamed a reality show diva. "You and Luciana must not quarrel, Peter," he said. "You make my head a rotten melon this morning with all your unpleasantness, *cara mio*. I am choosing the model for my own designs, only I."

Peter the ostrich stroked Luigi's cheek with a vermillion-tipped finger. "*Please,* Lu-Lu. Listen to me, dearest. I beg you—don't use Alberto for next fall's collection. Those bitter old warhorses at *Vogue* will crucify you for that. You know they haven't a working sense of real possibility between them. They'll hate it, simply hate it."

"Am I caring? Am I not Luigi Spada?" It *was* him.

"I am saying this once more." The paunchy designer touched the corner of his lipsticked mouth with a manicured, black-polished fingertip and smiled a condescending smile. "I will do as I will in this, though you and Luciana say I cannot. The new collection, it calls for a difference in the model, yes? I have done ladies for the spring, so-o-o . . . now I give autumn a new face! Let all be in love with a beautiful boy this time. The new *coccodrillo* designs must have a certain something, an attitude of go-to-hell that is *particolare*. And truly, only Alberto can wear my Adventure collection in the properly way for he tells me to go to hell all of the time. You are worried too much, *caro*."

The sister, Luciana, poked him on his bare, hairless chest with a big, bony forefinger. "*Attenzione, fratello mio*. For once, this Pietro is correct. No one will buy the collection if they think it is made for perverts. A *pollo* in skirts, I ask you! You don't even fit the samples on a girl yet, only that *transvestitismo*! The Adventure pieces are a challenge, this is true, but a certain species of girl can carry them off and make the look her own. Find such a one and all will be well, I swear it to you."

Looking relieved now that he had backup, Peter nodded emphatically. "Exactly so. For heaven's sake, you could simply use this girl here—the one who's been eavesdropping on us for the last five minutes."

They were talking about *her*. With a rush of hot blood to her cheeks, Lireinne's mouth fell open in shame.

"'Scuse me," she mumbled. "I wasn't really listening, not . . ."

As though she'd not said a word, Peter continued. "Put just one of next fall's designs on her, just one, and you'll see what we're on about. She's certainly fetching enough. Lord, I'll be completely gob-smacked if she's not a size two as well. Then afterward, if you must insist on this madness, you can use that little queen from Palermo and I'll not say another word."

Lireinne, aghast at this suggestion, had turned away from the window to escape, but white-haired Luciana yanked the sleeve of her coat, stopping her in her tracks.

"No, no—you must help Luigi. At once," the older woman declared imperiously.

"I'm sorry?" Not wanting to be any more rude than she'd already been, not sure she understood the woman's heavily accented command, Lireinne paused in the act of fleeing the scene.

Luciana didn't bother answering her. Like a red-taloned raptor, she captured Lireinne's jaw, turning her head to observe her from all angles. Lireinne had no idea how to react to this, frozen with shock and astonished confusion.

"The face, she is most good—even the scar," Luciana announced to her companions. Her immense sunglasses were black mirrors. She nodded briskly, as though the question were settled.

"Eh, Luigi," she said. "Come and see. Perhaps *here* is your something *particolare.*" And then, again before Lireinne understood what was happening to her, Luciana's big hands were busily unbuttoning Lireinne's coat, revealing the green silk dress underneath it.

"Pfft." Luciana made an impatient noise. "Cheap shit from Malaysia, this dress, but the color is good for you. Too, you are not overly fat. Excellent! This one is a two, I know it."

Placing her palm in the middle of Lireinne's back, Luciana gave her a quick shove in Luigi Spada's direction. *"You,"* she said to Lireinne, "will now make the angry face."

"You mean, pretend to be mad?" Lireinne asked, incredulous. Dumbfounded and practically paralyzed at the white-haired woman's having treated her like a department store dummy, she'd rebuttoned her coat in a hurry, but her confusion was turning the corner into outrage.

"*Sì, sì*—are you deaf? This instant, you must be angry," Luciana ordered.

Wait one damned *minute,* Lireinne thought. Outrage now obtained, she found that looking angry had already happened.

"Hey! Like, I'm not freaking deaf, okay?" she said with a threatening scowl. "And don't *touch* me. I'm going, get it?"

"More," Luciana commanded, ignoring her. "Be still more angry."

Angry? Never far from the surface, hateful memories of the snotty valet, of Tina and Jackie and Miz 'Cille and how they'd called her a whore, of Harlan and his near-rape, of Brett and his actual one, hammered Lireinne in that instant. And Con, the way he'd put his hands on her, and not being content to do that, was going to ruin everything with that *love* of his—God, she was done with the world thinking it could do whatever it wanted to her! Even in Paris, the world was still the same.

On the sidewalk of the Avenue Montaigne, Lireinne straightened her spine and grew two inches taller. Her eyes narrowed, her upper lip curled in fury.

"You want angry?" Lireinne's voice came from deep in her throat, dangerously close to a growl. None of Luigi's posse seemed to notice or care. "Okay, I'm freaking pissed *now*. Who do you assholes think you are?"

"Perfection," Peter pronounced, serenely oblivious to having been called an asshole. "Now walk, dearie." He seemed to be waiting for her to obey him.

Not having offered a word throughout, Luigi Spada raised a skeptical eyebrow and shrugged in disdain.

"She is *bellissima*, true," he acknowledged with a truculent pout. "But there are many such girls in Paris. Where is the go-to-hell, I ask you?"

Oh, Lireinne had plenty of go-to-hell at this point, enough for a whole yellow school bus packed with dropouts.

"Get a freaking *life*," she hissed through gritted teeth. "Go fuck yourselves."

Throwing back her shoulders, her head held high, Lireinne throttled down on her anger and gave it the gas. She shoved past Peter and Luciana with a stiff arm and stalked away from them in her modest heels. Everybody dissed her, everybody! Lireinne's thoughts were furious as she hurried to put distance between her and her tormentors. Even in Paris, she couldn't even take a damned walk without freakazoid famous designers and their bossy sisters getting in her face and treating her like she was nothing.

Her heart raced. Lireinne was riding a thundering wave, feeling as though she could ride that wave all the way across the ocean, all the way back to the trailer where her family, at least, had always known who she was—a human being like everyone else.

But Lireinne hadn't gotten twenty feet down the street before she heard flip-flops slapping behind her in pursuit. Oh, give me a *break,* she thought. Go away! Lireinne walked faster, lengthening her strides. If these people didn't leave her alone, she didn't want to think what she might do to *make* them leave her alone. For sure it wouldn't be pretty.

"*Signorina,* wait!"

Full of exasperation and on the verge of screaming, Lireinne stopped and whirled to glare at Luigi. "What?" she demanded. "What the hell do you want *now*?" She was still wearing the angry face. By now she was so goddamned mad she couldn't have worn another one if she tried.

The overweight designer struggled to catch his breath. "You are a-walking and . . . then I am . . . a-changing what I am thinking before. You are indeed a two, yes?" he managed with a wheeze.

"Yeah, last time I checked—not that it's any of your damned business," Lireinne said, no longer caring about seeming rude to *any-body*. "Why do you give a shit?"

Luigi snorted impatience at her question. "The samples, they are always the sizes two, sometimes the zero. Come!" he insisted. "Come now, exactly now. The time, she will not wait. And," he said with a careless wave of his hand, "Luigi Spada will pay, *cara*. I give an American tourist good money to wear my Adventure collection just for the day, good money for a few hours of your time."

Those kick-ass stilettos in the window at Prada.

Her anger rapidly cooling, Lireinne thought this offer over for a moment.

"How much money?" she asked.

Above the Luigi Spada store, the atelier was all the colors of dry bones—white walls, ivory floors, airy milk-colored drapery at the windows, and snowy leather couches. There, over the next three hours, Lireinne stomped, sulked, and stormed in front of the seated, impassive Italian designer, with her angry face firmly in place. If modeling meant wearing killer clothes and an attitude, she was good with that in *spades*. After all, Lireinne's many years of being dismissed, ignored, vilified, and used had created an almost bottomless well of go-to-hell, just waiting to be tapped.

And the collection—the alligator motorcycle jacket, slim jeans, and thigh-high boots in softly gleaming black, the cognac safari suit and chartreuse camisole, the dark-chocolate trench coat and slinky slip dress of shy pink—Lireinne loved *all* of it. Even though she'd never before imagined clothes like these made from gator skins, they were wildly gorgeous, unimaginably inventive.

It was past noon and Lireinne was starving again, but she was glad she hadn't eaten anything but the brioche earlier that morning. Luigi's designs fit almost as though they'd been made for her, but were so snug she hardly dared take a deep breath. That boy Luciana and Peter had been arguing about, Alberto-whoever, must have weighed only a hundred pounds in his shoes, she thought as she waited for the assistant to fasten the back of a sheath dress in flat, metallic gold hide.

But ever since she was first zipped into the leather's uncompromising caress, Lireinne had felt a heady sense of . . . *power*. It was an elusive sensation, one she was discovering she'd always craved without knowing what it was, having never really experienced power before. The alligator designs were an extreme fusion of sophistication and barbarity, and inside them Lireinne discovered she felt like somebody new, a girl who'd never have to take any bullshit from anyone. Glorying in this feeling, she ramped up the attitude another level, letting the power take her to a height she could never have imagined existed for her.

Attitude, power. They brought something with them, hand in hand. They brought a kind of *freedom*. Lireinne's attitude elicited Peter's soft claps of approval, Luciana's sighs of admiration—the outward manifestations of power. The freedom was humming inside, a clear, high song for Lireinne's ears alone.

And yet, his expression considering, Luigi hadn't said anything beyond a direction or two.

"Over here, by the light."

"Make the bigger steps. Luciana, mess up again her hair."

"Don't smile."

It was mid-afternoon in the cramped dressing room and Lireinne was worn almost threadbare. Modeling, she now realized, was harder work than she'd imagined, a lot harder. The girls in the *Vogue* photo shoot hadn't looked dead on their feet, but now she understood that they had to have been. She was as tired as if she'd hosed the barns clean on a Monday.

But only one design remained on the rack in the dressing room—an opalescent white, low-bodiced wedding gown hung with huge, gathered skirts, all of it in the same supple alligator skins. A stiff, armatured crinoline had to be fastened separately underneath the dress to give it volume, and between the foundation garment and the leather gown itself, Lireinne gasped as the assistant wrestled her into both pieces. The whole, layered costume was so heavy she staggered at the sudden weight of it. The voluminous skirts settling around her waist alone were an easy seventy-five pounds of alligator skin, lined with softest silk.

Good thing she was so strong from horsing the hose around the barns all day for months, Lireinne thought. Making the effort to stand erect, she found herself remembering enormous Snowball and her white skin. Luigi would need at least fifteen just like her for the skirt alone, but according to Con, there were only eight leucistics in the whole world. The skins for this gown had to have been bleached and dyed, good news for Snowball and her distant kin.

Lord, who'd have thought this morning that before the day was over Lireinne Hooten from Million Dollar Road would be wearing such an incredible gown, one that had to cost thousands and thousands of dollars? "This last one's for you, you big man-eater," Lireinne said under her breath, her hand stroking the shining white leather skirt.

Snowball. Her old friend, her sort-of good luck charm.

"Voilà, mademoiselle," the assistant said. She sounded wiped out, too.

"Merci." For the last time, Lireinne squared her shoulders and straightened her spine, determined to finish this day in the same style in which she'd begun—with attitude. Attitude was all she had left, she was so beat.

Both hands grasping the alligator folds of her skirts, sweeping from the small dressing room into the atelier, Lireinne suddenly halted before the wall of mirrors, stunned by her reflection in the glass. Her fatigue vanished.

"Holy freaking cow," she whispered.

Everything that had gone before was eclipsed by this dress. Lireinne raised her arms and lifted her long black hair off the white column of her neck, her breasts straining in the tight, scaled bodice. She almost didn't recognize the girl in the mirror. This was no fat chick, this wasn't damaged goods. This was no hoser.

This girl's eyes were glittering pools of black-lashed green, huge and fierce in her heart-shaped, amber-lipped face. Her slender waist rose from the shimmering gown's massive leather bell of gathered folds like a young sapling. And the crescent-shaped scar—the scar Bud hadn't had the money to get fixed—only served to underscore a cruel, almost snarling beauty. What had once been ugly now seemed a perfect punctuation mark, a signal emphasis to Luigi's bold, revolutionary design.

The room was silent, as though it held its collective breath. Lireinne pirouetted a slow circle in front of the mirrors, the wide alligator skirts rippling in dense waves around her black suede pumps.

Tapping her sunglasses against her yellow horse teeth, Luciana pronounced, "The shoes are not correct, but this *Américaine* has it—a hungry, dangerous innocence, most savage. And to think I am finding her like a lost dog in the street!"

Peter said with a sage nod, "I told you so. You never needed the boy, Lu-Lu."

Luciana said, *"Luigi.* I tell you a thousand times. Luigi!"

But Luigi said nothing.

Everybody waited; no one said a word. Silence mounted, like the fevered hush of the air before a storm breaks open the sky.

His face unreadable, Luigi got up from the low leather couch. In the quiet his rubber flip-flops slapped loud across the white wooden floor. He stopped behind Lireinne. His sharp little black eyes met hers in the mirror.

"Cara feroce," Luigi murmured.

Curtly, he nodded only once. Lireinne was as still as a girl made of glass when the man placed his hands on her bare shoulders. Luigi turned her around to face him. To her astonishment, he kissed her on both cheeks: *smack, smack.*

"This face," Luigi said with a grand bow, "is the new face of Luigi Spada. Now I call the fall collection . . . *Adventuress.*"

CHAPTER 24

Much to his irritation, Con hadn't been able to get another reservation at Marius et Janette for tonight, but Julien had pulled some obscure French strings and secured a late table at Michel Rostang, a classic restaurant not too far from the hotel. Instead of oysters, caviar, and blinis, tonight would be truffles and cream-laced vichyssoise, but Con wasn't thinking about dinner.

He was seated in Le Bar at the Plaza Athénée, and it was here he planned to give Lireinne the tourmaline earrings from Chopard. They'd be a splendid complement to the green dress she was wearing, and besides, a beautiful girl needed good jewelry to set her off, after all. She'd wear them to Michel Rostang and he'd be the envy of every other man in the room. Con fingered the small, dark-blue box in his jacket pocket, pleasurably anticipating her surprise and delight when she opened it.

But he hesitated. There was something different about Lireinne tonight, a mysterious something like the glint of luminescence in a deep woodland pool. Con couldn't put his finger on the change in her. If anything, she was more spectacular than ever—although she'd had barely five words to say to him since he'd sat down with her five minutes ago. Earlier she'd called him up in the room from downstairs, asking him to meet her here, which seemed odd in itself. And this difference, apparent from the first moment he saw her waiting for him in the bar, was becoming somewhat unsettling.

"What did you do today to top yesterday's hike? Climb three hundred stairs to the dome of Montmartre?" Con joked. But his attempt at wit fell into her silence with a thud. Lireinne only offered a half-smile, shrugging one shoulder in response to his question.

Con tried again. "How'd you spend your day?"

"Shopping." It was another one-word answer. Lireinne took a delicate sip of her aperitif, a *kir* he'd ordered for her. In the dimly lit, high-ceilinged room, at the lucent, handcrafted glass bar, a raucous trio of American businessmen howled laughter, something about an excursion to the Crazy Horse strip club later that evening. Laughter did little to cover the undisguised attention they were paying to Lireinne. She seemed indifferent to their comments and long, leering looks, but Con had already had enough of it. With luck, they'd leave soon.

"Shopping?" Con waited for Lireinne to elaborate but she didn't say anything else, only nodding her assent. "So why didn't you take the money I left you?" he asked. When he'd gone upstairs to change after his day with Julien, to Con's perplexity he'd found the bills exactly where he'd left them, an untouched, neat stack of euros on the table by the door.

"I didn't want to take it." Lireinne's reserve was impenetrable, but it occurred to Con that she seemed to be holding something back. What it might be, though, he couldn't fathom.

"Why?"

Lireinne shrugged again, almost irritably. "I told you already. I have my own money."

It was then that Con became fully aware of the seismological shift in her, the sea change. What had happened to the laughing girl of last night, effervescent as the best champagne, wind-blown and rosy-cheeked from her afternoon's adventure? Who was this enigmatic, beautiful stranger sitting in the gray leather club chair across from him? It was as though Lireinne was behind a wall made of the same heavy glass as the bar: he could see her, he could hear her, but he wasn't reaching her at all.

Digesting this disquieting realization, Con wanted another Glenmorangie and the waiter was nowhere in sight. He drummed the fingers of his right hand on the tabletop.

He was still learning about her, he realized. Lireinne had a needless independent streak, and might be easily offended. Con had attempted to keep his tone affable, but it was becoming a greater effort with each unsatisfying exchange in this terse back-and-forth.

"So . . . what did you buy?" he asked.

"These." Lireinne stretched an elegant leg from under the table and gestured at her shoe, a strappy, pointed-toe stiletto in gleaming black calfskin, stamped with a tiny brass logo on the instep. With a beatific smile, she said softly, "*Prada*. Aren't they cool?"

On Lireinne's slender feet the stilettos were very cool indeed, as well as incredibly hot. The shoe's thin leather straps braceleted the remarkable architecture of her ankles, the heels exaggerating the curve of her calf. And anything from Prada cost a pile of money, Con thought, his unease mounting by the minute. How the hell had she been able to buy them when she hadn't taken the euros this morning? No way she'd have had enough cash on her to buy a pair of shoes from Prada, not even if she'd saved every goddamned penny she'd ever made at the farm.

"They're knockoffs, right?" Those shoes had to be counterfeit.

Lireinne arched her scarred eyebrow, obviously irked at the suggestion. "No. I bought them this afternoon on the Avenue Montaigne, on my way back to the hotel." She swallowed the last of her *kir*. "Can I have another drink?"

"Oh, come on, Lireinne. How'd you buy them?" Con demanded. "You don't have that kind of money, not for shoes like those!" He swiveled his head, looking for the waiter. "And of course you can have another drink. For God's sake, you know I'll buy you whatever you want. What the hell did you do for money? Rob a bank?" Only half kidding, he was now impatient and almost alarmed at her evasiveness.

Lireinne's eyes had turned hard at his questions, her full lips compressed into an uncompromising line. "I earned the money, okay?"

"*Earned* it?"

"Earned it." Lireinne tossed her hair over her shoulder. "You didn't have to pay, so why do you care anyway?"

Why did he care? How could she ask such a thing?

Con rattled the ice cubes in his empty glass. "Because I love you, honey," he said with some asperity. It was an impossible story, her making the money for those shoes. Surely she hadn't *stolen* them. "Now look," Con said, struggling to find words that wouldn't enflame this rapidly escalating situation, "I don't want you involved in something . . . shady, not when I'm always going to take care of you. Exactly *how* did you earn the money? You better tell me the truth right now, babe, 'cause I can still fix it if—"

"Oh, for crap's sake," Lireinne interrupted. "I modeled, okay?" She folded her arms, her rose-leaf mouth turning sulky. "And that's part of what I gotta talk to you about."

"You modeled? You?" Con's face tightened.

"Yes, me. *I modeled.*" Taking a deep breath, Lireinne seemed to be preparing herself for what she meant to say next, but the waiter finally appeared at the table.

"*M'sieur, mademoiselle.* Would you have another cocktail?"

Her expression transforming from a narrow-eyed defensiveness to one that was considerably more charming, Lireinne held out her glass. *"Une autre pour moi, si'l vous plaît?"* The waiter bowed and took the long-stemmed glass from her with a nod of surpassing correctness.

"Me too, please," Con said. Inside he was seething, but made sure to maintain a pleasant demeanor in front of the waiter because he hated a scene, he hated a scene like he hated conflict. This disagreement had all the earmarks of turning into a messy scene in a public space.

Like hell, she'd modeled!

Young, uneducated, and unconnected, even though she was singularly beautiful, Paris was rife with pretty girls. The only way

Lireinne could've modeled for anyone would have been to take off her clothes. Con was nearly wild at the thought, only just able to contain his sudden, furious jealousy at the idea of someone other than him seeing her naked, but with a strenuous effort he managed not to react. Goddammit, Con thought, he'd have to march over to Montmartre first thing in the morning and buy up everything—photos, drawings, paintings, scribbles, every goddamned thing—from the scumbag who'd taken advantage of his girl's naïveté.

As soon as the waiter left the table, Con exploded. "You're talking about nude modeling, right? Like for some half-ass, piece-of-shit artist over on the Rue Montparnasse? What were you thinking?" Con shook his head, deeply frustrated at her heedlessness, all for a pair of shoes he could have bought for her himself. "Honey, you were taken advantage of, taking your clothes off for some creep with a palette knife!"

"Excuse me?"

Lireinne's eyes were green ice. In a low voice, surprising to Con in its sudden bitterness, she snapped, "Of *course* you'd go there! You're the exact same as everybody else. You think I'm some kind of *whore*. For your information, I didn't take off my clothes to get the money, you asshole. I worked hard for it, modeling for Luigi Spada, not for some freaking artist. God, like get over it, okay? You don't get to tell me what to do!"

"Luigi Spada?"

Con's mouth sagged in disbelief, both at this impossible story and how swiftly she'd become furious with him. He was only looking out for her, after all. This was nothing like the Lireinne he knew.

"You're mistaken." Con tried to be soothing. "Somebody lied to you. Darling, I love you with all my heart but . . ."

With an impatient wave, Lireinne interrupted him again, her tone level and deadly. "Okay," she said, "here's a big ol' news flash. You can knock it off with that 'I love you' crap, got it? You don't love me and for sure I don't love you! Go ahead, fire me now and get it over with. Luigi wants me to sign a contract with him; he wants me to be *the* model for his new collection. He says by spring I'm going to be famous, like Kate Moss. And here's another big news flash—I don't have to sleep with him for this job 'cause he's not like *you*. Luigi's gay, okay? He's got a boyfriend."

"What?" Con faltered, almost whispering. Like a great suspended chandelier breaking free of its moorings, the world as Con understood it crashed to the ground in jagged, heart-piercing shards of incomprehension.

"Slow down, Lireinne. I, I don't get any of this," he managed, barely able to say the words without stuttering. "What do you mean, me firing you? I would never do that to you. I don't know what happened today to make you even think such a thing, but, but . . ."

Con shook his head, struggling to understand this inexplicable . . . *tantrum*. He adored Lireinne, he'd do anything for her; this, at least, was solid ground. "Maybe you're not ready to love me yet," he said, his voice strengthening, "but I do love you, I'm crazy about you. You've known that for weeks. For God's sake, you couldn't *not* know."

"Yeah, sure." Lireinne nodded with a curled-lip disdain. "Face it," she drawled contemptuously, "since the moment you met me, all you wanted was to nail my ass, to use me just like everybody always tries to use me. Listen up, *Con*. You creep me out, touching me all the time, and I don't want you, okay?"

"You don't want me?" Con repeated stupidly.

"God, no—I don't want anybody!"

"So, okay, okay. I'll give you time until you . . ."

"I will never love you." It was a flat, cold declaration of immutable fact.

Con was stricken speechless. He was already drowning in Lireinne's spate of wounding words, but at this—*I will never love you*—he flushed a deep, injured red. Not only did she not return his feelings for her, she'd as much as told him he was a fool for thinking she ever would.

And she'd called him . . . *creepy*.

Him? Creepy? What, then, had these past months been about? How could he have been so deluded by her? Somewhere beyond the crashing waves of betrayed trust in his own blithe assurance of her, of what he'd been convinced was the love of a lifetime, a floundering voice wailed *wait*.

But Con couldn't listen, not now. Instead, he seized upon his injured pride, his hurt and bewildered pain, and turned it back on Lireinne in blazing scorn.

"So, let me get this straight," he grated. "You modeled for Luigi Spada and now, all of a sudden, you're telling me you can't—or won't—have me on a bet. News flash for *you*, little girl. You were a goddamned hoser. I gave you a chance no one else would've given some high-school dropout, no matter how pretty you are. No, I really put my ass out there for you and now that you don't need me anymore, you're telling me the last three months have been a lie? Who's using who, Lireinne?"

Her composure regained, Lireinne lifted her green silk shoulders in careless agreement. "Whatever," she said. "If you want to think about it like that, I guess we used each other, okay? But let's get it right, Con. You didn't promote me because you needed some freaking assistant. You just wanted to get laid. All this 'I love you' shit is something you made up so you can feel good about yourself. We both know what you're *really* after, and you can forget it."

She pushed her long, glossy hair behind her shoulders and gazed at Con, as implacable and dispassionate as a Vegas pit boss at a blackjack table. "Anyway, all that's over now. Luciana says I'm going to be huge after the collection previews. I'm gonna earn heaps of money, with nobody . . . *grabbing* me all the time."

"Oh, yeah?" Con raised a furious eyebrow, scoffing, "How much money? You're out of your mind if you think Spada's going to pay you enough to live on. Oh, and if you're bent out of shape, worrying that some people think you're a, a . . . whore, just wait until he expects you to put out like one! In this business, that's what happens to girls like you. I should know—every time I make a trip over here, models are always handed out like goddamned after-dinner mints."

Lireinne's lovely face was the picture of bored, youthful dismissal.

"That's so not going to happen to me," she announced. "I can look after myself, in case you hadn't bothered to notice. Besides, don't you get it? I'm gonna get to live in freaking *Paris*. Luigi's giving me an advance so I can get an apartment, so back the hell off. You don't know everything." She shook her head. "But this is stupid. It's going nowhere. I'm going now."

Lireinne rose from the table, collecting her purse and her coat. The Americans over at the bar pricked their ears, watchful as a hunting wolf pack spotting a lone, graceful deer poised for flight.

"Lireinne, wait," Con said helplessly, regretting his outburst and trying to salvage what he could, if he could. "Please, sit down. Let's go to dinner and try to talk this out."

"But I don't want to talk anymore," Lireinne said with exaggerated patience. It was galling: she sounded as though she were talking to a child. "Anyhow, it's not like I'm hungry. I had a late lunch with Luigi and Luciana this afternoon, celebrating, and now I'm going to her place to sleep on her couch. I'll come and get my stuff sometime tomorrow."

"That's *it* then?" He still couldn't believe it.

"That's it." Lireinne slung her purse over her shoulder. "'Bye, Con. Maybe I'll see you around sometime."

Scrambling to draw the shreds of his tattered pride around himself, Con could find absolutely nothing to say to her before she turned away from him.

Without a backward glance, Lireinne swayed on her brand-new Prada stilettos through the doors to Le Bar and turned the corner. She was gone. The wolves bayed their disappointment, but soon resumed their salivating speculation about the girls at the Crazy Horse.

From the other end of the bar, the waiter was approaching, carrying the tray of drinks Con had ordered. "*Mademoiselle* will return, yes?" he asked, placing fresh napkins, the crystal glass of scotch, and the rose-colored *kir* on the table.

Wait.

"No," Con said heavily. "I don't think she will." Fumbling for the bottle of pills in his jacket pocket, the fingers of his right hand brushed a small object: the box from Chopard. Con flushed. Popping the cap off the vial in a desperate hurry, he shook two Vicodin onto the table and, holding up one finger to indicate that the waiter shouldn't go yet, he picked up the pills and washed them down with the scotch in front of him, finishing it in a long, single swallow.

"Bring me another drink, please."

And another after that. Con raised his shaking, bandaged left hand to look at his watch and discovered that the whole scene, start to finish, had taken place in a fast ten minutes. Obi-Wan hadn't stood a chance, he thought. He had a stunned sense of having taken a slug to the head from his blind side. Even now he didn't dare admit how efficiently the girl had decimated his private understanding of himself, the easy, arrogant space he'd always inhabited.

Obi-Wan had failed: the lovely Lireinne had cut the old Jedi mind-controller off at the knees with a single, heartless stroke. He could have hated her for that.

But his anger with her, while it shielded him for a few minutes more, couldn't hold out for long. Even in the depths of injury, it had never been like him to hold fast to resentment. True also, this love wasn't so easily dead; he found he couldn't expel Lireinne from his heart. He couldn't seem to bring himself even to try. Con Costello had never had any experience with a love like this one, but he suspected it would be a long time, a very long time, before he could live with the way it had changed him.

So it was that Con set out to get thoroughly, suddenly drunk, alone at Le Bar with his humiliation, his spurned affections, and his ruined hand. From a wide world of love to a world of . . . nothing, all in ten minutes flat.

Wait.

Con had lost track of the time but the noisy American wolf pack had moved on, giving way to another, equally loud party. Down by the fireplace, five rotund, red-faced German burghers were enjoying round after round of beer and guffawing in high good humor. They offered up hymns to beer from the fatherland in beery baritones, happy and jolly and deafening. Con wished all of them would get the fuck out, go in search of wursts, Fräuleins, and accordion music and leave him alone.

At some point he'd lost track of how much he'd had to drink, too, although the drinks hadn't achieved the effect he'd hoped for. Sometime after the fourth scotch, counting had become pointless since Con couldn't seem to find oblivion no matter how many glasses of Glenmorangie the waiter brought. The Vicodin was having no discernible effect on his misery either, for there could be no rosy imaginings, no sweet warmth enfolding him into a dream of Lireinne. There'd be no repairing this, Con thought. Christ, apparently there had never been anything to repair in the first place and he'd been a goddamned idiot for ever believing otherwise. In a nod to small mercies, though, the hand didn't hurt at all now. Too bad the pills couldn't do their job on what was left of his torn-up heart.

Was she in bed? Had she turned out the lights and gone to sleep?

"Kill me now," Con muttered. He reflected blearily that far from his previous high opinion of himself, now it could be argued that he was, in fact, a loser. Proof? Oh, there was plenty of proof.

Lizzie was gone. She didn't even want his baby.

Lireinne didn't love him. She'd made that more than plain.

And then . . . Emma.

His thoughts turning to his first wife, Con had to admit her memory might be the most painful of all. If she knew of his current misery, he was sure Emma would shake her head in sorrowful incomprehension, wondering at his headlong, ultimately fatuous pursuit of a girl who was less than half his age. It hurt to think of Emma, but in that moment Con couldn't escape a keen longing for his old, unremarkable, now-suddenly precious life with her. Emma had loved him, he knew it, he'd always known it, but that hadn't stopped him from walking away from something that had once been very, very good. Tonight he wasn't sure he could remember why he'd left her for Liz if he tried.

Oh, yeah—the fun. That was it. Lizzie had turned out to be some barrel of laughs.

Ah, Em. What had he done? Had he ever been that stupid? Con

raised his glass to his ridiculous self and admitted he had been. Hard as it was to face, he'd badly misread them all. First Emma, then Lizzie. Now Lireinne. For a guy who always seemed to get the girl, Con Costello obviously didn't have a clue as to how to keep one.

All of his women. What a joke that was. After all she'd been through, Emma had to be too hurt ever to care about him again. Lizzie would find a soft landing in Binnings—if he'd read the signs correctly—and Lireinne was asleep on some Parisian couch somewhere. What was she dreaming of now? There could be no doubt: Lireinne was dreaming of her new life as a supermodel. How could she know what a perilous path that was, how so many young girls who flocked to Paris came to grief following the same dream? Exploited, underpaid, discarded after a few seasons when the next season's crop of adolescent Brazilians came to town? Though he tried to tell himself Lireinne wouldn't just survive, but would likely thrive, Con was troubled for her well-being even as he knew she'd want no part of his concern. Go on, say it, you fool, he thought. You love her still. You'll always love her.

Hell, you love them all. They just don't love you.

And in this way his thoughts circled the drain, deeper and deeper into the bottle of Glenmorangie.

It was well after midnight before the Germans finally paid their bill and departed in a back-slapping, hiccupping group. Con was alone at last, except for the bartender.

Alone, that is, until the woman entered the lounge from the lobby and sat down at the long glass bar.

"Martini, *s'il vous plaît*." Her voice was low and pleasingly cultured. The accent, the fitted, caramel-colored business suit, the graceful sophistication—it was unmistakable: she was a Frenchwoman. Moreover, that slightly simian, subtly made-up face and the blond-streaked mane falling in expert disarray to her shoulders proclaimed it like a French flag. Better than half drunk and sick of his own company as he was, Con wasn't so far gone as to miss the high, sharp breasts under her sheer white blouse, the slim waist flowing into sturdy hips. Her skirt slid up her thigh as she crossed her legs, and they were as good as the rest of her.

Nice. Unbidden, Con's predatory instincts hailed him through the fog of scotch. The woman was exactly what he needed, they said. That wailing, swept-out-to-sea part of him said to forget it. After Lireinne's utter rejection tonight, he was done with all that, maybe forever. Con was torn, but wondered what his future would be like if he were to listen to his loser-self now.

Ought to grab your lightsaber, Obi-Wan, he thought, if you ever want to look at yourself in the mirror again without shame. Get back in the game before it's too late. Just like always, a woman had crossed his horizon, a damned fine one by the looks of her. Con was on familiar ground when she lifted her eyes and gave him a frank, cool gaze of assessment.

But what if . . . he couldn't? What if this woman shot him down tonight, too? Con knew his ego wasn't just bruised and broken, it was in the ICU on life support. Another woman's rejection could pull the plug. Based on his recently proven capacity for self-delusion, he thought perhaps the safest course of action would be to sign his bar bill, go upstairs, and pass out.

Con sneaked another quick glance at the woman, met her eyes, and looked away. He hunkered over his scotch again, bereft of any confidence in his usual, unfailing ability to approach a potential pickup. Even considering it felt threatening.

But she *seemed* interested, didn't she?

"Jesus, go on. She can't hurt you," Con muttered under his breath.

You sure about that? the cast-away voice warned, querulous. Don't forget, it said, you've already been called creepy tonight. Why ask for more of that?

But deep in the broken heart of him, appetite opened its eyes and shook itself awake. Why not? appetite argued. Agreed: this woman might slap your face if you approach her, verbally if not literally, but you've never gotten anywhere in life by being a goddamned coward. Go on, appetite demanded. Don't just accept being a . . . *loser.* Not without making a last stand.

Having bullied himself in this way, with a resigned sigh Con opted for action. He slid out of his chair, lurched to his feet, and with a precariously attained, self-conscious balance crossed the room full of empty chairs to the bar.

She'd just finished her drink when he put his right hand on the tall stool beside her.

"May I join you?" Con's tone was careful, only a bit slurred. The woman's eyes, an unusual yellow-green the color of Pernod, met his in inquiry. Encouraged that she hadn't dismissed him yet, "Please don't leave," Con said, chancing the possibility that she spoke English. "I, uh, find myself at loose ends tonight."

"If you wish." Her tone was measured almost to the point of indifference.

"I do."

"Then by all means—sit, *m'sieur*. I make it a habit to avoid coming between men and their wishes. Yours is a simple one." She looked down at her empty glass with a small, polite smile.

Nonplussed, Con sat heavily on the stool and signaled the bartender for another round for the two of them. Okay, he thought in weary discouragement, maybe this wasn't such a great idea after all, but . . . what the hell, right? He'd give it his best shot if only to prove to himself that Lireinne hadn't killed him outright. Con keenly felt the absence of his old accomplice, Obi-Wan, though. The last time he'd done without Obi-Wan was years ago, with Emma. With a renewed sense of loss, Con realized that during their years together he'd never felt the need.

But the drinks came then, another scotch for Con and the woman's vermouth. They each took a sip, while the woman looked away, perhaps bored.

This was pointless, Con decided, and a deserved end for a resounding disaster of a night. He was about to make his excuses and go when, with a sideways glance, the woman said, "American, yes?" With that mundane question, she arched a groomed, dark eyebrow.

Con nodded in cautious relief. She was talking to him, at least. "Good guess. How can you tell?"

The woman made an amused noise that wasn't quite a snort. "It is not difficult. Rare, though—an American on his own. They seem to travel in pairs. Why are you alone tonight?" she asked.

Unsettled by her directness, Con wrapped his right hand around his drink staring with morose intensity at the sculpted glass surface of the bar. He tried vainly to think of a witty answer. He couldn't. Witty had fled the building hours ago with his old friend, Obi-Wan.

"Dunno, but I am," he said at last. "Alone, I mean. Maybe I made an asshole of myself." Con looked up to find her laughing at him.

"There, you see? Only an American would say 'asshole' like that."

Con's mouth twisted wryly. "Oh, yeah?" While it wasn't much fun being laughed at, she was still talking to him. "And so how do *you* say it?" he asked, feeling defensive and not liking the unaccustomed sensation very much.

The woman laughed, a delicious gurgle from deep in her throat. "I don't, but Americans say it all the time." She took a sip of her drink. "You see, in France we say 'shithead.' It's a custom."

Somehow Con found a weak chuckle. "Okay, then. I'll be a shithead."

"An improvement, no?" Her smile widened. "You can wash your head, but an asshole is what it is eternally."

Her good-natured teasing seemed to coax a pale flame of Con's charm into flickering life. It was a hollow, empty thing compared to his old blaze of talent, but still, Con carefully cupped that flame in his hand, grateful beyond all reason that he'd made this woman laugh. Even though it was at his expense, it was better than nothing.

"To shitheads," he said gallantly, raising his drink. The woman's eyes met his. They touched their glasses together.

"*Salut,*" she said. "To shitheads and their friends."

So then, as it often does in bars after midnight, the conversation really began, seamlessly sliding to the personal. Con gave the woman a condensed, censored version of his vital statistics—forty-three, divorced, alligator-skin-dealing lawyer for the world's largest farm. She seemed fascinated, but then everyone, Con had learned, was fascinated by alligators. Having exhausted that topic as quickly as he could, he learned that her name was Maxine—"Call me Max, everybody does"—she was from Marseille, was an amazing fifty years old, and she was married. A lawyer like himself, she was only in Paris for the night, having come to town to finalize a settlement for a client who'd divorced her husband of twenty years.

"He was more trouble than he was worth, apparently," Max said, one corner of her mouth lifted in a half-smile. "Sometimes it goes like that, yes?"

Con slugged back the last half-inch of his scotch and signaled for another. "Happens to the best of us," he said after a moment. "One minute you've got the world by the balls, and then . . . you're just another shithead. Still, it's better to have loved and lost, et cetera. Or so they say."

Those yellow-green eyes regarded him over the rim of her glass, amused and somehow understanding. "*Eh bien,* truly there is no argument. The experience for which one pays is better by far than the kind one gets for nothing. Everyone knows this is so."

Reluctantly, Con nodded. "Yeah, well—then I just got handed the experience of a lifetime. But if you ask me, I'm positive I could have learned the same damned thing without getting my ass kicked. That, as the recent, now-departed love of my life would say, sucks."

Max lifted her glass to his. "We are in agreement. Pain is an unforgiving tutor."

There fell a moment's silence, but this quiet between them was companionable. It felt . . . honest. Con would have been hard-pressed to say why, but he was thinking he'd never really known he could simply talk with an attractive woman, to be this relaxed with a potential bedmate. The conversation had a flavor strange to him, like that of enlisted men sharing war stories, but it was a welcome respite from years and years of the pressures of having to be Obi-Wan. Con hadn't understood that about himself, not before tonight, when Obi-Wan had taken a powder and Con had been left with none of his usual resources. Tonight, instead of being bent on seduction first above all things, he could enjoy paying attention to Max for its own sake. He was genuinely *liking* this confident, intriguing woman. She appeared to be a player equally skilled at his old game.

"So . . . what do you think about a man with a crippled hand?" Con found himself asking Max the question that had plagued him for weeks. He wasn't sure he was ready to hear the answer yet, but she seemed to be playing this straight, almost too straight. Still, in any case Con had nothing left to lose tonight by asking.

"Could you ever . . ." he hesitated. "Stand for someone like that . . . to touch you?"

Max tilted her head in inquiry. "Is this man a shithead? I have a weakness for them."

"Oh, I'm a shithead, all right."

"What courage. I wonder, is this a habit? Do you ask every woman this, or am I an exception?"

"You're the first," Con said, his mouth dry.

"Show me," Max said simply.

After a long moment's struggle and internal debate, Con removed his gauze-wrapped left hand from the safety of his jacket pocket and placed it on the bar. In the low, intimate light, the hand didn't look like anything human. It looked like a mistake at the end of his arm.

But Max didn't avert her eyes in shock or disgust. She didn't turn away in pity.

"And without the bandage?"

"Are you kidding? Isn't this bad enough already?" Con tried to draw his maimed hand away, but Max placed her well-manicured one over it, holding it in a soft, firm clasp.

"Show me," she said again.

"Nobody wants to see this, trust me. Nobody."

"*Vraiment,* I am sure you believe so. But you will let me see, yes?"

Could he really? Con wondered. And why was he even thinking about doing it at all?

One thing was certain, though: he couldn't wear a bandage forever. He'd likely never see her again, not after tonight. The risk was as low as it was ever going to get. And so it was, there in the bar at the Plaza Athénée, that Con Costello sighed and resolutely rode out alone to meet the new day. For the first time, he allowed another human soul besides his doctor to see what was underneath the slightly grimy gauze.

After he unwound the bandage, though, the left hand lay there on the glass bar between them, a naked, white, and helpless mess. Although he'd seen it before, Con nearly wept at the sight. Along the edge of what remained of his palm, the seam was an angry red, puffy with scar tissue, laddered with neat suture lines from the heel of his hand up to where the webbing of his middle finger had once been.

"That's . . . it." Con swallowed around a hard lump in his throat, scarcely able to speak.

Confronted by the evidence of his damnable injury, he'd broken into a sick sweat but forced a cavalier smile that was bound to look as false as it felt. Any second now, Max would turn her eyes away. Her mouth would turn down with pity, or revulsion. He would die inside then, knowing that this was the way it would be for him for the rest of his life—a crippled creep.

"Hazard of the trade." Con strained to sound casual. "I'm the guy who kills tens of thousands of alligators every year. One of them bit me back and ate most of my hand." Perilously close to tears, somehow he found a ragged ghost of a laugh. "It's a gory kind of karma, isn't it?"

Max traced a light finger over his ravaged palm, her expression grave. To Con's disbelief, she lowered her head and pressed her lips with a gentle pressure to the Mount of Venus below his thumb. She kissed his left hand. Con's breath stopped at the touch of her mouth, so soft, so deliberate. He was barely able to contain a bewildered moan.

Lifting her head, Max's yellow-green eyes met his and there wasn't an ounce of pity in them.

"*Mais non*. This is not fate, *cheri*. This was but an accident, a consequence of a life. You are still a man."

Still a man. Almost undone by her unflinching acceptance of the crippled hand he loathed, Con blinked back the tears threatening to spill into a sob. This was the last thing he could ever have expected; any words he might have possessed deserted him. Con dropped his eyes. He gathered up the bandage, stuffing it and his left hand back in his pocket, safe from view. Con wanted another drink then, really wanted one, but his glass was empty.

And so was his bed. Con's pulse leapt like a racehorse out of the gate at that thought, bounding past his confused attempts to understand what this long night had done to him. Still, he avoided looking at Max because he couldn't find the nerve to meet those wise eyes.

"Please." His voice was low and hoarse. Con fought his sudden desperation, afraid of his need. He might break down like a kid, lost in a crowd of strangers.

Ah—the agony of not knowing if he still could, but he had to try. Almost inaudibly, Con said it again. "Please. I'm, well . . . terrified, but . . . please."

"Yes."

Con looked up at her, barely daring to believe. "Yes?"

With a humid, sidelong glance and a smile, Max gathered her purse. "Let us pay for our drinks, and then . . . yes."

When she came out of the bathroom, Max had taken off her suit and thin shirt. She was wearing only a creamy, lace-trimmed, rose-gold chemise—the kind of intensely flattering lingerie that only Frenchwomen seemed to own, a luxurious secret beneath their clothes. Con had always wondered where they bought the damned things, so damnably seductive, so perfectly fitted they had to be hand-sewn.

His heart pounding, he waited for her in the bed while she removed her earrings and put them on the night table. Max fluffed her mane of hair in the mirror and then she turned, her eyes meeting his. She raised her arms to pull her chemise over her head, slowly, and she was naked underneath. Con's breath caught at the revelation of her body: the high, insolent breasts, narrow waist, and solid hips flowing to smooth, round thighs. Max paused beside the bed, letting him look, her knowing smile as intimate as a whispered confidence.

She came to him then and slid beneath the smooth linen sheets. Con reached to turn off the bedside lamp.

"No," Max murmured. "No darkness." She wrapped her arms around his neck, pressing the length of her body to his, and her breath was rapid and shallow in the hollow of his throat. "Kiss me now, *cheri*." Her skin was scented with vetiver, clover, and moss.

With a groan, Con enfolded Max into his arms as though she were his very last chance, crushing her sharp breasts to his chest. His lips found hers and they were soft and cool, warming quickly as the kiss intensified. Con stroked Max's narrow waist, his right hand exploring the long, flat muscles of her flank before it found the ripeness of her sturdy hips, cupping her full buttocks, and all the while the kiss went on and on. He broke it before she did.

"My God," Con gasped into her hair, burying his face in her neck.

Here at last was the oblivion he'd been seeking, he thought. His hands, good right one and the other, opened her round thighs and Con, lost in her, thought no more. Blindly, he lowered his mouth to her breast and then it was her turn to gasp.

Max's fingers were in his hair and then they were on him, guiding Con with sweet impatience to the cleft between her thighs. His body covered hers and, with a sudden inevitability, they were joined. Pleasure claimed them. It was good, it was better than good, and then it was better yet.

And after they had both found their way, Max and Con lay spent in a companionable tangle of drowsy satiation. His racing heart slowing to a trot, Con rolled over, bracing his forearms on either side of Max's tousled head. He looked down at her wise face, into her chartreuse eyes, a green so different from Lireinne's vivid emerald. She smiled up at him.

"Thank you," Con said. His voice was quietly intense. "Thanks for showing mercy to a crippled shithead."

Max's soft laugh was a chuckle of completion, ripening into a contented sigh.

Knowing it then, the honesty between them demanding the truth of him, Con said what was in his heart.

"I miss my wife."

Max turned her head to kiss his shoulder.

"I know."

CHAPTER 25

"Bonjour, mademoiselle."

This early Saturday morning the snotty valet's greeting was respectful to the point of obsequiousness, his bow practically a genuflection. Lireinne, clothed in samples from Luigi's fall line and her new Prada stilettos, ignored the uniformed young man holding open the door to the Plaza Athénée. She didn't bother returning his greeting.

Underneath the soft, black, cashmere sweater-coat trimmed with umber leather, she wore a white silk collared shirt, a tight-fitting alligator-skin skirt, and black patterned stockings. Lifting a long-fingered hand gloved in a gauntlet of olive-hued hide, she smoothed her careless chignon, its loose strands framing her face. Except for her underwear, the battered bag slung over her shoulder was all that remained of her own clothes.

As she cat-walked across the quiet lobby of the hotel, her heels sounding a brisk, light tapping that echoed in the hush, Lireinne was sleekly aware of the effect she was creating. All eyes, those that were open at this hour, seven a.m., followed her as she approached the bank of elevators.

Earlier this morning, before October's first hazy light dawned,

Luciana had carelessly tossed the ensemble onto the worn, brown velvet Empire sofa that had been Lireinne's bed the night before.

"These will do, *cara*," she said. "Now, have a *caffè* and hurry away, make done your business with this man. We have much to do today before Luigi and I must fly to Milan this afternoon."

Lireinne brushed her teeth with the First Class toothbrush and untangled her hair with the comb from the travel bag she still had in her purse. As she dressed, she stroked the rich fabrics and leathers, marveling at the way the alligator skirt slid onto her slim hips, clinging with a just-right combination of suggestiveness and style.

And like in the fairy tale, on her way out of the door, the long gilt-framed pier glass in Luciana's hallway told her that she was indeed the fairest of them all. For *real*. Bolstered by the mirror's tidings, Lireinne set out in a cab to return to the Plaza Athénée. She meant to collect the few things she'd left there, the last pieces of her old life.

Much as she hated to give her any credit, Lireinne had to concede that Emma had been right. Clothes mattered. This flower-filled lobby with its glittering chandelier and marble floors seemed an appropriate setting for the tall, beautifully dressed girl waiting by the elevator doors. Nobody here would take her for a whore now, Lireinne thought with proud satisfaction.

But when she got in the elevator and pressed the button for the fifth floor, her satisfaction was tinged with a stubborn anxiety. For all Lireinne's bravado, she hoped she'd be able to slip inside the suite, grab her things, and get out of there without having to encounter Con. With any luck at all, he'd be sleeping or have left already. Last night's confrontation in the bar was still raw in her memory. The things she'd said to him had been *harsh*.

Lireinne winced, sort of wishing she could take it all back. Okay, maybe everything she'd said had been the truth, she thought, but that didn't mean she hadn't hurt him—she knew she had and that wasn't something she'd set out to do. But there hadn't been a good way to tell him any of it, Lireinne argued with herself as the elevator traveled silently upward. There wasn't any way that conversation had been going to end up being anything but, well, kind of mean.

Still . . .

The doors slid open. After a second's hesitation Lireinne stepped out into the corridor. Did she really need her old clothes? Lireinne wondered, unsure if she was ready to do this. She thought of being dependent on Luigi and Luciana for *everything,* though, and decided she did. Besides, she'd paid good money for those clothes. Firming her resolve, she removed her gloves and stuffed them in her purse before she slid the key in the lock and turned it.

To Lireinne's surprise, the door swung open just as she put her hand on the doorknob. An older woman stood in the entrance, apparently in the process of leaving Con's suite. The woman, wearing a well-fitted business suit and heels, looked equally surprised to find Lireinne outside the door in the deserted hall.

Did she have the wrong room? Lireinne wondered. No, this was the right door. She was sure of it because the key had opened the lock. Removing her hand from the doorknob, she stood tongue-tied, feeling somehow at a loss.

With a lifted eyebrow, the woman studied Lireinne, nodding as though she'd just had a mystery explained to her. In lightly accented English she said, "Ah. You will be Lireinne, I think." She shifted her expensive-looking purse to her shoulder and extended her hand. "I am Max. *Enchantée.*"

Who was this Max and what was she doing, coming out of Con's suite at such an early hour? Lireinne wondered. How did she know her name? And *hell,* this meant Con had to be up.

More uncertain than ever, Lireinne found herself taking the woman's offered hand and shaking it. *"Un plaisir de faire votre connaissance,"* she answered automatically. In that awkward moment, some of her high school French rescued her.

Max smiled widely in frank delight.

"Vous parlez français! Merveilleux. Your accent is good—not French, precisely, but quite good for an *Américaine. Mais,* Con did not

confide this to me. He said you are *très* beautiful—and very young—but nothing about this. Where did you learn your French?"

Lireinne flushed under the older woman's yellow-green, assessing gaze. In spite of Luigi's supercool clothes and her new Prada heels, she felt impossibly childish and gauche.

"I didn't learn all that much." Trying not to be intimidated by this sophisticated woman, Lireinne struggled to reclaim her former attitude. "Just a year of high-school French."

"Now that you will be living in Paris, you will learn quickly, to be sure."

Exactly how did this Max person know so much about her? Con must have told the woman an awful lot. Was she a business contact, or was she . . . something else? That *dog,* Lireinne thought with grim amusement. He sure didn't waste any time.

Max must have read her mind. "Ah, *chérie*—Con spoke of you only *un petit peu,* and I am but . . . his good friend. May I say I find you charming? Such élan, so *comme il faut, parfaitement!* I see now why he lost his heart to you."

She stepped out into the hall, leaving the door to the room ajar. Tilting her blond head to one side, Max lowered her voice, her tone confidential. "Only a man made of wood could resist such a one as you, and Con is not such a man. Be kind, Lireinne, for his heart is not yet at peace. And now I must go."

So bewildered at this advice, before Lireinne could find her voice and long before she could figure out how she should respond, Max had stepped into the open doors of the elevator. *"Au revoir."* The doors closed, and Lireinne was alone in the corridor in front of the suite.

Be kind? *Kind?* To Con? Unable to make sense of this, Lireinne had no time to puzzle over Max's comments for Con's voice came from the other side of the half-open door.

"Hello? Lireinne? Is that you?"

Her confusion was instantly replaced with her earlier nervous apprehension, but nevertheless Lireinne straightened her backbone and pushed the door open wider. Reaching for the poise she'd been robbed of in the encounter with Max, she strode as confidently as she could into the sun-filled space of the sitting room.

"Hey," Lireinne said, wishing she felt as offhand as that had sounded.

Con, backlit by the morning light streaming through the windows, stood in the middle of the room holding a copy of the *International Herald Tribune*. Still in the hotel's white cotton robe, his red hair was disordered, as if he'd just gotten up. He was unshaven and his feet were bare on the room's carpeted floor.

"Lireinne," Con said evenly. His face could have been expressionless as he greeted her, but there was a subtle play of some emotion behind his blue eyes. "I suppose you've come for your clothes." He absently ran his fingers through his hair, smoothing it.

Lireinne nodded, relieved that she didn't have to explain. "Yes."

"Well, you look marvelous this morning. Great skirt." Con crossed the room and poured himself a cup of coffee from the silver pot on the room service tray.

Lireinne was startled to see that he'd removed the bandage. She'd never seen his hand without the gauze before. It didn't look as terrible as she'd imagined it would—bad, but not heinous. She shifted from one foot to another and clutched the strap of her purse, wondering what she should say now that she'd have to talk to him after all. Like, "Your hand's not as gross as I thought it was going to be"? Probably not a good move, she thought.

And besides, Con seemed . . . distant, changed somehow from the man she'd walked out on the night before. How the hell should she play this?

Find that attitude, girl, Lireinne thought. It had served her well before.

Con said casually, "And I like your hair that way, too."

Her hand going to her chignon, Lireinne lifted her chin, saying, "Thanks. I figured putting it up would make me look more professional."

Con made a noncommittal noise. He stirred his coffee. "I see." He didn't sound as if he cared, not really.

This was so weird. It was like Con was making conversation with someone he didn't know, as though last night's scene in the bar had never happened. In a way, this made things easier, but Lireinne felt oddly . . . deflated. At least Con didn't seem like he was still mad. She was glad about *that*, for sure.

"I assume everything is well *chez* Spada?" he said.

"It's all good," Lireinne said, striving for an airy tone. "Luigi says I need to lose five pounds, but I'm cool with it. Like, five pounds is nothing. I lost over thirty when I came to work at the farm, you know."

"Oh, really? I had no idea."

Lireinne's hand twisted the strap of her purse at Con's indifferent reply. Her regained attitude was holding, but it felt like an act and she was unsure of her lines. Suppressing an unaccountable urge to bolt, she wondered if maybe she should just go now and leave her clothes behind. There weren't that many of them and it wasn't like she was all that into those clothes anyway. She'd always keep the green silk dress because it had been lucky for her, but the rest, the gray skirt and sweater, her underwear—she'd never have to dress in clothes from Banana Republic or Walmart ever again.

Con took a sip from his steaming coffee. "Have you told your stepfather about your new job? Is he happy for you?" His tone was politely inquiring.

Lireinne shook her head. "Not yet. I'm going to call soon, though. I didn't want to use Luciana's phone and run up her long-distance bill. I mean, I'm a guest. That would be rude."

Con smiled a faint smile. "Knowing what I do about the House of Spada, you shouldn't have worried. That's an old Italian family that made its money generations ago, in olive oil. Luigi's couture business is a drop in that bucket, trust me."

"Seriously?" Lireinne found this hard to believe. Luciana's huge, dark-curtained apartment on the Île-de-France was crammed full of really old, dusty furniture and collections of weird stuff: tiny ivory carvings, cracked blue-and-white vases, and these murky little religious paintings. It was kind of shabby, in fact. "Olive oil?"

"The extra-virgin kind. In any case, you should let your people at home know what's going on as soon as you can."

Lireinne nodded reluctantly, knowing he was right. She'd wanted to call Bud last night, feeling like a lost Louisiana mouse tiptoeing through Luciana's crowded rooms overlooking the Seine. She'd told herself she'd find a pay phone to use this morning after she'd picked up her clothes. She still had some money left after buying her shoes.

"I'm going to call them later," Lireinne muttered.

"Well, I won't keep you then," Con said. He put down his coffee cup with a yawn.

This felt so freaking *wrong* somehow. Now that Con was being so cool toward her, Lireinne suddenly felt as though she wanted to clear the air. She wanted to tell him that no matter what he thought, she was always going to be grateful for the chance he'd given her, always. It wasn't like Con had done it out of the goodness of his heart, not at all, but still . . . he'd done her a huge favor. Lireinne knew then she'd never, ever forget him because her new life wouldn't have happened if he hadn't brought her to Paris. It wasn't her fault she couldn't love him for it, but that didn't mean she didn't understand what she owed him.

I mean, Lireinne thought, it's not like Con ever *grabbed* me, not totally. Unlike Harlan and Brett, when he'd come on to her, it wasn't like being attacked by a wild animal.

And to tell the truth, Lireinne realized, from the first she'd understood him well enough, she'd always known she could say no. She could have told him to stop it that night; he'd have respected that. He wouldn't have fired her either. That kind of mean wasn't Con's way. He was a dog when it came to chasing women, but he was basically a gentleman about it.

Maybe . . . in this strange tangle, they could just shake hands and call it even.

But she couldn't say any of that. Lireinne paused, wondering how to make herself understood, and in that interval Con's waiting silence was as loud as a jet engine. She was sure she had to say *something*.

So, "Thanks," Lireinne said. Everything she'd felt she needed to say, all of it, lay in that one heartfelt syllable.

Con's generous mouth quirked. "Thanks for what?" he asked.

Really? Lireinne's wave of insight broke and receded.

"For . . . everything, I guess." This last conversation between them was over, Lireinne decided, stung and somehow insulted by his reaction. There was nothing left for her here. She turned away, heading for the room that used to be hers, planning to grab her things so she could get away from the disconcerting, strangely depressing exchange.

"You're welcome," Con said to her retreating back.

Was she? Did he mean that? Lireinne wondered. And did she even care if he had? And when Lireinne had finished hurriedly packing her things and re-entered the sitting room five minutes later, Con wasn't there anymore. The door to his room was shut, but the sound of the shower running came from behind it.

So . . . this was how her old life ended. What the hell had she been expecting from him, anyway? Lireinne left her key on the gilt table and shut the door, leaving it unlocked, and waited for the elevator in the corridor.

But all at once, for no reason she could understand, her eyes filled with tears. Why should this feel like that day, over ten years ago, when her mother had left for the last time? Lireinne never allowed herself to think about that day, *never*, but that long-submerged memory owned her now. She was caught in its undertow, swept away in the tide.

"But where are you going?" Seven-year-old Lireinne begged, clinging to Mommy's hand. "Don't leave. Please, Mommy?"

Her mother yanked her hand free and grabbed the two garbage bags stuffed with her clothes. "Let *go*, Lireinne. You'll be fine. Look after your brother, 'kay?"

And then she ran down the steps to the trailer without looking back, without saying good-bye. Lireinne's mommy ran to the man with the white truck who had been waiting for her outside in the yard.

"Duane!"

The man threw Mommy's bags in the bed of the truck, they got in, and the truck disappeared down the drive, fast. Lireinne watched until it was gone, and without warning the trailer was empty-feeling, frightening. Before, it had felt like home. Her four-year-old brother, Larry, was crying, but he was too little to understand.

"Don't cry," Lireinne said. "She'll come back."

A veteran of many leave-takings, Lireinne had known better than to cry because it didn't do any good. It never stopped Mommy from leaving anyway. Besides, even though her mother had abandoned her before, she wasn't gone for forever. Sometimes it took a long time, days and days and days, more than Lireinne could count, but she always came back.

Only . . . this time Mommy's leaving didn't feel the same. Before, she'd *always* told Lireinne that she wouldn't be gone long, that she'd be back soon, even though more often than not that turned out to be untrue. This time she hadn't said anything but good-bye.

"Don't cry," Lireinne said again. Unconsoled, Larry's fat little legs collapsed. He sat on the floor and howled louder. Lireinne patted his heaving shoulders before she wandered down the hall to the room Bud and her mother shared. She looked in the closet at the empty hangers, the spaces where shoes had been, breathing in the last faint traces of Mommy's perfume—a musky, heavy scent—lingering on the few clothes that remained. In the front room her little brother was still wailing, but Lireinne wasn't going to cry because it hurt too much, like getting hit with rocks. It hurt because nobody ever came when you cried. Nobody was here to come to her anyway, nobody but Larry.

Lireinne closed the closet door and left the bedroom. She was going to try to comfort her brother once more. Larry would have to learn not to cry, just like she had.

Crying, the seven-year-old girl knew within the fortress of her now-cold little heart, didn't do any good at all.

Lireinne wasn't going to cry this morning either. Carefully dabbing her eyes with a fingertip, she stepped into the elevator and pushed the button for the ground floor.

She was *so* out of there.

Later that Saturday, after the Spada siblings had departed for Milan, a package was delivered to the shop on the Avenue Montaigne. It was addressed to Lireinne Hooten, care of Luigi Spada.

Taking the package from the shop assistant, Lireinne examined the mysterious courier parcel, full of excited curiosity. There wasn't a return address on the label. Who had sent it to her; what could the bulky plastic bag contain? Unable to wait, she ripped the package open.

Inside were two items: a small, rectangular orange carton and a much smaller, dark-blue leather box. There was an envelope as well.

Wanting privacy, Lireinne took the package and its contents and hurried up the winding stairs to the deserted atelier: Luigi and Luciana wouldn't be back in Paris until Monday. Throwing herself onto the white leather sofa, she opened the orange carton first and discovered it contained a small cell phone.

Oh my God, Lireinne thought. Her first cell phone! The *way* cute phone was the size of a deck of cards and came with a bunch of instructions in what was probably going to be too-hard-to-translate French. Lireinne laboriously figured out the basics, though, from the pictures in the manual. Slipping the battery into the back of the phone, to her happy satisfaction the screen winked into life. With a feeling of wonder, Lireinne debated: who'd send her a cell phone? After thinking the few possibilities over, she concluded that it had to have been either Luigi or Peter. They were almost always jabbering away on theirs, and with her new job she was definitely going to need one now, for sure.

But what had they put in the little blue box? It fit easily in the palm of her hand, the word *Chopard* printed across the top in gold script. She opened the box, and Lireinne's eyes widened, slowly turning to awed, shining green stars.

"Ooh," she breathed. Her lips parted with delight. This was the most incredible pair of earrings, more beautiful than anything she'd ever seen in her whole life—even in *Vogue*. When she took them out of the box they lay cool and heavy in her hand, so they had to be real, right? Heavy had to mean real, and real meant expensive. *Very* expensive.

For her? Real earrings for Lireinne Hooten? Lireinne checked the courier parcel again. Like before, there was her name, typed on the label. The earrings were for her, all right.

Holding the miniature chandeliers up to the sunlight pouring through the long windows of the atelier, she gasped with pleasure at the shimmering cascades of diamonds and tourmalines. She had to put them on now, right this minute, Lireinne decided. She wanted to see how they'd look on her, the ex-hoser from Million Dollar Road.

Jumping up from the sofa, Lireinne ran to the mirrored wall. With shaking fingers, she fastened the earrings to her lobes and the drops of cool green stones matched her eyes, the diamonds blazed like tiny bonfires.

What were Peter and Luigi thinking? All this, for *her*? These must be a kind of welcome-to-the-world-of-modeling present or something, she thought. Maybe everybody got a gift like this when they were starting out. Lireinne hugged herself with a shivering elation and shook her head gently. The earrings kissed her flushed cheeks, ringing like tiny chimes at her ears, ringing a promise just for her. This present was crazy generous, even for the olive oil–rich Spadas.

Damn, she was a lucky girl. Lireinne spun in the middle of the white floor with her arms outstretched, laughing.

Only the envelope remained. Her curiosity fevered by now, Lireinne ripped it open to find a folded letter inside. With a last, ecstatic glance at her new earrings in the mirror, she took the single heavy, cream-colored page over to the window to examine it in the light. Resting her dark head on the pane, she read the letter with a dawning amazement.

> *Lireinne,*
>
> *You need a cell phone and I've covered a year's charges up front, overseas calls included. You can call home whenever you want now, so please stop worrying about how to pay for it. I also took the liberty of asking my friend and business associate, Julien Moreau, to give you a call. If you run into any difficulties whatsoever, I want you to have him as a contact. He'll be ready to help you with anything you need, anything at all. I haven't forgotten that you told me you could take care of yourself, but Paris can be a big, cold place for new arrivals. It's a long way from Million Dollar Road.*
>
> *Please, Lireinne—be well, be happy, but be safe, too. I can't bear the thought of a world without you in it.*
>
> *And the earrings had to have been made for you, although I'm sure the jeweler who created them never dreamed that one day they'd belong to the most beautiful girl in Paris.*
>
> *Yours,*
>
> *Con*

CHAPTER 26

An owl hooted in the dusk this Monday evening.

Since dawn it had been a day of softly falling rain, the constant, misting scrim of silver washing over the earth, horizon to horizon. The old live oak's evergreen leaves were almost black with the cold water dripping onto the soaked ground, but the rest of the trees surrounding Emma's farm were a sodden brown-and-dull-gold cloud against the gray sky.

After having shed her raincoat, wet socks, rubber boots, and hat, Emma sat in the rocking chair on the front porch, damp and tired, but satisfied that her fall garden was off to an exceptional start. The showers had come at just the right time and all the winter greens were lifting their leafy heads out of the rich brown soil, the arugula, kales, and collards lush as a dappled velvet carpet. The chickens were cooped and fed, and Sheba lay at Emma's bare feet, the hound's nose on her paws, sleeping.

The rain-washed air was cool, verging on cold, but Emma was warm from her labors and enjoying the end of October. It would be Halloween in a week, and soon it would be Thanksgiving. Emma reflected that she had so much to be thankful for, she would hardly need to cultivate gratitude at all when that holiday rolled around.

Why, these mornings she woke up feeling at peace with herself, eager to start her day.

The rain fell on. Emma raised her arms over her head, stretching. Her shoulder muscles were tight from weeding the rows and wearing the wet, heavy slicker all day. It was always easier to pull weeds when the ground was soaked, though, and it had been a kind of exhilaration, being outside and wrapped in this gentle, constant weather. The farm seemed to be resurrecting itself from the long, dusty summer, sections of it coming to new life as others died: the season had turned once more and was headed for true autumn.

Soon it would be time to head inside and finish putting together the dinner she'd made for Bud and Wolf, started before she'd gone out to work in the garden. A cassoulet of creamy white beans, duck thighs, and garlic sausage was already in the oven, embarked on the slow, almost alchemic process of becoming a comforting, delicious meal for a rainy October night. She'd need to wash and shred the savory turnip greens later and make an apple tart, too, because men liked dessert and there would be two of them at her table in a few hours.

Emma smiled, thinking of Bud.

Without making too much of it, they'd begun to see each other every day. Bud would come by after working on the loading dock most evenings, but last night she'd made the trip out to Million Dollar Road, having finally been invited inside the trailer. While their time together was mostly spent around each other's tables, Emma was aware that with every hour she spent with Bud, she found she wanted to know him better. He was nothing like Con, but then, nobody was. She wasn't sure how Bud's fondness for country music, chewing tobacco, and the lack of conversation about books, films, or even current events was going to play out as yet, but for now her heart and life were warmed by Bud's goodness, his honest and open regard for her.

And perhaps, one day, it would be more than regard? Emma had begun to hope it would be.

Life had changed for him, too. For those long four days when he hadn't heard from Lireinne, Bud had been too quiet, wrapped up in concern for his girl. But Lireinne had called last Saturday afternoon, telling him of her decision to stay in France, and had phoned many times since then. With each conversation, Bud had come to a greater degree of acceptance, his spirits had seemed to lift, and now, to everyone's astonishment, it seemed that Lireinne was launched into a new life. She had set sail on a high-stakes adventure all on her own.

"*Modeling*. Do you think she's makin' the right choice?" Bud had asked, hanging up after the latest call from Paris. It was a coincidence, being there when Lireinne had phoned last night. Emma had gone out to the trailer, ostensibly to deliver a hearty meal of lasagna and salad from her garden, but in reality she'd come over to see Bud. The lasagna was an excuse to be with him and by now she didn't care if he knew it.

"She's so dang *young*." His voice was worried as he gazed out the window into the moonless night.

Not too young to seize her chance, Emma thought.

Her hands were full with the casserole dish and the salad bowl, and she'd just escaped tripping over the puppy. Lunchmeat danced on his little hind legs, begging at the aroma of the food. Emma set everything down on the table, debating whether she should tell Bud what she really thought, that Lireinne wasn't too young to take advantage of whatever unlikely circumstances had transpired to give her a shot at being a supermodel. Paris was going to have its hands full with Lireinne Hooten, in Emma's opinion.

But in the end she smiled and said only, "Well, it's an opportunity of a lifetime for her. Besides, she can always come home if she wants to. Down, Lunchmeat."

Still gazing out the window, Bud scratched his head thoughtfully. "Yeah, that's so. If she'd a stayed in school, she'd be away at college anyhow. Guess this ain't that different."

Busy gathering the silverware to set the table, Emma refrained from saying that modeling in Paris was a far cry from a freshman year at LSU. Lireinne was going to be on a steep learning curve indeed, but somehow Emma couldn't envision that tide of ambition contained in a dorm room, hitting the books, working on term papers, and making popcorn.

"True," she said. "No matter what, she'd have found a way out of here eventually."

"She asked after you, you know," Bud said. He turned from the window and put an arm around Emma's waist, kissing the top of her head.

"Really?"

"Sure did, right after she grilled me about the Saints game today and asked how Mose and Lunchmeat was doing. Wanted me to tell you thanks again for the dress. Said it turned out lucky."

The green dress. Emma had forgotten buying it for Lireinne on that trip to the mall. Returning Bud's hug, she said, "I'm sure she looked fantastic in it." Her heart gave a tiny lurch, though, thinking about Lireinne in that dress, about Con and Lireinne together in Paris. She'd never know what had happened between them, but now she understood that was for the best.

So Emma didn't ask any pointed questions about Con's possible influence in Lireinne's sudden rise to fortune either, but she wondered how he'd taken the news that the unworldly girl he'd sought to seduce had slipped the leash, bolted, and was gone. Too, since the night before Lireinne had left for Paris, Bud hadn't asked any more about Con. It seemed he'd made whatever peace he could with the situation and was once again stoically on the side of Lireinne's independent judgment.

Let the past lie quiet, Emma thought. Con would always be Con. She got out the plates for the lasagna, merely asking, "When's Wolf going to be home? We can always reheat this."

This rainy evening on the porch, thinking of Bud Hooten and Con, their many differences, Emma was reminded of other days, other meals she'd cooked that had gone to waste when her husband hadn't come home in time to eat them before they went cold and tasteless. It was always business, according to Con, but now Emma knew better. Con's business was then, as it probably always would be, another woman.

What would it be like, feeding two hungry men every night, two men who could be counted on to come to the table, happy to be in her company? What would it be like, being loved by someone who wanted her and only her?

Now she was ready to find out, Emma realized with a shiver of contentment. She was ready to raise her own sails, catch the wind, and explore the sometimes perilous sea of her life. Whoever said only Con could be a pirate, daring to venture for the curve of the earth?

But then Sheba raised her head from her paws and growled a low warning: a car was making its way along the gravel road to the farmhouse. On the porch, Emma got up from the rocking chair and peered through the misting rain, trying to make out whose car it could be.

Somehow, though, she already knew. Like a lost, wandering spirit, her thoughts of him had summoned him here tonight. Emma's heart beat a solid, quick rhythm as the car drew closer, her cold hands unconsciously clasped into fists.

The Lexus rolled slowly up the drive, splashing through the puddles in the graveled ruts. Something was missing, something she couldn't put her finger on right away, but then Emma realized that the usual muffled thud of music, turned up so loud as to be almost a physical presence, was absent. The car's progress seemed almost somber without it. As it rolled to a stop, the Lexus's engine shut off and then there was only the quiet dusk, the murmur of the rain.

Con got out of the car. He wasn't dressed for the weather. The shoulders of his leather jacket were dark and water-stained, his jeans wet to the ankles. Without approaching the porch, he stood beside the car in the rain, looking as though he'd been walking in it for hours. Con raised his head, his face glistening with beads of water, and gazed at her nakedly.

"Em." It was all he said, but there was a world of need in his voice.

Emma's heart pounded harder. She hadn't seen him since that terrible night, that last rainy evening from what seemed like decades ago. She shuddered. Who was that woman who'd so loved Con that she'd tried to kill herself when he left her? Where had she gone?

Why, she wasn't gone. That woman had *changed*.

With a kind of wonder, Emma understood that about herself now. Her heart slowed, her clenched fists uncurled. She knew what she felt for Con now was a tender affection, mixed with concern. Even at a distance his left hand looked every bit as bad as she'd feared it would. How he must hate that! She remembered Con's quick hands, their cleverness, the knowing intimacy of them touching her body, and Emma mourned for him then.

"Con," she said softly. There was no need to say anything more.

For a long moment they were locked together in silence. The rain continued to fall.

Can you? his sea-blue eyes pleaded. *Can you love me again?*

I never stopped, her gold-flecked gray ones answered.

Emma left the porch, running barefooted down the water-slick front steps, and without a moment's hesitation she took him into her embrace. Con caught her up in his arms and rested his forehead on her shoulder, a deep groan that was almost a sob escaping his throat.

"Dear God, Con," she murmured, stroking his red hair, wet under her fingers. "What have they done to you?" His arms tightened around her, so tight that she almost couldn't draw a breath before he let her go. Con rubbed his eyes with his right hand, the left hanging by his side.

"Mind if we get out of the rain?" he asked. "I just got in from Paris this morning and I, I really need to talk to you."

Emma realized that the rain had picked up and was falling harder. She'd be soaked in seconds. "Yes, of course. Come on inside. I'll get you a towel."

Inside the kitchen the light was yellow and warm, the air rich with the mouthwatering aroma of the cassoulet. Emma handed Con a thick, dry towel and he took it from her wordlessly, removing his soaked leather jacket. He was wearing a white T-shirt underneath, but that was almost wet through as well.

"Thanks." Con dried his hair and face with the towel, rubbing the strong arms and shoulders she remembered so well. He didn't say anything else. Emma went to the stove and put the kettle on for tea, and Con collapsed into one of the ladder-back chairs at her table, looking as exhausted as though he'd walked all the way from France to her farm.

"Tired?"

Con nodded but didn't elaborate. Waiting on the water to boil, Emma was aware of his eyes on her, hungry and searching, and for an instant she wished she was wearing something more flattering than her shapeless old wool sweater and worn jeans. Her bare feet were dirty and her silver hair was damp, limp with rain. She'd sometimes imagined that the next time she saw him she'd be at her best, but now that he was here she looked like a ditch digger after a long day of shoveling mud. What must he be thinking?

Stop it, Emma told herself with sudden impatience. She got two mugs down from the cabinet for the tea. Her self-consciousness was becoming something like an old acquaintance, one she'd recognized on the street but didn't want to acknowledge anymore. Dismissing it with a small shake of her head, she poured the boiling water into the mugs.

"It's been a while," Emma said, trying to make conversation. She busied herself with making the tea for them—one sugar for Con, skim milk for her. She smiled, thinking that there were some things you never forgot. "So what brings you out here on a rainy Monday?"

"You. Just you."

Emma nearly dropped the steaming mugs she was carrying, but somehow her hands stayed steady as she set the tea down on the table. Stunned and yet strangely not surprised at all, she eased into the chair across from Con, regarding his pleading, weary eyes with a guarded caution.

"Oh," she said.

At one time this would've been more than she dared allow herself to hope for. That hope had passed, however, in an incremental, almost impossible-to-measure progress. It had filtered through her heart and mind in the days and weeks since her near-suicide. "Oh" was the only response she could muster, for Emma hadn't truly known until this moment that her desperate yearning for Con had gradually grown into acceptance and a lingering regret, a deep process she'd not been aware of, not until tonight. This, Emma realized, was both a death, one she had to acknowledge, and at the same time a kind of rebirth. This was a second chance.

Con didn't say anything more and the unspoken hung there between them, thick with memory, heavy with the ghosts of pain, but there were no panicked wings in Emma's chest now, no jeering voices to distract her from this moment.

Finally, Emma took a quick sip of the scalding tea and asked, "And Lizzie?" Her tone was neutrally questioning. "What about your wife?" She couldn't help being curious, but she was also buying time, wanting to come to some kind of understanding of what that "you, only you," might mean to her after all this time.

His elbows on the table, Con buried his face in his big-knuckled right hand and rubbed his eyes. "We've agreed to part," he said quietly. "It wasn't working out."

"That's a shame. What about . . ." Emma took a deep breath. ". . . the baby?"

Con shook his head. "I honestly don't know what's going to happen, but Liz has told me that it's not up to me anyway. I guess I'll find out soon enough."

"I'm sorry," Emma said simply.

"I am, too, I think. Before now, I don't know that I ever saw myself as a dad."

No, Emma thought. Their baby had never been as real to him as it had been to her.

"And Lireinne?" she asked. She needed to learn this, too. "What happened with that?"

"You know about her?" Con looked up from his hand, his eyes surprised.

"Yes." Emma didn't explain how. Her brief time with Lireinne, her new relationship with Bud—she didn't owe Con any of this.

"Lireinne. Well, yeah." He sighed heavily. "There was nothing there, never was." Con avoided her eyes. "I was an idiot, okay? But now I know," he said, almost too low for her to hear him. "Now I know I never stopped loving *you*. Not for an instant." Con's eyes, his beloved eyes, the color of the sea at dawn, were glistening wet. "It's been a kind of hell for me lately, but I've always needed . . . you. Just you."

How long? Emma wondered. How long had she waited, praying to hear him say that? How long had she wandered through her days, lost without his smile, his generous spirit, his easy laugh that had lightened and lifted her? Con was so beautiful to her still, anchored so deeply in her heart, that before this instant Emma could never have imagined saying what she said to him next.

"I can't, Con." Ah, the regret in those words.

Con's face collapsed, a tear slipping free to his cheek. He dashed it with the back of his hand. "Em, please. It's true I hurt you, but you could forgive me. We could go back to the way we were. I know we can."

Emma reached across the table and wrapped his scarred left hand in both of hers. "I can't do it, I can't. I'm not the lonely girl you left, and I'm not the adoring girl who loved you, blind and heedless, for so many years. Not anymore. It's been hell for me, too, but that hell changed me. I've become a woman with a wiser heart. I'm responsible for my own life. I've learned how to be happy at last. No, there's no going back to what we were. I can't be with you again, not like that."

"I don't understand. What do you mean? What can you be to me if you can't be *with* me?" Con's questions revealed such desperation that Emma ached inside for him.

She thought for a moment, pondering how to answer him. "Something like . . . a friend?" she offered.

Con withdrew his hand. "You're telling me you want to be

friends? That's it?" He barked a bitter, disbelieving laugh. "Hell, it's just one goddamned irony after another. Since the divorce, all I wanted was your friendship, but that's the last thing I want now. Friendship would be . . . bullshit! No one's ever loved me the way you did, no one. I want your *love,* Emma." He grimaced at his left hand. "You asked what they'd done to me. Nobody did any of this to me but myself—okay, I know that's true, but I've got to have your love if I'm ever going to heal."

"You'll always have it." Emma found her own eyes welling with tears for him. "You're a part of my heart. How can I not love you? I'm still breathing, aren't I?" She brushed at the wet tracks on her cheek. "But I'm not the same person anymore, and you say you've changed, too. So . . . we'll have to love again the best we can—being friends, caring, wanting only the very best for each other."

"Yeah, right." Con's voice was leaden. "Be honest. There's someone else, isn't there."

Of course he'd think that. Con wouldn't be able to imagine any woman deciding all on her own to get over him. Dry-eyed now, Emma thought of Bud and suppressed a smile. Well, maybe she'd had a little help. Maybe a lot.

"That's not why," she said, her voice even. "We've outgrown what was left of us like a, a . . . swallowtail outgrows its chrysalis. We're here talking to each other, really talking at last. It's a good place to start, isn't it? We can do this."

Be here now. That New Agey advice had been slow to bear fruit, yes, seemingly fallow and empty for so long, but deep underground it had set roots, found its way up into the light, and bloomed at last. This newness between her and Con was as "here" as it could get, Emma thought, nodding in recognition of that truth.

"But I *need* you!"

Con's outburst blazed like a kitchen fire. It banished ghosts and echoes and her inward reflections, seeming to render the air in the room almost too hot to breathe. But tempered to searing heat in a restaurant kitchen, Emma waited. This was her time. For long seconds, Con's furious, wounded eyes scorched her from across the table, but then the fires in them flickered, and then they went out. He slumped in his chair.

"And you don't need me," Con said then, a note of discouraged wonder in his voice. He studied her. "Not anymore."

"Yes." Emma was tempted to tell him again that she'd always love him, but she didn't. This was a moment of real honesty and she meant to give it full weight, to honor it.

"So," Con said, with a tired sigh. "I guess I don't get a choice— again. It's going to be this friendship thing or nothing."

Emma smiled at his fatalism. "It's going to be good between us, Con. Just different."

Con's return smile was sardonic. "Oh, it'll be different, all right. You know, it's damned odd. Just a couple of days ago, I began to learn what it's like, being friends with a woman. I think . . . I think I'm almost good with that, but it's still really new to me. I'll probably suck at being friends, but please be patient. Don't give up on me."

"Never."

"Thanks for that." Con was quiet, his sardonic smile fading. "Oh, Em," he said, his voice low and passionate. "*You*. You were always wiser than I am. I should trust you, of all people. Even though I can't imagine being only your friend, I've got to believe that you've got this right." Con took a sober sip of his tea.

"I hope so," Emma said, although there was no doubt about it, not to her.

"But I will always, always love you. You can't make me stop." To her startlement, Con caught Emma's hand and pressed his lips to her wrist for a long moment.

And for that moment, just that one moment, it was as though the lost years between had never happened.

The rain had ceased when Emma walked Con to his car, but the evening air was still damp. The night had turned windy and cold.

"Be sure to get into some dry clothes as soon as you get home," she told him. She rested her hand on the wet sleeve of his leather jacket. "This is going to need to go to the dry cleaners."

Nodding, Con opened the door to the Lexus. "Got it—dry clothes, dry cleaners. Um, when can I see you again?"

Emma took her time, thinking about that. Con said hastily, "Don't worry. Nothing more than lunch, maybe, but I want to catch up, get started on the friend thing." He hesitated, visibly struggling to find the words to say something more.

"So . . . when can I call you?" he pressed.

Emma had to smile at his insistence. Con would always be Con, after all—a vital creature, impatient, single-minded, and relentless in the pursuit of whatever he desired. "I think I'd rather call you, but it won't be long. We'll do it soon."

"That would be good." His hand on the door to the Lexus, Con paused again, his eyes not leaving hers, as if he could hold her there with his gaze. Emma's return gaze was steady, waiting. Time slowed, and in that time, in that place, gradually it seemed that Con himself found something like acceptance. He turned from her and opened the door, fitting his tall frame into the front seat.

"Love you, Em." Con's voice was almost too quiet for her to hear him. He pulled the door shut then, and the Lexus, absent of music, drove away from the house, its taillights glowing red, dwindling until they vanished around the bend in the road and were gone.

"And I you," Emma said softly to the listening night.

But through the open front door the light was falling like a shining beacon across a dark shore, calling her back inside the house and out of the wind. With a last glance at the empty road, shivering, Emma hurried up the front steps onto the porch, into her warm home, to her kitchen where she'd make the pastry and peel the apples for a tart.

Bud and Wolf would be coming in an hour, and they'd be hungry.

CHAPTER 27

Mung bean sprouts, a big package of bright green baby spinach, asparagus out of season.

This Saturday morning in December, Lizzie had exhausted Maestri's produce department for sources of fresh folate, a nutrient her obstetrician had insisted she incorporate into her diet.

"Prenatal vitamins are good, but there's nothing like the real deal, Mrs. Costello. Eat your greens."

She could have picked up a mess of collards, too, but Liz drew the line at sandy bunches of field greens that required so much damned washing, chopping, and shredding it wore her out just to think about it. Lizzie had learned to pick her battles. She might still need to cook from time to time, but nowadays it didn't seem like the chore it had been, especially since she'd discovered that Skip didn't give a damn whether he ate at home or went out. To him, food was just another part of life, and Liz had happily concurred. If it weren't for the baby, she'd be content with only the power smoothies he whomped up for her in the blender every day for breakfast—strawberries, yogurt, bananas, and whey powder.

Lizzie smiled, thinking of Skip this morning. They'd woken at the same time, rolling toward each other in the bed. Skip had pulled her close. His eyes were sleepy and half-open but his kiss was warm, lingering on her lips.

"Morning, gorgeous. How're you feeling?" he asked. He always asked. Better, he always listened.

"Good." But the answer really should have been *lucky*. After all the years of longing to be adored, to be the only one, Liz was astounded at her good fortune to have found this man, this lover who'd unswervingly put her first in his heart. Skip made her feel beautiful, precious, and rare. To her delight, he even seemed to like how she looked at this point in her pregnancy—rounder all over, the swell of her belly more than merely noticeable now.

While not exactly into maternity clothes yet, Lizzie's waistline was growing apace and soon she'd be reduced to wearing baggy tops and sweatpants. She didn't mind this as much as she'd been sure she would. Her skin was glowing, she felt more full of her old restless energy than she'd experienced in years, and Skip told her every day she was the most perfect woman in the world. Besides, the bulk of the remaining months of her pregnancy was going to be during the winter and early spring: when summer rolled around, Liz planned to have shed the baby weight in time for swimsuit season. They could take the baby to the beach in June. With a secret smile, she dropped an outrageously expensive carton of strawberries from Mexico into her cart.

Skip loved strawberries.

Done in the produce department, she was wheeling her grocery cart around the corner to the meat section to pick up some salmon fillets (an excellent source of Omega-3 nutrients), when Lizzie spotted a familiar figure shopping at the cold case.

Con.

Hell. She hadn't seen or spoken to him in months, leaving the necessary correspondence to her lawyer so she wouldn't have to talk to him at all. Why did he have to be here, at Maestri's, today of all days?

Disconcerted but immediately on guard and ready to join the battle, Liz stopped dead in her tracks and the shopper following too closely behind her almost ran a buggy into her motionless back.

"Excuse *me*." The indignant older woman, wide as an oil tanker and decked out in a hideous Christmas sweater of red and green reindeer prancing across a starry maroon sky, swerved her cart around Liz as though she were an inconsiderately parked vehicle.

But Lizzie didn't notice because Con had just looked up from the selection of rib eyes, Porterhouses, and T-bones. She held her breath as he put his plastic-wrapped foam tray of meat back in the cold case, his eyes holding hers all the while. He raised an eyebrow and gave her a half-smile.

Why hadn't she done the grocery shopping yesterday? Son-of-a-bitch, Liz fumed. He was walking toward her right this minute. Lizzie resisted the impulse to turn her cart around, head back into the produce section, and pretend she hadn't seen him. It was too late for that anyway, and besides, she'd wash bushels of collard greens before she'd run away from this confrontation, Liz thought hotly.

"Lizzie," Con said, his voice warm and confident. "It's been a while. I'd been hoping to run into you before this."

Donning her chilliest demeanor, Lizzie narrowed her eyes in a frigid scowl. "Why?" she blustered. "It's not like there's anything else to say to each other. Whatever it is you think you need to tell me, you can tell my attorney instead. I don't want to have to get a restraining order."

To her irritation, Con seemed surprised. "That sounds a little uncivilized, Liz."

Lizzie arched a haughty eyebrow. "You're the one who hired Edith Gillette to represent you. If you wanted to be civilized, then you sure picked the wrong lawyer. She's a real *bitch*."

"That she is," Con agreed. "But Jerry Soames is a real bastard, so we're evenly matched. That's not what I wanted to talk to you about, though."

"What, then?" she demanded. Anything to terminate this odious conversation.

"I hear that you and Skip are moving to New Orleans. That could be something of an issue, Liz."

Oh, that.

A big Uptown plastic surgery practice had made Skip an offer, asking him to join their overburdened group. It would mean a big jump up from his already more than comfortable income, and Lizzie was currently looking for a house for the two of them in the Garden District, something with a pool and a yard big enough for the trampoline. It was going to be absolutely great to get out of Covington. There were too many people here with too many opinions about her and Skip's moving in with each other so soon, their decision to have the baby and raise her together. Lizzie was looking forward to a fresh start in New Orleans, a welcome change from this provincial backwater. She'd easily find work there after the baby was born, and the schools were much, much better than here on the north shore of the lake.

Wasn't it just like Con to try to stick his nose in her business? Wouldn't he ever learn he wasn't welcome anymore?

"And why is that an issue?" Liz lifted her chin and made an impatient, dismissive gesture, but she knew why: Con's lawyer had made it aggressively clear that Con expected to be a part of her baby's life, that he was going to be an *engaged* father or some crap like that. Lizzie wouldn't tolerate any resistance to her plans. She sure as hell wasn't going to let Con Costello dictate where she and Skip were going to live. "You can take the move up with Jerry," she said, her tone lofty, "if it's such a big deal to you."

Con didn't rise to the bait, though. "I'm not going to make trouble for you," he said. He ran his fingers through his hair, his expression thoughtful. "But we'll need to be on speaking terms at least. We're both going to be raising our kid for years to come."

"Daughter," Liz corrected him automatically.

"Daughter?"

Okay, it wasn't like it was some kind of dark secret, and Con would have had to know sooner or later. "The sonogram, you know. I'm having a girl."

Con's handsome face came alight with pleasure. "That's great," he said, his voice softening. "I love girls."

"I know you do," Liz said acidly.

Con flinched. "I guess I deserve that, but c'mon, Liz. You don't have to forgive me, but we could try to be nicer to each other. Believe it or not, I've kept Edith on a short leash so you and Skip can get married as soon as possible. I haven't insisted that you sell the house, or asked you to split the proceeds with me. I don't plan on making myself a fixture in your home, but I want—no, I *need* to be a part of our little girl's life."

"I don't care what you need."

"I really do need this though. Badly." Con's blue-eyed gaze was earnest.

Lizzie's curiosity overcame her better judgment. "Why?" she asked. "What's the big deal? Why *now*? Why couldn't you have been a, a . . ."

"Faithful husband?" Con finished for her.

He looked away, over at a stacked tower of canned Spanish tuna fish in olive oil, and blew a long, perplexed-sounding breath through his lips before he returned his gaze to her. He shrugged awkwardly, as though she'd asked him to explain quantum physics in ten words or less.

"I don't know," Con admitted. "I honestly don't know. Maybe it's a consequence of having grown up with nothing, so poor I never seemed to have enough of anything. Shoes that fit, a bed of my own. Even food. But it's like once I got out of there, I had to have it *all*. The job, the wives, the money. The girlfriends were just a part of it. Don't get me wrong—of course everybody's got a past to deal with, but mine has always been with me. All that . . . *hunger,* that appetite. I guess I could never say no to it."

Lizzie was too stunned to be angry. "That's it? You were hungry?"

Con nodded, his mouth wry. "Yup, that's pretty much it. I just got over a pretty healthy Vicodin addiction, so I've had a lot of sober time on my hands to think—what's left of them, anyway."

Liz's eyes dropped at the mention of his hand, but both of them were shoved in his pants' pockets. Con smiled a faint smile.

"Still getting used to that," he said. "You don't want to have a look, do you?"

Liz shook her head. She didn't need to feel sorry for Con Costello: he already felt plenty sorry enough for himself.

Appetite indeed.

"Will you think it over, at least?" Con asked. "Trying to find the best way to be parents to her together, I mean? I can't stand the thought of having to do this through the courts. She doesn't deserve that."

Much to her surprise, Lizzie found herself nodding. "Oh, all right. I'll try," she said, grudgingly thinking that, even though she hated to concede the point, he was probably right. All the parenting books she'd read had insisted that divorced parents needed to at least pretend to get along, unless they wanted to raise neurotic children. Lizzie didn't want a neurotic child.

"*You* could begin by telling Edith to back off," Liz countered. "You really don't want to name Skip as a correspondent. I don't want to have to drag that idiot girl, that Jennifer, into court, but I will if I have to. Don't think I won't."

Con shook his head, looking chagrined. "Damn. I told Edith to let that correspondent crap go. I never wanted to do anything like that anyway. I'm sorry, Liz. I'll see to it in the morning, first thing."

"Thank you."

An unusual quiet fell between Con and Lizzie while the steady flow of Maestri's credit-card-bearing customers parted around them like a river in flood, grabbing up rib roasts from Idaho and New Zealand lamb chops, Italian sausages and Texas-bred free-range chickens, wines from Bordeaux and Chile, tomatoes ripened in Florida hothouses, peaches and apricots and plums grown in California far to the west, blood oranges from Israel, almonds from Morocco, pecans from Georgia, and chestnuts from France—these and a thousand other things upon things shipped from the world over, part of the oceans of commerce destined to feed a vast, grinding hunger for something more.

Always, something more.

CHAPTER 28

"My name should be on the list—Emma Favreaux. I'm expected."

At the arched stone entrance, the uniformed guard studied a clipboard. He ran a gloved finger down the page, searching.

"*Oui, madame.* Welcome to the Caserne des Célestins. You may enter."

"*Merci,*" Emma murmured. She pulled her heavy wool coat close around her shoulders as she walked under the arch of the barracks. This Friday morning in Paris, the April air was damp and cold, especially after the warmth of the taxi. As Emma crossed the immense graveled courtyard, its flagstone paths bordered with bare-limbed trees just beginning to bud, the sky overhead lowered a smoky gray: it might rain later today.

There was another high arched passageway ahead and Emma paused for a moment, gathering her composure before she passed underneath it. She glanced at her watch. She was ten minutes early, but the trip from the hotel on the Left Bank to the headquarters of the Republican Guard hadn't taken as long as she'd feared it would. The traffic had been light and the Pakistani cab driver made excellent time, swooping down the motorway bordering the Seine like one of

Paris's battered black ravens, until he'd pulled up at her destination on the Île Saint-Louis. The walled gray-stone compound was the time-honored home of the last of the mounted French Cavalry.

Emma's breath was a white plume in the cold as she inhaled the unfamiliar smells of superheated steel from a nearby blacksmith forge and the pervasive, distinct scent of horses. It was time. There was no putting this off and she was as ready as she ever would be, she thought. Following the directions she'd been given, now she'd go inside the building marked MANÈGE, and then she would have to wait to see what happened next.

Be here now.

Emma smiled at the thought as she pushed the brass-hinged door open. Dear Margot. Her therapist would be proud of her: she'd come a long way in more ways than one.

Following the signboards in French, Emma climbed the dark, winding stone stairs until she emerged, breathless and blinking, to the top of the stairs and onto the gallery. It overlooked a high-ceilinged place of filtered light, wing-flapping pigeons, muffled hoofbeats, and a haze of dust—the indoor riding arena of the Republican Guard.

Below her on the hoof-printed tanbark surface, at least fifty riders worked the horses that were stabled here in the midst of the city. The riders were turned out in their everyday black uniforms and dull helmets, but almost all the horses were burnished golden chestnuts with short, neat manes and flowing tails. It was an arresting sight and for a long moment Emma could only watch, marveling at the graceful movements of the gleaming horses below her, at the skill with which the riders avoided collisions as they guided their mounts through their daily workout. This was what it meant to be in the presence of living history: these soldier-horsemen were successors to the regiments that had come before them. Throughout the nearly two hundred years since the Guard had first come to be headquartered at the Caserne des Célestins, this had been the routine of tens of thousands of mornings.

Down the steep steps from Emma, several other observers were already seated in the gallery. They were likewise bundled up against the cold, huddling together on the cement risers as they watched the spectacle below them with fascinated interest.

One of them, a girl, sat apart from the rest, her feet propped on the riser below her, chin in her hand. Emma took a deep breath of the dusty, damp air of the riding arena, crossed her fingers for luck, and descended the steps.

The girl looked back over her shoulder at her approach. She tossed long black hair, glossy and as well tended as the tails of the horses below her, and raised her hand in a tentative wave. Emma's heart beat faster but she mustered a smile.

"Lireinne," she said, her voice warm. "Thanks for meeting me here."

Lireinne gestured at the place beside her, an invitation for Emma to sit. "I come here most mornings when I'm not working. It's worth it, getting up early so I can watch the horses."

Emma settled on the cold cement of the riser with an involuntary shiver. "How did you find out about this place? It's amazing. I had no idea there were stables here, right in the heart of Paris."

Lireinne returned her gaze to the horses and riders below. "I told a . . . friend of mine about Mose. I still miss him, you know. I know he's in a good place now, but he was my best friend for years."

"I remember," Emma said softly.

Lireinne shrugged. "Anyway, my friend brought me here and introduced me to one of his old army buddies in the Guard. They let me come here after that, just so I can be around horses again. I love it. Most of the time, I'm so busy it's like I can't hardly keep up with my life. This gives me a chance to just sit, watch the horses work, and think about stuff. Sometimes I get to give my favorites carrots after they're done working, before I have to leave to head over to Luigi's."

"I almost didn't recognize you," Emma said. "You look fabulous, genuinely fabulous."

"Thanks."

Clothed in skintight tobacco-colored jeans and a mossy-textured, fox-fur-collared sweater, thigh-high suede boots, and a fringed silk scarf of muted blues, violets, and greens, Lireinne was the picture of a youthful sophistication informed by that indefinable yet unmistakable *something* that was the hallmark of a truly French sense of style.

Emma felt old and dowdy in her long wool coat, thick black stockings, and sensible Dansko clogs, but couldn't begin to hold that against Lireinne. The girl seemed so perfectly right, so at home in her clothes that it would have been like envying an exotic rain-forest bird its natural plumage. It seemed as though it would be enough, just catching a glimpse of such beauty, but as Emma glanced again at Lireinne's profile she couldn't help but notice the tension in her face and shoulders, her tight air of reserve.

It was understandable, of course: she and Lireinne hadn't exchanged a word since the day Lireinne lashed out at Emma, over seven months ago. Emma was at a loss as to what she should do next, but she knew better than to try to force the encounter. She'd have to be patient and wait for Lireinne to initiate the talk—if there was to be one—even if she had to sit here all day.

The two of them watched the scene below for several silent minutes.

"Bud still sleeping?" Lireinne asked finally.

She turned her head to look Emma in the eye, and the change in her came as a shock. Lireinne's face was thinner now than Emma remembered it, her cheekbones high and pure, her green eyes as huge and as brilliant as though she had a fever. They rivaled the glittering pair of tourmaline-and-diamond earrings almost hidden in her hair. Over the months, Lireinne's features had been clarified, distilled to an essence, her already lovely face transformed to something otherworldly and impossible to forget. The crescent-shaped scar through Lireinne's eyebrow was another part of that incredible, heart-stopping beauty, a necessary complement that made it somehow strangely . . . complete.

Not wanting to stare, Emma turned her wondering gaze away from Lireinne's face with an effort. "Well, yes. Bud was worn out from the trip. He basically passed out as soon as we got in the room this morning. It's good of you to let him rest. I left him a note, though, telling him you'd called, that I was meeting you here."

Lireinne nodded. "That's okay. I can see him later, when he's had a chance to crash for a while. I remember that flight from when I first came here. Me, I was too excited about being in Paris to sleep, but Bud's pretty old," she said with the unconscious arrogance of youth.

Hiding an amused smile, Emma said, "Being your age helps a lot when you're dealing with jet lag. Flying in First Class helped some. Bud's a big man and somehow I couldn't see him jammed into one of those economy seats. He was nervous enough about flying as it was, without feeling like he was caught in a bear trap. I wanted him to be as comfortable as possible."

Her expression cool, Lireinne gave Emma a long look. "Yeah, it was real nice of you to do that. I mean, you didn't have to take the time to come with him either, but I bet Bud needed you to show him the ropes. He's never been more than a few miles from Covington, just like me. I was glad to have Con around when I got off the plane that first morning. Immigration's a bitch."

"It is," Emma murmured. "I'm sure Con was a big help."

She didn't tell Lireinne that the plane tickets had been a present from Con, just as she hadn't told Bud whose money had paid for this trip to visit his daughter. She'd known Bud wouldn't have been able to stomach that, but her own finances hadn't been equal to a long weekend in Paris. Con's characteristic generosity—and frequent flyer miles—had made it possible for Lireinne and her stepfather to have this time together. Emma had offered to come along to help Bud, a first-time flyer, navigate the airports, flights, and the foreignness of overseas travel. She'd some prior experience with it, thanks to the long-ago trips she'd made to Europe with Con.

Grateful that she was accompanying him, nevertheless Bud had a hard enough time accepting this trip even though he was under the impression she'd put it on her own credit card.

"Don't know when I can pay you back, Emma." Bud had been

looking at their airline tickets, shaking his head. Lireinne had tried to buy him one, but he hadn't wanted her to pay for his ticket either, saying his stepdaughter needed to hold on to her money since she insisted on sending most of it home for Wolf's future school expenses.

Emma slipped her arms around Bud's back, resting her head contentedly on his broad shoulder. "It's something I *want* to do, darling. Look at it like, oh, an early birthday present. Besides, didn't Sarah say she's finally had enough of hauling water to her horses? Next month she wants y'all to dig her another well down in the pasture. After that, if you end up with money to spare you can repay me, but going to France with you is something I want to do."

Emma paused. "I've missed her, too, you know."

Her strained relationship with Bud's daughter was something they rarely spoke of, but even if Lireinne hadn't actually asked her to come, Emma hoped that by now the time might be right for something like a reconciliation. The girl might still reject an overture, and if she did, Emma planned to pass the days going to museums while Bud and Lireinne had some much-needed time together. Emma was under no illusions that she'd be welcomed with open arms, but she didn't want Bud to have to travel by himself for this first, all-important trip. Besides, she had always wanted to see Paris once more.

Bud nodded with reluctant acceptance. "Okay, I'll do it. Seems like years since I seen my little girl instead of only seven months, and she sounded like she really needs to see me, too. It's real good of you to do this for me, Emma, but you know I'm not gonna rest easy, not so long as I'm owing you a dime."

Emma had wondered at her newfound capacity for this loving deceit, but taking Con's money had been the best option for getting them to Paris. In the past months, what Con called "the friend thing" had become something real and good between them. Giving Bud and her the means to take this trip was Con's way of trying to be helpful and she was grateful to him for it. When Bud repaid her, she'd quietly pass the money back to Con. Later, if Bud's feelings about her ex-husband ever changed—which didn't seem likely—she'd tell him then where the tickets had come from.

A pair of pigeons took off overhead, their wings beating a quiet thunder. Thinking about the strange way events had worked out, Emma had to smile at the ironic circumstance. She loved Bud's quiet, stubborn nature, but she wasn't sure he'd ever appreciate Con's gesture, no matter how much time had passed.

"So it's you and Bud now, huh?" Lireinne's sudden question broke into Emma's thoughts.

"Yes, I believe so. Are you okay with that?" Emma asked. She was struggling not to betray her apprehension at this blunt, almost antagonistic inquiry.

Her scarred eyebrow raised, Lireinne lifted her shoulders in an impassive shrug. "Would it matter if I wasn't?"

Thinking Lireinne's question over, Emma couldn't answer right away. Finally, she said, "I don't know. I do think it would be a big problem for Bud if you told him you're against us . . . um . . . being together. He wouldn't want you to be unhappy about it."

"Yeah, probably. I'm not going to kick up a fuss about y'all, though, so you can quit stressing." Lireinne's voice was without emotion. Looking away from Emma, her narrowed eyes stared straight ahead, her full lips as compressed and tight as her clasped hands.

"But he's a good man," she said, "so don't you *ever* go fucking around with his feelings. You got me?"

"Look, Lireinne." Emma ventured cautiously here, trying to be as careful as though she were approaching a wild creature. "I don't know what to say to you. I'm never going to hurt Bud, not like I did you or any other way—not if I can help it."

"Yeah?" The skepticism in Lireinne's answer stung, but Emma knew it was deserved.

She said, "What will it take for you to forgive me, Lireinne? When I answered the phone this morning and you asked me to meet you, I wasn't sure what to think. I assumed you wanted us to be able to talk without Bud's being around. Please, just tell me—what do I need to do to make things right between us? I'm not asking this for me, but for Bud. I know neither of us wants him to feel like he's being pulled in two different directions."

As though she were a much younger girl, Lireinne leaned forward and hugged her legs to her chest. She rested her chin on her knees.

"Yeah, I've been thinking about that." She swallowed, her tensed mouth trembling. "I just gotta know one thing, okay?"

"Anything."

Lireinne didn't speak right away. "Like, how come you never called me?" The words burst from her mouth. "I wanted to talk to you, but you wouldn't even call me back." Her voice was small in the echoing space around them, but Emma heard the hurt in it clearly. In spite of her veneer of sophistication, her newfound worldliness, the girl's question was as plaintive as a seven-year-old child's.

Knowing she'd been the cause of the pain evident in that voice, Emma sighed with deep regret. "Oh, Lireinne—that awful day at the trailer, I wanted so much to explain, to apologize for everything but . . ."

Lireinne said in that same small hurt voice, "But I wouldn't let you. I know." She buried her face in her folded arms, and to Emma's sorrow she realized the girl was crying, her shoulders shaking with silent sobs.

"Lireinne, honey! I'm so, so sorry. I wasn't strong enough to understand you then, but I am now." Before she could stop herself Emma wrapped her arms around those slim, heaving shoulders, her lips pressed to the crown of Lireinne's dark head. She kissed her hair gently, stroking her back. "I'm listening now. Please don't cry."

Her face still buried in her arms, Lireinne fumbled for Emma's hand at her shoulder and found it. Holding on with a grip that felt like ice, her voice was muffled as she said, "I thought if I could get away, if I was ever here in Paris, everything would be *different.*"

Emma's eyes filled with her own tears, crying for the girl who'd run all the way to France to escape her memories, her pain. "And everything *is* different, isn't it? Aren't you happy here?" She squeezed Lireinne's cold hand. "You've come so far. Bud and I are very proud of you. How brave you've been, how independent you've become!"

But Lireinne didn't look up. Emma had to strain to hear her when she mumbled, "It's been sort of different, yeah. Nobody here calls me names, but almost everything's about work. If it weren't for my friend, if I hadn't gotten to know him, I don't know what I'd do. Sometimes I get scared, like everybody's going to decide I'm not really good enough to pull this model thing off. And it's hard, being so far away from home. That's weird, isn't it? Except for Bud and Wolf, I *hated* home. It was so freaking bad for me there."

"I always knew that," Emma said helplessly, her eyes streaming. She rubbed her face on the sleeve of her coat, still holding Lireinne close. "But you're not really alone anymore. I'll never desert you again, I promise."

"It's just . . . it's like I got lost a long time ago. Like nobody can find me."

"But we *did* find you. We'll always be here, whenever you need us." Emma hugged Lireinne's shoulders tighter, swearing to herself that she'd not hurt this child ever again.

Life had taught her that she could leap willingly into the void, and now she'd have to trust herself to be equal to the challenge of loving Lireinne. Emma would dare to love all the people in her life— every day, every hour, every minute—despite the knowledge that love would sometimes be hard.

"Isn't there something we can do to help you?" she asked. "Besides being with you this weekend, I mean?"

Lireinne lifted her head and shook it despondently. "I don't think there's anything anyone can do." She let go of Emma's hand and wiped her eyes. "God, I *hate* crying."

Thinking of all her own tears over the years, Emma said, "Me too. Crying always leaves me feeling wrung out, like I've been through the spin cycle in some giant washing machine."

"Yeah, that sounds about right." Releasing Emma's hand, Lireinne wiped her nose with her sleeve. "Look, I'm done being a baby. I'm just going to have to work this out on my own. I can do it. I always have. Don't worry about me, okay?"

Except Emma would. Even from across half the world, even during the months of silence, this girl had made her way into her heart. She lived there now.

"I won't worry," Emma lied. "I believe in you. Let's just call it . . . a loving concern."

"Whatever." Lireinne sat quietly for a moment. She rubbed her face with both hands, her expression turning thoughtful. "Hey, now that I think about it, there *is* something you can do for me. Remember when you bought the feed for Mose, and the grooming stuff? Remember how I said I'd pay you back when I could? Well, I've got plenty of money now and I'm going to make a lot more, everybody tells me so. Like, I want to make everything square. I don't want to owe you *anything.*"

Emma found a low chuckle at that. "Like father, like daughter," she murmured.

"What?"

"Nothing. Of course you can repay me, honey, if it's something you really want to do."

Lireinne sighed. "Good. I want to start off on the right foot with you now, 'specially if you're going to stick around this time."

"Oh, Lireinne," Emma said with a watery smile. "I'll always be here, even if I have to cross a whole ocean to find you."

"'Kay." Lireinne sniffled. "Hey, after the collection previews this spring, I can come home for a week or so, I think. Good ol' Louisiana in the summertime."

"That would be wonderful, even though it'll be hot. Wolf misses you, you know."

"Yeah, I need to see him, too. It wasn't cool, not being able to come home for Christmas, but I was just getting started and it would've been a problem." Lireinne paused, frowning.

"Oh, yeah," she said, "there's one more thing you could do for me."

"What's that, honey?"

Lireinne said in utmost seriousness, "Do you have a Kleenex? I need to blow my freaking nose."

Bud was awake and pacing the small hotel room when Lireinne and Emma returned that morning. His weathered face broke into a huge grin when they opened the door.

"Bud!" Lireinne ran headlong across the room and threw her arms around him. "Oh my God, I can't believe you're really here!"

The big man enfolded her in a bear hug. "Baby girl, I didn't know if I was gonna make it, but I swore nothing was gonna stop me from tryin'. Here, let me look at you." Holding her away from him, taking her in, Bud's eyes widened. "I'll be danged," he said. "Look at you."

"I know—it's great, right?" Lireinne turned in a quick, laughing circle, her arms stretched wide in delight. "Check me out. Like, this is what all the hosers are gonna be wearing this spring!"

Five minutes later the three of them were sitting in the hotel's lounge, a jewel box of a room with gleaming chestnut-wood paneling; deep, soft armchairs; and a small coal fire burning bright in the grate of the black marble fireplace. The concierge had been dispatched to bring them coffee. Bud couldn't keep his eyes off Lireinne, Emma noted fondly. His hungry gaze followed her when she got up to go make a quick call, watching as she stepped outside the hotel's glass doors onto the grimy Paris sidewalk with her cell phone held to her ear. She was talking with animation to whoever was on the other end, her face glowing in the cold.

"She's awful pretty these days, but she's too thin," Bud said gloomily to Emma. "Don't you think so? I mean, I know models ain't supposed to be fat, but there's hardly nothing left to her, in my opinion. It's damned cold here, too. What if she gets sick?"

At that moment, the concierge, an older, dark-suited Frenchman with a military bearing and a mustache as thin and precise as a pencil line, appeared. He carried a tray laden with a steaming silver urn of coffee, a smaller pitcher of hot milk, and a plate of buttery croissants. With a courteous nod to Emma and Bud, he placed the tray on the low table in front of the fire and went back to manning the front desk, leaving them alone together.

Emma poured the coffee, added milk, and handed Bud his cup. "She's lost some weight, but she doesn't look unhealthy to me. Her color's good and she seems to have plenty of energy."

In fact, during the cab ride back to the hotel Lireinne had been consumed with excitement about seeing Bud again, talking enthusiastically about the plans she'd made for the weekend. "We ought to go to Galleries Lafayette this afternoon." Lireinne eyed Emma's drab wool coat and heavy shoes with a scarcely disguised disapproval. "It's a fantastic place to shop, and you should get some new clothes. Tonight we'll go out to dinner and celebrate. Bud likes good food, you know, and there's so many *great* places to eat in Paris. I can't wait to take y'all to this bistro I know, just around the corner from the hotel. My friend made us reservations there, but we can go anywhere you want. It's going to be totally awesome wherever we eat."

"Do you go out often?" Emma asked, curious.

Lireinne shrugged. "I'm sure no cook. Besides, the kitchen in my apartment is about the size of a freaking plane bathroom—like, it's *tiny*. I love French food. It's not as fattening as you think, either, and I hardly have to diet at all, I spend so much time on my feet. Everybody in Paris walks everywhere. Luigi keeps me running, too. He's bat-shit nervous about the collection, but Luciana tells me he always gets this way before the premieres."

Noting again that Lireinne seemed thinner, Emma had to ask. "I see you've lost some weight. You are eating properly, right? You're not doing something . . . dangerous, are you?"

Lireinne laughed. "I'm fine, Emma. I'm usually hungry a lot of the time, but when I get a chance to eat, I chow down like a big dog. I'm not throwing up or some stupid shit like that. I've only lost five pounds, but on me it looks like a lot more. I'm really lucky that way. Some girls have it a lot harder." She added, "I know this isn't going to last forever. One day I won't model anymore, but for now keeping those five pounds off is just part of the job."

Remembering that conversation, watching Lireinne talk on her phone outside on the sidewalk, Emma said to Bud, "I believe you can trust her judgment. She's becoming wise about so much, so fast. I think Lireinne's really growing up."

Bud nodded. "I just don't want her to be lonely. This is a hell of a big town."

Outside on the sidewalk, Emma realized that Lireinne had been joined by a tall, angular, young man with a pair of narrow glasses perched on an aquiline nose, wearing what had to be a custom-tailored suit and a rich-looking tie. They shared a quick embrace, but Emma immediately sensed that this was no casual acquaintance.

"Ah," she said. "Don't look now, but I think our girl has invited someone to meet us."

Bud's honest face turned quizzical. "Like who?" Before Emma could answer, the hotel's glass doors swung open. The concierge looked up, smiled at the two young people, and went back to his newspaper.

The beautiful girl and the tall man walked across the lobby, their steps light, their hands clasped like lovers.

"Emma, Bud," Lireinne said, her smile as luminous as a dawn star. "You've got to meet Julien Moreau, my friend. He wants to take us to lunch at Hediard. Y'all ready to go? I'm, like, totally *starving*."

Late August, 2005

Snowball had acquired a taste that wouldn't be satisfied with alligator feed.

If any dared approach her now, she exploded from the water of her tank, jaws gaping, deadly and swift as though in this, her natural element. Snowball had fed on human flesh and found it good—and this more than once, for at first the rest of the Two-Legs had been unwary. Unnatural hunger had created a true monster, a creature out of nightmare with no shred remaining of an alligator's native shyness.

No, this beast had become something Other.

Blood and bone, ligament and sinew, muscle and fascia, rib and vertebrae. Snowball would wait in unspeakable patience to have it all.

And when the millennial storm came and the alligator barns collapsed like wet cardboard boxes in the winds, she fought her way out of the wreckage till she was free once more, loosed upon a world that had forgotten monsters. The surrounding wild took her into its shadows and dark places where she thrived.

Thus Snowball became a cautionary tale, a legend with crushing, savage teeth and an implacable appetite. Years upon years, she grew in size, power, and ferocity until she met her end. Then the legend passed into a myth to scare children—the monster white alligator of Million Dollar Road.

A half-remembered truth.

Million Dollar Road

Amy Conner

ABOUT THIS GUIDE

The suggested questions are included
to enhance your group's reading
of Amy Conner's *Million Dollar Road*.

Discussion Questions

1. *Million Dollar Road* is essentially a love quadrangle, a square, between a man and the three women he loves. Have you encountered a tangled romantic geometry before?

2. A theme in the novel is the range of options moneyed people possess versus those available to people living on the edge of real poverty. How do you see these options playing out as the story progresses? Did you learn about the characters through their options (or the lack of them) and the choices they made? If so, how?

3. Lireinne is a relatively simple person, but a complicated character: fairly inarticulate, but full of desire and determination nonetheless. At what point is the reader allowed to see beyond her dropout status, her menial job, and her poverty to the person she, with luck, might become?

4. When we meet Emma, we realize she's an extremely fragile woman. Over the course of the novel, do you feel her character grows into a new kind of resilience, or do you think she simply shifts her obsession with her ex-husband to a dependence on another man?

5. Lizzie is a challenging character in terms of likability, although we all know someone like her. Do you feel that she experiences a significant personal change in response to her pregnancy, or, unlike the others, is Lizzie a character impervious to life-changing events?

6. Another theme of the novel is that of appetite—a taste for something—as opposed to true hunger, set against the backdrop of the early years of the new century, before the Crash of 2008. Is Con's character emblematic of appetite, true hunger, or both?

7. Among other things, *Million Dollar Road* has been called a suburban morality fable. Do you find this to be an accurate estima-

tion, or did you experience it as a different kind of novel? If so, how would you characterize this book to a friend?

8. Snowball, the white alligator, is presented as a character with her own point of view. Why do you think the author chose to do this?

9. After reading *Million Dollar Road,* was there a character with whom you'd like to keep in touch? Did you feel that a kind of justice was ultimately achieved for all concerned? If not, why?